Lifeline Echoes

Kay Springsteen

δ

Dingbat Publishing

LIFELINE ECHOES
Echoes of Orson's Folly, Book 1
Copyright © 2011 by Kay Springsteen
ISBN 978-1-940520-14-8

First edition 2011 Astraea Press LLC
Second edition 2014 Dingbat Publishing

Published by Dingbat Publishing
Humble, Texas

This work is first dedicated to the Lord, my God, who is my ultimate Lifeline.

Also, with happy memories of my dad and mom, James and Audrey Springsteen, my shining example of what it means to be soul mates.

To my childhood friend, Sandy Roegner, who patiently answered my questions about what it feels like to be an emergency dispatcher holding the lives of others in her hands.

And dedicated to emergency workers everywhere. Thank you for all you do.

A special thank you to Jen, whose photography inspired the descriptions of some photographs in this story. The Photography of J.L. Gould may be enjoyed at http://www.jlgould.com/

There is no natural phenomenon which is held by all mankind in greater dread than earthquakes. Our ideas of permanence, solidity and strength are based upon the condition of the earth, as we daily see it; so that when the firm ground shakes under us, there naturally comes over the mind a feeling of abject helplessness.
~New York Times, April 9, 1872

Prologue

Seven years earlier...

Splat.

"Son of a—"

Sandy glared down at her double chocolate iced mocha. Pale brown slush slid off the toe of one white shoe to form a sticky puddle on the blacktop.

A quick glance at her watch told her she'd have to hurry or she'd be late for her shift as a dispatcher for Los Angeles City Emergency Services. She kicked the melting mush from her shoe and stepped around the puddle of yuck and raced across the parking lot to the low brick building. Behind her, traffic on the packed freeway growled and honked.

Good morning, Los Angeles.

Sandy yanked on the heavy glass door and stepped into the coolness of the air conditioned building with a sigh.

"Morning, Alley Cat!" greeted Rose from behind the reception desk. "Lunch at Del Rio's today?"

"Hi, Rose. Yeah, lunch sounds great. Gotta run. I'm late." With a wave, Sandy hurried past the desk and into the ladies' restroom. She set her oversized purse on the counter and grabbed several paper towels. Crouching, she dabbed at the mush, noting with dismay that it had worked into the seams of her athletic shoes.

"Gross," she muttered. She'd be lucky if it didn't stink like sour milk at the end of her shift. After she mopped off the worst of it, she pushed to her feet and staggered sideways. Her hand hit the cool marble wall of the first stall as she fought to steady herself.

"What the hell?"

A low primeval rumble surrounded her, invaded her midsection and radiated up into her heart and throat. Sandy stumbled to the left then the right. The fluorescent light overhead became a flickering strobe.

Earthquake!

The word registered in the recesses of her mind, and spurred her toward the door. She had to get out of the enclosed space before the ceiling collapsed and buried her.

Sudden blackness swallowed her as the lights lost the battle to stay on. The grumble grew to a roar and then a scream. She lurched to the right, pushed off the wall, and careened through the bathroom door. The scream grew louder before she realized it came from her own mouth. The floor beneath her rolled and writhed as her cries were echoed by a half-dozen coworkers at their workstations. Shelves toppled, notebooks tumbled to the floor.

The roar dwindled to a dull grating, the heaving slowed and finally halted. Sandy lay on her side, her back jammed against the wall. Her insides still quivered and shook like jelly, the remnants of the quake continuing in her viscera. Chills washed over her as she sat up and took stock of the dispatch room. Her coworkers moved slowly, sitting and looking around, dazed expressions gracing their faces.

"Holy cow," murmured Rose, pushing to her feet and doing a three-sixty. "That felt like an eight or a nine."

Fluorescent lights overhead sputtered then half of them winked on. That would be the backup generator, running nonessentials at half power.

More operators pushed to their feet, their faces all wearing uniform dazed expressions. Jabbering filled the air as a dozen people seemed to find their voices at the same time. The cacophony crescendoed. Any second her head would explode. She closed her eyes and attempted to sort out what was being said.

"...my kids..."

"I think my arm's broken..."

"Maybe we should get..."

"Comm's down!" called out Albert Torres, IT wizard and technical problem solving guru. "Switching to backup."

Phones began ringing. Frowning, Sandy oriented herself and located her desk. Someone had to answer the calls. And there would be calls.

She located her station and placed the headset over her ear, then punched the button. "Emergency services—"

A shrill scream came over the line and assaulted her ear. Forcing herself to speak calm words of reassurance as she wrestled open her desk drawer and pulled out an empty notebook and a black pen, Sandy managed to discern that the caller was an elderly woman who was merely disoriented and frightened.

The phone lines began to flash as more calls came in. Around her, more dispatchers followed Sandy's lead and began answering.

"Backup comms are on line," announced Albert, emerging from the computer room.

The first report of a fire came ninety seconds after Sandy started answering calls. The gas line alongside the Convention Center had burst and somehow ignited. Hell had erupted in Central Los Angeles.

Sandy couldn't stop the tremors running along the inner fault lines of her own neural pathways. *I'm a professional. People are depending on me.* She studied the older system that had just been replaced by a two million dollar upgrade, only months earlier, and re-familiarized herself with the buttons and switches. Then, in a voice that only barely trembled, she dispatched Fire Station Number 9 to the L.A. Convention Center.

The first shift after Sandy's vacation was off to a very rocky start. Before that shift was over, she would learn two important things. First, she was getting the hell out of L.A. Second, it was possible to fall in love with someone, sight unseen, in twenty-three hours and fifty-seven minutes.

Chapter One

Present day

Sunny and warm, the perfect day for mourning lost love. Maybe this would be the year she'd finally be ready to move on. Even as the thought teased her, Sandy suspected it might take another cataclysmic event to let go of the man she'd given her heart to in less than a day.

Summer was a handful of days off, but the mountain air was clean and brisk, nothing like the heavy smog of L.A., where she'd first met *him*. She had no memories of the man in this place except for the ones he'd painted into her mind while they'd talked. Yet Wyoming was where she felt his presence.

Her red roan colt pranced beneath her, needing to run off his teenage-intensity energy. Dry dirt kicked up by Domingo muffled the sound of his hoof-falls to dull scuffling *plunks*, which he punctuated with occasional impatient snorts.

As they traveled, the dusty ground became more firmed and flattened. Gray rocky outcroppings thrust upward amid a tan landscape dotted by the washed-out green of desert grasses. More of the same lay between them and the scrub pines along the swell of foothills in the distance.

Sandy pointed Domingo toward those hills, finally allowing the exuberant colt to set his own pace. He catapulted them across the plain, brawny muscles alternately flexing and contracting beneath her, racing at a full gallop. The denim jacket she hadn't bothered to fasten caught the wind and billowed behind her. Chilly air worked icy fingers along the exposed skin of her neck, bringing with it a wonderful ache.

They topped a gentle rise and a sea of yellow and purple wildflowers surprised her, God's own casually sown garden. The sky overhead was deep blue and cloudless. With the prairie behind her and the snow-covered peaks ahead, Sandy pulled Domingo up inside a cathedral of Ponderosa pines, closed her eyes, and inhaled the pungent scent. It was exactly as he had described it, which made it the perfect place to remember him.

Seven years had passed, yet her pain was an exquisite, fresh wound, probably owing to the fact that she revisited the memory once a year on the anniversary of that horrific day. In the hills of Wyoming that he had loved and missed so much, in the place he had brought her to with just his words, Sandy picked the scab off the wound she never quite allowed to heal.

* * *

The job was all that mattered now. Sandy made herself disregard the toppled shelves and scattered books. She blocked out all thoughts about the likely state of her own home. As she listened to the chatter on the official channels, she kept meticulous handwritten notes regarding the status of each unit checking in.

"Battalion 9-Alpha, this is Engine Squad 9-Bravo, do you copy?" The connection was filled with static and the voice was muffled, hard to hear.

Sandy waited for the response of the battalion chief on scene. None came.

The callout was repeated, the voice sounding a bit more urgent. "This is L.A. Engine Squad 9-Bravo, dispatched to the Convention Center—" Again static broke the transmission.

Following protocol, after the second unanswered call, Sandy intervened. "Copy you, ES-9-Bravo. This is central dispatch. Your transmission is breaking up."

She checked her watch and jotted the time in her notes: 0724 *hours.*

The response was drowned out by a loud burst of static in the earpiece.

"9-Bravo, be advised you are breaking up," she repeated.

More harsh squawks of static burst from the receiver. Sandy winced. If that kept up, her head might explode — or at least an eardrum. Then, amid the static, she clearly heard the code every dispatcher dreaded. "9-Bravo is 10-60, this location. Code three, code three, code three... trapped..."

The code for firefighter down!

Static filled the airwaves again as Sandy punched buttons on her console, frantically trying to boost the signal.

"Dispatch, are you there?" The voice was screaming. "Central! This is 9-Bravo in need of assist. The building's coming down around us!"

Afraid to switch over to relay, with the risk of losing contact altogether, she motioned to Ellen, the dispatcher sitting next to her. Quickly, Sandy wrote on her notepad in bold black ink: UNIT IN TROUBLE.

At the next desk, Ellen nodded and switched channels to contact the Battalion 9 squad leader over the comm.

"9-Bravo, this is Central Dispatch," Sandy acknowledged. Stomach-wrenching fear threatened to leak into her voice, so she bit the inside of her cheek. Dread shot out little tentacles of hopelessness to curl around her lungs, squeezing the breath out of her. "I'm reading you, sending help your way. What's your location?"

"Civic Center parking garage — A level. The building's coming apart! We need extraction." The voice was still urgent but the panic had faded.

She had to get her own terror under control and keep it that way, Sandy reminded herself, *or she couldn't help anyone.*

"Copy you, 9-Bravo. Who am I speaking with?"

"Mick-" More static, then, "Mic-key."

Sandy scribbled everything she could make out into her handwritten notes. "Mickey, you're breaking up badly. How many do you number? How long have you been trapped?"

"Two confirmed, dispatch, possibly three. I can feel my partner. He's not moving. I heard someone else moaning down here earlier. I don't know how long it's been. I think I've been unconscious — I'm pinned — can't move. It's dark — can't see a thing."

Sandy passed off the information to Ellen so her coworker could convey it to the battalion chief. The sarcastic part of Sandy's mind registered the irony of having crossed into the twenty-first century and being reduced to the mockery of a child's game of telephone.

With a pointed shake of her head, Ellen caught Sandy's eye and handed her a message from the battalion chief. As she read, Sandy's heart fluttered in her chest before moving upward to stick in her throat. Her free hand rose of its own volition and covered her mouth, as if to prevent her from saying the words she was reading.

The Convention Center had collapsed with several men inside. Some of them were buried under four floors of rubble, while above them the fire from the gas main explosion burned fully involved and uncontained. Rescue efforts would be delayed and prospects for extraction were grim. A chaplain was en route.

God help them all! How could she tell the man on the other end of the comm that he wasn't going to be rescued? What could she say to someone when her words were likely to be the last he'd ever hear?

* * *

Ryan kicked in the clutch and rammed the gearshift into second to take yet another turn on the series of switchbacks through the mountains. The 1967 Corvette Sting Ray had been a mess when he'd bought her, but she'd been his mess. And a bargain at the price he'd wangled. It had taken almost every one of his days off over the past two years, but he had fully restored her from the engine up. The work had been a welcome distraction from other aspects of his life.

Currently, on his first long trip in her, he was enjoying the way she held fast to the road, caressing the pavement around the twists and turns through the mountains the way a woman caressed a lover.

The throaty growl of the engine wasn't quite drowned out by the whoosh of the wind over his face. It was early in the year to drive with the top down in the mountains, but Ryan didn't care. The bracing cold reminded him he was alive.

It had been too long, the guilty whisper nagged. He should never have let his life get so far out of hand. It shouldn't have taken an emergency letter from his baby brother for him to come home and make things right with the old man.

Tires squealed just a bit when he took the downward curve a little sharply. He was in the foothills now, only a few miles to go. He'd be able to open his baby up on the two-lane once the last hill was at his back. Soon the sun would drift down into the shadowy embrace of the mountains behind him, leaving him the stars for company. Damn, he'd missed the mountains of home.

Halfway through what he recognized as the last switchback, Ryan downshifted again and punched the gas. His mind registered the apparition blocking the road in front of him a bare second before reaction set in. He stood on the brake, sending the car into a slow sideways skid and stalling the engine.

"Holy hell!"

Darts of adrenaline screamed through his veins, sending his heart into a staccato rhythm as he stared at the horse and rider in the road.

Washed in the golden blush from the setting sun, the horse reared, angrily striking out at the air between them with menacing hooves, nearly unseating his rider. With a toss of his head, the startled horse reared again, baring his teeth and screaming defiance.

The red roan colt had excellent lines, but he was clearly too much for his rider. Though the horse responded to her steady touch, it was obvious any sense of control she had was an illusion. Ryan shoved the car door open and jumped to his feet, ready to pick up the pieces when the rider was thrown. But when she swung her gaze in his direction, fury blazed in eyes the color of chicory blossoms. Her face mirrored the horse's defiance.

Sparks of awareness replaced astonishment, and a grin pulled Ryan's lips upward as he lifted a hand in greeting.

"Jackass!" The rider shoved at the wild mass of dark hair falling across her face. The motion distracted her, giving her mount the opening to misbehave.

With a clatter of edgy hooves on asphalt, the big colt danced and circled, threatened to rear again, but she recovered quickly and held him down. Then she tugged on the reins, steering the agitated horse away from the road, and sidestepping him down the steep, gravel-covered incline. Upon reaching solid footing, the colt wheeled sharply around. The rider cast a scathing look over her shoulder as the horse erupted into a reckless gallop across the prairie.

Pain shot through Ryan's neck, and he realized he'd been clenching his jaw. Absently, he rubbed the back of one hand along his chin, but he kept his eyes on the horse and rider until they were no more than a speck in the distance.

"Well," he said to the early evening sky. "I've just been schooled."

He wasn't sure if he was going to shake things up with his return or get himself shaken up. But he sure as hell planned to find out who lived behind those haunting chicory blue eyes.

Shaking his head, he started to lower himself into the car when he froze. Why was it sitting at such an odd angle? He strode around to the passenger side and groaned at the sight of the front tire, rolled right off the rim from his sideways skid.

* * *

By the time she had encountered the stranger in the fast car, Sandy's earlier upbeat mood had degraded, thanks to the dull heartache she'd given herself from lancing her old wound. Ordinarily she would have laughed off the incident and introduced herself once she'd realized no one was hurt. But the moron had just sat in his car staring in disapproval, apparently waiting for her to move out of his all-important way.

Wherever the aggravating stranger was going, she sincerely hoped he didn't so much as make a pit stop in Orson's Folly. She was pretty sure another meeting of that sort would result in her doing more than yelling at him. Pictures of strangling the shit-eating grin off his face popped into her mind.

Her heart raced with the need to dispel her jitters, and Sandy let the colt have his head again. Domingo calmed them both by doing what he loved most, streaking at breakneck pace over the plains of western Wyoming.

By the time they slowed to a walk alongside the fence leading to the stable yard, her ire at the stranger on the road had mellowed to a mildly bad memory. Whoever he was, it was likely he'd already hit Orson's Folly and driven on through. The sun rested in the cradle between the peaks of two mountains, sending lingering shafts of red to cast long shadows against the blue and white buildings. Sandy closed her eyes, bracing against the little pinprick of pain, and allowed herself to remember the reason she'd first come to Wyoming.

* * *

"*You hang on, do you hear me?*" she ordered. "*I won't go anywhere until they have you, I swear. But you have to stay with me. Promise!*"

"*Okay... promise.*" His words were slurred, his voice weary.

Sandy struggled to think of something to talk about — to keep him speaking and alert. "*Do I hear an accent, Mick?*"

His laugh was slow and soft. "*Yep, I'm afraid so. I can't seem to get the Wyoming out of my voice.*"

That worked! "*Tell me about Wyoming.*"

He sighed. "*There's nothing like a wild gallop across the plains on a fast horse. If you can be up on that horse at daybreak, you feel like you're flying up to meet the day. And to be in the Red Desert at sundown's even better. If you time it right, just a split second before the sun's gone, you feel like you're inside all that red and orange glow. Then in your next breath you're standing in pitch black. When you look up, the stars are already popping out. So many stars they blend together. And there's always shooting stars for making wishes.*" He laughed softly. "*I guess I sound a little pathetic.*"

"*No.*" She wished she could touch him with more than her voice. "*More like a homesick cowboy.*"

He was quiet for a time, then, "*I guess maybe I am, Angel. I am homesick.*"

His quiet admission brought tears to Sandy's eyes, and she prayed he'd see those sunrises and sunsets and stars again. "*So you lived in the desert plains?*"

"*I had the best of both worlds,*" he answered, his words filled with pride. "*Our ranch is in the middle of a finger of desert that's nestled between two legs of mountains and forest.*"

"*Why did you leave?*"

"*That's a story for another time,*" he said. "*I'll tell you when we're on our first date.*"

"*Are you asking me out?*"

"*Oh, we'll go out.*" His voice gave her visions of an easy cowboy grin. "*I was just making the plans.*"

Her lips twitched at his audacity.

* * *

Cooled and brushed, Domingo nickered a soft goodbye as Sandy left the comfort of the stable and walked into the cold night air.

Stars twinkled into view overhead, millions of glistening pinpoint lights fusing into a lacy curtain of soft illumination against the darkness. A trail of shimmery light tracked across the sky.

For the first time in seven years, her automatic wish wasn't for something impossible. "I want to feel alive again."

Emotionally and physically exhausted, she tore her eyes from the stars with a heavy sigh and climbed into the rusty Chevy pickup. It was older than she was by several years, so she counted her blessings it still ran. Driving past the main homestead, Sandy tossed a wave to Justin McGee, sitting on the wide front porch of the ranch house puffing on his nightly cigar. With a smile and a nod, the old rancher politely touched a forefinger to the brim of his battered tan Stetson.

Just as Sandy reached the cedar fenceposts marking the entrance to the ranch, a pair of headlights swung in from the main road. So, the McGee men were about to receive a caller. Maybe Sean had finally convinced Melanie Mitchell to drop by after her shift at the bar.

The two sets of headlights collided, the bright beams briefly joining forces and splitting the darkness. Then the moment was gone, leaving Sandy with a vague impression of something low and fast before she was engulfed by the cloud of dust chasing behind.

Nope. She coughed against the sting in her throat. Definitely not Mel, who tended to drive her ancient economy car with the caution of a grandmother. Tough break for Sean.

* * *

Ryan braked in front of the old ranch house and killed the engine. He popped open the door but took some deep breaths before climbing out of the car.

Though the land slumbered beneath a blanket of darkness, the nighttime couldn't mask his memories. He knew just beyond the edge of the light lay open spaces, fields of green and gold dotted by brown-and-white cattle and rolls of cut hay, all in the protective embrace of the Rocky Mountains to the west.

Closing his eyes, Ryan inhaled deeply, intoxicating himself on the aromatic blend of cow manure, freshly mown hay, and mountain wildflowers that hung in the air. The sweet, somewhat earthy scent of home.

Overhead, a shooting star blazed a fiery arc through the myriad visible stars. Ryan thought of a time, so long ago, when he and Sean had lain next to their mother on a sleeping bag, watching the stars overhead. Every time she saw a shooting star, she had urged them to make a wish.

The memory faded as suddenly as it had come. What the heck was he doing, coming back to Wyoming?

"Not much call for such a fancy machine on a ranch," admonished a gravelly voice from the porch's shadows. "But you always did love speed, didn't you, boy?"

Ryan stiffened as Justin took a step forward into the light cast by the moon.

"Hello, Dad." Ryan kept his response respectful and reserved. Leave it to his father to act like this was just another homecoming after a night in town. "You look good."

Justin chuckled. "Still spreading it thick, I see." But fondness had crept into his voice. "What I look is old." He nodded in the direction of the huge barns that had been standing since before Ryan was born. "Your brother's out there locking up... if you want to go find him, let him know you're here."

The statement startled Ryan. "Since when do McGee barns need locking?"

The old man leaned against the porch railing and examined the tip of his cigar.

Ryan waited. It was maddening, but no amount of pushing would get his father to talk before he was ready.

Finally Justin shrugged, fixed Ryan with a pointed stare. "A boy goes away for sixteen years, he's bound to see some changes when he comes back a man."

Same old shit with you, isn't, Dad? But Ryan held his tongue and acknowledged the well-deserved punch straight to the heart with a nod and a wry smile. Then he turned and strode toward the barns.

Strong floodlights, mounted at the corners of each building, lit the yard. Sean was clearly visible as he slid the barn door closed and set the lock. He walked toward the stable, a black-and-white dog at his heels.

Ryan stood just outside the light's edge watching his brother, looking for a trace of the kid he'd left behind.

The skinny boy's frame had become lean and muscular. Glow-in-the-dark blond hair had toned down some, but Ryan noticed it still had a tendency to curl at the ends even though his brother kept it cut short. Sean had been thirteen when Ryan had left. He'd grown into a man.

When Sean emerged from the stable, he ordered the dog to stay inside. Then with a flexing of his muscles, he slid the door closed. Ryan raised an eyebrow. His little brother had developed some broad shoulders and strong arms. While setting the latch, Sean's hands stilled. He eased around, his body tense, ready for anything. It had always been uncanny, the way the kid had been so acutely aware of his surroundings; it still was.

Ryan stepped into the light. Green eyes identical to his own met and held his gaze. Ryan marshalled his expression and waited, unmoving.

Sean's tension visibly drained. His smile started slowly, in his eyes first, then spreading to his mouth, where it bloomed into a full grin.

"Ry!" In two long-legged strides, Sean was in front of him. "Oh, man, it's good to see you!"

In a move too sudden for Ryan to dodge, Sean folded him into a bear hug and lifted him off his feet, his carefree laughter driving out the last vestiges of Ryan's uncertainty.

Welcome home, Ryan McGee.

Chapter Two

A clunky basketful of hygiene products weighed on Sandy's arm. She idly skimmed the magazine headlines while she waited at the checkout counter for Sarah Jessup to ring up Mamie Schmidt's order. It seemed the going rate for each item was a full minute of gossip while the two gray-haired women caught each other up on the goings-on in the small town since they had last talked.

Which had probably been no longer than the day before. Sandy shuffled her feet, crowding forward a couple of inches more.

"No mistake! It was Ryan, all right," Mamie was insisting. "Bold as brass he walked into Ed's and placed a considerable order for lumber and nails. Henky said he drove up all arrogant-like in his big city sports car."

Sandy shifted her attention from the dazzling picture of sexy summer sandals to the gossip at the cash register.

"Do you think the old man knows he's back?" asked Sarah in a loud whisper.

"If he doesn't, he will as soon as Henky makes the delivery. S'posed to take it out this afternoon."

Sarah glanced at the line, made brief eye contact with Sandy, and lowered her voice until it was barely audible. "What about the others?"

Mamie shook her head slowly. "I was wondering that myself." She opened her giant black purse and pulled out a crisp twenty dollar bill. The gossipfest was apparently over.

Finally it was Sandy's turn at the checkout, but Sarah no longer seemed in the mood to be chatty, which was just as well, since it got her out of the store about ten minutes quicker.

The line at the bank was even longer than the one in the drugstore. Apparently it was training day for new hire Bertie Higgins. Nate Graham was the youngish bank manager who had taken over a year after Sandy had moved to Orson's Folly. He was showing incredible patience, even when he had to void each transaction and repeat it himself. Given the direction in which his eyes repeatedly strayed, though, Sandy suspected he was more concerned with the young girl's deep cleavage than her banking abilities.

Standing behind Walt Blackstone and Leo Pickens, she gathered more gossip of the day.

"He just drove on into the garage with a mangled tire. Said there was an extra hundred in it if he got a new one by tomorrow," said Walt, owner of Blackstone's Auto Repair. "I had to send young Wendell up to Jackson to get one. Damned fancy things. Got no use for something like that on my racks."

"Came by my place, too," Leo announced. "Picked out some high-end tack. Ask me, the way he's taking charge, I think he's back to stay."

Walt shook his head as he walked up to the next teller, grumbling, "Never thought that day'd come. Now I s'pose there'll be the devil to pay."

By the time Sandy got to Valentine's Bar, she'd already learned a lot about the hometown prodigal son named Ryan, back after a long absence, and by all reports walking the streets like he owned them. Apparently, no one knew exactly why he'd left home fifteen or sixteen years back, though there was speculation it had to do with his father and the MacKay family. On two points, however, the entire town seemed to agree. No one had expected him to ever return to Orson's Folly, Wyoming; and now he was back, trouble had likely come with him.

Sandy was fairly certain she'd already had a taste of the man's particular brand of trouble the evening before. And she was beginning to wonder if that one taste might have only primed her appetite for more.

The snatches of conversation she'd overheard had been tantalizing but she suspected they were the tip of the iceberg. Maybe it was time to delve just a bit below the surface of that sleeping giant. And she knew just the person to ask as they prepped the bar for the Friday evening crowd.

"So what's the story on this gentleman who's come home... Ryan?" Sandy leaned one elbow on the bar, striving for nonchalance.

A cynical snort matched the inward rolling of Melanie Mitchell's lips as she shoved a stack of napkins into a holder. "I don't think anyone here's ever called Ry a gentleman before." Her short cap of pale blond hair flashed almost white in the glow of the neon bar sign as she glanced up with a grin.. "Lots of other references, though."

"So what's his story?" Sandy toyed with a bottle of mixer. "Lots of talk going around town."

"Talk's overrated." A scowl creased Mel's forehead. "I really hate gossip."

Time to turn on the charm, though Sandy had to admit *that* usually worked better with customers. And men. Still, she smiled. "Give me a break. I'm not on the main grapevine. So either I have to skulk around the supermarket or get it from you."

Mel's giggle echoed through the bar. "You wouldn't have to skulk if you gave a little information back once in a while."

A blast of chilly air whispered across Sandy's hand as she opened the mini-fridge and grabbed a bottle of water. "I never have anything to say."

One delicate eyebrow arched as Mel stopped fussing with the napkins and looked up. "Honey, you're the head bartender at the only watering hole in town. Trust me, everyone knows you hear the really good stuff."

The bottle cap twisted off with a tiny hiss, and Sandy took a drink before she answered. "Some of that's personal."

"Exactly. The good stuff." Another stack of napkins found its way into Mel's hands. Really, the girl worked like a mechanic on an assembly line.

"What do I have to do to stop being the outsider here?" Sandy took another drink and stared across the bar. She drew one finger along the polished brass edging the oak bar. It was one of the few things that had survived the renovation of Valentine's. "I'll bet if this bar could talk it would spill a lot of stories," she mused aloud.

Heaving a sigh, Mel toyed with a napkin, rolling it into a tube then smoothing it flat again.

A sudden tingle of awareness raced through Sandy. *She's trying harder than I am to be casual.*

"Look, there's really not much to tell." Mel flipped the napkin into the trash. "Ry was kind of the town bad boy. Got in a fair share of fights but it wasn't usually him starting them. He just never seemed to be able to walk away. He had girlfriends, but he wasn't the marrying type, you know?"

The guarded tone accompanying Mel's words alerted Sandy to something beneath the surface, something her friend wasn't saying.

Her gasp slipped out before she could stop it. "Mel, you and he weren't — were you?"

A short burst of laughter dispelled the thought. "Me? Oh, goodness no! I was just a baby when he left. Well, I was twelve. I guess I had kind of a crush, him being so handsome and bodacious. But I don't think he ever noticed me."

If he was male and breathing, he was certainly going to notice the pretty bartender now. *Won't that complicate the excruciatingly slow burn between Mel and Sean?*

The bottle of Kentucky blend was nearly empty, so Sandy pulled it from the rear shelf and replaced it with a fresh one from beneath the bar. "Everyone seems surprised he's come back here."

"Truth is, no one really knows why he left," Mel admitted. "Lots of speculation, but his family kept quiet, wouldn't talk about it. Wouldn't talk about *him*. Then, when he didn't come home, folks started thinking he wasn't going to."

The smile tugging at Sandy's lips bloomed into a grin, and she shook her head. *Gotta love small town mysteries.* Everyone had a theory and everyone absolutely knew his or her particular presumption was the one and only truth. She opened the dishwasher, leaned back while the steam spilled out, then unloaded the beer mugs and expertly stacked them behind the bar.

"You know..." Mel pulled a handful of menus from the wicker basket next to the old-fashioned cash register and began sorting through them. "He's probably still real easy on the eyes." She turned one of the menus to match the rest then swept her glance upward to meet Sandy's. "And he *is* rumored to be unattached."

"Whoa!" Sandy took a step back, holding up her hand. "I'm not looking for anything like that."

Tipping her head, Mel simply shrugged. Her light blue eyes seemed to dance. "Maybe you should. Go for a little human companionship instead of always hanging out with that wild horse of yours." She winked. "Get a little — you know — companionship of the right kind... scratch any lingering itches."

Heat swamped Sandy's face, but she resisted the urge to fan herself, though any minute her head would erupt like a volcano. "Domingo and I do just fine," she muttered. Maybe she should mention her encounter on the mountain road. What if that *had* been this man, Ry? Her heart began to beat a little faster whenever she thought about their sunset run-in. Right, definitely best not to mention it. Time to change the focus of conversation. "And speaking of my horse, I need to run out to the Cross MC to pay for Domingo's board. Unless you want to run it out for me?" Sandy wiggled her eyebrows suggestively and finished in a sing-song voice. "You could say hey to Sean."

"I'm just fine right here setting up," Mel murmured, her neck and cheeks stained a faint rose.

"I thought you liked Sean."

"I do," Mel answered steadily, without looking up. "And I want him to like me. Which is why I'll just wait for him to come in and see me tonight instead of me goin' out there lookin' for him." When Mel finally glanced up, her pale blue eyes twinkled. "I like to give him little opportunities to figure out he misses me."

With a good-natured chuckle, Sandy grabbed her purse from under the bar. "Okay, then. I won't be long."

* * *

The gas gauge on her truck dictated that Sandy would take a little longer on her errand than she'd planned. She swung into the gas station and swallowed over the knot of unease in her throat.

The huge white pickup parked at the inside island took up two spaces. The pump nozzle was jammed into the open gas tank door. The truck's hood was up, but the owner was nowhere in sight. Sandy eased her pickup to the other side of the island, casting a wary eye for Brody MacKay. Finally, she spotted him under the hood, the oil dipstick in his hand. He lifted his head from his task and met her look with a dark stare that froze her blood. Quickly, she averted her eyes, pretending she hadn't noticed him. She let the icy chill roll through her, accepting it for what it apparently was: an inexplicable sense of nervousness she always felt in Brody MacKay's presence.

Calling herself a coward for avoiding the man, she eased behind his truck and started across the parking lot to the mini-mart. For the first time, she was actually grateful that Stan Ocheski had never installed credit card readers on his pumps, like the gas stations in most twenty-first century civilizations. Who would have thought she'd one day appreciate Stan's tendency toward being old-school?

She set her gaze on her goal and kept walking. The same metal and tempered-glass door had probably hung at the entrance since the original service station had been replaced with a newfangled building in the late nineteen-sixties. According to the town's history, that had only happened because the state had re-routed the highway directly through the original service station Stan's grandfather had opened in the nineteen-thirties. Sandy pulled the heavy door open and stepped into the stuffy building. A thin layer of dust coated the bags of unsalted peanuts next to the register, prompting the outrageous thought that perhaps they had also been hanging in place since the sixties.

Sliding a twenty across the counter, she thought about the bottle of water she'd left sitting on the bar. "Hang on a sec, Stan. I need something to drink."

Sandy stepped around the end of the aisle, heading for the cooler at the rear of the store, and nearly barreled into Gloria Pratt, the sheriff's secretary, and — oh, just great. Alice MacKay stood next to Gloria, a scowl marring her face. Both women abruptly stopped talking.

"Sandy," greeted Alice in her well-modulated voice. "Are you in a hurry to get someplace?"

Sandy laughed, hoping she masked her unease. Why did she feel like she was interrupting some covert spy operation? "Oh, you know me. I hurry everywhere. I'm just on my way to pay Sean McGee for Domingo's board before my shift at the bar starts."

Was she imagining things or did Alice's lips thin just before she lifted them into a chilly smile?

"Well, then, we'll just let you pass so you can get going."

Sandy grabbed the first soda she laid her hands on, hoping it was something she could stomach. Then she forced herself to take more sedate steps back to the register, wondering how Alice managed to look and sound so pleasant and so disapproving at the same time.

* * *

If there was anything Ryan missed least about the ranch, it was mucking stalls. And yet there he was, using the rake to spread fresh bedding into the stall he'd just finished cleaning.

His early morning trip to town had been both productive and informative. It seemed some people, at least, were in a forgiving mood. Others apparently weren't, if the four-foot keying the driver's side of his car had taken while he was in the vet's office was anything to go by. As if it wasn't enough the veterinarian wanted nothing to do with the Cross MC, now Ryan would have an expensive insurance claim. The gouge was so deep in places, the fiberglass would need patching before the paint could be retouched. No need to wonder who had been at the heart of that, even if not directly involved.

He'd been back less than twenty-four hours and already he had more disturbing questions than anyone seemed inclined to answer. Maybe coming back had been a mistake after all. He saw no emergency on the ranch to warrant bringing him home. Of course, that didn't mean there was none. Sean was just like their father when it came to talking. They both got around to it in their own time and pushing only made them close down. Hell, with as slow to broach the subject as his family was being, he'd probably figure it out on his own first.

With a resigned sigh, Ryan turned his attention back to the stable. The ranch was a little more rundown than he'd expected. It appeared the major necessities were being handled but the small stuff seemed to be waiting. Some of the simplest projects were sitting so far on the back burner they were in danger of falling off the stove completely.

It felt to Ryan a bit like living from crisis to crisis, with no time or cash flow for anything but the next problem. As far as any extras went, there didn't seem to be any, not even the luxury of casual labor to help with menial chores. He thrust the rake against the wall and kicked at some errant straw. When had things gotten so bad for the ranch that Sean couldn't afford a couple of minimum-wage high school kids to help out part-time?

Snuffling sounds from the next stall told Ryan he would have to turn the occupant into the paddock. He grabbed a lead rein from the hook outside the stall. The last thing he planned to do was spend the rest of the day chasing an ornery horse. No sooner had he touched the door when hooves clattered against wood.

"I don't intimidate so easily, pal," Ryan said in a calming voice. He flipped up the latch and tugged.

A hairy mass the size of a semi barreled toward him.

"Geez!" He leapt backward to avoid the snapping teeth and slammed the door shut a bare second before one angry hoof connected.

His heart jackhammered, complementing the rhythm of the kicks coming from the other side of the stall door. What the hell was that demon of a red roan colt doing in the McGee stable? As Ryan sucked in air, trying to catch his breath, he considered the most obvious implication of finding the horse. His brother knew the woman behind the chicory-colored eyes. That his brother might have any sort of attachment to those eyes, Ryan refused to consider. Fate owed him one.

"Lost your touch with horses there, big brother?"

Ryan spun around. Sean leaned indolently in the doorway.

"Horses? No." Ry shook his head. "I can still handle a horse. *That*?" He jerked a thumb at the stall behind him. "Is not a horse. *That* is a demonic replica of a horse."

Sean pushed off the doorjamb and sauntered toward his brother. Inside the stall, the agitated snorts of the big roan continued, but the kicking had stopped.

"Domingo? This guy's a sweetheart. You just gotta speak his language." He held up an apple.

"You mean you have to bribe him," Ryan said flatly.

Sean smiled and held out his free hand for the lead rein.

Ryan stood well back when Sean eased open the stall door and stepped inside, apple first. When the horse took the apple, Sean clipped the lead to the halter.

"Sucker," Ryan mocked the big horse. "Trading your freedom for an apple. You should've held out for two."

Domingo's eyes rolled suspiciously as he passed, but the spirited colt nonetheless went easily with Sean.

Ryan followed, keeping a cautious eye on the colt as he pranced into the paddock. Leaning both arms on the top rail of the fence, he parked one booted foot on the bottom one. Sean came to stand next to him and together they watched the horse career around the enclosure.

"What's a horse like that doing in your stable?"

A troubled expression crept over Sean's face. "He's not ours. He's a boarder."

Ryan chose his next words with care. "Because... you're doing a favor for a friend?"

"For a friend." Sean spoke slowly, apparently considering his words with equal care. "But it's strictly a business arrangement." His direct look was a plea for understanding. "We have five other boarders and room for six more. It's part of the business now."

"The Cross MC runs cattle." Ryan never took his eyes off the colt bucking and kicking his way from one side of the paddock to the other.

Sean stiffened but held his silence. When Ryan swung his gaze away from the colt, they locked eyes and Sean spoke without emotion. "Price of beef's down, not likely to go up anytime soon. Cattle don't pay all the bills these days. The boarders fill in the gaps."

"It's a good idea," Ryan acknowledged. "What does the old man say?"

Sean's always-ready grin flashed again. "That the Cross MC runs cattle."

Ryan's bark of laughter startled the colt, who expressed his displeasure with flattened ears and a show of teeth.

"By the way, your delivery arrived earlier," said Sean. "The lumber's stacked by the barn."

Ryan shrugged and looked away. "I took care of a few needs. Some of the wood on the back barn's rotten, needs seeing to. I figured I'd make myself useful." He swung his gaze back to meet his brother's. "I found out we apparently don't use Dr. Davis any more when I tried to order cattle vaccines."

Sean lowered his eyes, staring at the ground. He kicked at a pebble with a well-worn boot. "We use the services of Dr. Pickeril up in Jackson."

"Jackson?" Ryan was genuinely surprised. "Why so far away?"

Sean lifted a shoulder. "He's the closest vet who has no ties with Brody MacKay."

Brody MacKay. The name turned his stomach as Ryan struggled to recall what connection the MacKay family had with the Drs. Davis, frowning when he came up blank.

"Davis Junior married some cousin of MacKay's," supplied Sean. "Anyway, Pickeril's good. Really good. He stopped an outbreak of what we thought was scours last spring before we lost too many calves."

What? With a jerk, he pulled his head out of his musing and focused on his brother. "We had scours?" Left untreated, the dehydrating illness could wipe out an entire year's worth of calves in a heartbeat.

Sean kicked at the pebble again, this time connecting and sending the stone flying across the drive. "Yeah, well. Turned out it wasn't really scours. There was some kind of toxin on the grazing in the south pasture. The cows were handling it okay but the calves were sensitive."

"What kind of toxin?"

"Never determined conclusively. Spring rains washed it away."

A sense of apprehension churned in Ryan's gut. "We ever have problems with that pasture before?"

"Nope." Sean shook his head. "State tested the soil and found nothing, but we haven't used the pasture since." He shrugged. "I prefer to keep things a little closer to home."

It didn't make sense. How would a short-lived toxin make it to one of their distant pastures? Before Ryan could press the matter, Sean's cell phone chirped. Judging from the grin on his brother's face, the call was from someone of the feminine persuasion. Someone important.

Pushing off the fence, Ryan headed back to his chores. He got to the door when Sean hailed him.

"Hey, Ry!"

Ryan paused and shot a glance over his shoulder.

Sunlight glinted off Sean's cell phone, still pressed against his ear. He flashed a grin. "It's good having you home."

With one finger, Ryan pushed his hat toward the back of his head and surveyed his brother, the rancher. "Thanks. Feels good to be here."

But I don't know if it feels right.

As he worked, Ryan gave some thought to his other life. It wouldn't be hard to leave it behind, except for *her*. His search had been a priority for so long it had become part of him. Maybe it was time to let her go, take his life back. How long was long enough to look for someone who obviously didn't want to be found? He was pretty sure he'd passed that mark a long time ago.

With the last of the stalls mucked, Ryan's aching muscles demanded a hot shower. Sean was going to give him grief about his stamina for ranch work if he didn't get his act together. Hoping to avoid his brother, he tramped along the side of the stable, stopping short when a feminine laugh from the direction of the main house drew his attention.

A rusty green pickup was parked on the circular drive in front of the house. Propped against the driver's side door, with one foot bent backward to rest on the fender, stood Ms. Chicory Eyes. Sean leaned forward, said something to her, and she threw back her head. Her melodic laugh echoed across the yard, spreading over Ryan like honey and heating his blood to one notch above simmer. He lingered in the shadow of the stable and watched.

She sashayed away from the fender and mock-punched Sean's arm. Then she reached for the door handle, but Sean said something else. With another laugh and a toss of her long chocolate-colored hair, she climbed into the truck. After she tossed a careless wave in Sean's direction, the truck's engine grumbled to life and left the ranch in a trail of dust.

No sign of a goodbye kiss. Good. Ryan counted to ten after her departure. Affecting a relaxed attitude he didn't particularly feel, he sauntered across the yard to the house. It had been a long time since his interest had been piqued by a woman. He hadn't realized how lonely he'd become until just that moment.

"Who was that?" he asked. *Good move, just keep it casual.*

Sean's eyebrows inched higher and one corner of his mouth pulled upward. "That would be Sandy, our best boarding customer. Domingo's owner."

"You two looked friendly."

"Yeah, I like her." Sean settled his hat back further on his head. "You want to meet her? She'll be at Valentine's tonight."

It took Ryan less than a second to accept the invitation.

* * *

"Bar's expanded some." Ryan scanned the parking lot, jammed to overflowing. "Always this busy?"

"Usually on Friday and Saturday." Sean maneuvered his pickup into a tight space between another pickup and a compact car. "Does a fair business the rest of the week but Friday and Saturday, there's a live band."

The marquee in front of Valentine's Bar and Grill advertised a band called Cowboy Blue featuring Ray Dan Beckley. The sound of lively music thumped across the parking lot. The last time Ryan had been to the bar, the music had consisted of a broken-down jukebox and good-natured arguments over which twenty-year-old songs to play.

He continued to scan the parking lot without realizing he was looking for anything. Then a jolt of pleasure raced through him at the sight of the beat-up green pickup near the side entrance. A smile of anticipation tugged at the corners of his mouth as he opened the door to go inside.

The color scheme was the same green, gold, and dark wood Ryan remembered but it had a richer feel. On walls that had once been Spartan now hung photographs of the town, the plains, the mountains. The expansions had been well thought out, with good use of space. An annex had been added, with a pool table and a row of electronic arcade games. A stage occupied one end of the main barroom and a huge plasma screen TV dominated the wall behind the bar.

Make that expanded a lot.

Ryan's smile widened in approval when he noted the ancient oak bar remained. He was momentarily warmed by some fine memories made at the far end of that scarred wood counter with the bar owner's somewhat more experienced daughter. But when he spotted dark hair and chicory eyes on the woman tending that same bar, his blood zipped from warm to hot.

Her hair was piled into a riotous dark mass on top of her head, looking deliciously bedroom-tousled. Ryan mentally calculated how quickly he could take it down and run his fingers through it.

Whoa, where the heck did that come from? Slow down, man. Slow down. No races here.

With the exception of glossy red lipstick coating what looked like very kissable lips, she wasn't wearing heavy makeup, giving her a classy natural look. The picture of small town barmaid was completed by large gold hoops dangling from exquisitely shaped earlobes.

Then she glanced up. Across thirty feet of crowded room, chicory eyes met his, holding him with a look that set off an immediate conflagration in his blood. The indignation of the previous night had been replaced by sparks of interest. He acknowledged her with a slow nod, somehow managing to stay upright as he followed his brother. Her very presence was unsettling in ways he wasn't certain he'd ever understand.

As Sean cut them a path to the bar, the band stopped playing and the lead singer began speaking to the patrons. "What do you think? Can we get our Friday night favorite up here?"

An approving roar went up from the crowd, loud enough to give a city rock concert venue a run for the money.

The lone spotlight rolled over the crowd, which was chanting a name: "Sandy! Sandy! Sandy!" Finally, the light settled on Chicory, still standing behind the bar. She shook her head and laughed good-naturedly, pointing to her watch and then back at the band.

The chanting continued, grew to a raucous level, and finally with a smile, Chicory surrendered and handed the cleaning rag she'd been holding to a pretty young girl with sleek blond hair.

Something about her called for a second look. "Whoa! Is that little Melanie Mitchell?"

Sean nodded, an eager grin splitting his face. So that was how it rolled.

Ryan whistled appreciatively. "She sure grew up well." The poke in the ribs confirmed his suspicions and went a long way toward reinstating his status as big brother. Ryan turned his attention back to the bartender as she sauntered across the room.

The lead singer held out his hand to give Sandy a boost onto the stage just as the band shot into a sultry opening with a heavy beat. Her foot, strapped into a gold sandal with an impossibly high heel, began to tap and she closed her eyes, as though feeling out the rhythm. When she popped them open again and her hips swung into the beat, an explosion of lust swamped Ryan's system and his libido kicked itself into overdrive.

Her voice was throaty and full. Sexy as fire. Interested in spite of himself, Ryan unashamedly ran his eyes over the whole package in the same way as probably every other man in the place and maybe a few of the women.

She wore a scrap of lavender silk, which slid over her body with the smallest of movements, taking a path his hands ached to travel. Faded blue jeans looked like they'd been painted on over nicely rounded hips and what details he couldn't make out, his mind had no trouble filling in. An amber-colored gem in her bellybutton played peek-a-boo whenever the lavender silk slipped upward. But when his gaze moved to her face, it was her eyes that held his fascination.

She sang in graphic detail about the destruction of a cheating lover's four-wheel drive, miming each action as she sang the words. Her hips rocking in time, she glided across the stage, openly flirting with everyone close enough to make eye contact. Every man there was probably considering the prospects for getting lucky that night, and about half of them would want to run out and check on their rides when she finished singing.

"Wow!" wheezed the overweight, balding gentleman seated next to him. One look at his excitement-reddened face had Ryan calling up the steps for emergency treatment of a stroke from his memory. The guy was breathing so heavily he could barely speak. "Wouldn't want to get caught cheating on that one."

Ryan mumbled something he hoped sounded halfway coherent and sipped the beer Melanie set in front of him. Chicory moved into another high-energy number with a heavier, even sexier beat. He didn't think cheating *on* her would be a problem. At least he couldn't imagine himself ever wanting to cheat on her if they were together.

She left the stage and worked the crowd, moving among them, touching arms and hands and faces, openly flirting with a few of the men as she sang about loving a good-time cowboy. The sexual energy in the room became even more tangible, yet somehow the atmosphere didn't flash over to raunchy.

Her eyes locked with his and Ryan lost his ability to think. Unexpectedly, she had become predator and he very much the prey in her sights. Without taking her eyes from him, she approached with a sultry cat-like walk, the embodiment of temptation. She stopped mere inches away and her body heat assaulted him like a five-alarm blaze.

While she rocked in rhythm with the thumping music and sang about a devil in disguise, Ryan forced himself to remain completely still. Sending him a cheeky grin of appreciation, the sexy singer reached up, plucked the hat off his head, and set it on her own. His gaze was imprisoned by luscious red lips singing about being addicted to love. Breath backed up in his lungs when she walked two red-tipped fingers in tempo from his belly up to his throat. All sense of his surroundings became lost in the steamy regard of those chicory-colored eyes.

She ran the tip of her tongue along her upper lip in slow motion. Then with a wink, she whirled around and presented her back to him while she flirted outrageously with Sean. Feeling needy, with a distinct sense of unfinished business, Ryan contented himself with watching the rhythmic sway of her behind. She was so close he jammed his hands in his pockets to restrain himself from doing anything to earn a boot of his sorry tail out into the parking lot.

Ryan kept ravenous eyes glued to the sexy bartender-turned-singer when she got back on stage, performing another number with the band's lead singer. When they sang a slow duet about being alone and needing someone, Ryan's heart gave a tug. Before he could figure out exactly why the song was having such an effect on him, they moved into another high-energy number. This time instead of working in the crowd, Chicory played off the band's lead singer, but she got the crowd involved with dancing and shining cell phones. She finished amid a roar of good-natured hoots and cheers, a couple of men near the stage gave her a hand down, and Ryan found himself tempering unexpected jealousy.

But then she was on her way in his direction again, chicory eyes holding him captive once more. Just watching her walk was seducing him. Her face was flushed, probably with the exertion of her performance, but he recognized the bold glint in her eyes as purely sensual. The hungry flame first ignited on the road in the mountains kicked itself up several levels, and at the moment, he could think of no reason to bank that particular fire.

Chapter Three

He'd entered the bar with Sean McGee moments before Ray Dan had called her on stage, and Sandy had deliberately punched up what was typically already a very sexy performance. She'd approached him with more overt sensuality than she'd ever shown in her life, intentionally sharking him, daring him to want her. And his motor had been running for her. Of that, she was quite certain.

Who knew, after years of having no real interest in dating, that one sexy performance directed at a stranger would jump-start *her* hibernating motor?

Now he was sitting at the bar, her territory, and her body was reacting as though it was very happy to see him. Wearing a Western-style striped shirt in shades of blue and a pair of ass-grabbing tight jeans, he looked even tastier than he had in the black leather jacket at the wheel of his vintage Corvette.

Having reclaimed her position behind the bar, Sandy gave herself permission to check out the tantalizing newcomer. So she'd been correct; the stranger on the road had been the mysterious, troublemaking prodigal son. At the moment, he wasn't making trouble, unless she could count the way her heart pounded a little harder as she studied him. He sat comfortably, half-turned outward on the stool, one hand on a mug of beer. Her eyes made the journey up and down his lean frame, openly assessing his sex appeal, which she suspected went hand-in-hand with his potential for trouble. When she got to his eyes, she was oddly pleased to notice he was observing her as she checked him out.

Lazily, he returned the assessment, heavy-lidded eyes lingering on her chest, traveling to her waist, her hips, then moving back to brush her throat. His look singed her skin wherever it touched. When his gaze caressed her lips, she could almost feel the scorch of his kiss, and with that on her mind, she cast a leisurely provocative smile in his direction.

He raised his mug in an apparent toast of appreciation.

Next to her, Mel trilled her tongue and poked Sandy in the small of the back. "I was beginning to wonder if you *liked* men. Get on over there, girl."

Sandy stopped herself from racing to the end of the bar. Barely.

She locked onto his eyes and found herself trapped in them as she concentrated on placing one foot in front of the other until she reached his end of the bar.

"We meet again."

"You two've met?" Sean's eyebrows skyrocketed.

"Last evening." Sandy hardly spared Sean a glance. "When he almost ran me and Domingo over with his car."

"You *were* standing in the middle of the road." Prodigal son Ryan ignored the obvious baiting.

"My horse and I were *crossing* the road," she corrected, laying elbows on the bar and leaning toward him.

* * *

Ryan suspected the droop of the lavender top to reveal the extra cleavage was no accident. But hey, he wasn't complaining. His eyes followed the curve into the intriguing shadows at the center of her chest.

"That explains a lot," Sean muttered under his breath. "Sandy, allow me to introduce my brother, Ryan McGee. He's mostly harmless — when he's not driving."

If he hadn't been watching her, Ryan would have missed the nearly imperceptible widening of her eyes followed by the quick flick of her tongue to her lips. His jeans tightened, and he fought the urge to shift and accommodate the reason.

"Oh, I'm sure he's anything but harmless," Sandy drawled. "But I'm willing to take my chances." With one elegant hand, she took his hat off her head and parked it back on his, setting it in place with a little tap.

He removed it again and set it between them on the bar. "Buy you a drink?"

She shook her head with obvious regret. "I'm working, sorry."

"Yeah, but you get a break, right?" He was aware he sounded desperate but was long past caring. "I can talk to your boss. See if you can take your break with me."

Sean opened his mouth but whatever he was going to say, he swallowed the words when Sandy laid two exquisitely manicured fingers on his wrist. The handful of shiny gold bands dangling from her wrist tinkled with her movement.

"You won't get anywhere." Sandy looked directly at Ryan. "The boss here's kind of a ball-buster. But I'll tell you what. Come by around eleven tomorrow and I'll buy you lunch."

With what might have been a wink, she was off to attend to other customers.

Well, it wasn't exactly a red light, more of a yield sign. Ryan amused himself by watching her casual flirtations with customers from one end of the bar to the other.

She stopped long enough to park another frosted mug of draft in front of him. "On the house. Welcome home." Her smile lit her eyes and Ryan temporarily lost his ability to speak. Then she was off again.

"Well, crap." Sean looked like he'd swallowed a bug. "What's Bull MacKay doing here? He almost never shows his face."

Ryan glanced over his shoulder following Sean's gaze. The burly man just entering the bar was as solid as he had been when he was a high school senior playing quarterback during Ryan's sophomore year. His face was weathered and his hair thinning, but the expression in his eyes was as sullen as Ryan remembered.

"Must've heard the grapevine buzzing," said Sean.

Ryan shrugged, unconcerned. "Bound to happen sometime. Relax. I won't start anything if he doesn't."

Deliberately, Ryan looked away and took a casual pull of his beer.

"I heard you had the bad sense to crawl back home." The goading voice came from behind him.

Ryan turned around to meet the other man's glaring black eyes. "Well, if it isn't Brody MacKay the younger."

"Rumor was you'd got killed," Brody sneered.

"Rumors are overrated." With a bit of effort, Ryan kept his voice even, punctuating the sentence with a swig of his beer.

"Still kidnapping little boys?" demanded Brody.

"Your old man still looking for kids to beat the shit out of?" countered Ryan in a soft tone that was in direct contrast to the general annoyance he felt.

So focused was Ryan on his old adversary that Sandy caught him by surprise, materializing at his elbow and inserting herself between him and Bull. She carried a tray holding a mug of beer and she lifted this in Bull's direction. Ryan didn't want her there, didn't want the ugliness to sully her.

But he was unable to stop her when she simply presented him with her back and touched Bull on his arm. "Hey, Bull, good to see you tonight. How are your mom and pop?"

A suggestion of intimacy between Sandy and Bull registered, and Ryan white-knuckled his mug of beer. But as much as he wanted to turn his back on the scene, he couldn't.

Bull shook off her hand and growled, "What are you doin', Sandy, associatin' with this?"

Sandy's laughter was a little too loud, her voice artificially bright. "Don't know what you're talking about, Bull. He's just a customer." Though he'd obviously had more than enough to drink, she lifted the tray with the mug of beer in his direction. "How about one on the house?"

The big man wavered, slowly releasing the fist at his side, finally snatching the mug and taking a long pull. Malevolent eyes glared at Ryan over the mug as he finished in one long gulp and then wiped his mouth with the back of his hand. "Next time you see me, you won't have a woman to hide behind."

"The next time you see me, try walking in the other direction," Ryan responded. "I'm not looking for trouble, Bull."

"Then you should have stayed away." After a final pointed glare, Bull swaggered off.

Ryan let his old adversary have the small victory, and concentrated instead on suppressing the adrenaline pulsing through his system. So much for thoughts of a mutually pleasant seduction. Ryan knew his eyes had hardened but he glanced at Sandy anyway, laying a hand on her forearm. "You seeing him?"

Sandy frowned, obviously not caring for the proprietary sound of the question. She jerked her arm from Ryan's touch and shifted her body slightly away from him. "First of all, I don't *see* married men," she replied in a voice gone cold. "Second, if I *was* seeing him, I wouldn't have spent the evening thinking about what it would be like to *see* you!"

With a toss of her head that loosened a tendril of hair, she spun around. The set of her shoulders advertised her tension, and Ryan winced. How many ways could he screw up tonight? "Wait. Please." Ryan felt the words being torn from him by a force he didn't recognize. He only knew he wanted no burnt bridges between him and the siren with the chicory-colored eyes.

Sandy hesitated then sent him a hard stare over her shoulder. The chill in her eyes was nothing compared to the icy fingers working their way along his nerves.

He drew a steadying breath and blew it out slowly. "I'm sorry. I took my mood out on you. Look, the man's dangerous. What's between us is... volatile." Ryan grimaced. "You should stay out of it."

He picked up his beer with an unsteady hand, unwilling to admit that watching her defuse the situation with kindness had sparked a slow-burning fuse of his own with pure jealousy at the core.

* * *

Slowly and deliberately, Sandy set the empty tray on the bar, turned to face Ryan, then stepped close enough to make her point without shouting over the band. "Obviously, the two of you have some kind of history. But I don't share that history. Bull and I have an understanding about how he'll behave in here. I don't care if you two go find a dark alley and pound the crap out of each other, but let me make one thing clear." She jammed her right index finger into his chest. "It isn't going to happen in my place. *Ever.*" Stabbing her finger harder to emphasize the last word, she used the motion to push herself away.

Just as carefully, Ryan set his mug of beer on the bar and folded his arms across his chest. "First, there aren't any alleys, dark or otherwise, in Orson's Folly. Second, what do you mean *your* place? What happened to Tom Valentine?"

What was the matter with her? She never put herself on display like she just had. Never. Yet as she watched his green eyes flash with surprise, she realized she wanted those green eyes on her again. Wanted any internal combustion he felt to be for her. *Only* for her. Sandy stuffed her hands into her back pockets, knowing full well the move would thrust her ladies front and center. His eyes instantly left her mouth and settled on her chest. Her lips curled into a lopsided smile. *Much better.*

"It's been *my place* since I bought it from Tom going on six years ago." She jutted her chin out in defiance. *Let's just see what he has to say about that.* "I put everything I had into this venture and then some. So trust me, wherever you take your argument with Bull, it had better be far, *far* away from here."

Ryan stared. His mouth opened, closed again. Finally he managed one sentence. "You told me the boss was a ball-buster."

Although she was standing so close that, even in four-inch heels, she had to tilt her head to meet his eyes, Sandy refused to step back. Instead, she leaned closer. "I am," she whispered with soft seduction in his ear. "You can trust me on that, too."

As she walked away, her hip brushed him in passing. He shifted quickly out of her way but not before she got a good feel. Since she doubted he was packing a gun... there, she was fairly certain his attention was back where she wanted it. On her.

* * *

Hours after the last patron had headed home and the light in front of the bar had been turned off, Sandy stretched out on her bed in the one-room efficiency apartment above Valentine's. But sleep remained elusive. Still feeling the residual heat from her encounter with Ryan McGee, she wore only light pajamas and hadn't bothered to pull down the covers on the bed.

So the returning bad boy was Sean McGee's brother. She hadn't seen that one coming. And Mel was definitely going to hear about her omission of that little detail.

She considered Sean's older brother. Not one mention within her earshot during the six years she'd made Orson's Folly her home. What did it take for a town to obliterate someone's existence from the circle of gossip? It must have been something drastic for the hard feelings to be so enduring even after such a long absence. She frowned. Maybe it hadn't been such a good idea to play up to him during her act. She still had a hard time fitting in, even after years of living in Orson's Folly. It might be better to remain neutral in the apparent ongoing dispute between Ryan McGee and Bull MacKay.

But something about Ryan intrigued her; something compelled her to want to spend more time with him. Emotions and physical sensations she hadn't experienced in years demanded permission to come alive again.

"Ryan McGee." Into the darkness she whispered his name, testing the feel of it on her tongue.

She wasn't worried about why he'd left Orson's Folly, nor why he had unexpectedly returned. None of that had anything to do with her. On the other hand, her over-the-top response to him confused her. He wasn't *her* returning prodigal anything. But something had drawn her attention in his direction from the start and she wasn't certain she could back off. Or if she wanted to.

For sure, he was easy to look at, with his long legs and fit muscular build. Wherever he'd been, he'd spent plenty of time outside. His skin was well tanned, his face not quite shaven. Sun-kissed dark blond hair feathered back and fell straight to touch the top of his collar. She always had been a sucker for that scruffy look.

She was intrigued by the way his expressive green eyes changed color with his mood. And she really liked the way he studied her with those eyes, especially when he knew she was looking back.

Touching him had been daring for her, even in the context of her performance. But she'd liked the feel of him. Even more, she'd liked knowing she had thrown him just a little off balance when she'd admitted in the heat of her anger that she had been thinking about him.

Tired, unsettled, just at the edge of sleep, she nevertheless found herself wondering if Ry was home to stay or just in for a visit. Either way, she figured her summer had suddenly become a lot more interesting.

* * *

With shaking hands, Sandy pushed the button to open the comm again. "Are you there, Mick?"

After a very long pause, the radio squawked and the voice answered, "I'm here. What's the status?"

She tried to keep it professional. "I've been advised you need to check your emergency locator signal. Help is on the way. And you should conserve your radio battery by turning the unit off and checking in every hour."

A lengthy pause followed. She could hear him breathing. Then she was surprised by a wry chuckle. "Good try, sweetheart. You get points for caring. But I know the score. I'm pretty sure the thing sticking in my back is an office chair. Since we're in the parking garage, that makes it at least a couple of floors of rubble on top of us."

A tear slipped down Sandy's cheek, and she lost the battle for objective professionalism. "Maybe it's not as bad as you think. Maybe a furniture truck fell on you instead of the building."

His laugh in her ear belied the gravity of the situation. "So you're a glass-half-full kind of gal, huh?"

"More like a grateful-the-glass-holds-anything-at-all kind of gal," she countered.

He laughed again. "I like you. Got a name?"

"Oh, it's um, Alexandra."

"Whoo-hoo! Ms. Yum-Alexandra. That's a mouthful," he said, exaggerating his Wyoming accent. More softly, he asked, "How 'bout I just call you Angel? That's what your voice makes me think of."

* * *

The ground underneath her trembled. *Quake!* With her racing heart threatening to hammer its way out of her chest, Sandy popped her eyes open. The blanket of blackness eased into shades of gray as her mind adjusted to wakefulness. The ground beneath her became the softness of her own bed. Another tremor rocked her, shaking the mattress beneath her, as shivers wracked her body.

Chilly waves of night breeze washed off the mountain, fluttering the ghostly pale chintz curtains framing the open window. Sandy stretched, enjoying the scents of pine and wildflowers wafting through her window. Give her the chill any day so long as it came with the fragrance of the mountains. She rubbed the goose bumps from her arms and rolled herself into the blanket, ready for another couple hours of sleep.

But her mind had plans that didn't include turning itself off to rest.

She sighed and watched a sliver of moonlight moving across the windowsill. The dream hadn't been unexpected. She'd grown used to her memories intruding sometimes. Thanks to the dream, though, she was now wondering if starting something with Ryan was a good idea after all. Maybe they could share a meal and it would be the start of a nice friendship.

Her erogenous centers twitched in protest as she recalled her sexy little dance for him the night before. Yeah. That genie probably wouldn't be stuffed back in the bottle so easily.

With the first touch of dawn, the colors around her emerged from the gray, as if the room itself was coming alive. Time for her to come alive, too. She pushed to her feet and smoothed the bed covers.

While the rushing water steamed up her bathroom, Sandy drank her coffee and painstakingly selected the makeup she would need in order to face the day. And her impromptu date with Ryan McGee. She stood naked in front of her closet for a full ten minutes trying to decide what to wear. She had no idea why she felt like a nervous girl going to her first dance, but she sure hoped the unaccustomed feeling went away, and quickly.

* * *

Excitement worthy of a teenaged geek about to date the head cheerleader tingled through Ryan as he found himself in the parking lot of Valentine's a full thirty minutes early. A couple of other cars occupied the parking lot, but either the lunch crowd hadn't arrived or she didn't do a large midday business.

His steps slowed as he approached the heavy wooden doors. Just beyond that entrance he would find the woman who'd been on his mind nonstop over the past several hours. It was no use reminding himself that he had no business being here. He knew that, yet here he was. Sandy's voice was like a siren's call. He couldn't ignore it. The moment she had crossed his path, everything and everyone else seemed to fade into obscurity. Even the search for the woman who'd once been the most important person in his life. He didn't understand it but he was powerless in the face of it.

The brass handle was warm from the midday sun. Drawing a fortifying breath, he pulled the door open and stepped inside.

She was sitting at one of the tables off to the side, concentrating on a red laptop computer. Ryan's heart rate picked up a bit as he let his eyes trail along the curves beneath a form-hugging pale pink tank shirt tucked into another pair of low-riding blue jeans. One leg was folded beneath her on the chair; a sandal rested on the floor next to her. Purple-tipped toes moved in rhythm to the jukebox music.

Captivated, he tipped back his Stetson and lingered against the doorway, watching her. And because he was watching her, he knew the instant she became aware of his presence. Her hand hovered over the keyboard then she pulled it back and sat motionless for a moment. Finally she angled a look over her shoulder to meet his scrutiny.

Her own gaze swept a fiery path down his body, then back up again and she greeted him with a leisurely smile that steamed his blood. "Have you been there long? I didn't mean to keep you waiting." Like a calculating cat, she rose to her feet in fluid motion and slid her foot into her sandal. Just watching the purple straps embrace her foot sent darts of jealousy racing through him.

* * *

With lazy movements, Ryan took off his hat and set it on the end of the bar, holding her eyes with his own as he sauntered across the room. "No hardship." His voice was low and sizzled with the barest suggestion of sex.

When he stood directly in front of her, well inside her bubble of personal space, she had to resist the sudden urge to lean in and kiss that incredibly sensuous mouth.

Then thoughts of resisting temptation faded to nothing as he took the initiative. Ryan leaned closer, paused, then finished the approach. Sandy lifted her face, her eyelids heavy, her breath hanging up in her throat. The first brush of his lips was subtle, a butterfly hovering. Only their lips touched. It was a relatively chaste kiss, but Sandy's reaction to it was anything but. She steadied herself with her hands on his waist as little zings of pure wow factor traveled to her brain.

Ryan deepened the kiss only slightly, but he lingered with his lips on hers. His hands slid up her arms to cup her bare shoulders, his thumbs drawing tiny circles which sent flashes of electricity rocketing to all the appropriate places. When he drew away, she moaned in protest. Her grip tightened on his waist, willing his mouth to return to hers. Ryan eased back another inch, running his hands down her arms to her hands, squeezing lightly before breaking the contact.

"What was that?" she whispered.

He touched a finger to her nose. "If you have to ask, I must not've done it right."

Sandy laid her fingertips against her lips. "Oh, no," she breathed. "You did it right." Maybe a little too right, considering she no longer maintained the upper hand in the encounter.

His eyes lit on her fingers and his roguish grin faded into a look of pure physical hunger which painted fiery brushstrokes of need into Sandy's brain. She wasn't used to needing. But her pulse skipped into high gear with the certainty he'd intentionally shown her his hunger, and just maybe that meant he was feeling as off-balance by whatever was happening between them as she was.

"Fact is, Chicory, I've wanted to do that since about two seconds after you called me a jackass." The playful grin returned. "Thought I'd get that first one out of the way so it's not hanging there between us any more."

She felt a little dizzy. "And now that you have?"

He tipped his head and slid a glance over her lips. "I'd like to go back for seconds at some point," he said softly. "Would that be a problem for you?"

"I'd say there's a good chance I won't have a problem with that. In fact..." Sandy pushed her hair behind her ear, leaning toward him. She froze, stepped back and looked up. "What did you just call me?"

Ryan winced. "Chicory. Bad habit of mine, so I'm told. Nicknames."

Sandy wrinkled her nose. "I remind you of a coffee *substitute*?"

He shrugged and then smiled one of those devastating, toe-curling, dripping-with-desire smiles. Sandy felt herself salivating and it had nothing to do with lunch.

* * *

Apparently she wasn't thrilled with being compared to a substitute anything, let alone a substitute some folks considered less satisfying than the real thing. "Not the root," he corrected. "The flower. Your eyes are the same blue as a chicory flower. It's what I first noticed. Out there on the road the other evening."

As he stood there, lost again in those eyes, they flashed with something that might have been irritation or arousal, or maybe something else. Ryan wished he knew which, but before he could discern, she was moving off.

He caught her hand and tugged her closer. "Hey, it's just a nickname. I won't use it again."

"No, no, it's okay. You can call me whatever you want. If I don't like it, I won't answer. I was just thinking about how much energy you're gonna take." She shot him a considering look. "And I'm trying to figure out if it's sweet that you compared my eyes to a wildflower or disturbing that you know the name of one."

Self-consciousness was an unfamiliar feeling, made him itch between his shoulder blades. "I know the names of a lot of wildflowers," he admitted, fighting the need to squirm the itch away. "My mom liked flowers. She spent a lot of time teaching me and Sean about things other than cattle."

"She sounds amazing."

"She was. She'd have liked you." When Sandy raised a disbelieving eyebrow, he nodded. "She would have liked your independence and admired your... spirit."

Sandy laughed. "I guess spirit's one way of putting it." With a pointed look at his hand on her arm, she added, "If y'all want to eat, you'd best let go."

Oh, he wanted to eat, all right, but it wasn't food on his mind. Reluctantly, he slid his fingers along her palm, lingering where their fingertips met. She drew a sharp breath as he dropped his hand, and he smiled. And when she ambled off toward the kitchen, he unabashedly followed her smooth sensuous walk with his eyes. Hell yeah, it was going to be fun. When was the last time he'd allowed himself anything solely for pleasure?

And how would Sandy do in the city? The thought was a mood-killer and he frowned. Did he really want to go back? Maybe it was time to stop doggedly pursuing a dream that was proving too elusive.

He pushed back the thoughts that dampened the moment and looked around the bar. Being nearly deserted gave it a different feel from the evening before. He wandered over to her computer. An expensive digital camera sat next to it, connected by a thin white cord. He didn't know what he expected to find. Maybe she was just doing the weekly accounting or balancing her checkbook. When he looked at the screen, though, he was immediately grabbed by the photo of a group of bison trekking single-file across a valley.

It was a technically good photo. Artistically, it was great. A still picture, yet it conveyed a sense of unrelenting lumbering forward. Curious, he rolled the mouse over the album, bringing up the next picture, a relative close-up of a bison in profile, lazy and unconcerned. He flipped through image after image, prairie dogs playing, a mother moose and her twins, black bears, grizzly bears, foxes, coyotes, rock formations, cloud formations, dead trees, budding trees, snow-kissed mountains, and a powerful red sunset over Diamondback Bluffs.

The pictures pulled him in. The pieces of home he'd missed. Over and over Sandy's images captured the Wyoming he'd once described to someone else with the hope of one day bringing her home with him. Once again past and present began a battle centered in the region of his heart, and Ryan considered making his excuses and leaving. Instead he clicked the mouse on the next picture. Then the next.

He was so caught up in the images, he didn't notice Sandy's return until she spoke. "House specialty burgers and fries coming up."

Heat swamped his face and he slowly turned away from the computer, expecting to see anger or at least irritation. Instead, she was setting up the table for their meal, completely unconcerned about his snooping.

He gestured toward the computer. "Sorry. I should have asked."

A gentle smile curved her lips, and her eyes, those amazing eyes, glittered with humor. "If it was something personal, I would have turned off the computer. They're just pictures from my rides with Domingo. I was wondering about framing some of them. Still a few bare spots on the walls."

Ryan took a moment to study the bar's framed pictures he'd seen but hardly paid attention to the evening before. "Those are yours?"

"They are," she acknowledged ruefully. Then she shrugged. "Just a few personal impressions of the area since I moved here."

"A woman of many talents." It didn't seem quite the right time to ask what other talents might be in her repertoire, but his body reacted to the fleeting thought, tightening his jeans for him. "They're really good. They remind me of everything I missed while I was away. Do you sell many?"

Sandy's hands stilled in the middle of arranging silverware. She blinked a couple of times in surprise. "That'd be a no, since they aren't for sale. They're just something I play around with."

Her tinkling laughter tiptoed across the air between them and settled against his ears with a little sigh.

"I'd buy them." He didn't realize he'd spoken aloud until she chuckled.

"Just tell me which ones you like and they're yours."

Ryan found himself grinning along with her as she told outrageous stories about shooting the photos he was browsing. He rolled the mouse over another album, surprised when he found pictures of wild mustangs. She had caught them running, grazing, with foals. There was even a series of photos illustrating a disagreement between two stallions.

"I know where this is," Ryan said, lightly tapping the screen with a forefinger. "This is Cross MC high pasture." He frowned. "We got mustangs running there?"

Sandy shrugged. "Apparently. At least they were there last week. I wanted to stay longer but it's a long ride and Domingo was getting ornery."

Ryan snorted. "When isn't that horse ornery?"

"He's a good horse," Sandy insisted.

"He tried to take a bite out of me." Ryan chuckled then related his experience mucking stalls.

* * *

"He... *might* be a little touchy," Sandy admitted. Why did she have to feel so damn defensive? Better to change the subject. "Anyway, I want to go back to see the mustangs. But I'm afraid of Domingo starting trouble with the bay stallion."

She stopped talking when she noticed Ry had stopped going through her photo albums and was sitting, his chin propped on one hand, watching her as though entranced.

"What are you doing tomorrow?" he asked.

"Not a lot," she drawled. "What are you doing tonight?"

Ryan stared.

Really, the look on his face was comical. Like he couldn't believe his luck and then suddenly realized he'd left his only condom at home in his other pair of jeans. "Relax, Cowboy, I'm not inviting you up to my room."

Yet.

"Okay." His voice sounded a bit strangled.

Sandy laughed. "Saturday crowd here's usually pretty fun. And it's the first Saturday of the month."

He angled a look at her. "What happens the first Saturday of the month?"

A slow smile tugged at Sandy's lips. He'd see... if he showed up.

Chapter Four

Singles night had once been fun. Watching the couples meet, sometimes leaving together, and sometimes drifting into longer term relationships had always appealed to Sandy's romantic heart.

But she'd gone and invited Ryan and now she was watching all the predatory single women in the county vying for the seat next to his at the bar. Worse, tending bar meant she was delivering the abundance of drinks the women who lost at the game of musical barstools invariably sent his way from across the room.

What had seemed like an opportunity to poke fun at Ryan was backfiring. Badly. He looked particularly pleased with himself as she slid yet another beer across the bar in his direction.

"From the lovely lady on the end," she said, forcing some brightness into her tone.

Ryan leaned forward and acknowledged the dark-haired woman, who was probably ten years his senior. With each drink, Sandy's mood became snippier. Almost as though she might be... jealous. Which, of course, was ridiculous. Wasn't it? She barely knew the guy.

"Can you do me a favor and start serving me just Coke?" He nodded at his glass. "I'd like to be able to drive home in one piece."

Sandy bent over the counter and motioned him to come closer. When he leaned forward, the subtle scent of leather and sandalwood tickled her nose. Fighting the urge to grab him by the lapels and pull him even closer, she whispered, "Or maybe you'll score and you won't have to drive home at all."

A grin flashed. "Offering?"

She allowed her gaze to wander downward, over the Western-cut shirt — dark blue — enjoying the way it hugged his wide shoulders and muscular chest. *Yum.* When she reached the silver belt buckle at his waist, she reversed direction until she met his eyes again. "Nope. Excuse me, I have another customer."

Ryan merely shrugged, a half-smile playing around his lips as his eyes settled on her mouth. Quickly, before she was tempted to linger, she walked away. Her step faltered just a little at what might have been his soft chuckle, but she pressed on.

Standing by the beer taps, Sandy watched him from the corner of her eye as he finished off his drink and said goodbye to the redhead who had occupied the seat next to him for the past hour. Her hands were all over his arm as she leaned forward, pushing her considerable assets against him, and slid a napkin his way. She said something and Ryan shot her a killer smile. Then she was gone.

"You should go on break, get the seat next to him before it's occupied again," Mel murmured, drawing another mug of beer.

"He's not exactly a sad country song when it comes to companionship tonight." Sandy glowered over her shoulder. "I've delivered more drinks to him than the rest of the single men here put together."

"But I bet he'd actually *drink* one from you." The smug smile on Mel's face was bad enough, but when she added a wink, she became Mad Mademoiselle Matchmaker. "He's been watching you all night."

Of *that*, Sandy had been acutely aware — and it pleased her. She pulled the tap on a house special for her next order and stole another sideways glance at the man of interest. He'd had a productive afternoon, apparently having visited the barbershop. Gone were the sun-tipped waves that had brushed his collar and made her want to dive her fingers through the spun gold, replaced by close-cropped hair that appeared more of a warm nut brown.

Wetness trickled over Sandy's fingers and she released the tap before too much amber liquid spilled down the overflow. "Damn it," she whispered, grabbing a rag. With quick strokes, she wiped down the outside of the glass. *Keep your mind on your work.*

"Oops, sorry, hon, too late." Laughing, Mel elbowed her in the ribs. "Bertie just took the open seat."

"What?" Sandy whirled. A young, willowy girl tossed her straight, honey-brown hair over her shoulder, laughing at something Ryan said. "Guess I'd better take her order."

"Wanna take me for a ride in your hot car?" Bertie walked her fingers along Ryan's arm and lowered her voice. "We could go someplace private."

"Hello, Roberta, nice to see you." Sandy smiled though she wanted to break the girl's fingers. "Ryan, have you met Roberta Higgins?"

Ryan took a closer look at the girl, obviously trying to figure out if he should know her. Bertie's engaging smile outlined her perfectly straight, gleaming white teeth.

"What can I get you?" asked Sandy. *Pacifier? Ride to kindergarten?*

"How about a rum and Coke for us both?" suggested Bertie, tilting her face toward Ryan.

"Certainly. Just let me check your ID real quick."

The perfect teeth disappeared as Bertie's luscious lips fell into a sexy pout. "Oh, come on, Sandy. You know my birthday's next month."

"Ohh..." Heaving a sigh, Sandy performed a mental fist pump as she outwardly feigned regret. "I'm sorry, Bertie. I can't break the law. You know how DC is about those things."

The sexy pout turned sullen. "My dad got you to do this, didn't he?"

"No, Roberta, it really is the law," Sandy corrected, cooling her voice as her temper heated. "But your dad *would* have a lot to say if he knew you were here, wouldn't he?"

Looking a little like a deflated balloon, Bertie directed a gaze at Ryan. "So, do you still want to go for a ride?"

"I'll have to take a rain check," Ryan said with an easy smile.

After subjecting Sandy to a narrow-eyed glare, the delectable — and underaged — Roberta Higgins slid from the barstool and left, her gliding walk leaking youthful sex appeal. Most of the men present watched her exit. But not Ryan, Sandy noted with approval.

* * *

Ryan chuckled. So Chicory had been jealous enough to interrupt a potential pickup. Interesting. "She seems like a nice girl." He shrugged and deepened his cowboy twang. "Pretty lil' thang. Who's this father of hers who'd have so much to say?"

"Bobby Higgins. Brother Bobby Higgins of the New Life Christian Church across the street."

Ryan jerked upright and stared in shock.

She snickered. "Yeah, you just got hit on by the preacher's daughter. Care to insert a joke?"

About to sip his soda, he reversed direction and set the drink down on the bar with a little thud, fairly certain he was about to be struck blind for even looking at the girl. He indicated the glass in front of him. "I think I need something stronger after all."

"Don't forget you still have to get yourself home tonight," Sandy warned as she walked away. A moment later, she was back with a tall glass of golden liquid, which she placed in front of him without a word and then walked away.

He sat nursing the beer and wondering how much longer she would let his torment go on. He didn't want any of the endless parade of single women hitting on him. He was only interested in one sexy single tonight.

Moments later, he felt movement as someone slid onto the seat next to him and closed his eyes, wondering what the opening line would be this time.

"Buy you a drink, cowboy?"

At the sound of the whiskey-honey voice behind him, Ryan's eyes flew open. His breathing skidded to a stop, the air backing up in his lungs. His heart bumped hard against his chest wall, pushing a massive amount of adrenaline through his veins.

When he was capable of movement again, he spun around, half afraid she wouldn't really be there. But she was.

She leaned toward him, chin propped on the back of one elegant hand, a near-smile tugging her lips. Her eyes said he was the only other person in the room.

He pulled in a slow breath, felt his unsteady world right itself. "Hello, Chicory."

* * *

The first gray light of dawn was nudging the night aside when the 'Vette's headlights sliced across the bar's empty parking lot. He'd stayed so late the night before, he'd nearly closed the place. Only the knowledge of their Sunday riding date had motivated him to leave so he could be well rested for their excursion.

Spending time with Sandy was becoming easy, almost second nature. What had begun as heated interest was rapidly moving to something else. Something he could neither define nor explain. He only knew being around her was comfortable. If he was honest, he had to admit that scared him just a little. What did it say about him that he could so easily move on?

He was halfway across the parking lot when his steps faltered. Silhouetted by the bar's exterior lighting, an ethereal angel emerged from the brilliance to join him in darkness. The image was oddly as disturbing as it was exciting. Shaking his head against the rush of baffling emotion, Ryan crossed the distance between them to relieve her of the heavy pack she carried.

"What's in here?" He tested the weight.

"Lunch, a few essentials, my camera. Why? Is it too heavy for you?" She reached for it, but he jerked the pack up, out of her reach, and she lost her balance. She saved herself from falling with a hand on his left hip. Ryan sucked in a huge gulp of air.

Sandy snatched her hand back. "Sorry. Did I hurt you?"

"No." He bit the word off, gritting his teeth against his exquisite excitement at her touch.

Ryan stepped to the back of his car, concentrating on cramming the overloaded pack into a trunk barely large enough to hold the spare tire. He had no intention of starting their day together with his obvious state of arousal between them. Only when control returned did he glance her way.

And immediately realized his mistake.

It wasn't the sexy singer from Friday evening staring back at him, nor the provocative bartender from the night before. In the predawn light, her face was soft, tender. Her incredible eyes wide, a sense of sweetness surrounded her, bringing visions of carousels and cotton candy to his mind. A smile played around full lips he already knew were soft and welcoming. But it was the morning wind lifting a tendril of dark hair escaping her ponytail that did him in.

He wanted to see the rest of her hair blowing in the morning breeze. He wanted to touch it, run his hands through it. *Control yourself, man. You barely know her.*

"Aw, hell," he muttered, tossing his inner caution aside. He settled his hands on her upper arms and dragged her up against him. Even as he registered that she came into his embrace willingly, he figured he'd probably regret giving in to his impulse.

But time enough for regrets later. He'd learned the hard way sometimes waiting held no reward.

With his knuckles, he grazed her cheeks on the way to his goal. As he combed his fingers through her silky hair, it sprang free from the elastic band and tumbled about her shoulders like a cloud, embracing him with the subtle sweet scent of her shampoo. Burying his head in that cloud, he closed his eyes and breathed in deeply.

* * *

"Oh!" Sandy giggled. "You're energetic this morning." She should push off, keep him at arm's length the way she normally did with interested men. Intending to do just that, she drew back and lifted her gaze.

The deep vulnerability reflected in his green eyes stalled her heart and held her breath in her throat. "I..."

Time seemed to freeze, suspending them in a single moment. When he moved, it came like the swooping of an eagle. One minute, he was meeting her stare; the next his lips crushed hers. Heat rose between them, swirled around them. This was no chaste good-morning kiss. This one packed the heat and promise of the rising sun. When he drifted back, she followed him, driven by the need to satisfy the deep hunger he'd awakened.

In a clever dance of kissing and caressing, pushing and leaning, they moved into and around each other. Sandy found herself pressed against the trunk of his fast, sexy car, while his fast, sexy hands found their way to the edges of her oversized man's Western shirt. He parted the garment and the heat from his palms branded her through the tank shirt beneath.

Sandy locked her hands behind his neck and held on, moaning deep in her throat. With a feral growl, Ryan lifted her and set her atop the trunk. He leaned against her, his mouth burning electrifying kisses along her throat. Her heart settled into a heavy, rhythmic beat, a primitive drum pushing heat through her system, stealing her ability to draw regular breaths.

* * *

Even through two layers of clothing, the sizzle emanating from Sandy slammed into him. Driven by need, he fumbled at the hem of her shirt. His fingers encountered soft, warm skin just as she settled herself more intimately into the embrace.

He could have her on the trunk of his car surrounded by the crisp early morning air. She was as eager and excited as he, and they could finish things right there where he'd started them, in front of her bar.

Across the street from the New Life Christian Church.

Where in mere hours, Brother Bobby Higgins would be preaching his sermon to his conservative congregation.

One of Sandy's hands lingered at Ryan's waist, her fingers making tiny movements. Remaining upright became difficult.

"You know, I have a room upstairs," she murmured against his throat.

Her husky invitation would have fueled many a teenage boy's dreams. But he wasn't a teenager. Hadn't been for many years. Sanity and reason filtered to the front of his rutting brain. With no small sense of reluctance, he pulled back and stood with his hands braced on either side of her on the trunk of his car. What was he doing? He'd known this woman for a handful of days — less than that. He stared down at her face, struggling for the right words.

Eyes heavy with unsatisfied desire, she gazed back, her lips drawn up in silent question. She snuggled closer, tearing a moan from his lips. He stepped away and pulled a hand across his jaw. It was on him to stop the madness.

"I can't believe I'm going to say this." Ryan tried to breathe but found himself inhaling huge gulps of air that smelled of her, of them. He was an adult, capable of self-control. But his hands trembled as he straightened her blouse, covering the parts of her he wasn't finished touching. "We should stick with the plan for the ride to the high country."

Ryan allowed himself one last caress of her cheek before he angled away from her and adjusted his own clothing.

* * *

"Oh." Heat rose from her neck and swamped her face. She moved her jaw, willing her tongue to work. "Sure. Okay." It took effort to stand on rubberized legs when she slid off the car. She tried to fasten the buttons of her shirt with fingers that didn't want to work.

Fear kept her from looking at him. Surely her emotions were parading naked across her face. What might he see in her eyes? What might she *not* see in his? So she studied the gravel at her feet and waited.

Ryan took hold of her hands, squeezing lightly until she looked up at him. "Make no mistake, Chicory." His Wyoming accent wound through a voice thick with the need reflected in his gaze. "This ain't finished by a long way. But if I make love to you, it won't be with my car parked in front of your bar and the majority of churchgoing folk in Orson's Folly noticing when they descend on that parking lot over there for their Sunday morning worship."

It was impossible to look away so she simply drowned in delightful desire, tingling in all the right places with his words. His voice held promise, and she shivered with anticipation. Something else was happening, something that went beyond physical. On one hand it felt nice. On the other, it terrified her.

A slow smile formed as she assigned a mental picture to his words. "Poor Brother Bobby has a hard enough time seeing most of his congregation parked here Saturday nights." She straightened her outer shirt with a little wiggle. "But it would be fun to see the flustered looks, especially from some of the women who wanted your attention last night." She sent him a playful little wink. "Don'tcha think?" Then she sauntered along the passenger side of the car, opened the door, and climbed in.

* * *

Ryan stared at Sandy's delicious rear view until it touched down on the seat. *Umm.*

"Washington, Adams, Jefferson," he whispered. Surely naming the presidents would dispel the heat. Not working so far. "Madison... Madison..." He frowned. Who came next? He'd known them all in order once. Committed it to memory in elementary school. How had he forgotten such a simple fact?

Sandy.

That woman could make a man forget a lot of things. Maybe even his own name. She'd addled his brain with a wink.

Huffing out the lingering warmth burning through his system in a long slow breath, he mostly staggered to the driver's door and tumbled into the seat.

The key was inches away from his hand but instead of reaching for it, he laid his hand on top of her knee. The move seemed more intimate than the moment they'd just shared, and Sandy's muscles trembled beneath his touch.

"Just so we're clear on one thing, Chicory. Right now, I don't care what any woman in the world thinks except you." As if to make him a liar, another woman's loving words floated to the surface, and he faltered. No, he'd deal with her later. He'd waited. She had not. A gentle mental nudge eased her back where she usually hovered, not quite out of mind but definitely out of sight. Ryan shook his head, as much to dislodge *her* from the moment as to make his point to Sandy. "But I do know firsthand what talk in a small town can do to a person."

"Yeah, about that," she drawled, and an unrepentant smile twisted her lips. "The gossip boat sailed inside the first year I was here, right after I brought live entertainment to Valentine's. All that gossip did was increase business. They can't hurt me unless I let them."

"Some would try," he said evenly. "I've been gone a while but some things — some people — don't change." He squeezed her knee lightly until she met his look. The effort of reining in his desire tightened his voice. "I do want you, Sandy. More than I've wanted anyone in my life."

She laughed softly. "That was pretty hard to miss, ace." Innocent blue eyes drifted to his lap where he was still in recovery mode.

"Don't," he whispered as his blood begin to head south again. "Please. Or I'm not gonna care about anything but getting you up those stairs and loving you so good you won't be able to walk after."

She continued to caress him with those eyes, his biggest weakness.

"For the love of mercy, don't do that!"

Sandy sniffed. "Crippling sex, huh?" Her smile scorched its way along his nerve endings. "Are you a gambling man?"

His mouth twitched and he offered a half shrug. "I've been known to place a bet or two."

A sly, knowing smile curved her lips. Leaning toward him just enough to give him a view of the valley leading to her personal Main Street, she spoke in a husky voice. "Good. Because I see you your crippling sex and I'll raise the stakes to mind-blowing sex."

Ryan drew a shaky breath. "You aren't going to make it easy, are you?"

Without saying a word, Sandy held him captive with her eyes and gave a slow shake of her head.

* * *

Fingers of pink and gold sunlight reached from behind wispy clouds and splashed the sky above the plains with vibrant color. The sports car dominated the road, utterly responsive under Ryan's capable hands. Sandy eyed them hungrily, those clever hands, and her body sizzled with the memory of his caresses, a flickering ember in the ashes of a blaze not fully extinguished.

Because she couldn't touch him, she stroked an appreciative finger along the edge of the leather seat. "This is a great car. Have you had it long?"

He downshifted on the curve between two low hills and kicked the speed up a notch, simultaneously shifting in his seat. "Couple years. Saved her from the scrap yard and brought her back to life."

An effortless smile pulled her lips upward, and she tilted her head to survey his profile. "So the man has his own talents."

"You have no idea." The mischievous crooked grin was a hair shy of an outright leer, bumping Sandy's pulse upward. "But I promise you will."

As they exchanged the two-lane highway for the long driveway to the ranch, the sun burst through the window and shards of rainbow-colored light danced over them both. Sandy gently captured the source of the prismatic effect, a tiny crystal angel dangling from the rearview mirror by a pale blue cord.

"Pretty." She glanced at Ryan to check his reaction, arching an eyebrow when he studiously showed none. She released the angel. "And a little... unexpected."

Ryan kept his eyes aimed on the driveway. A muscle worked in his jaw, but he said nothing.

"I don't look at you and think angel." Sandy threw a teasing glance in his direction. "More like cowboy-on-the-white-horse hero."

His lips moved upward but the smile never quite formed. After bringing the car to an abrupt stop in front of the stable, Ryan set the brake and cut the engine. He stared ahead for a moment then seemed to come to a decision and twisted in the seat until he faced Sandy, an inscrutable mask in place.

"You're mistaken," he said, the words barely audible. "I'm no one's hero." He reached out toward the angel, stopped just short of touching her, almost as though the touch might bring about unspeakable pain. "I put her there to remember someone."

Jealousy hit, more fierce than anything she had felt in the bar the night before. Like a welder's spark, it arced through her and landed in the pit of her stomach. Somehow she managed to keep her voice even. "Someone you love?"

Just before he smiled, she saw a spasm of pain shadow his features. "It was heading that way. Heading that way real strong."

Heat rushed into her face. "I'm sorry. I'm intruding."

Ryan shook his head. "It's okay. She was a part of my life, but — that was a while ago now. She said she'd be there and then she just — didn't stick around."

"And yet you want to remember her."

"Yeah." This time Ryan's smile came more easily, so not all the memories were bad. "Yeah, I do. I owe her that much. She believed in me, helped me through a bad time and I'm — grateful."

Sandy swallowed hard past the tightness in her throat. She didn't know what he'd been going to say but she got the feeling "grateful" had been a last-minute substitution.

He grasped Sandy's hand and cradled it in his. "I've been thinking of taking her out of here."

In silence, Sandy searched his face. Maybe not so much in the past as he liked to think. She was still very much in his heart. So apparently Ryan hadn't returned to Orson's Folly as unattached as the grapevine thought. Maybe not even as unattached as he thought himself.

More bad timing. Didn't that just figure?

"No," she said, warming her voice against the chill of disappointment that had settled in her heart. She liked the tenderness in his eyes. With a soft sigh, she touched the pretty bit of crystal with the tip of her finger, sending it into a gentle swing. "She's exactly where she should be."

* * *

Absently stroking his thumb over Sandy's knuckles, Ryan immersed himself in the eyes he found so compelling, finding he liked what he saw of the woman behind them. He enjoyed the glimpses she occasionally let him see of the inner beauty beneath the sexy packaging. Would she understand his feelings for the angel who had saved his life?

He thought about kissing her, really wanted to. But his emotions were suddenly raw with thoughts of the past, and it wouldn't be fair to Sandy. He wasn't certain if, in that moment, he would be kissing her or the woman who had once given him the will to live. Nor was he certain which woman he really wanted to kiss.

No, this wasn't the time or place to indulge in another kiss. But oh, he did want to, almost more than he wanted to keep breathing.

With a start, he realized she had gone quiet, and he looked up. In the golden light of early morning, her features were soft, the innocence in her smile almost angelic. And her eyes... he could spend forever looking into them and see something different every time.

Ryan gave Sandy's hand a light squeeze. "Ready? I'll get us a couple of horses. You can load your kitchen sink pack into a couple of saddlebags."

"You'll appreciate my efforts when lunchtime comes around," she called after him. "Unless you want me to throw together some trail mix and you can rustle us up a rattlesnake."

Ryan kept walking, tossing her a wave and a thumb's up sign over his shoulder without looking back.

This was going to be one interesting ride... if he could get through it in one piece without crippling his manhood. He picked his hat off the peg just inside the tack room, deliberately ignoring the off-white Stetson in favor of the black.

* * *

The bank of windows overlooked the parking lot. Once, it had been a favorite place to check the weather before going home, or traffic conditions on the freeway on the other side of the blacktop. Sometimes she had enjoyed just standing and unwinding after a difficult call. The view of the outskirts of L.A. was nothing to write home about, but up close it offered a postage stamp sized patch of green grass, a row of palm trees, and sunshine. Or it had once.

At the moment, the normally bustling freeway outside was dead. A line of cars stood unmoving; the road was probably impassable at some point and closed down. The horns had stopped blaring an hour earlier, just before many of the occupants had set out on foot. A few people had shown up at the dispatch office, but most appeared to be trekking west along the off ramp.

Angry plumes of black and gray smoke clawed the sky to the north, an appalling beacon marking the place where lives had been lost... where one life was struggling in a futile attempt to hang on in the face of impossible odds.

As if her thoughts had summoned him, the light above her workstation popped on, indicating radio activity. Sandy raced back to her seat. "I'm here, Mick."

"Got some time to keep me company?" he wheezed.

Sandy looked around the office, noting every station was occupied, every operator talking and writing. "I've got some time. It's slowing down a bit here," she lied.

"Do you know how long we've been down here?"

She checked her notes, though she knew the answer without looking. "A couple of hours," she said. "You should turn off your radio, save the battery."

"It'll be all right for a while yet." He was obviously reluctant to let go of the human contact. "It's black as pitch down here, Angel. Disorienting. Knowing you're out there helps some with that."

"You just stay strong and hold onto me. We'll get through this together."

"Will you talk a bit?"

"What do you want to talk about?" She rolled her pen between her fingers, concentrating on the way the clear plastic picked up the outside light.

"What do you do for fun?"

"Mmm, lots of different things. I read just about anything. Go for walks, watch old movies on cable. I do community theater."

"An actress, huh? You're in the right city for it."

"Oh, no. I'm not looking to be discovered," she assured him. "I can't imagine a worse life than acting for a living. It's just a fun little storefront group."

"What plays have you been in?"

"I did some Shakespeare in college," she told him. "Romeo and Juliet, The Taming of the Shrew."

"'Kiss me Kate, we will be married o' Sunday.'"

"Quoting Shakespeare?" She giggled in unexpected delight. "You've managed to completely surprise me."

"Good. I like my women off balance," he said. "Tell me more."

"Okay, I played Marian the Librarian in The Music Man last year."

"A musical. So you sing?"

"Just something I dabble at." Heat rushed her cheeks.

"Sing something for me," he pleaded.

"Sure. When you get out you can come see me in Oliver!"

"I don't want to wait. 'If music be the food of love, play on,'" Mick quoted softly.

Sandy chuckled. "I can see I shouldn't have told you about singing. Or about Shakespeare." Though she silently admitted her heart would always melt for someone who could quote the Bard of Avon so easily.

"Too late. You did. Now you have to sing."

"You make my head spin," she said, only half joking. "I'll bet you're a real tornado on a date."

He laughed. "You'll find out. Stop stalling."

"Okay, let me think. Um, do you like Bette Midler?"

"Sure."

Sandy looked around the office. The other operators were engaged; no one was paying attention to her. A little self-conscious, she quietly sang about the nature of love, and how hope grew from nurturing love's seeds. When she finished, the line was quiet and she thought maybe she'd lost him.

But then a soft sigh whispered in her ear. "I love your voice," he said after a minute. "I'm gonna want to hear a lot more of it. Maybe you'll do a private concert." He chuckled. "Makes me really want to kiss you, though."

If only their meeting could really go somewhere. She'd never felt so easy with a man before. "Maybe your voice makes me want to kiss you back."

"Tell me more about you," he begged. "I'd sure like to get to know you, Angel. Get a head start on those kisses I'm giving you as soon as I get out."

In between bursts of static they talked, sharing the inane bits of information two people getting to know one another often exchanged, as if they were meeting for the first time over coffee.

He liked the color of the sky on a clear day in the mountains. She liked ice cream in the winter. He liked to go for runs on the beach at sunrise. She liked puppies and kittens. He didn't have any pets but he'd saved a mother dog and her pups from a fire once and she'd gone crazy kissing his face.

"My hero!" Sandy sighed in her best Southern belle voice.

After a long pause, he finally whispered, "Naw, I'm not a hero. I'm just a man stuck under a building, talking to an angel he'd really, really like to kiss now."

* * *

"Here you go, Chicory." Ryan emerged from the stable leading a pair of horses. "You ready to ride?"

She flashed him a grin. "Now that kind of depends what I'm going to be riding."

His startled blink signaled a direct hit by her double entendre. Score!

"I noticed you go out without a hat. Not a good idea to ride without protection." He tossed a white Stetson in her direction.

Those green eyes of his lit with mischief when she caught his own double meaning and she licked her lips.

"Nice to know you're thinking about me," murmured Sandy, setting the hat in place. Especially since she'd been thinking about him nonstop for the past few days.

Ryan gave her a leg up onto a small but sturdy sorrel gelding named Galaxy. With a carefree grin, he mounted a buckskin gelding with the rather unimaginative name of Buck. Side by side, they moved onto the trail without speaking. Early morning sun slanted across dew-coated fields of hay ready for harvest, turning them the color of fresh honey.

The silence between them swelled to its own life, and with it Sandy's uncertainty. What was he thinking? Why didn't he talk? Why didn't she? What was she doing here? As soon as they came to even ground, they opened up to an easy, ground-eating lope. Still they didn't talk, but the ride began to work its magic and Sandy started to relax. She contented herself with watching Ryan.

He sat easy in the saddle, his hand light on the reins. His own movements were the perfect counterpoint to those of his horse, and he didn't look like he'd spent any time at all away from the ranch. He was taking in the scenery the same hungry way he'd been looking at her. Sunlight flashed off the bright red shirt that pulled a little too tightly across muscular shoulders, but it didn't seem to bother him and it gave her a bit of eye candy to admire.

Enchanted by his boyish eagerness, Sandy raised her camera and discreetly captured some shots. When he glanced at her, she sent him a sweet smile, fairly certain he hadn't caught her snapping his picture.

* * *

Climbing back on a horse had been another given of returning to Orson's Folly. Like all the other facets of his homecoming, Ryan moved easily into it but once again found himself wondering if it was right. He hadn't expected the simple act of having a horse beneath him to generate such overwhelming emotion. He wanted to talk, craved the human companionship he'd been finding with Sandy, but he found himself fascinated by the land, how much and yet how little it had changed.

And he'd become uncharacteristically tongue-tied with her.

To the north, a series of bluffs came into view, and the trail led them into the shadows of a narrow canyon. The walls were close. When he'd chosen the route, Ryan hadn't realized how much the tight quarters would bother him. Little twitches between his shoulder blades grew stronger as the passage between the rock walls grew tighter.

If anything should happen there, the canyon walls would render the handheld radio in his saddlebag useless.

A movement on the bluff above them sent a barrage of gravel sliding down the cliff. Probably an elk or a bighorn. Buck shied and Ryan flinched. The sound of falling debris prickled at his nerves, scraping along old memories and drawing them to the surface.

Ryan glanced over his shoulder to warn Sandy about the mini-avalanche but she had already guided Galaxy to the far side of the trail. She waved a reassuring hand then tilted her head to look upward, squinting at the edge of the cliff overhead.

"Is there another way out of here?" Her voice trembled, an echo of the tremors in Ryan's gut.

"Yeah," he said, a little more brusquely than he'd intended. "We'll take a different way home."

* * *

The walls of the canyon finally began to open up, the single narrow path widening and flattening into a trail of loose shale. Sandy's tension eased.

Slowing the pace, Ryan pointed to the left and urged Buck upward through a break in the trees. The path was lined with sediment washed down from the heights through years of spring rains and winter melts.

Gravel crunched and rolled underfoot as the two horses climbed the steep wash. Sandy never would have chanced it with Domingo. Any second, she expected Buck or Galaxy to lose footing and tumble back to the bottom. So far, though, the seasoned geldings proved sure-footed.

They burst into the sunlight on a high crest.

"Oh, my..." Sandy drew in a deep breath. The view was certainly worth the case of nerves she'd used up on the trail getting to it.

The valley was long more than wide, bordered on two sides by dense pine forest stretching toward the distant shadow of the heliotrope mountains. A creek meandered through the center, edged by tall grasses and yellow and white wildflowers.

Each direction held more wonder and she snapped at least a dozen different pictures without moving. "I thought you said this was open range."

Ryan scanned the deserted meadow, a puzzled frown shadowing his face. "It is. It's where Cross MC turns the herd out for the summer."

"Where are the cattle?"

Sandy snapped a picture of Ryan looking over the valley. His love for the land was reflected in his expression. He drank in the sight like a very thirsty man drinking from a well.

"That seems to be the question of the moment," he said after a long time.

Chapter Five

On horseback, Sandy followed Ryan, amused when he would cast a look over his shoulder as if to assure himself she was there. She was expecting one of those glances any minute now. And there it was. With a laugh, she squeezed the camera's shutter and captured his impatient *hurry-along* look before nudging Galaxy to catch up.

After only a few more yards, though, he unexpectedly pulled his horse up. When Sandy edged Galaxy beside him, he held up a hand to warn her into silence then pointed ahead and to the right. A bay stallion stood regally on a low bluff, overlooking a sizeable herd of mares and foals grazing peacefully in the valley below.

Sandy almost forgot to breathe. She caught a few wide shots of the whole herd and then zoomed in to capture the majestic stallion watching over them. The breeze lifted his mane and pushed his tail as he stood stiffly, nostrils flared, ears pricked forward. He was in every way the king watching over his kingdom.

The wind shifted and the stallion's nostrils fluttered. Could he smell them? Tossing his head, he cried a sharp warning and his obedient mares perked up their heads then began to trot away. The thud of their hooves blended into one continuous roll of thunder as they gained speed and moved up the valley. Sandy shot pictures until they were out of sight.

"That was incredible," she breathed, snapping a picture of settling dust spinning in the sunlight.

"Unforgettable."

Sandy swiveled in Ryan's direction, saw his contented smile, the glint in his eyes. Her gaze lowered to his awkward seat in the saddle. She smiled. "You weren't watching the horses, were you?"

His smile widened and the green of his eyes darkened. He shrugged, sweeping his eyes downward, pausing occasionally to rest on her lips, her chest, her legs where they met the saddle. "I can't imagine why I'd want to watch horses when I can look at you."

Never in her life had Sandy felt like she was in a perpetual state of excitement. But with Ryan McGee, every look ignited a conflagration of need that burned through her body like sizzling summer lightning. Sandy forgot the mustangs as an urgent need to be touched insinuated itself in her center.

"What are you thinking about all of a sudden?" Ryan asked softly, shifting his gaze back to her eyes.

One searing look had taken her from zero to oversexed in less than sixty seconds. Awesome! "I'm thinking that *you*... are a force of nature."

* * *

Something tugged on his memory but before he could think it through, Sandy shuddered. It wasn't an overtly sexy move. He didn't even think it was intentional. But it signaled her responsiveness to him on a fundamental level, and in turn he became even more aware of her.

Inhaling sharply, Ryan took in the rock-strewn ground, the dense bushes encroaching onto the narrow trail. He blew out a frustrated breath and urged his horse forward. "Come on. It's not much further."

"You aren't thrilled about the mustangs up here," Sandy said as she followed him along the trail.

That was quite a subject change. Deciding to go with it, Ryan shrugged. "I didn't say that."

"You didn't have to. It was obvious the first time you saw my pictures."

"I think they're beautiful. I like watching them. I admire their adaptability and how they handle adversity."

"Those are all the polite answers," she challenged. "What's the 'but' that I'm not hearing?"

"They compete with cattle for the best grazing. So ranchers consider them pests." Ryan pulled his mount up when he reached a small crest. "And that stallion's obviously comfortable, at home, so they've been here awhile."

Sandy pulled up next to him and put on an exaggerated show of looking around. "Weren't we just discussing the lack of cattle up here? So what's to compete with?"

"That's just it." Ryan couldn't ignore his sense of disquiet. "There *should* be cattle up here, and Sean should be concerned about the mustangs on our range." He shook his head. "Something's off."

Ryan set Buck in motion again, leaving Sandy to follow.

* * *

Sandy could tell the apparent mystery of the open range was eating at Ryan. Were Sean and Justin keeping something from him? That would likely disturb him more than not being able to figure things out.

Was the Cross MC in trouble? She'd known the ranch was having some setbacks. Every ranch in the county was experiencing difficult times, though. The MacKays had sold off a third of their breeding herd the previous fall and had just put a prime piece of land on the market. And Colt Ford had made a few cutbacks as well.

She resolved to ask Sean if he needed some help. He might resist, but Ryan would flat-out turn her down. She didn't have to know him longer to be certain of that.

"Where are we stopping?" she asked as they passed an old rotten log blanketed in pale blue pine butterflies. *And when can I explore on foot?* She settled her gaze on Ryan's rear end. Not that she was complaining about the horse's eye view or anything.

"Almost there," he tossed over his shoulder.

"Have you been up here since you got home?"

Ryan shook his head. "Nope, first time back on a horse for me."

She nearly choked. "In sixteen years?"

"Yup."

Did he realize how quickly his accent and attitude had slipped back to his Wyoming roots? The cowboy sitting the horse in front of her was as far removed from the dangerous city slicker stranger she'd first glimpsed behind the wheel of his fast sports car as he could get.

Ryan pulled up just inside a clearing, and Sandy nudged Galaxy alongside him. The rustic log and stone cabin nestled in the shade of the tall pines was something out of another era.

"It's like a postcard from the Old West," she murmured. "All it needs is smoke coming from the chimney."

Only the trills and whistles of the birds replied. Sandy sighed. It wasn't the first time during the ride she'd felt like she was talking to herself. But something about his stillness made her turn in his direction.

His face was marred by a scowl of deep confusion as he surveyed the clearing. He eased his horse forward, a step at a time.

"Ryan, what is it?"

But he only shook his head. "Nothing. Place is empty."

Odd, it didn't seem like nothing. But maybe he was coping with emotions. Obviously the place meant something to him. "Where are we?" She aimed her camera at the front porch of the structure.

"It's the cabin we use as a base when we come up here to check on the herd." He rubbed at his jaw. "Part of the original homestead. Dad had it restored before I was born."

The dusty cabin didn't look particularly welcoming with its boarded-up windows. "Doesn't look like anyone's been here in a while."

"They must not have moved the herd up here." Still staring at the cabin, he eased himself from the saddle then rounded Galaxy and offered her a hand down.

Once on the ground, Sandy followed his gaze as it drifted to the tall grass near the cabin. It had obviously been cut back recently. And even she could tell the trail in had seen some recent use.

The thump of his booted feet on the wooden planks of the cabin's covered porch broke into the birdsong. Ryan withdrew a key from a hook on one of the overhead beams and slid it into the lock on the door.

"Seems a little pointless to board it all up and lock it if you're leaving a key out where anyone can find it," Sandy observed.

His hand on the door latch, Ryan chuckled. "It's locked against the elements and the wildlife, Chicory. But if someone happens on it when we're not using it — hikers, hunters, whoever... they might need to get inside. Nothing particularly valuable here except the shelter itself."

After Ryan entered the cabin, Sandy waited a moment to be certain he wasn't going to pop right back out then made a face at the empty doorway.

"I can think of a better use for that tongue," he told her, materializing at the side of the cabin.

Sandy's yelp echoed across the clearing. Both horses stamped their feet and tossed their heads in protest. "You just went in there! Where the heck did you come from?"

Ryan set his hat back on his head with his familiar cocky grin. "Originally from my parents after a stolen night in the middle of cattle branding."

A picture formed in Sandy's mind of clandestine love in a sleeping bag, of secret moments and steamy covert glances between lovers. She smiled when she realized the faces she had mentally put on the couple belonged to her and Ryan. Casting the object of her daydream a glance from veiled eyes, she decided that was a fantasy she'd like to try.

He looked dangerous and arrogant, and... thrilling, standing there with his black hat cocked back on his head. Quickly, she raised her camera and snapped several pictures in rapid succession.

"Seriously," she pushed while she continued to shoot. "What did you do? Walk through a wall?"

"I walked through the door in the back wall. Does that count as walking through a wall?"

"Okay, smartass, would it have been too much trouble to just say, 'Sandy, there's a back door'?"

"Sandy?" His grin widened; his eyes were twin emerald glints of trouble. "There's a back door."

Muttering a particularly graphic suggestion about what he could do with his back door, Sandy snapped one last picture before moving off, pointedly ignoring him while she shot pictures of Galaxy and Buck.

* * *

She did love to capture things with that camera. No wonder she did such great work that it could hang on the walls at Valentine's.

Mom really would have loved her. Vague memories of Bethany McGee dancing around the meadow, shooting pictures of his dad playing with their old three-legged border collie, laid themselves over the present moment. Her Pentax had always seemed to be around her neck or in her hand like it was attached to her.

His mom's memory faded, blended into Chicory as she crouched near the river and took a picture of the mountains upstream. She'd be occupied for a while. He hoped. Keeping one eye on her to be sure, Ryan walked to the rear of the cabin again.

The trampled grass near the back door bothered him, especially since he'd found the door unlocked. Maybe hikers had come upon the place and forgotten to lock up when they left. But he doubted hikers would have scoured the place clean. The strong smell of bleach and pine cleaner in the enclosed space made his eyes water.

Nothing appeared to be damaged, though, and he wasn't certain being too clean didn't sound like an oxymoron. But he rubbed the back of his neck, unable to shake the unsettled feeling. After a quick scan for footprints turned up nothing, he huffed out a breath and retraced his steps. Nothing was being accomplished by staring at the ground and fretting over the oddity. He'd much rather enjoy Sandy's company and fret over his growing attraction to her.

Ryan came around to the front of the cabin and once again found himself spellbound. She was sprawled on her belly, apparently trying to capture the perfect photo. He shifted his stance for about the millionth time since picking her up. She was definitely having a profound physical effect on him. But there was something deeper there as well, something emotional he wasn't quite sure about yet. Something he wasn't sure he was ready for, no matter how strongly his body reacted.

Right on cue with his lascivious thoughts, Sandy rolled onto her back. Balancing herself with one knee flexed, she looked along the length of her body. "Hey, Mr. Wildflower Expert. Tell me the names of some of these." With her thumb out, she arced her arm, indicating the field beyond her.

All Ryan saw was the way her curves strained against her shirt with the motion and the way her jeans hugged her legs as they guided his eye straight to the Promised Land. Flowers were the last thing on his mind.

With enormous effort, he pulled the names his mother had taught him from his memory. "The lavender spikes are lupines. The orange and pink are poppies. The yellow flowers are prairie daisies."

"What about the tiny white and pink ones?" she asked.

Ryan's lips twitched, and he tore his gaze away from the sensual woman lying on the ground before he forced out the answer. "Those are called — pussytoes."

Her sultry laughter resonated like a drumbeat pulsing through his blood. He considered crossing the space between them and teaching her about more than wildflowers, then decided not to make it so easy on either of them.

Lowering himself to the porch, Ryan settled his back against the wooden railing and tipped his hat over his eyes. He dangled one leg lazily over the edge, kicking at the tufts of tall grass next to the step as he set his thoughts free to roam.

When he'd first made plans to come home, he hadn't considered staying beyond the time it would take to help his family. That had all changed on a mountain road at sunset before he'd even pulled onto the ranch. *And now?* Well, that was one of the questions to be explored, wasn't it? At the moment, he didn't have any idea of what he wanted to do. Or with whom.

Sandy's unique fragrance, an exhilarating blend of candy, fruit, and spice, tickled his nostrils, and his awareness of her was instantly heightened to an exquisite level. His body began stirring in response to her proximity when he felt the barest brush of something tickling his cheek then moving his lips.

Slowly, he opened one eye and peeked out from beneath the brim of his hat. Sandy was on her knees in front of him, igniting his very explicit imagination along with the corresponding part of his anatomy. With lips curled into what he could only think of as a naughty smile, she held a chicory blossom and had obviously been tickling his face.

When Ryan snaked a hand out and clamped onto her forearm, Sandy's squeal of surprise morphed into a peal of carefree laughter, washing over him and tugging once more at long-dormant emotions.

With his free hand, Ryan tipped his Stetson back to get a better look. "You're playin' with fire, Chicory."

"Really," she drawled, her blue eyes gleaming with mischief. "And here I thought I was playing with a cowboy." She moved closer, and one soft breast brushed against his knee.

"Sweetheart, you've got about five seconds to stop before I finish what you're starting." *Four. Three. Two. Too late.*

Sandy removed his hat and tossed it carelessly onto the porch behind her. Her gaze scorched a devastating path upward to his mouth. Like a serpent, she leisurely slithered her body upward along the same track her eyes had just taken.

His body drank in the feel of every blessed soft curve she pressed against him.

When her mouth was less than an inch from his, she whispered, "Do I look like I want to stop?"

* * *

His muscles tensed under her touch, stirring the waiting embers of her yearning. Sandy brushed her lips across his, pressing little feathery kisses over his jaw, down his throat. Molded against him as she was, nothing was left to her imagination. He was not immune to her advances. Still, he made no move except to slowly release his hold on her arm.

Drawing away just enough to meet his gaze, Sandy slid her hands to his shoulders. Those green eyes were filled with a heat that matched hers, but they also contained unexpected emotion and longing. She wavered, uncertain how she felt about what she saw. Her emotions answered with a tug of their own. Embers deep within sparked to life. She touched her tongue to her lips, willing him to kiss her.

"Hey," she murmured when he remained frozen. "Please don't tell me you're afraid of what the wildlife will think if we make love."

Ryan's lips twitched and something unreadable flickered in his eyes. He shifted, bracing one hand on her waist. Lifting his other hand to her face, he caressed her cheek with his knuckles. The butterfly touch sparked an ache of intense longing and stole her breath.

"More like wondering what you'll think after we make love, Chicory." His voice was roughened by the obvious battle between desire and self-restraint. "Feels like we're about to jump headfirst into a bonfire. I want you. It feels like I've wanted you for—" He shook his head helplessly then sighed. "For longer than I've known you."

The passion in his look became like a physical touch. He'd just expressed her own thoughts. She couldn't keep her voice steady. "Are you worried I'll complicate things by wanting a commitment?"

Ryan shook his head slowly, still holding her eyes with his own. "No. I'm not worried about that at all." His hand lowered to her collar bone, where his fingers teased. A shudder of need rocked her. "Actually, it might just be me complicating things that way. Chicory, something's happening between us. I like it. A lot. But it's happening real fast."

She understood. It was bigger than both of them. That made it downright scary. One of the horses whickered and she shifted her gaze over to where they grazed. Their obvious contentment stood in direct contrast to her tumultuous emotions. Things *were* happening fast with Ryan. But somehow they felt right. Sandy swung her eyes back to him, met his hot green stare head on. "I want this. Can that be enough for now?"

Ryan drew a shaky breath but when he spoke his words were steady. "I don't know. Because right now it feels like I'm gonna want more. A whole lot more. I'm not looking for friendly benefits, Sandy."

Pleasant warmth erupted from a pinpoint spot in the center of her chest, radiated outward until she felt it would engulf her. Sandy leveled her gaze to meet his. With a slight shake of her head, she whispered, "No. I'm not either."

He traced the line of her jaw, stopping at her chin and stroking the hollow below her lip with his thumb. "I don't know what it is, either, but I do feel... something with you that I haven't felt since—" He shrugged.

"I know," she said quietly. "I feel it, too... something. A kind of connection with you. But I don't know what it is and I don't know what to do with it."

Ryan closed his eyes, slowly letting out his breath. When he opened them again, they were darkened with a mix of desire and need that sucked the air from her lungs. Sliding a hand behind her head, he pulled her toward him. She was inches from his mouth, and his lips curved into a gentle smile. Her heart began a slow melt.

Then the heat flared between them, and his lips were on hers, possessing, giving, taking, thrilling. His ardor exploded and hers responded, adding her own fire into the combustible mix.

Frenzied hands grasped the edges of her outer shirt and stripped it from her shoulders, using it to catch her arms together behind her back while he leaned forward and feasted on her throat. Driven by need beyond anything she might have imagined, she arched into the touch. His kisses alternately seared and soothed, and rendered her helpless against the onslaught.

Finally he peeled the shirt off the rest of the way, tossing it aside. His hands were already sliding under her tank, running up both sides, over her heated skin. One settled at the small of her back, the other grazed the side of a breast and then hooked around to her midback as he compelled her closer.

Sandy could only fist a hand in his shirt and hang on as his caresses carried her toward an end she refused to fear. When Ryan's mouth moved over hers, she nipped at his lower lip. His velvet tongue pushed between her lips, stroking, tasting, taking.

She lost herself at the intersection where physical sensation met emotion, helpless to stop anything — even if she'd wanted to. She didn't want to.

In one fluid movement, he pulled back. His gaze swept over her, as hot as his touch. Needy. Bold. Possessive.

* * *

Ryan's pulse jumped to heart attack levels at the sight of her fair skin beneath his sun-bronzed hand. The deep need to feel more of her against him set his frantic fingers to work clawing and tugging at his shirt. When he became aware of her working the buttons, he retreated, giving in to her not-at-all-gentle touch.

The vibration emanating from her throat when she ran her hands over the bare skin from his waist to his chest stoked him to flashover and he felt an answering groan issue from his own throat. He knelt, hauling her up against him until her skin glided along his. They held each other that way, face to face, skin to skin, heat to heat, the beginning of a firestorm. Sandy fisted her hands in Ryan's hair and drew him even closer. It was all the invitation he needed. Every touch, every sensation, every response fueled his fervor.

He would never get enough of her. He bent his head and captured those soft lips in a deep, slow kiss that drove them both senseless.

Something tickled the back of his neck. A fly or maybe a spider had dropped from the rafters. He interrupted his exploration for just a second to brush at it.

Sandy's whimper drew him back. The subtle floral scent he'd caught during their embrace back in town blended with a splash of the outdoors and he followed it, let it lead him to her shoulder, her throat, then lower...

The tickle returned, a little stronger, built into more of a sting. Ryan shook his head, tried to shrug it off, but the sensation erupted until it crawled like a line of insects from the base of his neck on a direct line to the center of his brain. It was the kind of feeling he'd often had before discovering someone watching him.

But unless it was an antelope or one of the horses, that couldn't be the case.

Still, the awareness grew, and Ryan pulled away. He gathered his feet and pushed into a crouch then stood, drawing her up with him and walking her backward, farther beneath the porch roof. Raising a finger to his lips, he silently warned her to stay put before he moved to the end of the porch and looked across the field.

Everything seemed serene and idyllic. Nothing disturbed the horses. Birds sang and chirped. There were no frantic squawks, no eerie silences. But something was off, something just at the periphery of his awareness, raising an edgy, calm-before-the-storm feeling along his nerve endings.

And it wasn't going away.

He glanced over his shoulder at Sandy, regarding him with unvoiced questions in her eyes. She'd pulled her shirt back over her shoulders. He sighed. It was just as well. The mood was pretty much shot anyway.

Chapter Six

"Much better than rattlesnake." Ryan popped the last of a spicy tortilla into his mouth. Stretching out his long legs, he rolled onto his side, propped his head on one arm, and took pleasure in watching Sandy's hands as she chopped a pair of mangos into bite-sized pieces.

Sitting cross-legged in front of him, she drew her sharp knife through the rind of a lime, cutting it in half before looking up. "Says the man who didn't pack anything *or* rustle up a rattlesnake." She squeezed both lime halves over the chopped mangos with a motion that had Ryan thinking of more sensual digital pursuits.

He tore his gaze from her hands and lifted a shoulder. "I didn't have to. You brought a whole kitchen with you."

She plucked a cube of mango from the bowl between them. When she held it to his lips, he took the fruit into his mouth, then snagged her hand, bringing it back to his lips and licking the sweet stickiness from her fingers. When he swirled his tongue over the tip of her index finger, she touched her tongue to her lips. Ryan's blood began a quick drain southward.

With a tiny smile, Sandy slipped a chunk between her lips. "Did you know the mango tree is sacred in India? It's a symbol of love, and some people believe it can grant wishes."

Keeping his eyes on her, Ryan bit into another piece and chewed slowly. He'd put the brakes on their interlude, and suddenly she seemed intent on setting a more leisurely pace. Whatever had started her engine, maybe she'd worked the heat from her system, which might be a good thing — so long as she didn't work it out too far.

She lifted another sliver of orange and sucked on it, closing her eyes in obvious delight. Watching her eat was becoming an excursion into exquisite sensual torture.

"Do you have wishes, Sandy?" Time for a different kind of distraction.

She shook her head. "No, not anymore. I think I've used up my quota of wishes. What about you?"

Silence fell between them while he contemplated the woman across the blanket. For just a minute incredible sadness had shown on her face, but she'd recovered quickly. He chose his words with care. "I think we've got the beginning of something nice here. I'm really wishing it'll keep going."

* * *

Sandy opened her mouth and accepted his offer of mango. Closing her eyes, she chewed slowly, savoring the splash of sweet juice washing over her tongue while she considered the odd combination of pleasure and fear his words gave her. "It's having a pretty good start. I don't see any reason to stop."

"It's also going fast," he reminded her.

"So you've said. A couple of times." She scooted across the blanket and right-angled her body against his, supporting the back of her head on his chest. As pillows went, it wasn't soft enough, but subtle heat caressed her neck, and the distant thump of his heart brought a sense of comfort. Rocking her head sideways, she glanced up at his face. "Too fast for you?"

Surprise registered briefly in Ryan's eyes then was gone. He drew lines along her wrist with one finger as he spoke. "I don't think so. We obviously have physical chemistry."

She couldn't hold back a laugh. "You do have a gift for understatement."

Ryan said nothing. He was looking right at her but she wasn't convinced he was seeing her. She allowed the peace of the clearing to settle over her and waited. The trills of blackbirds harmonized with the river's bubbling in the distance. It was the rocks that allowed the water to sing, creating obstacles and detours that gave the river her song. At the moment, she sang a happy song... other days, would it be angry? Ever changing, but always singing.

Story of my life.

With a sigh, he toyed with the ends of her hair then laced strands between his fingers. "I'm thinking maybe we should get to know each other."

"I kind of thought that's what we were doing."

His gentle laugh rumbled beneath her cheek. "I'm talking about the other-than-sexy stuff."

She reached up and touched his jaw, enjoying the oh-so-deliciously masculine scratch of light stubble beneath her fingertips. "I want to take a long time to get to know you, Ryan. I don't want to find out your favorite color is blue because you tell me. I want to know it's blue because it's the color of your car, and it's the color of every shirt I've seen you wear except this one."

Ryan gave a little start, and she smiled. *Direct hit.*

"I plan to learn all about you," she continued. "And that includes the sexy parts. I want to find out what you like by your reaction when I touch you."

She ran her thumb over his lower lip, smiling at his sudden indrawn breath. The muscles in his chest tensed, but he didn't move.

She fought the sadness that could so easily overwhelm her. "But I also want to pay attention to the music you listen to and what movies you watch." A tear slipped down her cheek and she swiped at it impatiently. "Because I've done it the other way, Ryan, with the questions and answers. And I promise you the ending to that one sucked."

Mortified that she was breaking down in front of him, Sandy tried to roll away but Ryan tightened his grip and she ended up half curled into a ball against his chest.

"Who hurt you, Sandy?"

She couldn't quite meet his eyes. "No one hurt me. Sometimes life just hurts. Things don't work out. You think things between you and me are moving along fast? Try falling in love in twenty-three hours and fifty-seven minutes and having your heart ripped apart in just under sixty seconds."

Confusion clouded Ryan's face. "What?"

"That's how long it took me to fall in love for the first time in my life." She shrugged, and sent what she only hoped was an encouraging smile to show him she no longer lived in the past. "And how long it took for my heart to be completely shattered by circumstances no one could control. Especially not him," she finished in a whisper.

Sandy studied the emotions streaming across his face, as readable as a Wall Street ticker. He didn't like the thought of another man in her life any more than he liked finding mustangs on his open range. Any more than she'd liked thinking of him with another woman. What did that say about them? If they couldn't accept that each had a past, could they really expect to build a future?

"Ryan, have you ever wished for just one more day with someone?" She hesitated, frowning. When had she started needing him to understand who she had become seven years ago? "Have you ever wished you had a day when you could tell that person exactly how you feel and have him know without any doubt that you mean it?"

A spasm of pain flickered in Ryan's eyes until he forcefully pushed it away. "Yeah." He nodded. "Yeah, I have."

"But all we have is now," she said softly. "We can't go back and change things to make them come out better, and we don't even know for sure we'll have tomorrow, so we need to live today. That's what loving him taught me. To live in the moment. If something makes us happy, and it doesn't hurt anyone else, we should embrace it."

"For as long as it lasts," he qualified for her.

Sandy shrugged. "For as long as it lasts."

He looked at her with nearly unbearable kindness. "What happened, Sandy? What happened to break your heart?"

Sandy raised her eyes and met the uncertainty she saw in Ryan's. "He died," she said calmly.

* * *

Her emotionless disclosure sucker-punched the breath from his lungs. She spoke of it like she was announcing she'd been to the market, but the pain rolled off her, waves of it slamming into him.

He wanted to hold her and soothe her. He wanted to bear her pain for her. All he could do was close his eyes and absorb the agony that flowed around her like a tangible entity. "Sandy, I'm sorry. I'm so sorry."

"Don't!" She sat up. This time he let her go. "It was a while ago. I'm glad you know about it, because it's part of who I am now. But Ryan," she said, her gaze showing no emotion, "I don't sing the blues about it. And I'm not looking for you to sing them for me. Are you okay with that?"

Would she run if he told her he wasn't? Very slowly, Ryan nodded once, and Sandy settled comfortably back into his arms.

"I didn't expect it to be so hot up here," she observed suddenly, firmly closing the door on the subject of her lost love. "I'm thinking of wading in the calm part of that river over there."

With a lazy turn of his head, Ryan glanced over at the bubbly stream meandering through the clearing. It was running fast but not deep. "You could do that," he agreed. He lifted his chin, indicating the white-topped mountains behind her. "But the water's all runoff from the snow up there."

She wrinkled her nose. "Never mind, then."

This time the silence was comfortable, broken only by the gurgling stream and the occasional call of a blackbird. Ryan laced his fingers through her hair and combed down to the ends, eventually settling his hand at the nape of her neck. She sighed softly. It was a contented sound. He watched her eyelids flutter downward.

* * *

"Hey, what kind of food do you like?" asked Mick. "We'll go to dinner. Just tell me where you want to go."

Sandy's breath caught as she heard the sickening rumble before she felt it. Aftershock! A bad one. It seemed to take forever, though it was probably less than a couple of minutes before she heard the radio squawk in her earpiece, but no voice came across the comm.

"Mick! Are you there?"

Another moment of silence, then, "I'm here, Angel. Dropped — the radio. Few more chunks fell is all."

He sounded so normal and casual.

"So how about that dinner, Angel?"

"Italian. With breadsticks and we can share some cannoli. And... and when you pick me up, you can bring me flowers. I like daisies. The white and yellow ones growing by the side of the road near Big Bear Lake."

His chuckle was laced with pain that she felt along with him.

"That's a deal. Angel?"

"I'm right here."

"You want to go to Vegas with me and get married? I figure we've already spent most of the night together."

She giggled. "What kind of half-assed proposal is that? You do know how to sweep a gal off her feet." Really, he did.

A breathy chuckle filled her ear. "Sorry... I can't get down on... one knee just now with a building on top of my ass."

Sandy's pain was exquisite, lancing straight through her heart. It was getting harder to do, but somehow she kept her voice light. "So, Mick, do you always just jump in with both feet?"

"It's the only way, sugar." She could hear his smile. "You're not really living if you're always looking at life from the outside."

"Don't you ever think about how you could get burned?"

He was silent for a moment, then soft laughter filled her earpiece. "Every time I climb on the truck when we're called out, sweet stuff."

Color flooded Sandy's face. "I'm sorry — I didn't mean — that was incredibly insensitive of me."

His laughter grew a little louder. "Relax, honey, I'm messing with you. I knew what you meant. Look at it this way. If you don't take chances, you won't get any rewards." He finished softly, "And right now, I'm thinking marrying you would be one really great reward."

"You know, you're taking a heck of a chance asking me to marry you when you don't even know what I look like. I could be paper-bag homely."

"Then I'll have to lay up a good supply of paper bags," he teased. His voice softened. "'Love looks not with the eyes but with the mind.'"

She laughed. "It's hard to fight with a man when he's quoting Shakespeare."

"That would be the point of doing it." He laughed softly. "It doesn't matter what you look like on the outside, Angel. I think you're beautiful."

She had no idea how to respond.

"Angel?" His voice was just a bit louder than a whisper. "I was serious about getting married. We don't have to do it in Vegas. You can carry white daisies when you walk down the aisle to me."

"I know you were serious," she said. "I was mulling it over."

He chuckled. "And?"

"Yes, Mick. I'd love to marry you." She closed her eyes against the pain of knowing that day would never come.

* * *

Ryan shifted to get a better view of Sandy while she slept. A week ago he hadn't even known her. Now he couldn't imagine not being with her. In sleep, her vulnerability touched him even more deeply than her sensual playfulness when she was awake. He was at a loss to explain his reaction. He'd never expected to feel so strongly again.

"Ryan," she murmured as she stirred against him.

Sitting up, she threw back her head and raised her arms, stretching like a cat in the sun. The movement thrust breasts against the soft, thin fabric of her tank top. Her body invited his touch, but he sat still, drinking in the sight and allowed his hunger for her to spiral upward.

Lowering her arms, she caught his eye and smiled. "I know who I'm with, Ryan. I've been alone in every sense of the word for a while now. It's always going to hurt when I wonder about the might-have-beens. But I'm here with you right now because I want to be with Ryan McGee, not because I'm looking to replace someone I can't have."

She bent to lay a tender kiss against his throat, lingered there for a breath then moved along his neck to his chin and then on to his mouth. Her lips tempted; his cried out for more. Hers teased; his sought and found. His hand rested against her just above her left breast. Her heart beat like a hummingbird's wings beneath his fingertips.

The guttural, bawling scream was not of the earth. Emanating from the thick woods, it echoed unnervingly across the once tranquil clearing.

Sandy leapt away from Ryan, her eyes wide with alarm.

"What the hell is *that?*"

Ryan was already on his feet, grabbing the Winchester from his saddle holster and sprinting toward the sound. "Calf in trouble! Stay here!" he shouted over his shoulder before he pushed into the woods.

* * *

Paralyzed with fear for several heartbeats, Sandy finally unstuck her feet from the ground and followed Ryan. The brush was thick. It clawed at her, leaving painful lacerations along her arms and back as she struggled to get through. It grabbed her hair and wouldn't let go. She twisted and freed herself from the painful grasp of a thorny bush. Where was he? Where was Ryan? Which way had he gone?

She forced herself to stop and listen. The bellow rang out again, followed by thrashing in the undergrowth to her left. Resolutely slowing her rapid gasps for air, she calmed herself enough to see the trail of broken branches.

The bushes directly in front of her parted and Ryan stepped through. Sandy sprang backward, swallowing her cry of alarm. He had a fair-sized calf cradled in his arms.

"Take her back to the clearing," he ordered in a brusque tone as he shoved the calf at her.

Without a second thought, Sandy took the calf into her arms. He was stern, all business. Nothing at all like the mellow, sometimes playful man of earlier.

The calf's weight was much less than she expected, and she overcompensated, stumbling into a thorny shrub.

"Ry, what is it?"

He caught her arm and steadied her, then shot her a pointed look. "Just do it," he barked. "And don't leave the clearing. Don't follow me under any circumstance." Then he was gone, swallowed again by the thick brush.

His words and attitude shot terror right through her as she fought the tangled underbrush and made her way back to the clearing. The squirming calf bellowed frantically in her ear.

"Shush, baby. Shhh..." She set the calf down on the blanket where she and Ryan had shared their picnic, and dropped to her knees. Rubbing between the little one's huge brown eyes seemed to calm her, and the bawling quieted.

If only Sandy could still the trembling assaulting her muscles. Unable to do anything else, she sat staring at the bushes, awaiting Ryan's return. The sound of a nearby rifle report tore through her as though the bullet had physically ripped into her flesh. She was halfway across the clearing before she realized she'd jumped up. But Ryan had been explicit with his instructions not to follow him for any reason. She sank to the ground again, making no effort to stem the tears cascading down her cheeks.

* * *

"How badly are you pinned?" Sandy asked when Mick checked in. "Is there any possibility of working yourself out some?"

"Not a chance," Mick told her easily. She could almost picture a grin. "Got a cement beam across my legs and a chunk of something across part of my chest. Pretty sure at least one of my legs is broke. Feels like a couple of ribs bought it, too. Kind of hard to catch my breath. I can hear my partner breathing but he's not answering. Don't know how bad off he is. It's hard to just lie here, Angel."

Mick's labored gasps tore at her heart. "I know it is. I wish I could be there to help you."

"Oh, sweetheart, you're helping from where you are. Nothing you could do here."

"I could hold your hand, at least."

"You know, Angel, it kind of feels like you already are holding my hand. It's real nice knowing someone's out there who cares. I'm glad you're on the other end of the line."

"I'm glad, too," she said truthfully. "I'm not letting you go, Mick."

* * *

Ryan surveyed the scene, struggling for objectivity. The cow was a mess. Once, her hide had been a honeyed tan, but it was now caked with layers of blood which had run freely from a wound on her flank. The trampled, blood-stained grass told the story. She hadn't gone down easily, but finally had lost so much blood she couldn't stay on her feet.

He looked from the flank wound up to the animal's head, into which he'd just put a Power-Point from his Winchester. It was the only comfort he'd been able to provide.

A muscle worked in his clenched jaw. He might have fired the kill shot but he hadn't been the one to bring about the cow's death. It still hurt to his core.

Ryan estimated she'd been shot within the past twenty-four hours. He supposed it was possible she'd been mistaken for an antelope or an elk, but since it wasn't hunting season, that meant someone was possibly poaching. Based on the absence of the Cross MC herd from prime grazing land, though, his gut told him he'd stumbled onto a very different picture.

Screw Sean for keeping critical information from him. *Little brother, you owe me answers, and you* will *give them.*

With his teeth clamped against emotional pain, Ryan crouched next to the carcass and pulled a folding knife from his pocket. The blade was short but sharp and it was all he had, so it would have to do. Knowing of only one way to recover the slug in her flank, Ryan began methodically slicing into the cow's flesh.

* * *

Sandy heard him fighting his way through the thick brush. When he emerged, he carried his shirt bunched up in one hand. His eyes met hers, and her tension drained. He was okay. His long strides carried him directly to the cold mountain creek, where he tossed his shirt onto the bank next to the fast-running water.

Her eyes skimmed over him. His hands were coated with sticky-looking crimson. Streaks of red stained his abdomen, and another smear ran across one cheek.

With her heart lodged in her throat, she rushed toward him. "That's blood! Where are you hurt?"

"I'm okay," he assured quickly, but he held up a hand to stop her approach. "It's cow's blood."

She slowed her steps but didn't stop. "What happened?"

Ryan presented a façade of calm, stooping to bathe his arms and chest in the icy water. But his hands shook when he grabbed his shirt from the bank and used it to scrub at his skin. "She was badly injured. There was nothing I could do. I had to put her down."

Understanding dawned quickly, and she closed her eyes. "The gunshot."

He nodded. "She'd lost too much blood. There was nothing I could do," he repeated dully.

Sandy laid a hand on his bare shoulder, squeezed lightly, and then crouched next to him to study his face. She dipped her hand in the creek and used her thumb to scrub away the line of blood along his cheek.

Ryan closed his eyes and leaned into her touch. "Aw, Sandy. It's been so long since—" A spasm of pain contorted his features. "Thank you."

Sandy pushed her hand around the side of his head and grazed her thumb over his ear. "Hey," she whispered. "I'm glad you're okay."

He gave a start, and his eyes brightened with emotion. Standing, he pulled her up with him. His arms settled around her and he held her tightly, burying his face in her hair. His breath was warm on her neck. Her arms stole around his waist and she hung on, rubbing her cheek against his chest. A long time later, his shaking slowed and he leaned back, peering down at her. She gazed back, drawing on experience to force a calm she was far from feeling.

"There's a lot I want to say to you, Chicory." He shook his head.

She was pretty sure she had the same things to say back. It seemed they were both going to complicate things after all. She kept her hands on him, unable to sever contact.

"I know stuff like this happens, but it's hard to think about." Gesturing toward the calf, she asked, "Will she be all right?"

Relief eased its way into his features, and he gave a quick nod. "Probably. She's hungry but still strong. Sean'll have provisions for orphans so I'll carry her back to the ranch."

"What would have happened to her if we weren't here?"

"If she was lucky, predators would have gotten her. If not, she would have starved to death." He spoke in a matter-of-fact tone that didn't match the tension in his body.

Sandy shuddered; neither scenario was appealing.

Ryan took up the shirt and made a face. Dirt and blood had ruined it. "Sean's gonna be pissed about this."

A piece of puzzle fell into place, bringing a grin to Sandy's mouth. "That's Sean's shirt?"

He angled a gaze in her direction and answered her grin. "You were right about the color blue. It's all I tend to buy. I figured it'd be prudent to wear a bright color out here so I raided his closet."

Sandy stared down at the garment and wrinkled her nose. "You'd think the red would have hidden the blood a little better."

With a sigh, Ryan tossed shirt in the creek and swished it around. Then he used it to clean the dirt and blood from the orphaned calf. "It's okay, little one, you're safe now." He ran gentle hands over the baby's brown-and-white hide, checking for injuries. Under his soothing touch, the calf drifted to sleep.

Sandy picked up her camera. As she watched Ryan from behind the lens, she realized the calf was not merely meat on the hoof for him. He hadn't saved the baby as part of some plan to salvage the ranch's profit margin. She mattered to him, on an intensely personal, very human level. And killing the cow, no matter how merciful, hadn't come easy to him.

Chapter Seven

Checking the cinch on Sandy's saddle, Ryan froze when her arms slid around him from behind. She laid her cheek against his back, her breath spreading little feathery sensations of warmth across his bare skin. He closed his eyes, enjoying the contact. Splayed across his abdomen, her hands were warmer than the sunshine.

Beneath her tender caress, emotions Ryan couldn't name erupted like a long-dormant volcano. He looked at his hands, still resting against the saddle, and realized he was trembling with the force of the feelings sliding through his system.

"Since Sean's shirt is trashed…" she murmured.

That honey-smooth voice never failed to capture his attention, but at this moment, it was coursing through his heart.

When she drew back, the mountain breeze chilled his flesh. She slid something over his arms and onto his shoulders. Ryan looked down and recognized the man's shirt she had been wearing earlier.

"It's going to be a bit small on you but it's better to be covered."

Sandy's essence embraced him as he shrugged his shoulders the rest of the way into her shirt. Her warmth lingered and her scent clung to the pale cotton, rising up to tantalize, drawing him in.

It was a simple move, turning into her arms, but it felt somehow complicated, like another lock opening — or another one closing. He pressed one simple, soft kiss to her lips then stepped back. Rolling his shoulders, he tested the fit of the shirt. It caught a bit across his back, but if left unbuttoned it would suffice. Smelling her for the whole ride back, though, was going to be a test of will.

"Thanks." Mischief demanded outlet. "Should I be wondering why you have men's clothing in your closet?"

Blue eyes twinkled at him. "Jealous?"

Ryan flexed his muscles against the confines of the shirt. The seams strained beneath his broad shoulders. He raised an eyebrow. "I don't think so."

She laughed. Man, how he loved that sweet sexy laugh.

"Relax, cowboy, you've got everything I want." Resting her hands on his hips, she leaned in and gave him a swift kiss. Everywhere she touched felt like a hot iron branding him. "I'm all yours," she said against his lips. "I got into liking big shirts during my men's-shirt-short-skirt nightclubbing days."

Ryan inhaled sharply at the picture her words conjured. His fingers tightened reflexively on her shoulders.

"Sometimes I wear one when I ride instead of a jacket." Reaching past his shoulder, she removed a pink T-shirt from one of the saddle bags and pulled it over her head. "There. Now I'm covered, too." She winked.

Ryan's lips twitched. He was so gone over this woman, liking the way she was almost innocent and vulnerable one moment and sensually playful the next. He'd been pleasantly off balance around her since their first meeting.

His gaze landed on the calf. "Sandy, things got a little crazy. This isn't how I pictured our day together." He'd hoped for a slow, sensuous romantic interlude with a mutually pleasant end later in the evening.

She responded with a sexy chuckle that hit right below the belt. "You do know how to show a gal a good time." And then she lifted one exquisite shoulder and let it fall. "The days won't all be crazy. If things were too mundane, we wouldn't know what to do with ourselves. And I'm sorry about the cow. But Ryan, about the rest of the day..." Her sweet smile completed the picture of perfection. "I wouldn't change anything."

With a groan of regret for all the moments lost that day, Ryan ran his hand along the back of her head and steered her toward his lips for a tender kiss. "We have to get back. Will you save some time for me tomorrow evening?"

He boosted her into the saddle, resting his hand on her leg. When she looked at him, she wore a sweet smile. "Will you wear your black hat?"

* * *

The sun barely held on in the sky by the time they reached the ranch. Laser beams of crimson shot out from behind silvery-gray clouds edged in gleaming gold. The plains around them glowed red, reminding Ryan of the first night he had seen Sandy.

He slipped out the radio and checked the frequency.

"Where did that come from?" asked Sandy.

"We carry them when we go out on the range. In case of emergency. " He frowned. "Sean never gave you one?"

In the dimming light, he almost didn't catch her silent headshake.

As they closed in on the ranch, the radio finally registered a signal. Ryan called Sean to alert him about the calf. His brother met them in the yard with Gus Hanson, the Cross MC foreman. He was a grizzled troll of a man who had been on the ranch since Ry's granddad had been the head of the family. Ryan gratefully slid the calf into the old man's waiting arms.

Ryan handed Sandy his car key and grinned. "Warm her up for us? Sean'll help unsaddle."

Her start of surprise told him he hadn't been as smooth about excusing himself to talk to Sean as he'd intended, but she took the key without protest, smiling once over her shoulder as she sauntered to the car.

Ryan handed Galaxy off to Sean, keeping his hand on the reins a bit longer than necessary. "You have any inkling why I found a cow shot to hell and gone up there?"

Sean stiffened, inhaled deeply, then slowly blew the breath out and nodded. "Yeah. I do."

"We need to talk." Ryan shot his brother a pointed look, a silent warning to stop dodging.

"I know. Tomorrow, okay? Go ahead and take Sandy home. I'll settle the horses. And, Ry. Don't bring it up in front of Dad."

So much for getting answers, Ryan thought on the drive to town. The warning not to involve their father had only raised more questions, and Ryan was certain he wasn't going to like the answers.

* * *

"You're awfully quiet." Sandy struggled to keep her voice casual.

"Tired."

"Umm, yeah." She watched him set the brake and turn off the engine, moving as if in slow motion. *Not just tired. Drained.*

Their feet thudded heavily on the open-backed wood steps as Ryan walked her up to her apartment. After she unlocked the door she turned into his arms. His kiss went from soft to heated then back to gentle.

She leaned into his embrace, enjoying the strength of his muscular arms beneath her hands. She hated having to let him go.

"I wanted to watch the stars come out with you, Chicory," he whispered.

She looked up. Even with the ambient light from town, the sky was overflowing with visible stars. "I love stargazing. There are so many here they almost..."

"... blend together."

Electrical current raced along her spine. "Yes," she whispered, wishing she could see his face.

Ryan gently spun her so her back was to him and slid his arm around her waist while they enjoyed the view from her tiny balcony. "My mom used to tell us stories about the sky and the stars," he murmured, his breath warm against her neck. "She said the night sky was one of God's favorite old blankets, keeping everyone here on Earth safe and warm. And the blanket has these tiny pinholes worn in, like some comfortable blankets do. The lights we see are little glimpses of heaven on the other side of the blanket."

Her throat tightened. "Then I guess... we're sharing a little bit of heaven right now." Any moment she would surely turn to warm mush.

"Next time we'll get it right." In a flurry of smooth moves, he shifted and suddenly she was facing him. With almost agonizing slowness, he angled his head and pressd his mouth to hers. The kiss was soft and filled with sweet longing, and his gaze lingered when he drew back. "I'll see you tomorrow, Sandy."

After Ryan left, Sandy closed the door and leaned against it, her fingertips pressed against her lips while her body hummed with residual electricity. "Pretty sure you got that last bit right," she whispered. She'd come within inches of begging him to stay.

Her T-shirt landed on the sofa. She unfastened her jeans and loosened them on the way to the bathroom. While the hot water splashed into the tub, she tossed in her favorite bath beads. Then she heard the soft knock on her door and flew across the small apartment to answer, her heart tripping into a happy dance.

"Hey, cowboy, you gonna spend the night—?" She pulled up short at the sight of the brawny man lounging against the railing outside her apartment. "Bull, hey, what are you doing here?" Hastily, Sandy pulled the edges of her gaping jeans together, cursing when the zipper jammed.

"Heya, Sandy, I came by to apologize for Friday night," he told her gruffly, stepping inside on his own invitation.

His greedy eyes crept along the length of her bare arms, skimmed her neck, flicked over her chest, slid lower to where her jeans weren't quite fastened. Sandy knew he couldn't see much and forced herself not to clutch the denim closed. Chills settled everywhere his inky black gaze touched. He was creeping her the hell out. He'd never come on to her before, had always treated her with respect.

But Bull probably wasn't thinking of the wife he habitually left at home as his eyes shifted once more to her breasts and he licked his lips. His eyes slid to the unmade bed behind her, and he rubbed his thumbs and fingertips together. Sandy's heart lodged itself in her throat, beating madly with foreboding.

"It's okay, Bull. I accept your apology." Why did her voice have to shake? She held the door wider, praying he would just leave.

As a thin film of perspiration formed along his upper lip, his mouth fell open and his breathing grew shallow.

Apprehension gave birth to alarm, slithering along the route Bull's eyes traversed and clawing at her gut with fierce talons. Bull was a big man. She was completely alone. If he tried anything, she wouldn't be able to stop him.

Adrenaline rushed, and she drew a deep breath. She'd just have to make sure he didn't try anything, get him to refocus his attention.

"Bull, it's getting late. Brenda's probably waiting up for you." Her suddenly constricted throat barely allowed the words out.

He nodded, pulling his gaze away with obvious regret. "Maybe I'll come in to the bar one night, have a drink with you."

"We'll talk soon." She knew her promise sounded false, but if Bull noticed, he said nothing.

Finally, by stepping through the doorway herself, she managed to entice Bull over the threshold.

"I'll, ah... see you at the bar sometime, then." As he paused and looked around, apparently stunned to find himself outside, she quickly stepped back in, then closed and bolted the door. Heavy footsteps thumped down the stairs and she released her pent-up breath. The distant growl of an engine had to be his truck starting. *Please let it be his truck.*

The shakes slammed her, and she pressed her back against the door as if to keep it from opening. Almost in slow motion, her legs gave way, and she melted into a pool on the cold, hard tile. Tears squeezed from behind closed eyes as huge shudders wracked her body.

What the heck had that been about? She could go weeks, even months, seeing nothing of Bull. He generally took his play to the hookers up in Jackson and did his drinking there as well. But with Ryan's return, she'd seen two incidents with the troubled man in three days and Sandy couldn't help but think the explanation for that rested with Ryan.

She scrubbed the tears from her cheeks, but didn't get up until long after the engine sounds had drifted into the night.

When she pushed to her feet and staggered into the bathroom, she discovered the water of her forgotten bath had sloshed over the edges of the bathtub, swamping the floor, saturating the pretty lilac colored rug and soaking into her favorite pink fuzzy slippers.

* * *

Sean had developed a particularly skillful disappearing act since Ryan had begun to ask more pointed questions. But Ryan could be skillful, too, and this time he was determined to keep Sean from dodging him by riding out early. Spending the night in the tack room waiting to ambush his brother wasn't particularly appealing, especially when Sandy had made it very apparent he would be welcome in her bed. But Ryan knew it was time to corner Sean for answers.

Sandy. Dang, their relationship had been intense right out of the chute. Being with the woman was like sitting on a crate of firecrackers. It was impossible to know when it would detonate, but explosions were inevitable. And he always *had* loved playing with matches. At some point, he'd started feeling things he'd never expected to feel again. When had that happened?

He knew the answer. It had begun when he'd nearly collided with an otherworldly vision on a mountain road. Never in his life had head, heart, and physical interest all happened at the same time for him. And now they were doing just that, life was pretty freaking amazing.

Forcing what he'd rather be doing from his mind, Ryan took a rough inventory of supplies, noting the worn leather, the scraps of unusable equipment set aside for salvage. Much of their equipment had long ago seen better days. Working with his hands had always relaxed Ryan, so he settled on the old barstool in front of the little workbench and repaired tack while he waited for his brother and some answers.

"You're up early," Sean said when he walked into the tack room a few hours later. If he was surprised to see Ryan there, it didn't show in the pleasant smile on his face.

"Never slept."

"You used to going without sleep?"

Ryan shrugged. "Sometimes. When it's necessary."

"Guess you're saying I made it necessary."

Ryan didn't look up. In silence, he concentrated on folding the leather strip into a loop around the harness buckle then securing it with neat stitches.

Sean shuffled his feet back and forth. "Come on, Ry! I hate it when Dad pulls that no-talk bullshit. Do you have to be just like him?"

Ryan frowned, irritated by the comparison. With deliberate care, he tied off the thread then hung the repaired harness on a hook behind the bench along with several others he'd finished.

Just as deliberately, he reached into his pocket and pulled out the scrap of material he'd cut from his shirt the day before, unwrapped the slug he'd retrieved from the dead cow, and set it on the workbench.

Then he turned and regarded his brother in silence, pointedly waiting for the answers to the questions he'd been asking for days.

Sean regarded the spent bullet like it was poison. "You got that from the dead cow?"

Ryan cocked his head to the side and raised an eyebrow. "Is there someplace else I might have found it?"

Sean stooped and picked up a stray buckle from the floor. With exaggerated care, he placed it on the bench. "We had some trouble up in the high pasture this past spring."

"Some *trouble*?" Two words that offered nothing in the way of explanation. "Come on, Sean! You gotta do better than that. Why did you ask me to come home?"

Sean averted his eyes.

Ryan rocked back on his heels and blew out an irritated breath. "I don't get it. You literally summoned me home, hinted that you need help." He shrugged. "And for some reason, you don't want to have a simple conversation about what's going on around here. So I guess the real question is, why should I stay?"

"Dad had a heart attack. About three years ago."

Ryan's head came up sharply, as though Sean had just popped him in the jaw.

"It was mild, pretty much over before he even got to the hospital. But he had to have tests, meds. And there were bills. A lot of bills" He paused, seemed to struggle for words. "We had... a rough patch."

"You never said a word." Rage constricted Ryan's voice as he barely checked his temper. "Did you think I wouldn't care?"

"He didn't want you to know. I kept hoping you'd see the quarterly reports and..." He spread his hands helplessly. "Notice something."

With a little prick of conscience, Ryan visualized his desk drawer with the neat bundle of unopened white envelopes that arrived from the accountant every three months. He scrubbed a hand over his face as the frustration of years spent avoiding reminders of the life he'd once left behind caught up with him. If he was truthful, he had to admit to himself he'd come back exhausted from living a life he shouldn't have been living. And he'd nearly been too late getting home.

"Dad thought — hoped you'd come back after Mac... died." Sean picked up a scrap of harness and began rolling the leather between his fingers. "When you didn't, he didn't want to drag you back here on his account."

"I couldn't come back. Not then. I was injured myself, and..." Ryan closed his eyes against pain he'd spent years hiding from. Mac, his cousin with the unruly red hair and the splash of freckles across his nose that kept him a perpetual kid even as a man doing a man's job. The grin that flashed even in impossible circumstances. The vision gelled in Ryan's mind, became so clear he might as well have been twisting the knife in his heart. He forced his eyes open and focused on the tack room. Harnesses, buckles, wood, straw... But no red hair. No Mac.

Tamping back on the raw feelings, he focused on Sean and returned to the conversation. "I could've helped in other ways. I would have sent money. Geez, Sean, I've got more of that than I ever use. I was Mac's beneficiary on his life insurance and he died on the job, so the payout was tripled."

One side of Sean's mouth twisted upward into a wry smile. "Wouldn't Bull and old Brody just love you investing Mac's insurance payout in McGee land?"

"Who cares about what they'd think?" Ryan leveled his gaze at Sean. "It's what Mac would have wanted."

"Is it?" Sean tossed the scrap of leather onto the bench. "Dad said he had good reasons for running off."

Ryan winced. "I didn't think Dad ever understood any of it. I figured he'd have tried to stop us, so I never gave him the opportunity, never told him much."

Sudden motion and a whoosh of air sent Ryan flinching backward as Sean drove a violent punch into the wooden beam next to his head.

Sixteen years worth of anger simmered in Sean's green eyes. "You don't give Dad enough credit," he grated. He unfurled his fist without as much as a glance at the torn skin on his knuckles. "He may not have known until later why you left, but he had your back the whole damn time. He trusted you. Covered for you. When he knew you'd gone to Texas, he told the FBI you were always yammering about going to

Alaska, so they should start looking there." Sean's eyes became enraged slits. "Pretending to hate you was the best way to take the heat off Dad. *And* off of you. Only he never expected you would hate him back for real."

Under the weight of Sean's words, Ryan staggered and gripped the workbench behind him. "I don't — I never hated Dad. I didn't know what he did."

"You didn't want to know." Sean flexed his fingers as though itching to form new fists. "I was watching it kill our old man to write you off so he could protect you from being picked up for kidnapping, and you never even asked how he was the few times you bothered to call."

His brother stalked to the other side of the tack room and stood, back straight, shoulders heaving, his back to Ryan He'd always had a hot temper, and it had always bugged him when it got away from him.

Ryan stepped away from the bench, forcing his hands to remain open and loose. He had no reason to feel defensive, or maybe he did, but he wouldn't fight his brother. "Sean, I was hurting, too! I was just eighteen. I was arrogant, thinking I could save the world and there wouldn't be any consequences. By the time I realized there were, it hurt too much to talk *about* home, let alone call and hear your voices."

"And I was thirteen!" Sean whirled, wearing an incensed glare that seemed capable of shooting flames. "Old enough to know you left, but not old enough for anyone to trust me with your reasons for leaving."

Old enough to feel abandoned.

Ryan took several deep breaths, seeking calm in a river of rage. "You're right. I'm sorry."

Sean slumped. "They made life bad for a while." Sadness replaced the temper in his voice. "The MacKays. They spread lies about you, about Mac, even — about Mom. And people were listening. But Dad wouldn't talk about it, wouldn't talk about *you*. Finally people stopped caring about the stuff Alice was spreading in town. Mostly."

"If anyone deserved to die in that family, it wasn't Mac." Fury he'd never quite banked began to swirl again.

"Dad said his old man beat him up."

"Someone sure did." Ryan picked up the long black knife he'd been using to cut leather and twirled it baton-style. "I found him sleeping in the little barn. He'd been there probably three, four days. He was sneaking into the house when we were out so he could steal food to feed himself." Ryan's voice hardened. "Three or four days, and no one came around looking for him."

"Was he in bad shape when you found him?" Sean paced to the door, stopping to stare out into the stable yard.

"Both eyes were blackened, one was swollen shut. His nose was broken, teeth were loose." Ryan waited for the picture to fill Sean's head the way it was filling his own. "And someone had put out a cigarette on his tongue at some point."

Sean whipped around and Ryan caught a glimpse of shock in his brother's eyes. "Why?"

"Because he had red hair and he stuttered maybe." Ryan slashed the air with one hand. "Shit, I don't know. Why the hell does that family do any damn thing?"

"Couldn't you, I don't know, call someone? Report it?"

"Report it to who?" demanded Ryan. "Sheriff Russell MacKay?" He slammed the knife point-first into the scrap leather Sean had been playing with.

Sean whistled low and long. "Mac's uncle. I forgot."

"I was just going to take Mac into Jackson, see he got help then come home," Ryan said, swallowing back the bitterness the memories had dragged up. "But he was afraid they'd send him back. He begged me to stay with him, to take him away from Wyoming, from his family." He leaned forward and captured Sean's eyes. "Do you know how bad shit must have been for a kid to beg someone to keep him safe from *family*?"

A muscle worked in Sean's jaw but he said nothing.

"I never stopped missing this place," Ryan said quietly, allowing some of his rage to dissipate. "But I couldn't come home until Mac made sure I was cleared of kidnapping. And Mac was always — different. Kind of fragile. He couldn't come back here, and I couldn't leave him in the city."

"Why did you stay away after Mac died?"

"I told you I was injured. I just about had to learn to walk again, Sean." Ryan closed his eyes and allowed different, even more painful memories to surface.

"You never told us it was that bad," accused Sean, his face showing horror.

"I was in rehab for months. Then... I wanted to come home, but I didn't know how to ask. And... I was trying to find someone."

Sean frowned. "Who were you looking for?"

"I'll tell you about her sometime," Ryan promised. Needing a distraction, he scooped the spent bullet off the workbench, rewrapped it, and returned it to his pocket. "She was with us when Mac died. I've been looking for her since I got out of the hospital, but... no luck."

"Long time to be looking for someone," Sean observed. "So what now? Are you here to stay or are you here with one foot still in the city?"

Easy... one breath in, another out. "I want to come home, Sean. To stay if you'll have me. I've missed this place, Dad... even you." He sent a grin across the tack room. "Maybe especially you."

Raw torment traveled across Sean's face, and he choked out his answer in a thick voice. "I've missed you, too, big brother."

Something Sean had said earlier registered anew. Ryan leveled him in his sights. "Dad said I was 'yammering' about Alaska?"

Sean chuckled. "In the thickest hayseed accent you ever heard."

The first bit of happiness since the conversation had begun brought on a smile. Their father, with his Master's Degree in Agricultural Science from Wyoming State, playing country cowboy.

For me. The thought was even more humbling than it was comical.

"So, how much does you wanting to stay have to do with the local barkeep?" Sean's grin was back in place.

That old brotherly feeling surfaced again — it came easier each time. With an answering smirk, Ryan stalked across the distance between them, hiked Sean onto his shoulder in a fireman's carry, and walked out into the stable yard. With no remorse whatsoever, he tipped his younger brother into the stock watering trough.

"Hey!" Sean sputtered as he sat and blew water out of his mouth. He stood, shaking the droplets from his hair. But the huge grin remained plastered across his face. "Paybacks, bro!" he called out. "You know what they say about 'em." Then he let out a whoop before bending and retrieving his hat, floating in the trough next to him.

"Yeah, yeah," Ryan muttered around a yawn. "They're a real bitch." With a lighter heart, he spun away from the happy scene and strode to the house.

* * *

A plush dark towel slung around his hips, Ryan was using another to dry his hair while he contemplated the insanity of having stayed up all night. His bed now looked mighty appealing.

He slid open the dresser drawer and grabbed a pair of dark briefs, pausing when he saw the folder. With one trembling finger he traced the upper edge. The bold black lines of the capital A on the tab sliced through his conscience like hot wires. Ryan squeezed his eyes shut against the onslaught of thoughts and emotions he preferred to keep buried.

He popped them open again, making himself dizzy as the colors around him swirled into focus. Damn it! What had he done by getting involved with Sandy? It felt a little like... cheating.

He picked up the folder and opened it, swallowing past the thickness lodged in his throat. Pages and pages of his own handwriting were clipped together. Notations of leads which hadn't panned out; her name, given to him by one of her sympathetic coworkers — Allie Whitman. Beneath all that, more pages of handwritten notes, the details he remembered of all their conversations, written when he'd been unable to walk, just so he'd have something to hold onto when he'd realized she wasn't coming to the hospital. He shuffled through them once again, those well-worn sheets of yellow paper.

He'd fallen in love with her, asked her to marry him. Yet he had nothing tangible of her. He'd needed her, but she hadn't been there as she had promised. She'd completely disappeared, almost like she'd never existed. The guys had teased him for months about hallucinating until he'd gotten more careful and sly about looking for her.

And now... Sandy made him want to throw it all away. Seven years of searching for someone who must not want to be found. Who was he cheating on if she'd left him first?

"Sandy," he whispered. He was cheating Sandy if he moved forward with her before letting go of the past he still struggled with.

"You and your brother square things up?" Justin's gravelly voice came from the doorway.

Ryan jumped. "Stop my heart first next time, will ya?"

Reason told him he hadn't been doing anything wrong, but he stuffed the papers back in the folder, then shoved the whole mess back into the dresser and slid the drawer closed.

Throughout Ryan's life, his father's commanding presence had filled every room he entered. Some things never changed, even after a heart attack, so Ryan was glad when Justin made himself comfortable in the chair by the window. It lessened the effect ever so slightly.

"I want to talk with you. I know your brother warned you to keep me out of it." He snickered. "Thinks I'll live longer if I don't get upset."

Ryan rolled his eyes. "Can this wait until I'm wearing pants?"

"We can talk while you get dressed."

Ryan stared.

His father shot a pointed look at the towel. "What? You got something under there you didn't have when I was changing your diapers?"

"A few more inches," he muttered under his breath, pissed at the invasion of his personal space. Ryan averted his stance, hoping his dad enjoyed the view of his ass, and stepped into his briefs then hauled on a pair of well-worn blue jeans with holes in the knees.

Justin ran a critical eye over the choice of attire. "You know, you can get a decent pair of jeans at AJ's General Store for under twenty bucks."

"These are my favorite." Ryan shoved his wallet into the only pocket without a gaping hole. "I'm just breaking them in."

Justin shook his head. "Looks more like you're breaking out of 'em, but suit yourself." He drew a deep breath, let it out slowly. "I figure your brother caught you up on some things."

Ryan fastened the button on his shirt cuff without looking up. "What he told me, *Dad*, was you had a heart attack and wouldn't let him call me."

"Wasn't any point. It was over as soon as it started. I wasn't in the mood for any deathbed nonsense."

Ryan forced his gaze up, taking in the weathered skin on Justin's face, the deep lines etched into the corners of his eyes. The shadows beneath those eyes. "I could've helped. I still can. We can get this place back on its feet."

Justin flashed a crooked grin. "I wasn't aware it was completely off its feet."

"I can help get it back to where it was before—"

"You know Sean's gotten into boarding some horses?"

The smooth change of subject was so typical of his father that Ryan didn't lose the beat. "It's always been horses for him. He's got a solid plan. We have the space, and the extra income it generates will help." He pulled his wristwatch into place.

"I agree," said Justin in an agreeable tone. Too agreeable. "But let's not say anything to your brother just yet. You know, your pretty young lady's the one who got him thinking about boarding. She bought that colt at auction last summer. Turns out he's so crazy no stable would keep him."

"No stable should keep him." Ryan shuddered at the memory of snapping teeth. "Including this one. Sandy shouldn't even have him."

"You plan on telling her that, I want to be there to see it." Justin cut loose with a hoarse chuckle. "Thing is, the colt'll do anything for that girl. Sean's been helping her train him, but she's got horses in her blood, herself, and that colt loves her." Justin's expression softened. "She reminds me some of your mother."

Just great. So his father saw it, too. Ryan could already see the matchmaking gleam in his dad's eyes. Never mind any potential interest he might have in that direction himself, he needed no help from his daddy on that score. So he shrugged. "I don't know. I've only just met her."

Justin's pointed glance told Ryan he still understood a great deal about what made his sons tick, even the one who'd just returned home after years of being absent. "You won't find a better match. She won't take your crap."

"My—" Ryan let out a long slow breath, relaxed the hands he discovered he'd balled into fists. No, not getting drawn into a conversation he couldn't win.

Justin went silent and closed his eyes. Good. Ryan considered leaving the room but experience told him they hadn't gotten to the heart of the conversation yet. So he waited it out. As usual.

"I don't suppose your brother got 'round to telling you the real problem here." Justin's voice bordered between heightened concern and outright worry.

Ryan shook his head. "Baby steps with him. Gotta take baby steps. I hurt him — hurt you both — when I left."

"You did what you had to do, son." Justin said. "Right now we got some problems a mite harder to deal with than simple cash flow. I know you went to the range yesterday with your girl. You're too smart not to have noticed the absence of cattle."

Finally. The answers he'd been looking for. "I noticed. What happened?"

"Sean planned to open up more range farther west," said Justin. "He was going to expand by about five hundred head to start. He was talking about going modern, bringing in a helicopter like a couple of the outfits out of Laramie. We've had a couple good years. He made some good investments. Bank was all set to loan him the rest of the stake he needed."

A half-hour and many words later, Ryan found his world rocked off its axis. And not in a good way.

More than a hundred head of cattle slaughtered by high-powered rifle shot. Before that, a series of little things which might have been accidents or a run of bad luck, but when pieced together, they looked less like random events and more like well-thought-out malicious acts.

"When did all this happen?"

"April. Right after we moved the herd up there. Sean had a couple of hands up there watching the rest of the herd, but a few more cows got picked off and he brought the whole lot down off the mountain. Couldn't risk more cattle, or worse, the lives of his men."

Ryan pinched the bridge of his nose then drew a hand down his face, stopping at his jaw, while he considered the impact of his father's words. "Geez, Dad. I should never have taken Sandy up there."

"You're right. It should have been the three of us riding up there, with you knowing what you were riding into."

"And whose fault was that?"

"Mine." Justin sighed. "It's mine. I wouldn't let your brother call you when things started happening."

Ryan's gaze flashed to his father, for the first time seeing a hint of defeat in the tired green eyes. His anger evaporated.

"I'm sorry."

"You've got nothing to be sorry for," Justin told him, returning his gaze.

"No, Dad, I do." Ryan blew out a long breath, realizing the choices he'd had to make sixteen years earlier would never sit easy with him. "I left for good reasons and I'd do it again. But I left a man and a young boy to run a family business I was part of. I stayed away too long, and I came back, started giving orders and taking over without earning— What?" he asked when Justin began chuckling.

The chuckle became a full-out laugh. "I remember your grandmother saying something along those lines once in regard to me. When I started trying to tell my dad what was what after one year at college."

Chapter Eight

The answers were finally trickling in. But with every one answer came two more questions. It was like being on a perpetual and very irritating quest against a hydra.

He turned onto the deserted highway, shifting quickly through the gears. The raw power of the car thrummed into his feet, pulsed through the steering wheel into his hands. He downshifted once and rounded a curve. The highway would lead straight on to town, so he opened his baby up. It wasn't quite the same as having a horse under him, but it was a close second.

Close second? How many times had he settled for a *close second* over the last decade and a half? Memories of Sandy astride the horse next to him as they'd raced across the plain the day before sent heat spiraling through him, followed quickly by a dousing of ice water. Too many times. Way too many.

Shoving aside the unsavory thought, Ryan began instead to play around with the idea that had stirred while talking with his father. Something that expanded on Sean's concept of modernizing to increase the herd but also involved giving Sean his own niche with the horses he loved.

"Sean's not afraid of failing, Ryan. He knows business and he's got a head for it. He's afraid of not measuring up to what you might be expecting from him." His father's last cryptic disclosure wasn't sitting well.

So would Sean see the benefit of Ryan's proposal or would he only see his older brother trying to take over? He'd have to tread carefully. Hell with it. Sean would have to get used to him being home, being part of the Cross MC. And they'd either learn to work together or kill each other.

Ryan stabbed the hands-free button on his cell and dialed L.A.

"Hey, Ry! Have you gone cowboy on us yet?" asked the deep voice on the other end.

Ryan felt the grin splitting his face at the sound of his best friend's voice. "Missing me yet, Joe?"

"Only taking most of your paycheck at the Friday night poker game."

"Ah, I don't miss that." Ryan took a deep breath then dove in. "I'm not coming back."

Joe chuckled. "Yeah, I figured. I want out myself. Got any openings in Cowville for a hotshot helicopter pilot?"

"Maybe," said Ryan. "Have you ever considered herding cattle by helicopter?"

The outskirts of Orson's Folly loomed — as much as a sprawl of one- and two-story buildings *could* loom — as Ryan finished outlining his proposition to a very interested Joseph Griffin, EMS helicopter pilot.

"So, what about prospects for female companionship?" asked his old pal.

Sandy's face floated into Ryan's thoughts. He affected his thickest accent. "I can probably rustle you up an invite to the Sunday church social to meet our one-eyed, bucktoothed schoolmarm."

"My dream girl." Joe chuckled. "I'll start packing tomorrow."

"Pool drying up out there, buddy?"

"Not exactly. I went on a blind date with an actress last week. And she's not averse to going out again. Of course, it's kind of like dating a box of rocks without a lid, but she's not hard on the eyes."

Ryan snickered. "I'm sure you can figure out what to do with her *rocks*."

"I'm sure I will." Joe sighed heavily. "Ryan, I don't know how to—" Another puff of air sounded over the phone. "Look, Cara got her start in community theater."

The back of Ryan's neck heated up. "And?"

"And she remembers a girl she used to work with when she first started out. Said she had a beauty of a singing voice, was a good actress but not serious about it. And she left L.A. very suddenly some years ago in the middle of a production. Cara thinks she went back east to her family."

Braking to a stop in front of the sheriff's office, Ryan forced himself to keep breathing. "Okay, I see you still like to bury the lede."

"I'm sorry," Joe apologized quickly. "I wasn't sure if you were still looking. I've seen what the dead ends do to you, man."

Memories of drunken nights and morning-after hangovers with Joe doing the male equivalent of hair-holding played in Ryan's mind like an old movie reel. "Not my finest moments."

"So I didn't know what to do with the information." Joe's voice was heavy. "Do you want me to dig further? Are we still looking for this girl?"

"I..." Ryan hesitated. *Was* he still looking? The dead ends were exhausting as well as heartbreaking, but as clues went this was the most solid they had come up with in a long time. He thought about Sandy. The woman in the flesh and now. He was definitely falling hard for her. The sun flashed off a passing lumber truck, inciting an answering sparkle from the crystal angel hanging on his mirror, reminding him there were things left unsaid.

The truck rumbled past and was gone.

"Ry?"

Ryan inhaled, blew out forcefully. "Yeah, sure, go ahead," he said in a rush. It couldn't hurt to ask around, could it?

After severing the phone connection, Ryan began to rethink his decision.

The angel swayed gently on her cord in front of him, mocking his indecision. He watched her until she was still again. A dream forged in loneliness and desperation. A dream which had been about hope and survival and beating the odds.

His eyes drifted to the passenger seat where Sandy had sat just the day before. Vibrant, alive, happy. She hadn't even been on his radar before that mountain road. And now... even though she wasn't physically seated next to him at that moment, she was real. She was a tangible presence in his life, not the dream that the angel dangling from his mirror represented.

Ryan reached up and yanked the angel until the cord snapped. He held her in the palm of his hand for a moment, ran his thumb over her face in a gentle caress.

"Parting is sorrow, darlin', but there's nothing sweet about it. Whatever your reasons for not being there, wherever you are now, I sure hope you're well and happy."

His decision made, he leaned over, opened the glove compartment, and dropped the angel inside with a feeling akin to adding the last period on a shift report. The slam of the little door echoed through the car. He considered calling Joe back and telling him to drop the hunt, then shrugged. As with all the other leads, nothing was likely to come of it anyway.

* * *

Melanie finished clearing the table from the last lunch customer and picked up a tray of beer mugs. "Whooee! That was a bigger-than-normal lunch crowd."

It certainly had been. But why? Sandy shrugged. What did it matter? Business was business. "If it keeps up, I'll see if I can find someone part-time for lunches."

Balancing the bus tray on the end of the bar, Mel popped open the dishwasher and added the mugs. When she looked up at Sandy again, she wore a speculative expression. "How did your day out with Ryan McGee go?"

"It had some interesting twists." Sandy tilted her head and surveyed her friend. "Speaking of twists, did I miss the part of the story where you told me the prodigal son was Sean's brother?"

Mel smiled and shrugged. "Did I forget to mention that? Huh."

Sandy huffed an impatient breath. "Mel, what's the real story there? With Bull and Ryan?"

Shaking her head, Mel looked away, her eyes clouded with doubt. "I can't answer that."

"Can't or won't?" Sandy asked, irritation sharpening her tone.

Mel shoved the tray further onto the bar. Drawing a deep breath, she whirled to face Sandy and settled her hands on her hips. "Can't. Because it's not mine to tell. Besides I don't know all the details. The families haven't gotten along since Sean and I were kids. Ryan left when I was twelve and Sean thirteen. I knew Sean was upset, but he wouldn't talk about it, and my mom told me Ryan went to college. Then, the next year I — left Orson's Folly myself. By the time I got back, things were different between me and Sean. He doesn't tell me so much now." Fine lines pinched Mel's forehead, and she didn't quite meet Sandy's eyes.

Obviously something deep was happening, something her friend found troubling. A twinge of remorse for having pushed her spurred Sandy forward. "I'm sorry. I didn't mean to make you feel uncomfortable." She picked up the bus tray and sighed. "I'm just a little spooked, I guess. I know *something* is going on, but the town seems pretty closed up about it."

Like a switch had been pulled, Mel's smile flashed with a grin. "You know who you should ask, don't you? If you want the whole truth, you need to ask Ryan himself."

That couldn't be disputed. But how would Ryan react to direct questioning about an obviously sore subject?

"We probably won't get anyone in before dinnertime now," said Mel, tapping the end of the bar. "I'm going on break so I can run to the bank."

The breath stalled in Sandy's throat, and fine tremors overtook her hands. She stuffed them in the pockets of her long pink sweater. It would be okay. Besides, Charlotte Hains was just on the other side of the silver kitchen doors, prepping for dinner. The cook would have her back with the sturdy baseball bat she kept behind the door.

"Um, yeah, go ahead." She stooped and pretended interest in the shelf of beer mugs beneath the bar, hoping Mel wouldn't notice her reluctance to be alone.

Apparently her act fell short. "What's up with you, being all edgy? And what's with the granny getup? It's a bazillion degrees outside and not much cooler in here. At least unbutton the sweater."

Sandy repositioned a few of the beer mugs before looking up. "I must be coming down with something. Go on to the bank, Mel. I'll cover."

After a long stare filled with doubt, Mel shook her head and left through the kitchen doors.

Alone in the bar, Sandy tried to work out her agitation by fussing with a pyramid of beer mugs. After her third attempt to line them up evenly, she impatiently slid them all to the side. The sound of clinking glass was a welcome interruption to the silence. Drawing a deep, calming breath, Sandy started over.

She arranged the first layer, cursing Bull for his late night visit. He'd invaded her home, her sanctuary. She added another layer, then a third. She had no idea what had set his eye in her direction but it was a fair bet it had something to do with Ryan.

After stacking the last layer, she stepped back. The pyramid of beer mugs looked like a child had built it, but Sandy couldn't bring herself to care, directing her attention instead to the rack of margarita glasses.

* * *

"I sure could go for a cold beer." Mick's voice was getting hoarse.

"I'll have one waiting for you," promised Sandy. "Or we could go for margaritas."

"My heart! I've met the perfect woman."

But his words were slow, seemingly spoken with care. Perhaps he was experiencing fatigue... or worse. She wanted to cry but stemmed the tears and forced brightness into her voice.

"I'm far from that. But I can get a thirsty man a beer."

"And I'll take that beer, Angel," he said, his voice stronger. "Then I'll kiss the most beautiful gal on earth! After that we'll go find dinner and that pitcher of margaritas, and we'll spend the night watching the stars. 'Cause I won't want to be indoors anytime soon. You ever make out under a starry sky?"

Heat assaulted her face. "No, but I'm thinking you plan to show me what I'm missing."

"You smiling, Angel? You sound like maybe you're smiling."

"I am." Then she laughed.

"Give me something to picture here. What do you look like?"

"I'm average everything. Average height and build, brown hair, blue eyes."

"I'll bet you have a killer smile."

"I have a crooked smile," she assured him.

"How long is your hair?"

"Short. Really short."

"Dang, you got me, girl." He chuckled. "I was picturing running my hands through it, all chocolate silk, falling around your shoulders."

"You'd be a day late for that. I just got it cut yesterday. I like it short in the summertime."

"Do you dance?"

"Not very well."

"Too bad," he said. "I wanted to dance at our wedding."

"I'll take lessons," she offered. "Just for you. Besides, after a pitcher of margaritas you might not care how I dance."

* * *

When the front door opened, Sandy's hands jerked, knocking two of the margarita glasses to the floor, where they bounced once, hit the base of the bar, and shattered.

Her heart leaped against her throat and she cast a startled glance at the door, breathing out a slow sigh when she recognized the tan uniform and the gold star. Glass crunched under her feet and she muttered a ripe curse under her breath as she stooped to pick up the mess. The sting of glass piercing her flesh brought on a new round of cursing as she watched the drops of blood well like red tears from the base of her thumb.

"You okay, Sandy?" Sheriff Dirk Cooper, affectionately known as DC — since childhood, according to the rumor mill — hurried over. He took her hand and hissed in a breath through his teeth.

"It looks worse than it is," Sandy assured him.

Emitting a noncommittal grunt, he nodded. "Yep, you've got two little cuts here. They don't look deep, but they ought to be cleaned out. Got a first-aid kit?"

She pointed to a green box beneath the sink as she dumped the pieces of glass into the tall trash. "I can't believe I'm such a klutz!"

DC pulled her to her feet, turned on the faucet, and held her hand under the running water, running his thumb lightly over the parallel red lines. "Does it feel like you've got anything stuck in there?"

His touch against her palm created an urge to snatch her hand back and rub at the feathery sensation. A giggle slipped out. "No, but that really tickles."

DC applied a couple of band-aids then pulled her hand to his lips and made a show of kissing it.

"Lisa insists this makes everything feel better," he said very seriously. "Last night she fell off her bike and suggested rather strongly I needed to kiss her backside."

"Your toddler essentially told you to kiss her butt?" Sandy didn't bother to fight a smile. "How does a parent handle that?"

"The same way I handle all the dad stuff that scares the crap out of me," DC replied. "I sent her off to find her mother."

* * *

Sandy's laugh rang across the bar and slammed into Ryan at the door. His steps faltered briefly when he saw the sheriff holding her hand and pressing a kiss to her palm.

"DC, I heard you went to the dark side," Ryan said from the end of the bar, stemming the prick of jealousy.

Recognition took a few seconds. Then Ryan's old friend was crossing the distance between them. "And I heard you went to the hot side." DC clapped Ryan on the shoulder. "Welcome home, man."

"I was just at your office," he said in a voice meant only for DC to hear. "Got something I need to show you but..." His eyes slid toward Sandy as she approached.

DC caught the signal and gave a sharp nod. "I was just about to order some lunch. Why don't you join me?"

"What can I get you two?" Sandy slid a menu in front of DC with a smile. She slapped one in front of Ryan with a little more force.

Startled, Ryan shifted his eyes in her direction. Anyone else might have missed it, the hint of some indefinable emotion in her eyes; anger or fear or sadness? Or doubt? She covered well, but her eyes mirrored something troubling inside. And not even her perfect makeup covered the deep shadows beneath eyes that looked like they hadn't known any more sleep the previous night than he had. His conversation with the sheriff would have to wait.

Glancing over at DC, Ryan answered, "How about a table for three and your company for lunch?"

Sandy stiffened and he thought she might refuse. Finally she shrugged and set another place. She didn't talk much through the meal and Ryan found himself giving responses of one or two words to his old friend as he tried to pin down the emotions that occasionally played across Sandy's face.

They were midway through the meal when DC received a call from his office.

"That's just great!" He slid his cell phone back into his pocket. "Someone went and started a fire at Lantree's Lumber." Standing, he took a last bite of his hamburger. "I gotta go."

When he reached for his wallet, Sandy waved him off. "You know your money's no good in here. Now go save the world!"

Ryan watched her through a narrowed gaze. That was her first honest laugh since he'd arrived. And it didn't last long.

"You're paying the sheriff off with free meals?"

Guileless blue eyes began to twinkle again. "Of course!"

She was coming back, he thought, but wasn't quite there yet. Reaching over the table, Ryan took one of her hands in his. "Hey, you," he said softly. "I missed you last night. It took me less than a mile to wish I'd stayed."

Again a flicker of trouble floated back into her eyes, but it was gone too quickly for him to discern what it was. She said nothing, merely sighed and averted her face.

The door opened behind her and Sandy jerked, nearly knocking her drink from the table.

"Sorry I'm late," Mel apologized. She breezed through to the kitchen without waiting for a response.

"Okay, what's up? You're jumpy." His eyes swept over the body she had wrapped beneath layers of baggy clothing. "I don't know what you're wearing, but it's not you. And your eyes... sweetheart..." He leaned forward to kiss her gently, trying not to read too much into her obvious flinch. "Is it — are you having second thoughts about seeing me?"

Sandy's breath caught. "No! That is — I — it's not—" A tear spilled over.

He felt like a jerk for making her cry. "Chicory, I'm trying to understand what's going on, but you aren't making much sense here."

"Last night, right after you left, I was going to take a bath. The water was running and I was getting undressed when I heard a knock on the door." She gulped in a breath.

"Who was at the door?" He brought her hand to his lips, keeping his gaze focused on her face.

"I thought it was you but it—" Another deep breath.

Her fingers were cold as he stroked them with his thumb. "Whoever it was, you're safe now."

"I opened the door with some smart comment about you missing me and spending the night and—" She swallowed convulsively. "Bull was there."

Ice enveloped Ryan and he tensed, ready to commit an act of violence. "Did he touch you?" Anger and alarm fused to form a band of steel, squeezing his chest, compressing his lungs, making it impossible to breathe while he waited for her to answer.

A shudder rocked her body, but she shook her head. "No, but he wanted to very badly. I saw it in his eyes." She clutched the edges of her sweater, tugging them closed. "I could feel it. When he looked at me, it felt like he was already touching me."

He leveled a stare at the table to his left, unable to watch her while he struggled to control the rage searing its way through his psyche. His free hand clenched. Each ragged breath he drew was like inhaling flames. He should have been there. He shouldn't have left her alone.

He caught her gaze again. "Has this happened before?"

"No." A resigned sigh accompanied the toneless word. "He comes in here sometimes. We've met around town. I hired his son to do landscape work this spring. But Bull's never come by my apartment, and mostly he's just... pathetic." She pulled away and ground the tears from her cheeks with the heels of her hands. "He's never caused any problems until..." She swallowed hard.

"Until I came back."

When she raised her face again, sparks of anger mixed with apprehension. "Ryan, is there something I should know?"

What his massive efforts to check his temper couldn't do, her question accomplished. The rage bubbling under the surface couldn't hold on as compassion nudged it aside. She did deserve to know the truth. *Shit.*

"Yeah. There is." He stood, maneuvered around the table, and drew her to her feet. With gentle hands, he cupped her cheeks, raised her face so he could look at her, wiping away the last of her tears with his thumbs. Recognizing the war between anger and hope being waged in her eyes, he groaned and pulled her against him. She held herself rigid, but he refused to loosen his grasp, and finally she relaxed into the embrace.

Burying his face in her hair, Ryan breathed deeply, filling himself with her scent, before pulling back to meet her eyes again. "Sandy, listen to me. You expected it to be someone you trusted at your door. You had no reason to think otherwise. If it had been Sean, or DC — anyone but Bull, you probably would have had a good laugh about it. Bull and me—" He huffed out a breath. How did he explain the unexplainable? "Our history is — it's complicated, and it's not pleasant. And I'm sorry... so sorry that it's touching you."

"I'm sorry, too, Ryan," she whispered, her eyes clouded by what could only be doubt. "I feel like I should just trust you — that I shouldn't need to know—" She took a step back and he let her go. "If you don't want to tell me about you and Bull, it's okay."

"Sandy, listen. Just don't — underestimate Bull MacKay." Ryan looped a strand of hair behind her ear, leaving his hand against her neck. "He's not pathetic, he's dangerous. He gets off on hurting people. And obviously associating with me has painted a huge target on your back."

She shuddered. "I just never saw that side of him before."

"It's there," Ryan assured her. "It's been there." He leaned in for one more quick kiss. "Don't go anywhere, and make sure you aren't here alone. When I get back, we'll talk." The second he released her, his body cried out against her absence.

Eyes wide with fresh alarm, she reached for him. "Where are you going?"

"I have some ranch business I can't get out of," he answered, tapping the back of her hand before he moved off. "I came in to report the downed cow and arrange for removal. After that I'm all yours."

"You're not — you won't—?"

Ryan tipped Sandy's face upward. "I won't lie to you, Chicory. I want to hurt Bull MacKay right now." *For even thinking about touching you.* "But I won't go looking for him."

He made no promise, though, of what the outcome would be should Bull find him.

* * *

The door closed behind Ryan and still Sandy sat without moving. He'd run out without telling her anything, with only a vague promise of talking later. That left her feeling a little unsettled and out of sorts. What was wrong with her? She barely knew him and she had managed to come on to him, nearly have sex with him — three times. And currently she was feeling sorry for herself because he hadn't made any promises.

"I'm a freaking psych case," she told the empty chair across the table.

Mel popped her head through the kitchen doors. "Sandy, that pipe under the main sink just blew out."

Of course it did, because the day isnt already going bad enough. "I'll call Parsen's Plumbing," she called out with a sigh.

"I already did. Glenn's out on a call, not expected back until after five."

"Of course he is," muttered Sandy.

* * *

"I've told you a lot about me. Tell me what you do for fun," suggested Sandy.

"Well, Angel, I like fixing things."

"Things like...?"

"Cars, houses."

"Okay, the cars I get. But houses? Whole houses?"

"A few of the guys and I got together and bought a house. We lived there during our off-time and fixed it up. Then we flipped it and sold it for twice what we paid."

"So you flip houses?"

He chuckled. "Not so much these days. But we still get together and help out on some of the community projects."

"And what part of the fixing up do you do?"

"You name it, I've done it. A little carpentry, a little electrical."

"And plumbing?"

"It just so happens plumbing is one of my specialties."

* * *

Lying flat on her back beneath the sink, Sandy applied the wrench to the slip nut on the blown trap, twisting the handle with a grunt. Nothing happened. She was getting nowhere.

She dropped her arm to allow circulation to return. "Sure could have used you here, Mick."

"Did you say something?" asked Mel.

"Just talking to a ghost." Sandy lifted the wrench again.

* * *

For the second time that day, Ryan's Corvette hit the tiny parking lot of the Orson's Folly Sheriff's Department, spewing gravel from beneath wide tires. DC's brown patrol car pulled in from the opposite direction before Ry's dust had settled.

DC exited the cruiser, a clipboard in his hand and a warning on his lips. "Some folks around here would just love it if I had to give you a ticket for reckless driving in your fancy little sports car."

Ryan ignored the sheriff, rounding his car with angry strides. "Bull MacKay went after Sandy."

"Okay, slow down. I know he tried to start something at her place but I thought it was you in his sights."

"He was knocking on her door late last night." Anger added an edge to Ryan's voice. "Probably less than ten minutes after I dropped her off. Would've been fairly close to ten-thirty or eleven." Nearly choking on the words, he filled DC in on the events as Sandy had related them earlier.

The sheriff swept a look of speculation over Ryan. "You and Sandy Wheaton, huh? I thought I picked something up back at Valentine's. You two sure you know what you're doing?"

"Are you getting at something, DC?" Ryan inserted a chill into his words. "Because I'd sure like you to get around to it if you are."

A pained expression crossed his old friend's face. Sighing, he leaned against the back of his patrol car, folding his arms over his chest. But the tapping of the clipboard against one hip belied the relaxation behind the move. "You know, Ry, no one ever expected you to come back to Orson's Folly. Now you're here, about fifty percent of folks don't think you'll hang around, and forty-nine percent are afraid you will."

"Where do you stand?" Ryan asked softly.

"I'm the one percent willing to wait and see how things go," DC replied with a snort. "Thing is, you and Sandy hooking up, well, that's going to upset the balance a bit. Town's still pretty well divided about her, too. Used to be no one wanted her here at all. But she's proven herself part of this place by bits and pieces, and things are balancing out. Now she's the darlin' of most of the men here..." He cocked his head to the side, a smile twisting half of his mouth upward. "'Ceptin' Brother Bobby, of course. The teenage boys follow her like bees to clover. The teenage girls all want to *be* her, and most of the women wish their men would stay home with them on a Friday night. But they've come to trust Sandy doesn't have designs in that direction." He paused for a beat, pinning Ryan in his stare. "Add a black sheep into the mix, things are gonna get complicated."

Ryan pulled his mouth into a smile to match his sarcastic response. "Is this the part where you warn me to leave the saloonkeeper alone or get out of town?"

DC's sharp laugh echoed off the front of the building. "As if I had that power." He leaned back onto his elbows and drew a deep breath. "Seriously, Ry, you had to know you'd be watching your back when you came home."

Ryan studied the sheriff for a long, silent moment. Had their friendship suffered so badly in the years of his exile? He supposed that had been inevitable. Was DC giving him a subtle politically correct warning about life in Orson's Folly?

The poker face staring back gave Ryan nothing to go on. When he spoke, his impassive tone matched his expression. "I don't guess you plan to stop seeing her?"

That answer required no thought. "Snowball's chance in hell."

DC nodded. "Thought you'd say that. Then watch out for her. Don't go looking for Bull. In fact, stay out of his way as much as you can. Just take care of your woman and... enjoy being together." The sheriff stood, began heading for the office, but stopped, glancing over his shoulder with a thoughtful frown. "What was it you wanted to show me?"

"Did Sean talk to you about the cattle on our open range?"

"He did. That why you're back?"

Ryan parked his hat further back on his head. "It's one reason."

"The state police took over the investigation," DC said with a nod. "Your brother should have the contact information."

"Such an attack could be considered personal." Ryan kept his voice even against the rage that boiled just under the surface.

"You know, I'd agree with you but you weren't here at the time. And things have been pretty easy between your family and Mac's these days." Shaking his head, the sheriff shrugged. "The state police are looking real hard at a coal mining company out of West Virginia. There's been some interest in purchasing land along the Green River vein."

"Why would anyone do that? Green River's old news. It's unreachable."

DC scratched his jaw. "It *was* unreachable. Technology gets developed all the time, and with the energy crunch rich veins of coal like that are gonna get a second, even a third look-see."

"Someone's been up at the cabin since my brother brought his cattle off the mountain," Ryan said. His gut told him the threat was local, but how to convince the sheriff? "Fairly recently. It's clean. Too clean for a two-month stretch. The grass outside's been trampled a fair bit."

DC shrugged again. "Hikers. Rangers, maybe."

"And they what? Got a sudden urge to clean? You could eat off the floor once you got past the smell of pine cleaner and bleach."

"I can pass the information on," said DC coolly. "But on the surface it just doesn't sound like it means anything." He started walking again.

"Another cow was shot up there," Ryan said quietly.

DC stopped, his hand on the door to the office, but he didn't turn around. "When?"

"Found her yesterday. She was alive but down. I had to finish her off. Flank shot, within a day, maybe day and a half of me finding her. She had a calf and probably took care of her as long as she could." Ryan pulled the piece of ruined shirt from his pocket and unfolded it, revealing the recovered slug. "Dug this out of her."

DC eyed the object in Ryan's hand with obvious frustration. "Flat point .44 Magnum. This is consistent with findings in the state police investigation." With a sigh, he held the door open for Ryan. "You'd best come inside and make a statement."

Ryan tried to lose the scowl as he followed the sheriff inside. As successes went, it wasn't much of a bone, but he'd take whatever scraps he could get.

"Hey, Gloria," DC said, letting the door to the office close after they entered. He dropped the clipboard on her desk. "Got an arson report to be typed up here." He lowered his voice but the room was small, and Ryan had no trouble making out his next words. "There's no positive ID, but Henky swears one of the boys running away had red hair."

Gloria Pratt was a plump woman with a roadmap of wrinkles on her face. Her shoulder-length hair had once been strawberry blond but was now heading strongly toward white. At DC's words, she wilted in her chair and her face took on even more wrinkles with her frown of apprehension.

"Now, there's no evidence as yet. I'm telling you so someone can get control over the boy before he gets hurt or hurts someone else." DC's tone was stern, but his eyes reflected concern. "If I get another report that sounds like him, I'm going to have to start looking at him real hard."

"I understand, DC," Gloria answered in a defeated tone. "I'm not askin' for a break. I'm just worried about Brenda. I don't think she knows what to do with the boy. Sometimes I think she wishes—" She broke off as she caught sight of Ryan.

Removing his hat, he nodded a greeting.

"Hello, Ryan. I heard you were back in town for a spell."

He smiled and met her stare head-on. It didn't take a genius to realize Mrs. Gloria Pratt was among the forty-nine percent crowd, the folks afraid he wasn't leaving.

DC took Ryan's statement and logged the spent round into evidence. "I know it's frustrating, not getting answers, Ry."

Fatigue was creeping up on him. Ryan rubbed his forehead. "Kinda feels like I keep stepping in it these days. And all I wanted was to come home."

Finally, DC gifted him with an understanding nod. "You know, if you really plan to stay, a good way to start out might be to put those skills of yours to work with the OFVFD. They can always use an extra hand, 'specially if that hand's got experience."

Ryan stiffened at the mention of the Orson's Folly Volunteer Fire Department, but then drew a deep breath and slowly expelled it and gave a nod. "I expect you're right. I'll look into it."

"It is good to have you back," DC said quietly.

On his way out, Ryan caught sight of a grouping of women's pictures on the bulletin board, all under the heading *MISSING*. One in particular drew his attention, a black and white picture of a woman with dark wavy hair and pale eyes. Her hair was piled loosely on top of her head with stray tendrils escaping. Large hoops dangled from her ears.

He spun on his heel. "What's this?"

Looking up from his desk, DC grunted. "Ongoing FBI case. Some women gone missing from up around Jackson in the past couple years."

Ryan read the specifics listed beneath the photo. Waitress in a small diner in Jackson, lived alone, no current boyfriend. Missing since the middle of May.

"You ever notice how much this one—" He bent and checked the name. "—Frances Henry, looks like Sandy?"

DC frowned. "Now you mention it, I do recall thinking something along those lines when those came in."

Ryan tapped his fingertips against the picture. On closer inspection, the resemblance to Sandy wasn't as apparent. Frances Henry's lips were less full, her face slimmer, her smile more forced, nose too angular, and her eyes too widely spaced. Pretty, though. He wondered what had happened to her.

Tipping his hat to Mrs. Pratt again, Ryan moved for the door. The late afternoon sun was hot when he stepped outside. But he couldn't shake the chill at the thought of working with the Orson's Folly Volunteer Fire Department. *It wouldn't be the same,* a voice inside reminded him. His old hometown wasn't a big urban environment filled with skyscrapers.

Chapter Nine

He returned to the bar, mentally shored up for the conversation he knew he had to have with Sandy, but the only person in evidence when Ryan walked through the door was Mel. She was doing something with beer mugs behind the bar and he hung in the doorway, about to ask where he might find Sandy, when a streak of mild curses erupted from beyond the double doors into the kitchen.

Mel looked up and smiled. "If you don't know anything about plumbing, I suggest you don't go in there."

"Plumbing, huh?" Speaking of lucky breaks… One side of Ryan's mouth curved upward as he sauntered through the double doors. The curses leaned further into the graphic zone, and he raised an eyebrow. Chicory had more of a temper than he'd realized.

The kitchen was new and very modern, stainless steel everywhere. Looking up from where she was chopping onions, Charlie Hains shot him a silent grin then nodded and pointed to the other side of a long food prep island in the middle of the kitchen.

Ryan edged his way around the counter. A pair of long denim-clad legs emerged from a cabinet beneath the deep sink. One leg was straight, the other bent at the knee. Every few seconds, the flexed knee pushed against the floor, as though bracing against something beneath the sink.

"You *will* turn, you damn piece of—!" The words morphed into a low grunt.

Crouching next to her, Ryan tried to see beneath the cabinet but the dim light hid all from his view except for some nice curves pushing against Sandy's sweater. Or maybe those were just more interesting...

Gently, he touched Sandy on her bent knee. She jumped and propelled herself from under the sink, sitting up and casting him a blinking stare. "You're back."

"Looks like." He craned his neck to get a better look at what she was doing. "Plumbing problems?"

She smiled, showing no trace of the agitated plumber. "Looks like."

"Want a hand?"

Her smile became crooked, and she held out the wrench. "If you know what you're doing, have at it."

Ryan grinned. "It just so happens plumbing is one of my specialties."

Sandy stared. The wrench slipped from her fingers, landing with a clank on the ceramic tile floor.

"You okay?"

A shudder wracked her body. Then she recovered with a shake of her head. "Um, yeah... it's just... someone else said that once and I was just thinking about him. You startled me."

The muscles in his jaw tensed. No need to ask who'd said it. Her twenty-three hour love. Jealousy stabbed like a needle in Ryan's gut. *Relax. No point in fighting a ghost.* Unless that ghost was still a tangible presence standing between them.

He forced the thought down and reached for the wrench. "Move on out of there, woman, and let an expert show you how it's done."

* * *

"I can't believe you got that pipe off so easily." Sandy glared at him through narrowed eyes then suddenly broke into a good-natured smile that brought life to those chicory-colored eyes, reminding him of flowers dancing in the wind.

"And I can't believe you pulled the trap without having a replacement." Ryan tugged the strand of hair that had escaped her loose ponytail.

The exaggerated pouty face made her look about ten. "I had duct tape."

A smile tugging on the corners of his mouth, Ryan handed her the silver roll. "You're going to want to repair that the right way by tomorrow. I can do it for you."

She tilted her head back and grinned up at him. "Got lots of experience, have you?"

"Hey, anyone can repair a sink trap." He chuckled as they entered the main bar. "But it just so happens I've re-plumbed an entire house."

Next to him, her steps faltered. Then she stopped. When he looked over his shoulder, she was staring at him again.

"What?" he asked.

"You just keep surprising me," whispered Sandy.

If her smile seemed a little too bright, Ryan wouldn't dwell on it. A deep-seated need to touch her drove him. Turning, he held her gaze. Her eyes widened when he cupped her face in his hands, caressing her cheeks with his thumbs. Then he bent and teased her with a butterfly touch, rubbing his lips back and forth along hers. She sighed, and he took the kiss deeper by inches, coaxing instead of demanding, giving instead of taking. Her breath caught and her hands settled on his waist. Ryan took his time, lingering until he felt her tension dissolve.

He ended the kiss, laying his forehead against hers. "Hey, you."

"What was that?" she whispered.

Ryan laughed softly. "I guess I'm still not doing it right."

The roll of tape dropped to the floor with a dull thud. Sandy's arms slid around to his back and she pulled herself against him. "You've never *not* done it right."

After a quick, hard hug, Ryan stepped away, moving his hands to the buttons on her sweater.

"What are you doing?" She tugged the edges back together.

Ryan stilled his fingers but left them at her buttons. He leaned in and kissed her once more, a little harder this time. When she finally relaxed against him, he worked at the buttons again.

"You don't need this." Leaning out, he tugged the sweater off her shoulders, then straightened, folding the soft garment and laying it on the bar. "That's better."

Ryan looked her over head to toe. Her flowing white blouse had wide gauzy sleeves, which ended just above her wrists. Light and airy, it covered nearly every inch of skin. But Ryan knew what lay beneath. Just the memory of that wonderland he had yet to fully explore made his body thrum into awareness and clear his mental dance card for the evening.

Her head was angled as she looked at him. Her eyes gleamed. A hint of a smile played around her lips. Oh yeah, she was aware of him, too. And maybe, just maybe, a little less aware of the ghost from her past.

Music filled the room, a slow easy number about the intent behind a particular kind of kiss. Ryan looked up and caught his brother tipping his hat from next to the updated version of the jukebox in the corner.

Sandy held out a hand. "Dance with me?" Her smile promised much more than a dance.

Want and need held hands and skipped through his system. He answered with the most profound statement he could think of. "Okay."

Ryan laced their fingers together and tugged her against him. This time, his mouth closed over hers in ardent possession. With a throaty moan, she returned the kiss with the same passion, sliding her free hand up and tickling the sensitive spot at the nape of his neck.

But she had a sensitive spot of her own, and he knew where it was. In moments of finding and licking the tender place below her left ear, she went nearly limp in his arms. Smiling with the minor victory, he edged them onto the dance floor where they moved into an easy rhythmic sway. Sandy hooked her arms over Ryan's shoulders and leaned back to gaze into his face. In the dim recesses of his mind, he felt the sensual glide of her body against his as they danced, but his whole world swirled in those incredible chicory-colored eyes. Did she know her heart shone in them?

"If you don't stop looking at me like that, sweetheart, we're going to have to find a preacher and get married."

He didn't realize he'd spoken the thought aloud until her startled expression pierced through him.

"What?" Her fluttery laugh pricked at the edges of his nerves.

Ryan scanned her face. Was she frightened or was she turned off?

"Whoa, rewind and delete. I'm on fast forward again." He kissed her lips softly and followed up with a peck. "Just ignore me, sweetheart. It's a saying around here, like telling someone to get a room."

Her lips curled gently upward and fear eased its grip on his heart.

"I have no intention of ignoring you." She stroked her fingers over the shell of his ear. "We can rewind. But we don't have to delete, do we? Maybe just… hit pause?"

He hugged her more tightly to him and wound one hand into her hair, tugging gently until the soft waves spilled freely around her shoulders. "So much better." The scent of strawberries embraced him as he buried his face in the waves of softness and inhaled.

Around them the dinner crowd began to filter in, no more than a handful of people to start. Sandy seemed content to let her staff run the place without her. They moved into the next song together, prolonging the connection. When the song was over, Ryan captured her lips in a gentle kiss, spinning them into a prelude to fulfillment. Applause sounded from the dozen or so people seated at the tables on the edge of the dance floor.

"I'm sorry, Chicory. I'm afraid we just went about as public as we can."

"And I told you yesterday." She cupped his cheek in one hand and held his eyes. "I. Don't. Care. I love being with you."

* * *

Shadows created by the flickering candle between them played across Sandy's face. She speared a roasted redskin potato chunk on the end of her fork and dragged it through the garlic sauce coating her plate. Ryan followed each motion, mesmerized by the way she grasped the utensil and the scrutiny she gave the potato just before she popped it into her mouth.

Maybe she'd had something when she's suggested they learn about each other over time rather than telling their stories.

But some things had to be told, not discovered. They needed to talk, but he couldn't find the words to start. So he smiled and stuck to light teasing instead. "You never seem to be the same person twice."

Sandy giggled. "So, what, you think I have multiple personalities or something?"

A smile pulled at his lips. "No," he said softly. "You've just got a lot of facets. I'm wondering if I've seen the real Sandy yet, or if you've only managed to show me a string of disguises."

She swallowed hard and looked away for a moment. Had he lost her? Doubt twined through him. But then she smiled and he became lost in her gaze. "You found me out. When things matter I get nervous."

"Nervous?" Ryan scratched along one eyebrow, thinking about the easy way she moved through life and living, how she took most things in stride. "You must have an interesting definition of *nervous*."

Sandy laughed. The sound affected him the way it always did, with a rush of warmth and heightened awareness. "I'm mostly an act, Ryan." She shrugged and picked up her water, watching him over the glass while she sipped. When she set the glass on the table, she ran a finger around the rim. "I did some amateur stage work before I came here. Enough to put on a pretty convincing act of Wild West barmaid. It, um... entertains the regulars." She shrugged. "And it gives me some clout when I need to discourage troublemakers."

Ryan couldn't pull his gaze from that finger, but his thoughts flickered briefly to the way she'd diffused the situation with Bull. If that had been an act... His mood souring fast, he pushed MacKay Junior out of his mind. That ass wasn't going to ruin his evening. Reaching across the table, Ryan took hold of her hands and rubbed his thumbs over her knuckles.

Her eyes swept up to meet his, filled with questions and uncertainty. But burning with intensity that sparked an answering heat inside him.

"And how are you feeling right now?" he murmured.

Her smile was slow and sweet and did things to his heartbeat. "Not as nervous as Friday night when you came in here the first time."

There was something about her voice that nagged at him sometimes, but when he was with her, mostly all he could pay attention to was her eyes. "I've been trying since we met to figure out your accent."

She looked at him with a sly smile of her own and shifted in her seat. When her bare foot brushed along his inner thigh, he choked on his next breath. Apparently she didn't mind taking advantage of the seclusion afforded by their corner table, seating courtesy of Matchmaker Mel.

Sandy giggled. "I'm sorry. I was distracted. What did you say?"

As soon as some blood made its way back to his brain he might be able to remember. "I... wondered where you came from. Your accent."

"I don't have an accent. You do." She frowned. "Only your Wyoming cowboy is mixed with something else."

"You *almost* don't have one," Ryan corrected. "Just certain words sometimes. The way you say 'you' like it starts with an E and ends on a question mark. It's cute. I've heard it someplace before but I can't place it. So where did you start out?"

Sandy smiled. "Southwestern Virginia. Blue Ridge Mountains."

That explained why she was comfortable with the mountains in Wyoming. Newcomers often weren't. "So how did you end up moving from one mountain range to another?"

"There were a couple of stops in between, but the short story is I made someone a promise."

Twenty-three hour man — again. Her face had started closing off the minute he'd asked the question.

"You have family back in Virginia?" Ryan asked.

"Only child," she said easily. "My parents died in a car accident when I was nineteen."

Crap. Zero for two. "I'm sorry."

"Thank you."

So, no denying the pain with statements of how long ago it had been, no insanity about how they'd had a good life and at least they went together.

But she wasn't struggling with their loss the way she was with her twenty-three hour man. The thought was a quick stab to his heart. There were a million ways to screw up and he'd just stumbled onto the top one.

* * *

"Hey, Angel, are you particularly attached to L.A.?" Mick was starting to slur his words.

"It's nice. It's not really home. I came out here with some friends."

"Good. 'Cause I was thinking after we get married I want to go home. Back to Wyoming. Will you come with me?"

"I'd love that. I like to travel, see new places, but I kind of like the idea of making a home." She checked the log. More *than twenty hours had passed. It was a miracle his battery had lasted so long.* "Why don't you see if you can get some rest? I promise I'll stay. I won't go anywhere."

"Feel a little like... I'll have lots of time for resting later." *Listening to him struggle for every breath was torture.* "Angel..." *The radio sputtered but didn't go dead. Still he didn't talk.*

"Mick?"

"Angel, I don't think they're gonna get here in time." *His voice sounded stronger, resolute.*

Her heart thumped against her chest wall, an unsteady staccato beat driven by fear. That was supposed to mean something, wasn't it? People often got stronger, more lucid, right before they died.

"You listen to me. You proposed to me. You can't just leave me here."

His familiar chuckle took a little longer this time. "I'll hold on as long as I can, but I think — I think I'm pretty torn up inside. And my leg. Something's shifted and I can feel it again. I think it's bleeding pretty bad."

Her breath caught. With so much rubble to get through, there was little hope he would be alive if he was bleeding out.

"Can you move at all? Can you find where you're bleeding from?" *She tried to keep the panic from her voice.*

She heard him gasp. Then he uttered a soft curse. Then nothing.

"Mick?" *she called into the radio. Then more insistently.* "Mick!"

"I'm back, Angel. I got some pressure on it. Not... an artery... I don't think."

* * *

Sandy watched Ryan pop the last of his fried potatoes into his mouth with a sense of awe. His plate was completely empty. The man had an insatiable appetite.

"What's on your dessert menu?" he asked.

Sandy wrinkled her nose. "A pretty limited choice. People around here seem to have more simple taste. So we have three basic flavors of ice cream, and either lime or orange sherbet, strawberry shortcake. And on your personal menu, there's always... me."

Before Ryan showed any sign of reaction to her invitation, the front door opened, admitting two more people.

"Oh, man," he breathed. "I'd really hoped to avoid this. I'm sorry. I'm sorry this has to go down, sorry you have to see it, so sorry they brought it here to your place."

Sandy followed Ryan's troubled gaze and caught the unmistakable flash of light auburn hair just starting to go gray. Brody MacKay had made a grand entrance, followed by his wife.

"They come in sometimes." She tried to instill an easiness she didn't feel into her voice. "They're quiet, keep to themselves." And she almost always asked Mel to serve them when they did.

"Not this time," murmured Ryan.

Brody scanned the room, his eyes finding and locking on Ryan. Clearly the old man had an agenda, and it wasn't dinner.

Sandy snapped to attention and drew in a sharp breath, taking in the set to MacKay's jaw, the open hostility in his dark eyes. She held her breath. There was still time for him to turn away. *Please turn away.*

He didn't.

He was propelled on waves of tangible aggression, his wife trotting in his wake, like an obedient lapdog on a short leash.

Sandy bit her lip. Brody MacKay on a mission of obvious malevolent intent increased her sense of uneasiness tenfold. Somewhere in his fifties, he was a formidable antagonist, as big as his son but with a coldness that never failed to chill Sandy to her core. Avoiding a confrontation in the community was one thing. In her place of business, it wasn't as simple as taking a longer path around a parked truck.

Sean stepped into Brody's path, but the old man brushed him off, his eyes never leaving Ryan.

Ryan made a barely perceptible hand motion, warning Sean to stay out of it. The younger McGee stepped back, but he didn't go far. He had his brother's back. But would it be enough?

Around them, the soft conversation in the bar spun into silence, broken only by the sweet sounds of a crooning country artist on the jukebox. Something in the quality of the silence crawled along the edges of Sandy's awareness. She looked around, taking in the expectant looks.

"Crap," she whispered. Dread inched its way under her skin. This was apparently the confrontation the entire town had been waiting for. She locked eyes with Sean as he inched closer to their table.

"You shouldn't have come back to Orson's Folly." MacKay wasted no time getting to the point. "I warned your father to keep you the hell away."

"Oh?" Ryan's voice was cool but his eyes were slits. His hands were balled into loose fists. "It must have slipped his mind when I asked for my messages."

"Now you know," said Brody. "So turn yourself around and go back where you came from. Where you took my boy when you kidnapped him."

Cold dread curled in Sandy's belly. For the second time a MacKay had accused Ryan of kidnapping. It couldn't be true! She refused to accept it. A glance around the room, though, showed at least half of the patrons present put stock in Brody's words. She shifted her gaze to Ryan.

Bright green eyes flashed with anger. His face was hard as he returned MacKay's fierce stare in equal measure, but when he spoke, his tone was cool. "I'll tell you what I told your son, MacKay. I came home to be with my family. I didn't come here to start trouble."

"You got it wrong, boy." MacKay leaned over the table and jabbed a finger at Ryan. "You found all kinds of trouble just by coming home. You and yours don't want more of the same, then you'd best leave before someone gets hurt."

Ryan and Brody MacKay glared at each other in a silent battle fueled by palpable, deep-running animosity. It was obvious Ryan had things he wanted to say.

Sandy held her breath, holding her eyes on Ryan as he struggled with fury. His mouth clamped tightly closed; small muscles worked in his jaw. His breathing was rapid and shallow, through flaring nostrils. Not an expression Sandy would want directed at her. But MacKay seemed unaffected.

Ryan broke the stare-down, picking up his water glass and drinking, then shifting his eyes away from MacKay in dismissal. "I'll consider your advice."

Brody's lip curled into a snarl. "You'll do more than consider it, if you don't want to see everything your family owns wiped out."

Sandy's stomach rolled into a knot. Her heart hitched somewhere in her throat, making even the simple act of breathing nearly impossible. She gripped the edge of the table to stop the terrible tremors from becoming apparent. The hostility she'd seen between Bull and Ryan had been nothing compared to what was happening here. Suddenly she understood why Ryan had wanted her to steer clear of his argument with Bull. She swallowed hard, wondering if the MacKays really had the ability to destroy Ryan and his family. With a start, she realized if sides were to be drawn, she was already firmly on the McGee side of the street.

"Let me explain this in terms you can understand." Ryan narrowed his gaze and lowered his voice. "You *don't* want to jack with my family, MacKay. That'd be your second mistake."

Brody snorted. "My second one, eh? Want to tell me what my first was?"

"Drawing your first breath the day you were born." Tension rippled in Ryan's arms as though he was preparing to spring.

Next to her husband, Alice shifted, drawing Sandy's attention. Her jade green eyes glittered with malevolence. But she wasn't looking at Ryan; she was looking at Sandy.

"Hello, Mr. MacKay, Miz MacKay." DC seemed to materialize behind them.

Anxiety eased its grip on Sandy's gut. She could breathe again, but the knot remained in her throat. Alice MacKay had been less than civil for the past couple of days, since even before Sandy had met Ryan. What was that about?

"Someone call the sheriff to defend this piece of shit?" demanded MacKay.

DC smiled. "As a matter of fact, I came in here to pick up some dinner and heard you hollering over here. Now I'm going to do you a favor and see you get headed for home. Because if you don't, Mr. MacKay, I won't have a choice but to put you in jail until you're sober."

Keeping Sandy trapped in her hard-eyed stare, Alice tugged on her husband's arm. After a last long look at Ryan, MacKay spun on his heel and stalked to the door.

DC watched the couple leave then looked at Ryan, speculation in his eyes. "Enjoy your evening, Sandy, Ry." With a nod at them both, he followed the MacKays.

"I'm sorry." Resignation colored Ryan's voice, but his gaze into her eyes was unwavering, not quite a challenge.

Sandy kept her eyes leveled on his. "That wasn't your fault." When she laid her hand over his and squeezed gently, the tension in his arms drained. Thank God. "I don't know what the trouble is between you and them, but I trust you, Ryan."

She waited, hoping maybe he'd tell her it was nothing, a misunderstanding. But it was apparent it went deeper than that. Far deeper.

His mouth worked soundlessly. Finally, he managed to speak. "Thank you."

She smiled. "What do you think, Mr. McGee? Do you want to take dessert up in my apartment? It'll be quiet and we can talk there."

"Seems a little like running," he murmured, darting a glance around the room.

"Maybe. But if we leave together, it becomes a question of whether you're running away from all the ruckus or running away *with* me." She ran a tantalizing finger down his arm. "Personally, I'd prefer to think of it as running off with me." She stood and held out her hand. "So... wanna come raid my... kitchen?"

Ryan slipped his hand into hers. "You have a talent for turning things around."

The hum of conversation picked up as they abandoned their table and crossed the room. Sandy led him through the kitchen and out the side door, then up the long wooden staircase at the back of the building, turning just before they reached her door.

A bright flash trailed across the sky and Sandy pointed. "Look! Make a wish!"

She closed her eyes but when she tried to think of a wish, none came. Unsettled, she opened her eyes again to find Ryan watching her with an intensity that took her breath.

"Not all wished out after all?" he asked softly.

Sandy gave him a sad smile and shook her head slowly. "Actually, I couldn't think of one wish just now."

Standing one step above him put them at the same eye level. His eyes looked darker green beneath the combination of security lights from the parking lot and the moon high overhead. His lips curled upward and he cocked his head to one side. Slowly, he moved toward her. When she moved back, he followed, walking her one step at a time until her back hit the door. He crowded her there but stopped just short of touching her.

Need drove her to slant her body toward his in invitation. Unresolved questions hung between them, but at that moment she couldn't find it in herself to care. Time to talk would come later. Instant hunger erupted, sending her body into a hot burn for his. She needed him. She needed to move forward with Ryan in order to move on from Mick.

Ryan brought a hand up and laced his fingers in her hair, cupping the back of her head. As he drew her close, his lips brushed over hers and Sandy's breath caught.

He pulled away slightly then moved toward her again.

"Please," whispered Sandy.

Ryan froze in place. "Please?"

Sandy trembled, recognizing the point of no return. "Come inside."

Ryan groaned. When he crowded her into the wall again, he didn't hold back. He molded his lean body against hers. She forgot what they'd been going to talk about, forgot they were going to talk at all.

He breathed heavily as his hands roamed up and down her ribs, each caress a gentle promise. "Key," he murmured against her lips.

In answer, Sandy reached behind her and turned the doorknob. The door opened easily.

"You shouldn't leave your door unlocked."

Sandy laughed and nibbled at his lower lip. "You've been in the city too long." She tugged him to the edge of her threshold, then across. Without needing to look, she flicked the switch upward and the tiny room was washed in a golden pink glow from the lamp next to her bed.

"Wow." Ryan surveyed the small apartment, a neutral mask in place. "It's..."

Sandy winced, wishing she'd taken more time to tidy up. "Messy, I know." Her eyes slid to her unmade bed. Why hadn't she changed the sheets? "And it's small but—"

"Cozy, private, efficient, convenient..." A huge, somewhat leering grin spread across his face. "But I was actually going to say it's nice to have someplace where you're comfortable leaving your underwear hanging in the kitchen."

Heat rushed to her cheeks. She followed his glance at the tiny bits of lingerie hanging on the makeshift clothesline, stretched along the length of her kitchen countertop.

"Okay, you get to go park yourself on the settee over there while I tidy up. Obviously you don't understand the concept of a bachelorette pad." She snatched up her lingerie and stalked over to the dresser, shoving it all into a half-open drawer.

"Guilty. I'm only familiar with the male equivalent of said pad and that was..." He chuckled, spreading his hands helplessly, then broke into easy laughter. "Actually it was pretty freakin' disgusting." Retrieving a red silk camisole from the floor, he dangled it on one finger. "And the underwear wasn't even close to this interesting."

Sandy grabbed the garment. "Go sit down, caveman. There's a large TV hooked to a satellite dish over there. That ought to keep you occupied for a couple of minutes."

Ryan twisted his head in the direction she pointed. "You do have your surprises," he murmured, sauntering over to the TV with a tuneless whistle.

Sandy gathered various pieces of discarded clothing, stashing them in drawers and shoving them into her closet. She kicked a dozen half-pairs of sandals under the bed, the likely resting place of their mates. Cleaning up her overflowed bath the previous night had led to scouring the bathroom, but she poked her head in to make sure she had picked the wet towel off the floor after her shower that morning.

When she returned to the main room, Ryan was checking out the stereo, and the sultry sounds of a slow jazz number began to play. Anticipation edged into her sensual centers. Sandy yanked the sheet straight and felt around for the blanket at the foot of the bed, pulling it up and squaring it off with efficient movements.

When Ryan's arms closed around her from behind, she stiffened in surprise, then relaxed and let her head fall back against his shoulder. His hands rested lightly at her waist in a grip she could easily have escaped. His breath played along her neck and he teased the sensitive skin beneath her ear with his lips.

"Watching you is making me crazy." His silky whisper in her ear turned up the hum of awareness, which didn't seem to have an off switch when he was around.

His hands didn't move and she leaned backward into him, longing to touch his muscular, heated body, but he held her still. Finally he pulled back a half-step and gently spun her to face him.

"Sandy?"

It was her name. It was a question. It was a promise.

She understood. She could say no. She could stop him right there and that would be the end of it. The power to choose the evening's outcome was completely in her hands. Except she wasn't certain the power to choose had ever been in either of their hands.

There was no seduction in his eyes, only tenderness. Her heart thumped against her chest. Her eyelids burned with unshed tears she was at a loss to explain. She might think about it later, but just for that moment she wanted it to be them, only them. So she held his gaze, liking the way he was looking back at her, enjoying the awakening sensations she had never expected to feel again.

He held her with a look, a silent question hanging between them. Slowly she nodded, stepping closer.

"You're sure?" His voice was husky, his eyes dark with desire.

"Never more sure in my life." She leaned up and touched her mouth to his, running her tongue along his bottom lip, enjoying the hint of beer that lingered.

He took over the kiss, branding her with his desire. It wasn't nearly enough, and she moaned, slipping her arms around his neck, straining against him, parting her lips and opening herself to him.

Energy surged between them, lighting a fire of fervid desperation. His fingers tickled as they settled at her waist and then pushed beneath her blouse and lifted the hem. She drew back slightly, tugging on his shirt where it met his jeans until it came free. His skin was hot under her palms and something deep inside her answered with explosions of desire. She took a step back and fumbled at his buttons, giving a little cry of triumph as they came free one by one. He raised her blouse and air blowing through the open window nipped at her skin. Then he whisked it over her head and tossed it aside.

Sandy eased down onto her bed, pulling Ryan with her. Bracing himself on his elbows, he dipped his head and pressed molten kisses to her neck, her left shoulder, trailing lower until his mouth rested in the valley between her breasts. A shudder raced through him, inciting an answering tremor within her.

* * *

On the coffee table, where he'd emptied his pockets, Ryan's cell phone hummed with an incoming call. Ignoring it, he nudged the scrap of lace covering her breast aside. With Sandy in his arms, nothing else mattered.

He wanted to take his time, savoring the moment at the brink of love. She was everything to him. She filled his empty places and made his broken places stronger. She balanced his strengths and weaknesses. He didn't understand it, but her name was somehow burned into his soul. She moaned and arched into his touch as he teased one pebbled pink bud with the tip of his tongue.

The cell phone buzzed again, this time with the tone indicating a message. Sandy stiffened and Ryan groaned. He should have turned the damn thing off. She'd gone completely still beneath him, applying the brakes on their romantic interlude, but he didn't move. If he touched the phone just now, he'd probably smash it in frustration.

Chapter Ten

The lamp next to the bed cast a warm radiance over her face. Cradled in his arms, she was soft, contented... vulnerable. What would it be like to see her face every night before he drifted to sleep and again when he woke up in the morning? He wanted to find out. Would she want the same thing? If they weren't going to make love, at least they could indulge in some pillow talk before he called it a night and headed for home.

"Ah, Chicory..." he sighed, wrapping a strand of dark hair around his forefinger. "I'm going to want a lot more than just one night. If I spend the rest of my life getting to know you, I'll still find something new every day."

She opened her eyes and smiled. "I'm not going anywhere."

As her assurance washed over him, Ryan's heart began to race. They were just words. She would have no idea that to him they were false promises. Only words. But his breath caught in his throat, and liquid fire flushed through his system only to be doused by instant ice water flowing in its wake. He hadn't experienced such a reaction since PTSD had dictated his life. The tremors would come next. He didn't want to have to explain everything to her. Not yet. He squeezed his eyes shut, nearing panic, fighting to force the beast back into the darkness where it belonged.

Sandy poked him in the side. "Your cell's going off again."

The trigger was broken, but the episode left him shaking. Ryan rolled to the side, allowing her to sit, and drew a calming breath. He made no move to retrieve his cell. He probably wouldn't be able to walk. Maybe she hadn't noticed his lapse into mental instability.

Gentle fingers trailed a whisper of a touch along his jaw. "Ryan?"

He sighed. She'd noticed.

* * *

Ryan's eyelids fluttered open, and the shadows in them tore at her heart.

"Ryan, what's on your mind?"

She'd barely finished speaking and already he was closed down, his expression shuttered against her concern. His groan was followed by a slow smile. Heat replaced the darkness in his eyes. "You."

Apparently some things were still off limits. Arguing the point would be useless, so she simply waited and watched.

His breathing slowly returned to normal but he showed no inclination for talking. Satisfied that the shadows were fading, Sandy bent over and pressed a kiss to his forehead. As she drew back, his hand snaked out and grabbed her by the wrist, keeping her with him. He flipped her hand over and pressed a kiss to her palm.

Green eyes met hers. "I lived away from here for a long time. Not everything is about my history *here*, and there are some things that are hard to talk about."

An abrupt memory of the crystal angel dangling from Ryan's rearview mirror stalled her heart. She smiled and looked away, putting a mental band-aid on the little stab of pain as she backed off. Didn't she have her own painful past, after all?

"I see." She disentangled her hand from his grasp and stood, unwilling to share this particular vulnerability. Maybe it was a good thing his cell had interrupted them. He wasn't ready for a relationship and she wasn't ready if he wasn't being a hundred percent open. "How about we check out that dessert then?"

She righted her bra, aware of her body's protest at the unsatisfied hunger. His eyes followed her as she located her blouse and pulled it over her head. But she might as well preserve a bit of dignity. She stumbled to the kitchen on wooden marionette legs and yanked open the freezer.

Her hand was on the carton of chocolate ice cream when the first tear spilled over. What was she doing? Had she just become the other woman in a messed-up triangle with Ryan and his missing woman?

Strong arms stole around her from behind and she stiffened against his touch.

"Hey, what is it?"

Gentle hands settled on her shoulders and turned her away from the refrigerator. He'd pulled on his shirt but hadn't fastened it or tucked it in.

She couldn't meet his eyes. "Nothing. I thought I had some whipped cream but I can't find it."

Placing the backs of his knuckles beneath her chin, Ryan tilted her head up. He pressed a gentle kiss against her lips but Sandy held herself rigid. When he looked into her eyes again, she noted the sadness in his.

"We're moving too fast," he murmured.

Sandy nodded. "I think — maybe yes. I'm sorry. I must be driving you crazy. Hot, cold, yes, no."

His thumb worked back and forth across her cheek. It was a long moment before he spoke. "Let's take a step or two back."

A wry chuckle slipped from Sandy's lips. "Is that even possible?"

Green eyes lit when he smiled. "Chicory, I'm counting on it."

"I don't know what's happening here," she whispered.

His smile deepened. "I'm pretty sure I'm falling in love."

Her heart lodged in her throat, threatening to explode outward. "Don't say that."

Ryan looked like he wanted to say more but his mask floated down instead. "Okay." He released her and bent to look in the refrigerator. "Let's check out your dessert menu here. Ah, here you go." He held up a blue and red can. "One can of spray whipped cream. What else do you have?"

The moment was gone, the shut-out complete. Sandy gestured toward the sofa. "Sit down. I'll find something."

Raising one eyebrow, he looked between her and the sofa, then shrugged and padded across the floor.

A hiccup of emotion bubbled out as she realized they'd been in such an intimate position yet neither had removed their boots. That could well have ended up in an even more awkward moment. She smiled and set about gathering some dessert, not the best substitute for mind-blowing sex, but all she had at the moment. Then she followed Ryan to the couch.

"Should I be worried about the reasons for your smile?" he asked as she knelt on the edge of the sofa.

"Surely a big strong man such as yourself isn't afraid of a woman bringing him dessert."

He nodded at the bounty she was laying out on the table in front of them. "No bowls, Chicory, and only one spoon? Makes me wonder if I'm going to *be* the dessert you promised."

Holding up the can of whipped cream, Sandy laughed maniacally. "You found out my devious plan."

She shook the can then made as if to lather his body with it. "First I'll spray your belly, and then—"

His arm snaked out and grabbed her wrist, tugging her down onto the sofa next to him.

"Oh!" She landed awkwardly, half against Ryan's chest.

"Stop teasing me and feed me the dessert you promised when you lured me into your lair, woman! I'm starving over here."

Sandy sat, laughter on her lips. "We can't have that when I have access to multiple types of chocolate. It doesn't cure everything, but it helps. Let me show you."

After popping open the top of the ice cream carton, she sprayed on a good measure of whipped cream, then added a handful of strawberries and topped it all with a drizzle of chocolate syrup. After swirling the spoon through the mix, she aimed it for Ryan's mouth.

* * *

Fruity sweetness and chocolate splashed across his palate, and Ryan moaned out loud at the sugar overload.

"See? See?" Sandy angled a look, studying him as he chewed. "I told you it was good. Deny me now."

Her almost childlike giddiness captivated him and he couldn't resist teasing. "It's not a combination I'd have chosen, since I was raised on the simple Orson's Folly fare..." He nodded and cocked his head sideways, pretending to consider the taste. "...but yeah, it's okay."

A smile worked its way onto her face as she gathered more of the icy confection on her spoon.

Ryan's mouth watered in anticipation.

But the second bite disappeared into Sandy's mouth and she sucked on it like a lollipop. Childlike? Giddy? Forget those! The sensual siren in front of him rolled the spoon over and thoroughly licked the back, keeping her eyes on him as she caught a stray smear of whipped cream from her upper lip with the tip of her tongue.

Ryan's blood went from pleasantly warm to boiling in the space of a breath. Maybe he should rethink his dismissal of her proposed alternate use for the whipped cream.

The strident blare of an incoming call on his cell phone jarred the thought out of his head, and he frowned, already hating the caller. "Ignore it."

But Sandy was already leaning forward. "It could be important. Your dad or Sean."

He checked the phone. It wasn't his father or his brother, so he tossed the phone aside without answering. "It's just a friend who's been looking into something for me."

Sandy's hand, already lifting another spoonful of chocolate and strawberry, hesitated. She lowered the spoon back into the carton and cast an assessing stare in his direction.

Too many interruptions, too many secrets between them. Ryan didn't want to talk about his reasons for leaving Orson's Folly, or about Mac, or his time away. And he really didn't want to talk about the search for Allie Whitman that had consumed the last several years of his life. Not tonight. He was finished looking, and if he hadn't been with Sandy when Joe had called, Ryan would have told him so. But from the sadness in her eyes before she looked away, she already knew who the call was about.

"You're quiet," he murmured, willing her to meet his gaze.

"What happens when you find her?" Sandy studied the ice cream a moment longer then flashed a look up at him. "What happens to you and me?"

Ryan blew out a breath. Easing the carton of ice cream and the spoon from her fingers, he set them on the coffee table next to his phone.

"Sandy." Ryan took her hand and kissed the tip of each finger. "I... don't want to be with her. Once, I thought — maybe. But she wasn't there — and now..."

* * *

The metallic taste of blood tainted Sandy's tongue. Crap! She'd bitten her cheek. But the ache blooming in her heart soon overshadowed the sharp pain in her mouth. Did Ryan understand what he was saying? That he was with her only because the other woman had disappeared from his life?

"Ryan, please." *Stop talking*.

He shook his head. "She's very special to me and I'll tell you about her sometime. But I'm with *you*. I *want* to be with you. She's never going to be an issue between us." He pressed his lips to her palm. "I know who I'm with, too, Sandy Wheaton."

Sandy regarded him in silence, caught like an animal in the glare of oncoming headlights, unable to move, unable to do anything but wait for the disastrous impact that could only bring death. Yes, he knew who he was with; knew he was with his second choice... and had just admitted that fact out loud. The fist around her chest slowly squeezed the air from her lungs.

He moved his mouth to her wrist where he pressed tiny kisses. "Sweetheart... you're amazing... you're beautiful... you're everything I never knew I wanted and never hoped I would find. Never deserved to find. The dream of her is nothing compared to the reality of you."

Sandy blinked. Had he really just replaced those looming headlights with sunshine and rainbows? She must be out-of-her-head crazy. How could she believe him? Did Ryan even really know what he wanted?

He held her hand against his cheek and Sandy looked into his eyes, promptly tumbling into the vulnerability he revealed for her. She still had all the power. She held their future. Could she live with the revelation that she was his second choice? In a sudden moment of perfect clarity, she recognized her own weakness; nothing mattered because she didn't want to live without him.

Sandy inhaled deeply, drawing in the spicy woodsy scent of him that had become so familiar. She slid her hand around to the back of his neck and played with the soft skin at his hairline. Almost in slow motion, she advanced, hesitating just a hair's breadth from touching his lips. Ryan remained still, waiting, she understood, for her to make the next move.

"Will you hold me tonight?" She brushed her lips across his, just a hint of a touch. "I just need some time."

"Darlin', take as long as you need and I'll hold you for as long as you let me."

* * *

Sandy awoke to find the room cloaked in darkness. Whispers and rustles of stealthy movements jolted her heart rate and she rolled over. Warmth and a woodsy scent clung to the sheets. Ryan. She eased out a breath, alarm replaced by curiosity. "Where are you going?"

"Shh... Go back to sleep." He laid a tender kiss on her forehead, brushing back her hair. "I'm going to help Sean with the stock. He's been doing it all on his own for too long."

Sandy pushed up onto her elbows and pushed the switch on her bedside lamp, blinking as the light cut a path to her optic nerves. "Let me help."

But Ryan shook his head and turned the lamp back off. "No, go back to sleep. I'll be by later. Promise."

"I don't—" She didn't want him to leave. She didn't want him to leave without her. But he seemed determined to go back to the ranch alone and it wasn't fair to push.

He bent and nuzzled her ear and then kissed her, slow and deep. "Chicory, in case I forgot to tell you," he whispered, pulling away, "I'm real glad you decided to come to Wyoming."

Then he was across the floor and out the door, closing it behind him with a soft click, and she was alone. As usual. Doubt edged its way back into her consciousness. Would Ryan ever really love her the way he loved his mystery woman?

* * *

The aftershocks still rocked the building. He had to be feeling them, too.

"Still here, Angel," he assured her after a strong jolt.

She let out the breath she'd unconsciously been holding.

"Listen," he said, enunciating the word with care. "I'm not — giving up. But I want you to promise me something. Can you do that?"

"Maybe." She lost the battle to keep her voice steady.

"I was thinking about the song you sang for me. I want you to live, Angel. To really live, like the song says. Whatever

happens here or — doesn't, I want you to promise you'll do something you want to do. If you like singing, I want you to sing every day. If you want to travel, promise me you'll travel. And if you want to settle down, do it in a place you love. With or without me, I want your life to be good." For the first time in a couple of hours, Mick's voice was steady and strong. "Can you promise me?"

Sandy closed her eyes and drew in a deep breath. The request was obviously important to him. "Yeah, I can promise that. Mick, is there someone I can call for you?"

He was silent for a long time. "No. There's no one. But thanks anyway, Angel. And thanks for staying with me."

"I like talking to you. So get used to me. I'm sticking." As a wave of exhaustion hit, Sandy pulled off her sweater and balled it up on the desk, leaning into it and using it as a pillow.

The radio squawked again.

"Mick?" She shoved the sweater aside and sat up straight, rubbing her eyes.

"Yeah, it's me. Angel? They're not coming for me, are they?"

"They are, Mick. They are, I promise. But there's a lot of building to get through."

"It's okay, Angel. We're trained for this. Have to be realistic here. I smell smoke and it's getting stronger. I don't think the fire's contained. And I've got no O₂ left in my tank."

"They are working on it, Mick! You have to hang on. If you give up, you — just don't give up. Hold onto me."

"For long as I can, Angel."

"You stay! And when they get you out, I'll be waiting for you! I keep my promises, Mick."

"Make one more promise, then. See Wyoming just once."

"We'll see it together when you take me," she said. "You can show me all the best places."

"But if I'm not with you, see it anyway, okay? I know you'll love it there. And think of me when you see it the first time, okay? Promise."

"Promise." Tears rolled down her cheeks, hot, stinging drops plopping onto the fists she pounded into her balled-up sweater.

* * *

Sandy came awake with a start. Memories of a night filled with perplexing secrets and feelings of being cherished surfaced. For once it wasn't the man in her dreams plucking at her emotions. It was something — or rather someone — else, someone very present in her life.

* * *

Sean hurled the broken padlock across the stable yard. Wood splintered when the lock struck the door to the stable. The black and white pup on his heels yipped and skittered sideways. Beyond the door, several horses called out in protest. One set of hooves connected with the wall a couple of times as though answering the call to arms. That would be Domingo, Ryan wagered with a disapproving shake of his head.

"Trying to finish what someone else started?" asked Ryan.

Sean's blue streak of curses shattered the relative peace of the stable yard. "What's the point of dumping all the feed?"

Gus emerged from the feed shed shaking his head. "Good and wasted. They pissed in it, wet it down good, and then tossed shovelfuls of manure from the pit all through it. You'll be lucky to salvage a handful." He glanced at the dog, shaking his head. "Where were you last night, Patch?"

As Patch covered his face with one paw, Sean snorted. "With Dad, probably at the foot of his bed."

"Dad lets dogs in the house?" Ryan pushed his hat back and stared at the border collie.

"Lets?" Sean choked back a laugh. "Hell, no, he sneaks him in every chance he gets unless I get him first."

"I'll be..." whispered Ryan. His whole life, dogs had been relegated to the barn, had never been allowed in the house. "Guess things changed."

Gus cleared his throat. "I think we got us a situation."

"Yeah..." Sean scrubbed a hand over his face. "What's happening here?"

Ryan leveled a look at his brother. "You know the answer. This is personal."

"But why after all this time?" Sean kicked at the dirt beneath his boots.

Ryan blew out a breath, exhaustion catching up with him. "We'd have to crawl inside Bull's head to figure that out." He shook his own head. "I don't think I'm ready to do that."

* * *

Singing a song about lucky hearts with the stars on their side, Sandy dashed down the stairs. It was an upbeat song, light and happy. Not her normally heavy sensuous choice, but it warmed her heart to sing it. She'd have to see how to fit it into her act. For the moment, however, she was ready to hit the day with a list of errands and a plan to take Domingo out for a short ride. And just maybe she'd be able to track Ryan down. The light of day had reined in her insecurities.

As she rounded the corner of the building and headed into the parking lot, her nose began to protest, and the song died in her throat. She would never understand what it was about being drunk that made a person decide to take a leak in a parking lot. Now she'd have to call one of the kids who did landscaping for them to spray down the sidewalk before they lost the lunch crowd to the odor. When her suspicions were confirmed by the sun glinting on the telltale crystalline residue along the side of her truck, she only rolled her eyes.

"At least they could pee on their own ride."

She frowned at a whitish substance gunked across the hood. "What the heck is that?" Visions of people having raunchy sex on the hood of her vehicle presented themselves, turning her stomach. "Ew. This is just nasty," she muttered to the empty parking lot. "And wrong. Get a room, folks."

As she reached for the door handle, the word *WHORE* carved in big block letters leaped out at her. "Geez..." Rolling her eyes, Sandy slumped. "Great, we're back in middle school."

It wasn't worth repainting her rusty old truck, but she certainly couldn't drive around town with *that* on her door.

Something about the door's angle was off, and she realized the truck was leaning. She'd paid good money to have the potholes graded out of the gravel parking lot, so it must be another flat.

"Son of a bitch!" Was anything going to go right? She was going to have to invest in new tires all around since they'd all seen better days. She couldn't risk a blowout on a patch when she was driving the desolate roads out to the ranch or up to Jackson. She walked around the rear of the truck and ground to a halt.

The deadly black blade sticking out of her tire was a pretty specific threat, not to mention incredibly intimidating as such things went.

"Oh, wow." Irritation turned to alarm and sent her heart into a tailspin of thumps against her chest. Did someone want to do that to *her*? She looked around uneasily. She couldn't write it all off as a drunken prank any longer.

No one was watching her as far as she could tell, but Sandy did spot DC at Blackstone's. If she could catch him before he left, she could save herself some waiting time. Ignoring the crosswalks, she made the direct trek diagonally through the intersection.

DC looked up from his clipboard. "Sandy, don't be making me write you a ticket for jaywalking." A wide grin took the sting out of his words.

Sandy surveyed the deserted road with disdain then swept her gaze back in DC's direction. She peered at him over the top of her sunglasses. "Don't make me hurt you, DC. Not one car has gone by in the past fifteen minutes."

DC shrugged. "The law's the law. What can I do for you?"

"Someone did really disgusting things with bodily fluids all over my truck, carved some free advertising in the door, and then murdered one of the tires with a hunting knife. And in case that sounds a little too Chicken-Little-Sky-is-Falling for you, the knife's still in the tire."

DC blinked, stared at her. He shoved his hat further back on his head. "Aw, geez, Sandy. It's too early in the day for this crap."

Sandy examined the parking lot with a critical eye. An assortment of tires lay scattered like oversized donuts burning black in the strong morning sun. A tire rack was toppled, and one tire had been tossed onto the hood of an antique cherry-red Cadillac convertible. Mayor Bennett wouldn't be thrilled with that.

"What's going on here? It looks like a baby giant had a temper tantrum."

But DC had gone silent. He cast a speculative look in the direction of the bar, then back at the chaos surrounding them. Frowning, he stooped, picked up a tiny tan cylinder, glancing back across the intersection as he stood. With a shake of his head, he walked a few feet and looked down again, then crouched to pick up another cylinder.

"Heck of a thing, ain't it?" Walt announced, joining Sandy. "Got in here this morning and found all my new tire stock slashed. Never had to lock it up at night before. I knew he'd bring trouble, coming back here like he did."

Sandy stared at the old auto mechanic. "I'm sorry, you lost me. Who brought trouble?"

Walt shook his head as though he couldn't believe she didn't already know. "Why, young McGee, of course."

Apparently, Walter Blackstone had already tried and convicted Ryan.

Irritation sparked. She fixed Walt with a narrow-eyed glare. "Mr. Blackstone, do you seriously think a responsible man in his thirties vandalized your shop?"

The mechanic remained stubborn in his notion. "Just making the obvious connection. He's back and now there's trouble. The fire at Ed's yesterday, now this." He took out a pack of cigarettes and plugged one into his mouth, then pulled out an ancient silver lighter with a fading U.S. Army emblem on the side.

As the sunlight glinted off the lighter, Sandy realized what DC had been plucking from the ground. Cigarette butts.

"You know, Ryan was having lunch with me and DC at my place when the fire started," Sandy argued. "He couldn't have been responsible."

But there was no swaying Walt. "Someone with his know-how would be able to rig it for a delayed start."

Not enough coffee to process the input. She squinted at him, struggling to put it all together. "Know-how?"

"Oh, yeah..." He became animated, using his hands and gathering momentum as he talked. "He used to work putting out fires on oil rigs, you know. Them fires most often get put out with explosives."

Actually, she hadn't known what Ry had done while he'd been away, but fighting oil fires would have suited him. There would be no winning the argument, so she made a noncommittal sound and changed the subject.

"Did they get all your stock?"

Walt nodded his head. "Every last one of 'em."

"How soon can you get a replacement tire ordered up for me?" Sandy asked.

"For your truck? I can send Wendell up to Jackson today, be ready to put it on tomorrow." Walt leaned sideways and peered over Sandy's shoulder. "Why? Did you get hit, too?"

She nodded without going into detail, though from the way his eyes strayed between his ruined tires and the parking lot across the street, Walt clearly would have appreciated the gossip.

Fortunately, it became a nonissue when her cell phone signaled an incoming call. Sandy checked the caller ID and answered with a smile. "Hey, Sean, what's up?"

"We need some supplemental feed. Were you still planning to stop by the feed store for Domingo's blend?"

"Actually, I'm going to be delayed."

"Delayed, huh?" Sean chuckled. "My brother's out here at the ranch so it can't be good lovin' delaying you."

Before she could think of an appropriate comeback, she heard the telltale *oomf* of breath being pushed from his lungs, probably with a gut punch. She winced for him. Then she heard a masculine voice in the background, and Sean was suddenly apologizing profusely.

She laughed into the phone. "I'll pick up your feed as soon as I can, Sean. Tell Rocky I'll see him after I change a tire."

"What happened to your tire, Sandy?" Sean asked sharply.

She sighed, afraid she knew what would result when she answered. "I had a visitor last night who decided to leave a hunting knife in my rear tire. I'm here with DC now, so—" She broke off with another sigh as Sean relayed the information to his brother.

"Ryan'll be there in forty minutes," Sean said before the phone went dead.

Chapter Eleven

Ryan made it to town in twenty-five minutes. As his car roared to a halt next to the sheriff's cruiser in front of Blackstone's, DC just shook his head.

"Keep driving like that," he said in a stern tone as Ryan climbed out of his car, "I'm going to be forced to deputize you just so you can write your own citations. You two are a pair."

Ryan shot Sandy a questioning look. "What did *you* do?"

Sandy shrugged, slid her sunglasses off her face, and hooked them into the front of her off-the-shoulder top. "I jaywalked at rush hour."

Ryan's gaze lingered on the front of her shirt, where she had parked the glasses. Then he looked at her face. Her eyes held no shadows, only a flash of temper. The tightness in his throat eased. His heart rate returned to as normal a pace as he'd ever had in her presence.

Little things edged into his awareness. How the breeze lifted the wisps of hair escaping from her loose ponytail. How the turquoise of her shirt contrasted with her peachy skin. How the shirtsleeves rode off her shoulders, exposing a path his lips remembered following all too well, while the rest of the fabric embraced the curves he had yet to explore to his satisfaction. And... there went the heart rate again. Six inches or so of peach delight above the waist of her low-rise jeans and below the hem of her shirt.

A delicate gold lizard dangled from her belly button.

He swallowed, but his throat was dry.

Echoes of feelings from the night before stirred. She was the perfect blend of sexy and beautiful, and just being near her was a fantasy come true. But they had a lot to talk about, and he didn't know when or where to begin.

DC's nudge broke into Ryan's contemplation. The sheriff's mouth was moving, and presumably sounds were coming out, but nothing Ryan could make sense of.

He blinked. "I'm sorry, what did you say?"

With an exasperated sigh, DC rolled his eyes. "I'm going to have to look at Sandy's truck, get the knife out of the tire. But I'm guessing this is all connected." He gestured to a cluster of evergreen bushes. "There's a pile of cigarette butts on the ground over there, looks like almost a whole pack. Someone sitting just right wouldn't be spotted from the road, but sure would have a good view of Valentine's."

"Why would anyone be watching my bar?"

Over Sandy's head, Ryan met DC's troubled eyes, reading in them what the sheriff was unwilling to say out loud. The violence was definitely escalating. And it was bleeding over to stain Sandy's life.

"What happened, Sandy?" asked Ryan.

"Oh, someone decided to leave a couple of calling cards in the form of various bodily fluids on my truck, along with a love note carved into the door. And then they murdered one of my tires with a hunting knife." Her voice was drenched with sarcasm. She angled her head and met his gaze. "How's your day been so far?"

She was being flippant but she kept toying with the strap on her purse. She was definitely beginning to take things seriously. Good.

"We had an incident with a broken lock and dumped feed." Ryan addressed his next words to the sheriff. "Still think it's not personal, DC?"

"Getting harder to discount that theory," DC admitted. He motioned for them to follow him. "Heading to your place now, Sandy."

On the walk to Valentine's, DC made it a point to demonstrate the proper use of the crosswalk.

"Whoo-ie!" DC muttered about the time a distinctive sour stench greeted Ryan. Screwing his face into an expression of disgust, he pointed at the sidewalk in front of the truck. "You two stay right there. I don't want you messing up the crime scene."

While he stared at the messed-up truck, Ryan balled his hands into fists he knew he would plow right into Bull's ugly face if his old adversary made the mistake of crossing paths with him any time soon. Relieving himself on Sandy's truck might have been the drunken act of settling the score with her for rejecting him Sunday night. Or it could have been a way of marking territory. Either way, it was a threat they couldn't ignore. The single word labeling Sandy's character was gouged into the truck's door, and it only added fuel to Ryan's slow burn. But it wasn't about her; it was about him. The same way the crap at the ranch ultimately came back to him.

DC had ordered him to remain on the sidewalk but he hadn't said anything about getting a better look at things from there. Ryan took a couple of side steps and peered at the damaged tire.

The sixteen-inch knife jammed in the sidewall sent his blood from fiery to icy in a heartbeat. Fury turned into fear for Sandy's life.

Donning a latex glove, DC pulled the knife from the tire and popped it into an evidence bag. The last of the air in the tire escaped with a viperous hiss.

The sheriff crouched and examined the puncture. "Looks like the same marks as the ones on Walt's tires." He touched the double-serrated blade near the hilt with the tip of one finger. "I'll send this to the state folks. There're some numbers etched here. They might be traceable to the owner. Maybe we hit it lucky when this guy left the knife behind."

Was it too much to hope that two people in the county might have the same knife? *Yeah, because that was so likely.* "Shit," he whispered. Then he shook his head. "Nope, not so much. You'll find those numbers will be my army serial number."

Sandy's startled gaze shot over to Ryan and she studied him, her features unreadable. Great. She was probably trying to determine if he was a sore loser who'd defiled her truck in retaliation for the brakes she'd put on their romantic interlude. Sighing, Ryan grimaced at DC and rattled off the digits from memory.

"Damn moth—" Red stained DC's face as he bit off the rest of his streak and slid a glance at Sandy. "Sorry." He turned and squared off with Ryan. "You want to explain what your damn knife is doing in Miss Sandy's tire here? Or do we need to go to the office for a discussion?"

Ryan held his old friend in a long glare, but DC didn't budge, just stood there balancing the damning knife across his palm, one eyebrow cocked upward in query. So that was the way it would go down?

The breeze shifted and the fetid odor intensified. Trying not to gag, Ryan drew a shallow breath and broke the stare. "The last time I saw it was at the Cross MC. I used it in the tack room the other night when I was doing some leather work." Picturing Bull's face, Ryan balled his right hand into a fist, grinding it against the palm of his left. "That son of a bitch Bull probably took it when he ruined our feed."

DC nodded at the fist. "Calm down, McGee. We'll sort this all out. But the fact is, we got no actual suspect here. Not yet."

His blood pounded in his ears as the anger he'd kept in check exploded. "What the hell! DC, you know this was all Bull. What else do you need?"

Sandy gasped and stepped forward but then clamped her mouth shut.

"Catching someone in the act would make a nice tidy case." DC scratched his chin. "But for starters, conclusive evidence would prove helpful. Maybe we'll find fingerprints on the knife. But officially, Ry, I can only consider him a person of interest based on the history between your families, the incident here last Friday, and what happened last night. And since the knife turns out to be yours, that puts you and yours on the short list as much as Bull, maybe a tad higher." DC's tense jaw belied his calm voice.

Ryan snorted. "You think I took a leak in our grain then came here to use my knife on Sandy's truck?"

Before DC could answer, Sandy spoke up in a soft voice. "Ryan spent the night here, DC. Since I have a perfectly usable bathroom upstairs, I doubt he felt the need to relieve himself on my truck and slash the tire as he was leaving."

It took him a second for her words to set in, and when they did, Ryan stared in horror. What was she doing? Didn't she realize the picture she was painting of herself? Not to mention placing him at the scene.

He shifted, but froze when she touched his arm and shook her head. Then, rolling her eyes, she faced DC and gestured to the truck's hood. "And given what we were doing most of the night, I also doubt he felt the need to whack any monkeys on my truck — or whatever you guys call it these days."

Oh, crap. Ryan's jaw dropped as the horror of her words caught up with him. *Say something!* But his brain was fried. No words presented themselves.

DC focused a narrow-eyed gaze on Sandy, assessing her silently for a moment before he answered. "Sandy, you just admitted Ry was here, and it's his knife we found."

Twin spots of pink decorated her cheeks, turning cherry red when she tossed her hair and the sun fell upon her face. "I just told you we had crazy monkey sex, too, so he didn't have anything left for—"

"Yeah, I got your meaning!" DC held up a hand as though to ward Sandy off. His face was even redder than hers.

"Geez!" Ryan finally sputtered. "Sandy—"

With a single defiant glare, she forced him to swallow back his words.

Breathing a little heavily, DC took a step back and continued in a tight voice. "Even if you want to file a complaint about Bull's visit here Sunday night, suspicion's gonna bounce off him and back onto Ryan because of the crap between the two of them." He shrugged and some of the tension drained from his stance. "At least that's how a lawyer'll spin it. So until we've got something, we've got nothing. I don't like it either, but—"

"How did you know about Sunday, DC?" Without waiting for an answer, Sandy whirled and flashed a glare at Ryan, temper flaring anew in her narrowed gaze. "You went to the sheriff?" The heat chilled and her eyes never left him. "I told you... he never touched me. You can't arrest someone because I thought he wanted to — touch me. I didn't want him to know I was afraid of him. I didn't want to give him any power, so I didn't report it." She shivered in the eighty-degree heat and from several feet away, Ryan felt it.

He understood her anger. By going to DC, he'd stolen her sense of control over her encounter with Bull. Understood it and didn't care. Just as her tenuous control of her horse was often an illusion, so was her control over any situation with Bull. Ryan tightened his jaw, prepared for the fight.

"Can I change my tire now, DC?" Her tone was calm, flat actually. But Ryan could still see anger in her rigid stance, the impatient way her fingers twitched against her leg. And her eyes still shot sparks in his direction.

An itch developed between his shoulder blades then ran the length of his spine. *Probably wants to do more than call me a jackass this time.*

DC sighed and shook his head. "Ah... Sandy, I'm going to have to impound your vehicle as evidence. I'll try and get it back as quick as possible but the state police need to process the... ah..." DC cleared his throat and stared at the ground as he finished speaking in a hushed voice. "The, uh, DNA evidence."

Sandy's eyes narrowed. "Oh, that's rich. Someone attacks *my* truck, leaves it covered in nasty filth, and now *I* can't even *drive* it? How am I supposed to get my errands done now?" She kicked at the gravel, sending a few stones flying through the air to land about ten feet away.

A strangled sound garbled past Ryan's lips despite his best effort to hold it in, and he swiftly looked away, pulling his hand down his face, trying to wipe away the smile he couldn't contain. He wasn't nearly fast enough.

"What's wrong with *you?*" Sandy fixed him with a glare. "You think it's funny? I've got a ton of errands to run and no way to get them done."

"No," he said a little too quickly.

Sandy straightened, settling her hands on her hips. "Then why are you laughing like a jackass?"

DC's eyes slid between Sandy and Ryan. "Plead the Fifth. Seriously."

"Yeah, pretty sure it's too late for that," murmured Ryan.

"DC, go Mirandize yourself." Sandy's blue eyes leveled on Ryan. "I'm waiting."

He could think of no way to make it sound good. "When you kicked the gravel, you reminded me of the way your horse kicks when he's pissed off. Only his kicks are generally followed by snapping teeth."

DC sighed and eased back — out of range, the jerk.

Angling her head, Sandy raked Ryan from head to toe with a harsh stare. His skin stung as though he'd been dragged through a field of nettles. Then a slow smile began to light her face, and her eyes slid to the Corvette.

Ryan followed her gaze. "Oh, *hell,* no! You're not driving my baby while you're in this mood."

"Fine. I get it. You don't want to share your toys."

Oh, well, that just made him feel selfish. He didn't want to lose the argument, but she sure as heck didn't fight fair. "You can borrow Dad's truck. He doesn't drive any longer."

"Thank you." She smiled sweetly and he knew he was in trouble. "But since Justin's truck isn't here, are you going to drive me out there to get it so I can come all the way back to town to run my errands?"

DC cleared his throat and handed them each a sheet of paper. "Receipts for your property. So are you two okay? Getting things worked out? Anyone gonna die in the next few minutes?" He held up a hand when Sandy drew a deep breath. "Just checking."

"Yeah," Ryan said slowly. "I guess I'll be driving Sandy on some... errands."

DC snickered and clapped Ryan on the shoulder, looking him in the eye. "Friend, you should have pled the Fifth about the horse." To them both, he said, "Do the best you can to keep this from interrupting your life. It could be just something random. I can't think of a reason in the world why old Walt got dragged into it if it's not."

Ryan leveled a stare at DC. "He sold me a tire last week."

The sheriff gave him a hard, unreadable stare in return. Finally he nodded and looked away, and Ryan knew he'd at least given DC something to consider.

Ryan held out his hand to Sandy. After a hesitation so brief he might have imagined it, she slipped her hand into his and they walked to his car.

"Use the crosswalk!" called the sheriff.

Lifting his hand without looking back, Ryan refrained — just — from making it a one-finger wave as they stayed carefully between the lines.

"Where to?" he asked after Sandy secured her seatbelt.

She slid her sunglasses back on her face and rattled off her list of errands with a sigh. "Thanks for the lift," she muttered, apparently still miffed.

Ryan slid an appreciative glance over her body. "I can think of a lot worse things I could be doing right now." Like dealing with her cantankerous horse.

"Still, I know you're busy and I really do appreciate the help," she said a little stiffly.

Her formal tone was already grating on his last nerve. Ryan started the car and peeled out in a spray of gravel. As they blew past the bar's parking lot, DC tapped his badge and shook his citation pad in the air.

* * *

"I just sent out a substantial order to the Cross MC last week." Leo Pickens scratched his head. "I can fill a partial for you, let you have about a quarter of this here order, but if I wipe myself out, I'm not going to be able to take care of other customers. I'm liable to lose business."

Sandy stared at Leo, wondering about the chill in his voice when he spoke. Ryan's deeply furrowed brow and grim mouth matched the storm brewing in his narrowed eyes. Arms appeared to be benignly at his sides, but his right hand was alternately clenching and relaxing. Didn't Leo realize he was about to lose the McGees' business? Did he care?

"How fast can you get an extra order from the supplier?" Ryan was either oblivious or ignoring the message behind the cold attitude. Given the set to his jaw, Sandy's money was on ignoring it.

Pickens shrugged. "I don't usually special order as a rule, so I don't know how fast they can deliver." He looked into his storeroom, avoiding Ryan's eyes. "I'm expecting a delivery end of next week."

Ryan's eyes narrowed. "Most of your regular customers must already have made their monthly purchases."

"Look, McGee, I don't want any trouble here." Pickens shifted his stance backward and cast a look in Sandy's direction. "What about Domingo's blend? I have plenty of that in stock. Maybe you'll want to upgrade."

Ryan stared at the older man, one eyebrow raised. "Change their diet without a transition period? Sounds like I'd be asking for a stable full of sick horses."

Sandy couldn't stand it any longer. For whatever reason, both Leo and Walt had apparently decided Ryan was trouble walking, and they weren't going to make things easier for him. Where was that famous small town, close-knit fellowship?

"Ryan, Colt Ford sometimes uses a feed and tack in Oslow. Why don't we take a run up there?"

Leo stood up straight. "Well, you know, I don't want to put you out, either." He rubbed his jaw. "I can put up about half this order and I'll call over to Oslow myself, see if Ned can spare the rest, have it to you by tomorrow or day next."

Ryan glanced at Sandy, then back to Pickens. He nodded, reaching into his back pocket and sliding out his wallet.

Pickens eyed the gold credit card in Ryan's hand. "So you won't be needing store credit?"

Ryan's eyes glinted and he smirked, sliding the card across the counter. "Nope. But thanks for the offer."

* * *

"I usually take the feed out myself when I pick up Domingo's blend to save Sean the delivery fees," said Sandy as they crossed the parking lot.

She was almost running to keep up and Ryan slowed his steps to accommodate her shorter legs, though all he really wanted to do was put immediate distance between himself and Leo Pickens before he plowed a fist into the old geezer's sorry mouth. He'd known it wouldn't be easy, coming home. He'd known his welcome wouldn't be warm. Apparently gossip and propaganda were still running Orson's Folly. Sean had described things as having been worse for a while. It must have been damned near intolerable right after he'd left. A twinge of guilt stabbed at his heart. If he could go back... But he couldn't.

"Well, since it won't fit in my car, today it's all going to be delivered instead." He winced. She didn't deserve his temper. He shot her a weak smile as he opened the car door for her.

"Ry..." She rested one hand on the roof of the 'Vette. She obviously had something to say but she remained silent, just looked at him with those incredible blue eyes.

The breeze toyed with her hair, mesmerizing him when one strand wouldn't stop teasing her face. The third time it tickled her nose, his hand got there before hers and he tucked it behind her ear.

The tip of her tongue touched her upper lip. "Do you really think all this — the stuff here, the things that happened at the bar — is about your history with Bull?"

If anything, he was less surprised that she'd asked than by how long it had taken her to pose the question. Ryan tapped his fingers against the top of the car door as he looked across the parking lot to the veterinarian's office. Recalling his chilly reception there and Sean's explanation for it, he nodded once. "Yeah, I'm afraid it might."

She stared at him for a long moment with pleading in her eyes. He should tell her about the grudge now, give her a chance to make her own decision about whether she wanted to stick it out with him. No words formed. Darts of cramping pain shot up his arm. He released his white-knuckled grip on the door and stepped back.

She dropped into the seat and he shut the door, then rounded the car and settled behind the wheel.

"One more stop?" Sandy pointed to the drug store, her expression carefully benign.

With a shrug of agreement, Ryan put the car in gear and changed parking lots. When he turned off the engine and opened his door, she shot him a pleading look. "Let me go in alone. I'll only take a minute."

"I was thinking of picking up some, um, protection. In case, ah..." Heat rose at the back of his neck. Now, why was trying to do the responsible thing making him feel like he was sixteen again?

Sandy regarded him with an arched eyebrow. "Ryan, this drug store has the biggest gossip chain outside of Sundays in front of Brother Bobby's church. I'm aware the town knows we're seeing each other by now, but given what I told DC, do you really want to go in and pick up condoms while I'm refilling my monthly birth control? Can you imagine the talk?" Stepping back, she folded her arms across her chest, which had the effect of directing Ryan's attention there.

His mouth went dry. How did he answer that? Why was she on birth control? And why did he even think that was anyone's business but his own?

Sandy leaned over and forced him to meet her eyes. She chuckled. "When you think, sometimes I can literally see your mind working. At the risk of over-sharing here, the pill is for medical purposes. I'm not — and haven't been — seeing anyone in a way that requires it for actual birth control."

Ryan slowly nodded his head. "Okay." *Stupid! As if she needs your approval.* Still unable to find his voice for a more profound statement, though, he did the next best thing. He winked, tipped his hat, and leaned against the fender of his car to wait for her. Just as she reached the door to the drug store, she tossed a frustrated look over her shoulder. His body reacted instantly.

So did his heart.

* * *

He didn't have to stand out there looking all sexy and self-satisfied. Sandy fumed, reaching for one of the double doors of the old drug store. She threw one last glance over her shoulder as she yanked on the handle. Alice MacKay fell through the door into Sandy's arms, her shopping bag flying through the air and spilling the contents on the ground between them.

"Goodness, I'm sorry, Sandy." Alice stooped and began picking her purchases off the ground.

"No, I'm sorry. I wasn't watching where I was going."

Alice glanced up at Ryan, still lounging against his car. Her lips formed a cool smile. "I guess I can see why."

No mention of the previous evening — as though it had never happened. Well, that wasn't so surprising. Sandy was never quite certain if Alice played down her husband's behavior because she didn't want the attention or because she saw nothing wrong in his frequent drunken outbursts.

Saying nothing, Sandy bent to grab a carton of Reds then stood and held it out.

"Thanks." Alice tucked the carton of cigarettes into her bag. She chuckled, her glance darting around the parking lot, never really settling in one direction. "Disgusting habit, smoking. I keep trying to get Brenda to quit but she's a nervous thing without 'em. That grandson of mine 'bout makes her crazy." Her smile didn't quite reach her green eyes. "You have yourself a pleasant day now."

Sandy entered the store with an edgy sense of disquiet. Alice MacKay had never been particularly chatty with her. Generally a nod was all she doled out unless witnesses were present. The sudden U-turn didn't ring true.

* * *

As they started out of town, Sandy laid her head back on the seat and let her eyes drift shut. The growl of the engine and the whine of the tires on the highway became white noise, comforting as a lullaby.

The timbre of the engine changed and the road vibration dulled then stopped. Drawing in a deep breath, she opened her eyes and sat up. She must have fallen asleep.

Ryan had parked in the shade of a cottonwood tree at the baseball field just on the edge of town.

"Why are we here?" As she had done most of the morning, she was careful to keep her voice neutral.

"We need to talk." Ryan sank back into his seat and twisted slightly toward her.

Interest stirred. Sandy pushed herself straight. So he was going to open up finally. Strange place for it, but long past time. "Okay."

"You were mad earlier."

Me? Is he seriously going to make this about me?

Sandy frowned. Best to negotiate around icebergs with care. "Of course I was mad. Someone's messing with us. I was happy when I left my apartment this morning. Dealing with someone's damn tantrum didn't figure into my plans."

"At me," said Ryan. "You were pissed at me because I told DC about Bull coming by your place."

So he wasn't going to let her in after all. Sandy opened her mouth, ready to deny his claim, changed her mind, and huffed out a breath. "Maybe. A little." She leveled her gaze on him. "Some."

"Progress." His mouth curled into a crooked smile. "Which is it, Chicory?"

"I'm getting over *that*." She steepled her fingers together and brought her hands up to rest her chin on her fingertips while she considered her reactions to Ryan. Her body wanted to move full speed ahead. Her heart seemed to want to follow. But he was so closed off even when he didn't seem like it; what did that say for their future?

She drew a few deep breaths to steady herself then faced him. "I know you meant well when you went to DC. But I should have been the one to go to him."

Irritation sparked in Ryan's eyes. "We're in agreement there. You *should* have told DC. Hell, he was in your place having lunch with us and you didn't say a word."

"I would have. Eventually." She shrugged. "Probably."

Staring out at the bleachers lining the ball field, he drummed his fingers on the steering wheel.

"Ryan, I don't need someone to take care of me. I don't want you riding up on your white horse — or in your blue car." Sandy blinked back tears. "Especially if you're still—" She whipped her head around to stare out the window.

Oh, man. She'd almost trodden right into the territory she most wanted to avoid with him.

"If I'm still... what, Sandy?" His voice was quiet and too calm.

When she turned back, he was watching her, his expression guarded.

"You close off whole pieces of yourself. I get that we don't know each other well yet. We haven't had a lot of time. I know I said I wanted to take time to learn about you but — there seem to be so many unfinished things in your life." She shook her head. "After last night, what we shared, I thought—"

Ryan pinched the bridge of his nose. He pulled in a long, slow breath, then blew it out through pursed lips but said nothing. Typical.

"I'm sorry, Ryan. I tried to tell myself it doesn't matter. But it feels like there are a lot of secrets between us."

She scrubbed at the tears spilling onto her cheeks, angry with herself for being so vulnerable.

Ryan ran a finger along the top of the steering wheel. "What's between me and Bull goes back years. Ever since I can remember, he's hated me."

"Why?"

He huffed out a breath. "You'd have to ask him."

Disbelief spoke before she could temper her irritated tone. "Someone hates you and you have no idea why?"

From the center of his dashboard, Ryan's cell phone chirped. He checked the readout but made no move to answer. Nor did he answer her question.

Thoughts of the woman he sought generated a slightly dirty feeling. It wasn't the mystery woman who was intruding. Sandy swallowed. *It's me. I'm the other woman.* "That was your friend again, wasn't it? The one looking for your..."

He nodded once, his eyes never leaving hers.

"See, sometimes — like now — when I'm with you, it feels as if there's another person here with us."

He made an impatient noise. "Just you and me here, Chicory."

"And our respective memories." She sniffed. "Maybe — maybe this is a mistake."

He stiffened. "If you really felt like that, you wouldn't be here now."

"I'm sorry. I don't want to fight with you. But I do feel like that. Ryan, you can't have us both. And as long as you *want* us both, you can't have me." Shaking with emotions even she couldn't name, Sandy flopped back into her seat. Her gaze drifted toward the windshield.

How had she not noticed the empty space? "Where's your angel?"

He met her eyes, irritation replaced by a guarded expression. "I put her away. Yesterday. *Before* I came to your place the first time."

"Oh," she whispered.

* * *

Ryan locked his gaze with Sandy's and traced a finger along the neckline of her shirt.

Wherever he touched, she quivered. When he reached the middle of her chest, he hooked a finger in her collar and used it to pull her toward him.

His lips hovered over hers, not quite touching. "We *are* alone, Sandy. Very much so. This isn't about Allie. And it's not about secrets I haven't had a chance to share. It's about what you want. Or don't. When you figure it out, I'll be right here. But you've got to tell me the difference between you caring about my issues with Bull that go back years, and me worrying about danger you're in from him *right now*." He drew back without kissing her, hating the look of shock and hurt filtering into her eyes, knowing he'd put it there.

She didn't answer. He forced himself into stillness, waiting her out.

Finally she drew a deep breath and spoke. "What if— What if I say I want *you,* need *you*? But it scares me to want and need anyone this much?"

Ryan stiffened. "You're afraid of me?"

A tear splashed on her hand. Another rolled over her cheek. Ryan reached out and brushed it away. His eyes drifted to the tiny, mesmerizing pulse beating madly at the base of her throat.

"No, I'm not afraid *of* you, I'm afraid *for* you. Afraid if I love you—" She shook her head.

Afraid she'd lose him? The thought sucker-punched him. Ryan shook his head. The sad part was, he got where she was coming from. The same fear of losing her coiled like a rattlesnake in his gut, just waiting for the right moment.

"Oh, baby." He bent and pressed a kiss to that fascinating pulse. "I can think of a thousand ways I could screw things up between us. But I promise you, me leaving you isn't one of the scenarios."

Even if, by some wild trick of fate, Allie resurfaced in his life, it was Sandy he was falling in love with. But how did he explain that to her when he didn't completely understand it himself?

She pressed herself against him and sobbed into his neck. "You can't say that. You can't make that promise, and I don't think I can survive losing you."

Surprise catapulted him back a few inches. "You're *pushing* me away because you're afraid of *losing* me?" Ryan scrubbed his face with one hand. Temper edged into his voice. "Do you have any idea how freaking ridiculous that sounds?"

"I didn't say it made sense!" Crimson bloomed on her cheeks. "It doesn't have to make sense. It's how I feel!" She slapped a hand across her chest. "Here."

Fresh understanding dawned. It wasn't about jealousy and secrets. He'd never considered how his problems with the MacKays could scare Sandy, not for *her* safety, but for *his*. He gentled his voice. "No, Chicory. I can't promise not to die." He wiped another tear with his thumb. Emotions pelted him from every angle, old ones, new ones, hers, his own. "No one can." He kissed her gently. "But I will never *want* to leave you. All I want is to know you're safe and for you to know you are the most important person in my life." He smiled. "Chicory, I want a million more days with you, but if I only have one, I want you to know I mean it when I tell you how much I care for you."

Sandy sniffed, wiped her eyes, then drew back just a little. "It is so like you to use my own words on me," she finally said, a tremulous smile breaking through her tears.

Ryan took her lips in a kiss she met with equal passion. Her lips parted. His tongue teased hers. He'd only ever needed one person as much as he needed Sandy. And that ship had obviously left the port without him. Or maybe it had never been there to begin with. It no longer mattered.

He stroked her cheek with one hand then combed his fingers through her hair, releasing it from her messy ponytail. She shifted in the seat, leaning over the gearshift and straining against him, all softness and curves. He found his hand on a firm breast and used his thumb to stroke her nipple through her blouse. When she moaned and arched against him, he felt an answering stirring deep inside and his jeans were suddenly two sizes too small.

"Come on, you two," said DC's voice from over Ryan's shoulder.

Ryan jerked upright and broke the kiss.

"I know you two like hot monkey sex, but you do both have homes. Why don't you take this to one of them instead of making out where kids are playing?"

"Sorry." Sandy hid her face against Ryan's shoulder.

"Yeah, sorry." Ryan angled himself toward the sheriff with a sheepish grin, blocking DC's view with his body to give Sandy time to adjust her shirt. A flash of red hair caught his eye. Ryan nodded toward the ball field, where a teenaged boy was trying to look like he hadn't been staring. "Who's the kid?"

DC looked over his shoulder and heaved a long-suffering sigh. "That young man is Ricky Brody MacKay. Bull and Brenda's boy." He zeroed in on Ryan again. "Uncanny resemblance, eh?"

Ryan's gut began a slow roll. He went completely still as tension crept into the back of his neck. "Brenda was Mac's girl. She wouldn't even have been sixteen when we left. How did she get twisted up with Bull?" His eyes followed the boy, who was walking away, a baseball bat and glove dangling from his hands. "How *old* is that kid?"

DC placed his hands on the car door and leaned over. Ryan saw his own angst reflected in the mirrored lenses of the sheriff's sunglasses.

"Don't go where your mind's going." DC was calm but firm. "Things are already tangled up enough. Decisions had to be made all those years ago. Decisions you and Mac had no part in once you left. This is one thing you should just leave alone. Don't think about it, don't even wonder in passing. It's not your concern."

The sheriff stood, tapped twice on the door where he'd been leaning. With a final pointed look at Ryan, DC turned and ambled back to his patrol car. "And go home," he called over his shoulder. "No outdoor monkey whacking on my shift."

Though Ryan heard the words, they barely registered. He watched the redheaded kid disappear into the distance, suspecting that his past and present had just collided. "Oh, shit."

* * *

Sandy checked the front cinch. "You are exactly the therapy I need, big boy."

Domingo tossed his head and kicked up dust, dancing sideways when she led him to the fence. Sean met her in the yard.

"Hey, Sandy. Need a leg up?"

"I've got her." Ryan stood in the doorway of the stable. His preoccupied expression said he wasn't finished with his brooding. Well, she was finished with waiting for him to get over whatever had started eating at him when he'd seen Ricky MacKay back at the ball field.

He settled his hands on her shoulders and met her eyes. "I can't ride out with you today. I know you can take care of yourself. But I'll feel a lot better if you don't go too far on your own, okay?"

Sandy noticed the fine stress lines at the corners of his mouth and the shadows in his eyes. She gnashed her teeth together, determined not to let his vulnerability sway her. He was worried for her but had yet to tell her why. Until he found the time to talk, she wasn't giving him the right to worry about her. "I don't need you to *ride* with me, Ryan." She needed him to share his secret bits and pieces with her. "I'll be fine. I'll stick to the main trail and turn around at Diamondback Lookout."

After his easy boost into the saddle, she blew him a kiss, then whirled the horse around and took off at a trot, shaking with the effort of not looking back.

* * *

Ryan watched her disappear, not surprised when she didn't turn around. He knew she'd been thrown because of his reaction to Bull's son. He should have explained it to her but he hadn't known how to begin. How could he explain to her that seeing the teenager had been the equivalent of seeing a ghost?

From behind him, Sean cleared his throat. "Things at her place that bad, or did you put her in that mood?"

Ryan heaved a sigh but didn't turn around. "This one's all mine."

Sean's sharp laugh rang across the yard. "You've known her less than a week and you've managed to piss off the most un-piss-offable woman I've ever met. You sure you're my brother?"

Ryan pulled a hand down his face. Damn, he was tired. Blowing out a breath, he swung around and fixed Sean in a pointed stare. "I saw a kid at the ball field today."

Sean's grin turned to a frown of confusion. "What were you doing at the ball field?"

"I pulled off the road there to talk, to find out why Sandy was so prickly." He shook his head. Sean didn't need the full explanation. "Thing is, DC stopped by, and then I saw this kid. DC said he was Ricky Brody MacKay."

The name registered on Sean's face immediately. Regret clouded his eyes and he looked away, a muscle working in his jaw. "Oh, geez. I'm sorry, Ry." He swung his green gaze back to meet Ryan's. "You shouldn't have found out about him that way. I should have told you when you got here."

One side of Ryan's lip pulled upward in a sarcastic half-smile. "Or, I don't know, maybe someone should have told me fifteen years ago. Or let Mac know. He *is* Mac's son, isn't he?"

Sean shook his head slowly. "No one's ever called him that out loud. Speculation on that stopped ten or twelve years ago. Still, if I had to say one way or the other..." He shrugged. "I'd say there's a good chance."

The conversation DC had held with Gloria Pratt the day before began to make sense. Regardless of his paternity, Brenda was his mother. Was the kid a troublemaker like Bull?

Looking up at Sean, Ryan knew he should let it all go, but he had to know. "The fire at Lantree's yesterday... I overheard DC mention a kid with red hair to Mrs. Pratt."

Sean winced and rubbed the back of his neck. "I don't think he's a bad kid, but there are rumors he gets into a little trouble now and then."

"A little trouble? Someone set a fire in the lumberyard." Ryan bent and picked up a stone. He held it loosely in his hand, weighing it while he weighed the thoughts tumbling around in his head.

"Maybe more than a little." Sean shrugged. "Folks have kinda given the boy a pass on things... growin' up with all the questions—"

"Damn it!" he yelled, flinging the rock. The crack of wood as the stone slammed into the side of the barn echoed across the stockyard, followed by snorts and thudding hooves from the horses inside the barn, spooked by his temper tantrum. "Can things get any more screwed up?"

"Ry." Sean's voice was soft but firm. "Folks around here were aware we knew where you were, how to get in touch with you. And that included Brenda."

Ryan pinched the bridge of his nose. "So if this kid is Mac's, she must have kept quiet for a reason."

Sean inclined his head and shrugged. "Once the subject dropped, Ry, I never thought about it again either."

Ryan grimaced. "I probably wouldn't have either." He stared along the trail Sandy had taken. "Sean... are there any other surprises?"

When his brother didn't answer, Ryan looked over his shoulder to meet Sean's steady regard.

"No. That's about it."

* * *

Domingo opened up when she gave him his head. Hot sun blasted over her back as his powerful muscles bunched beneath her. He carried her without extra effort as though she were simply a part of him. They'd covered a lot of ground before the horse worked off his energy, but when he slowed back to a fast walk, she began to think.

How could she know Ryan so well yet know next to nothing about him? When had he been in the army? Had he run away to join? What else had he done over the years he'd been away?

Walt's words about Ryan fighting oil fires made sense. He did carry himself like the firefighters she'd once worked with. Confidence without arrogance. She suspected something big had happened to him on the job. Something to cause a posttraumatic stress reaction the night before. Yet he'd refused to talk about it. His life was a graveyard of mysteries and secrets, and she might never find out about some of those. Then again, she had a mental graveyard of her own.

* * *

"Did you grow up with dreams of being a fireman?"

His sharp bark of laughter ended in a cough. "No, Angel, I was going to be a rancher. I never wanted the city life. Shit just happened."

"Shit" as in the reason he'd left the home he loved.

"What's it like? Fighting fires?"

"It's part physical, part mental, and part emotional. Sometimes you have to get intimate with a fire before you can kill it. But you can't let yourself get caught up in it or you'll start making... mistakes." He gave a wry chuckle. "Like being where you shouldn't be when the building falls in."

Her heart fluttered. She had to change the subject, but not so it was obvious what she was doing. He'd already proven too smart for that.

"What was the weirdest run you ever did?"

He laughed again. "This is L.A. There've been a lot of weird runs."

"Tell me." She lifted the water bottle to her lips.

"I think the strangest was the time the house began shooting at us."

Sandy almost choked on her water. "Um, yeah... that would be pretty memorable. What happened?"

"We got a call about a trash fire. Nothing big, so we only rolled one unit."

A spasm of coughing interrupted him. In the middle of taking another sip of water, Sandy paused. The bottle cooled her palm. She scraped her thumb along the rippled ridges. Drops of water clung to the inside, but with a little shake of her hand, they fell to the waiting pool below. How many things had she blissfully taken for granted all her life? Like drawing her next breath or quenching her thirst. She should tell Mick to stop talking, save his strength. But his voice came over the radio again, mesmerizing her...

"We pulled up to this house and there was a trash can on fire. But behind the trash can, the house was involved, shooting flames out of one of the bedroom windows. We couldn't get there, though, because the driveway was filled with clay pots of huge burning marijuana plants."

"That's one way of getting rid of the evidence," murmured Sandy, her lips twitching with humor despite the situation. "And a good way to get your local firefighters stoned on the job."

Mick chuckled. "Even burning green, it did have a very distinctive aroma. We found out later the grower's girlfriend had come home from work early and found her boyfriend bang— ah, engaged in sexual activity with her best friend. So she dragged his plants onto the driveway, doused them with barbecue lighter fluid, and lit 'em up."

"I guess the grower would have been upset."

"He told the investigator that when he jumped up to save his plants, he knocked over a candle, which caught the bed on fire." Mick drew another labored breath. "His companion tried to extinguish that with the bottle of whiskey on the nightstand and succeeded in catching the curtains on fire." He gave another chuckle. "And that left her in a quandary since she wasn't dressed."

"Did she run out nekkid?"

"No," he said with a raspy chuckle. "She grabbed a blanket which, unfortunately for her, kind of..."

"Caught fire."

"Yep, and that led to her running through the house to escape it, spreading the fire behind her. In particular, some curtains in a utility room leading to the garage caught fire when she breezed through. We were just on the scene when she came running out of the garage. About then she managed to lose the burning blanket. Kind of made all of us pause to appreciate the view."

Sandy's laughter echoed across the dispatch office. His words painted the picture so well she felt like she was there.

"By that time our backup had arrived and we dispensed with the burning pot. It, ah, didn't fare so well. We were just moving into position to assault the house fire when the garage started popping like popcorn. Seems the grower had been stockpiling small arms and ammunition with the idea of protecting his little farm. Bullets explode when they get hot. We had to take cover and pretty much watch the house become fully involved before that ammo stopped burning off. No one got hurt so we all cracked jokes while we waited it out."

"What happened with the naked woman? Did you give her your coat?"

"Me? Heck, no! I wasn't going to spoil the view. My partner did. He's always had a chivalrous streak."

* * *

Domingo snorted and balked, tossing his head in violent up and down motions. The acrid scent of burning grass clung in the air, growing stronger with each step toward home. The horse danced sideways, pulling hard on the reins. Then he half-reared and Sandy nearly slid from the saddle. Leaning forward, she murmured calming nonsense in his ear as she peered along the trail ahead. The barns should have been visible in the distance, but the only thing ahead of her was a writhing black serpent waiting for her to ride into its jaws. Fire!

Chapter Twelve

Another paroxysm of coughing tore through Sandy's body. Her throat was scorched from the smoke she was already breathing. Ash fell like a hot summer snowstorm. Agitated horses raced back and forth along the rear fence of the paddock. Fear-crazed bulls bellowed in the stockyard. The fire was burning at the front of the property, so the animals were frightened but safe. She turned Domingo loose in the corral next to the stable without unsaddling him. Then she sprinted toward the heaviest smoke.

The blaze was low and mean. It crept along with an evil sputtering hiss, consuming the dried grasses in front of it. In its wake lay the blackened remains of what an hour earlier had been a lush field of hay nearing harvest.

The fire pushed its way along the fence with nothing to stop its steady march to the homestead. Justin was using a garden hose to wet down the roof against flurries of sparks being carried on the wind, but if the fire reached the house, he wouldn't have a chance of stopping it. Gus Hanson and Sean frantically pitched dirt at the base of the flames, beating them back. Sandy's jaw dropped when she recognized Ricky MacKay working alongside them.

She finally spotted Ry working with the volunteer fire department, expertly moving equipment from the pumper truck, directing the firefighters with an air of command. He pulled more hose and pointed to the hot zone close to the house. One of the younger firefighters grabbed the end of the hose, waiting for the pump to start sending water along the line.

Snapping to life, Sandy picked up an abandoned shovel and went to work next to Ricky. It felt like a losing battle right from the start. With every shovelful of the dry dusty earth tossed onto the fire, a flame sputtered out, only to find a fingerhold in some of the dry grass a little farther on. Sandy wrinkled her nose against the stench of the heavy smoky air and coughed as it ripped at her already raw throat. If only she had just one drink of water.

Thrusting the thought of quenching her thirst aside, she resolutely attacked each tendril of fire as it danced on to the next patch of brown vegetation. It was impossible to orient. She was aware only of the onslaught of gluttonous flames and knew she had to drive them back.

She never noticed the shifting wind until the fire's tone changed from snapping puppy to snarling wolf. The rusty amber glow swirled into a vortex of smoke and flame with Sandy in its eye. Promising exquisite torture, the monster fanned her with its hot breath. Greedy licks of orange and yellow stretched toward her, as if eager for a taste of tender flesh. Invisible flames charred the tips of the dried grass at her feet and heat scorched her lips and mouth. If she breathed too deeply, her lungs would be gone in seconds.

Sandy stood transfixed by the beauty and power of the blazing entity. Smoke stung her eyes and tears blurred her vision. Heat seared along her nerve endings, the pain breaking the fire's spell. She spun frantically. Which way was out? Pillars of flame blocked her path in every direction. Sandy was in the devil's domicile, with no idea which direction led to safety and which led her deeper into hell.

Gasping for each breath, her vision began to film over with a purple-red mist. Thickened blood pounded hard through her carotid arteries, struggling to carry oxygen to her brain. Her arms and legs were clunky, hard to move. Her neck didn't have the strength to hold up her head.

She was going to die in the devil's embrace.

Ryan came for her on the gush of artificial rain, pushing back the firestorm, her personal white knight rescuing her from the grip of the enraged dragon. She felt his confident touch as he pulled her into the safety of his embrace. He used his own body as her shelter against the ravenous inferno.

She followed his guidance with complete trust. His muscles contracted around her as he launched them both into a desperate leap through the blast of heat. They landed with breath-stealing pain and he rolled them over the muddied ground, in the wash of spray from the pumper truck.

Ryan pushed to his feet, hauling Sandy up with him, swiftly pulling her away from the fire. She clung to his arm as coughing wracked her body, nearly knocking her back to her knees. Once she had her bearings, she nodded and stepped away from him.

"I'm good," she shouted over the angry howl of the fire.

He pointed her toward Justin and gave a little shove, then left her and returned to the battle.

Through eyes that burned, Sandy watched Ryan work. He was a man used to facing down fire. He knew the beast, knew exactly where to hurt it the most. When the wind shifted again, pushing the blaze back toward the path it had already taken, the flames sputtered. Ryan and the other firefighters moved in for the kill and the beast was slain.

A glass of cold liquid was pushed into her hand. Sandy looked up. Justin. Covering her hand with his own, he guided the glass to her lips. Tart lemonade flowed over her sandpaper tongue and nurtured her irritated throat.

"A little more," he encouraged after she took one long pull. Only after several sips did he set the glass aside.

Ryan's father gently wiped her eyes with a bandana soaked in cool water. When she struggled to see what was happening, he simply moved with her so she could watch while he continued wiping her face.

"We've got some eye drops in the house that'll help." He handed her the bandana and was gone.

Out of commission because of her own stupidity, all Sandy could do was observe the mopping-up process.

Wisps of white crept upward from hot spots in the blackened field, and volunteers used shovels to check each smoldering heap for errant sparks.

Ryan assisted with rolling hoses and packing gear, showing an easy camaraderie with the other firefighters. He might say he'd come back to Wyoming because he wanted to run the ranch. He might even believe it. But fighting fire was in his blood. And once it got that far into a person, it wouldn't easily leave. He was as much in his element fighting the flames as he was in the saddle. Would he be able to straddle both worlds or could he choose one? And if he chose fighting fire over ranching, would she be able to live with his choice?

When the VFD pulled out of the driveway, Ryan turned his attention to the redheaded teenager who hovered near the fence. He spoke to Ricky for several minutes. Then he shook the boy's hand and patted him on the back. When the boy began walking toward the road, Ryan watched him for a few minutes before turning to meet the approaching state trooper.

Justin returned with a small bottle of drops and Sandy stood motionless while he efficiently flushed her eyes. She blinked with the rush of fluid, grateful when the sting began to ease.

"Umm, feels good," she murmured. "Thank you."

She permitted herself a last long look in Ryan's direction before walking to the stable to care for her horse.

"Another firefighter," she mumbled under her breath. "I must be crazy."

* * *

Coated in layers of soot and dirt and sweat, Ryan pulled off another ruined shirt and used it to mop his face on his way to the house. Exhaustion had made him its bitch, but it was so much more than physical weariness that put the drag in his steps. Fury rose again, mingling with despair and angst, in a triple play surge demanding instant outlet. He kicked at a sizeable stone partially embedded in the gravel drive, cursing under his breath when it didn't budge. Really? He'd just beat back a fire and rock was going to best him? He crouched and with a little effort managed to work the rock out with his fingers. Round and white, it left a matching hole in the ground when he stood, but the minor victory was his. Too bad no satisfaction came from the win.

Pausing, he stared into the ruined field. Nothing remained of the hay they would have harvested in the next several weeks. Worse, the blaze had almost made it to the house.

"Damn you, Bull!" he called as he hurled the white rock into the scorched field. A blackbird sitting on the charred fence squawked its protest and took off in a flutter of black feathers.

When Ryan raised his eyes from the dusty gravel drive, he locked onto Sandy's face. Flinging the shirt aside, he started walking, quickening his steps, the need to reach her driving his pace. It had been a new experience for him to feel so torn between duty and emotion. He hadn't liked it.

They met at the top of the drive. A half-step between them and he opened his arms. With a tiny cry, Sandy entered the embrace, rubbing her cheek over his bare chest. Her silky hair caressed sensitive skin, sending him into an impossible spiral of erotic demand to affirm life.

But as her arms encircled his waist, Ryan's world righted itself.

"I knew you were on the other side of the fire," he whispered into her hair. "I didn't think I'd get to you in time. When I saw flames all around you—"

Abruptly he pulled back and stared into her face. Streaks of soot were difficult to distinguish from smudges of dirt. Her hair now lay in loose disarray about her bare shoulders, bits of leaves and grass caught in the tangles. "You look like you just fought a fire." Tenderly he extricated a dry twig from just above her ear and cast it aside. "I've never seen you more beautiful."

"I couldn't find my way out," she said shakily. "All I could see was more fire and smoke. It's like the fire was alive."

"That's one of the first things they teach you at the academy," he said. "Fire is alive. It breathes. It moves. Sometimes it even seems to think."

"For a minute I felt like—" She shook her head. "Never mind. You'll think I'm crazy."

"Like you were under a spell?"

She nodded slowly, her eyes wide.

He rubbed his thumb over her cheek, wiping away a smudge of soot, glad the skin beneath was unmarred. "That's common. Lots of good firefighters get trapped. You can't fight a fire without getting to know it, but getting intimate with fire is — risky."

"Yeah..." She stiffened and frowned, then shook her head and snuggled close.

Closing his eyes, Ryan nuzzled her neck and breathed in the acrid smell of smoke mingling with Sandy's scent. She'd come damn close to losing her life. He'd been in situations where he'd barely made it out of burning buildings, been forced to stand by helplessly while friends had lost their lives. He'd seen prairie fires form tornados in the blink of an eye, watched them dance over the ground.

Seeing the fire form a twister around Sandy had nearly killed him. He'd been certain she was gone. Only by some miracle had they gotten out of that conflagration relatively unharmed.

* * *

With her arms locked around his waist, Sandy caressed Ryan's chest with her cheek. His skin was warm and a strong aroma of smoke lingered, but his heart pulsed beneath her cheek. He was alive. She shivered and squeezed him tighter, then looked up at him.

"How did the fire start?"

He stared at the lost field for a few beats before meeting her gaze. "It was arson. They found a cigarette lighter next to a can of gasoline and some Black Mountain beer cans loaded with fertilizer and cotton." His bark of laughter contained no trace of humor. "The Wyoming version of a Molotov cocktail."

"It wasn't random, was it?" she asked softly.

He pulled back, trouble clouding his eyes. His terse headshake and grim expression said it all. "We should talk, Sandy. There're some things you need to know. You almost died today because you're involved with me."

Sandy blinked. *Involved?* What kind of piss-ant lukewarm word was that?

She looked down at her soot-covered shirt. "Okay. Let me see if I can clean up a little first." She regarded him critically. "You could use a spray-down yourself."

Needing the contact, she laid her hands on Ryan's shoulders then traced twin paths downward toward his hands.

He hissed a breath through clenched teeth.

"What is it?" Carefully, she turned both arms over, gasping at the gaping jagged gash on the back of his left upper arm that began at his shoulder and ran almost to his elbow. The skin around it had blistered and reddened. The outer edges of the wound were black.

"Got caught by a piece of burning fence." He winced as she ran a finger alongside the injury. "A rookie mistake."

"You need an emergency room."

Ryan shook his head. "It'll be okay."

Sandy tilted her head and sent him a sideways stare while they walked. "Really? Have you seen it?"

Awkwardly, he tried to look at the back of his arm. "Can't see it, but I don't feel it— Hey!" He dodged her questing fingers, only half playful as he slapped at her with his other hand. "—unless someone touches it."

Sandy tugged him over to his car by his good arm and angled the rearview mirror upward. Without a word, she gently steered his injured arm so he could see its reflection.

He shrugged. "It's nothing. Gus has some first aid training. He can patch me up. Won't be the first time."

"Can he give you a tetanus shot, too?"

"I'm up to date."

Sandy felt her heart give a little squeeze and realized she would do anything for Ryan. Even tap into expertise she'd hoped to never use again.

She groaned, hoping she wasn't about to make a huge mistake. "Lord, save me from stubborn men. Come on, I've had some training. I can patch you up." She led him to the front porch, where his father and brother waited, grumbling under her breath, "Just don't expect me to shoot you up with cow antibiotics."

"Not at all," he answered smoothly. "Horse pills will do just fine."

His soft chuckle soothed the tension from her nerves.

* * *

Like most ranches, first aid on the Cross MC ran somewhat more sophisticated than the average suburban American household. Sandy wasn't surprised when Sean produced a disposable irrigation and suture kit with surgical wash, topical anesthetic spray, and latex gloves.

Seated at the kitchen table, Ryan was breathing in short gasps. Fine lines fanned from the corners of his eyes. Beneath streaks of soot, his skin appeared a little pale.

"I wish I could give you a shot of lidocaine." Over Ryan's head, she directed a pointed look at Sean. "There's no way to do this without causing some pain."

Either Sean had excellent intuition or he had honed the power of telepathy. Without further direction from Sandy, he stepped next to Ryan and offered himself as a brace.

Still, Sandy hesitated.

"Just do it," Ryan said through gritted teeth. "I've had worse."

No doubt he could tell some horrific stories. And she would listen if he did tell them. But at the moment she only sighed, seeking out some inner strength. "Maybe you have, but I wasn't the one hurting you then."

Astonishing even herself, Sandy kept her hands steady as she irrigated and debrided his injury. After trimming away some of the charred flesh, she carefully sutured the deepest part of the gaping wound.

A low moan emerged from deep in his throat when she touched the burned area. But other than repositioning himself more firmly against his brother, he didn't move.

"Okay," she murmured. "It's actually good you felt that. Less chance there's nerve damage. I don't think the burns are full thickness. But there's not enough skin left here to hold. We'll have to put a good dressing on you and watch it for infection. It'll leave a big scar."

"I wasn't planning on entering any beauty contests," he ground out.

"I was more worried about the scar impairing movement," Sandy snapped as she applied antiseptic salve, then a layered gauze dressing. "You should see a doctor."

At her nod, Sean released his brother.

Sandy peeled off the latex gloves and pulled Ryan's hand into her own. She checked the circulation in each finger then finished by taking his pulse. It was a little quick but steady and strong. Finally, she studied his face. He was pale but his eyes were clear and his pupils matched.

"How do you feel?"

"Like a crazy woman just did embroidery on my arm," Ryan said, emphasizing each word.

"Where did you learn to do all that, Sandy?" asked Sean.

Maintaining her calm with effort, Sandy shrugged. "I was an EMT in another lifetime, while I was in nursing school."

"You're a nurse?" asked Sean.

She shook her head. "No, I dropped out."

"Our little bartender has skills. Guess we should keep her." Sean chuckled and sent his brother a suggestive wink.

"Get your own girl," mumbled Ryan.

"Why'd you quit?" Sean collected the 4x4s she'd used to clean the skin around Ryan's arm and dumped them into a plastic bag.

Air backed up in her lungs, but she puffed her cheeks and forced out a long, slow breath. "Sometimes stuff happens and life doesn't quite work out the way you thought it would." *Please don't ask any more questions.* She angled away from Sean but found herself up against Ryan's broad, bare chest. His right arm closed around her. She didn't care that he was sweaty and dirty and smelled of smoke. Slipping her arms around his waist seemed the most natural move in the world. Sighing, she leaned her forehead against his warm chest and hung on. *Another fireman...*

Ryan brushed her hair behind her ears. With his thumb under her chin, he tipped her face up and brushed her lips with his. "Thank you," he whispered, then pressed a kiss to her temple, and just like that, the comforted became the comforter. He glanced over his shoulder. "Hey, I could go for some hundred proof. You?"

Sean was already at the kitchen cabinet. "Way ahead of you. Got a little medicinal Jack right here."

Almost by magic a bottle of whiskey and three tumblers appeared. Sean poured generous measures into the glasses. Sandy accepted the drink he handed her and knocked it back, appreciating the burn as it went down.

"I'm going to go see to the stock." Sean set his glass on the counter with a soft thunk. "Dad's out front with Gus."

When they were alone, Ryan lifted the glass from Sandy's hand and set it next to his and Sean's. "You doing all right?" He laid a kiss on Sandy's forehead, almost as though he couldn't bear to keep any distance between them.

"A little numb," she admitted, leaning back and sending him a smile. His face looked less drawn, a good sign.

Mischief, not pain, danced in his eyes. "I'm going to get cleaned up. Want to borrow some clothes?"

Sparks had turned her shirt into a scorched rag. She poked a finger through one of the holes and wiggled it. "Ya think I need to? This could be a great new style."

Ryan swallowed hard, looking like he wanted to say something, but instead he leaned forward and captured her mouth in yet another a tender kiss, his right hand moving convulsively against her back.

Sandy swayed against him and slid her hands upward along his chest to his shoulders. With gentle back and forth movements, he brushed feathery kisses on her lips. She moaned and pressed more urgently against him.

From somewhere deeper in the house came the distant chime of a clock, and Sandy pulled away with a sigh. "Do they know?"

Stepping back, Ryan stared, obviously thrown by the question. "I'm... going to need a little more information. Does who know what?"

"Sean and your dad. Do they know you spent the night at my place? Do they think we—"

Ryan rocked back onto his heels. Then he huffed out an easy laugh. His green eyes sparkled. "Chicory, I haven't felt the need to ask my father's permission to spend the night out in a while now, and I haven't had any burning desire to have a conversation with Sean about what's between you and me. But I'm a healthy man and you're a beautiful woman. I breezed in here at about five this morning after Sean saw us leaving the bar together last night. It's a fair bet they're thinking along those lines." One of his killer smiles curved his mouth, shooting warmth to sensitive places. "Not to mention DC's likely to bring up monkey sex to someone at some point and that's definitely gonna get back to Dad and Sean."

A giggle slipped out. "I forgot about that." She rolled her shoulders to ease the strain. "So, hopefully no one'll be shocked if I take a shower here."

Tension visibly drained from Ryan's body. He grinned and held out his hand. "No, Chicory, I don't guess they will."

* * *

The bathroom Ryan led her to was painfully neat. The array of soaps and shampoos numbered two of each, not discount products but not top end either. Sandy smiled as Ryan showed her around. It was exactly what she would have expected.

"I share this bathroom with Sean." Ryan set a couple of towels on the counter. "He won't come in while you're getting cleaned up." Pushing open the glass shower door, he gestured inside. "Pretty basic but the water'll be hot. Use whatever soap and shampoo you need." He looked a little sheepish. "Sorry, it's kind of masculine."

Sandy's smile widened. "If they were feminine, I'd be a little worried." She touched him on the arm. "Are you going to join me?"

Her words seemed to throw him off balance. He lifted a hand to caress her cheek, searching her eyes for a long moment before he finally spoke. "I'm going to use my dad's bathroom."

Grazing her lips with a butterfly kiss, he then pointed her toward the shower and slipped from the tiny room.

Sandy reached into the shower and turned on the water, oddly grateful for Ryan's resolve. They'd just been through a few hours of terror. Now was definitely not the time to take their relationship to the next level. Before she could dwell on that particular need for too long, she stripped out of her clothing and stepped under the spray, enjoying the pulsing beat of warm water. She knew by smell which was Ryan's soap and she closed her eyes as she pulled the wash cloth with his scent across her body, dreaming of a time when it would be his hand following that path, when she could enjoy in every way the man who now held her heart.

* * *

Most of the guys he'd once worked with had sought sexual outlets for their excess adrenaline after a run. Ryan had never done that, but he struggled now. The warm shower had relaxed aching muscles; knowledge of Sandy's proximity stimulated his ever-present awareness of her. The contradicting sensations were intensely erotic. Not surprising, he finished his shower before she did, not because she dawdled, but because he'd rushed.

He'd pulled on a pair of athletic shorts he wore when he worked out, and was rummaging through his top drawer, seeking something he could give Sandy to wear, when the door opened.

"Ryan, about earlier..."

He glanced up and caught sight of her in Sean's blue flannel bathrobe, the belt at her waist somehow keeping her from drowning in the garment. Laughter spewed, and he didn't bother reining it in. Her hair was wrapped in a dark blue towel and her face was scrubbed free, not only of soot but also of the makeup she'd no doubt meticulously applied earlier in the day. She should have looked like a comical depiction of a nineteen-fifties housewife. Instead she was a lovely vision of everything he wanted in life. Without shutting the drawer, he closed the distance between them.

"Shh." He touched a finger to her lips. "We'll work it out."

"I, um..." She shook her head, apparently speechless. "I have to say this. I'm... falling for you." Her voice was laced with amazement.

Ryan froze. Emotions skidded, tangled, crashed inside him like a massive traffic accident. He'd only begun to hope she was tripping along the same path with him. To hear her say it out loud was as mind-numbing as the little touches he'd come to crave from her. He scanned her eyes, noted the doubts in them, but then she smiled. His heart stalled for a split second before it started beating again. Nothing could be more beautiful than a woman on the threshold of love — even if she wasn't quite ready to call it love.

She wrapped her arms around her waist, seeming to shrink within herself as she sent him a shy gaze. "The thing is... I don't know where this is going, but... if it's not going to go anywhere, I can't — it's not casual for me anymore." Gone was the bravado, the overt sexual innuendo, the playfulness... all the things she'd once told him she hid behind when something was important enough to scare her. The real woman had unmasked herself for him.

His lungs tightened, became too full as the breaths he took backed up. Did she think that's what it was for him? Had she even listened to him when he'd told her he wasn't looking for just sex? "Chicory... it's never been casual for me." He took her lips in a long, sweet kiss, pleased when she opened her mouth and invited him home.

When he slid his lips along her jaw to tease her earlobe, she sighed, her soft breath like silk on his skin. "I'm too emotional."

"You're allowed. You nearly died." She'd been worried about losing him, and he'd nearly lost her. He tightened his arms.

* * *

Ryan's shoulder muscles were bunched in knots that had to be painful. Sandy kneaded at them, but her reach was awkward and her efforts ineffectual. "Come here," she murmured, leading him toward his bed.

"Sandy..." He balked, shaking his head.

She laughed. "My oh-so-sexy cowboy, I want to make love with you very badly. But when it does happen, it's not going to be in your bedroom in your father's home, with Justin and Sean downstairs wondering about it." She tugged on his hand again. "Come on! Your shoulders feel as though they're made out of rocks. I'm just going to give you one of my killer massages."

He obediently flopped backwards onto the bed, grabbing the light blanket lying across the foot and drawing it over his bare legs.

"Are you cold?"

He sucked in a sudden deep breath then nodded his head once.

"Well, I'll have to warm you up. Okay, on your stomach."

He managed to take the blanket with him as he rolled over and she chuckled.

Sitting next to him wearing only a thin flannel bathrobe was awkward, but straddling his back struck her as too forward. The tension in his muscles eased as she rubbed and squeezed along his shoulders. She put a little extra effort into working a particularly tight knot in his left scapula and he moaned out loud.

"I think you need a muscle relaxer or maybe just some aspirin or something. You're gonna be really sore." She brushed a hand down his back and knocked the blanket from his leg.

He jerked a hand down and snatched at the cover, pulling it back into place.

"Easy, ace. I already told you I'm not after your virtue. What gives?" She tugged playfully on the blanket. "You got chicken legs under here or something?"

With a laugh, she lifted the edge, ready to tease him about legs that never saw the light of day.

"Oh." It was all she had breath to utter at first. It wasn't a new wound but it had been major. "Ryan, what happened to your leg?"

"It's nothing." He started to roll, moving the leg away from her, but she stopped him.

The puckered scar slashed a jagged line along the inside of his right leg from just above the knee almost to his groin. She traced the whitish line with one finger. Ryan jerked as though her touch hurt. She lifted her face and met his steady gaze, seeking permission to continue. He held her in a long stare before nodding.

Sandy ran her hand the length of the injury. He was missing muscle mass, and it was a miracle he didn't walk with a limp. It was anything *but* nothing.

"Were you in an accident?"

Ryan's eyes flickered with a hint of dark emotion, then the shadows fell over his face and he carefully set his mask in place. His voice, when he finally answered, was raw, choked with the emotions he was trying to hide. "Yeah. Got hurt at work. If you don't mind, I'd rather not talk about it. Not just now."

She swallowed hard against her natural curiosity. Just another facet to the mystery of Ryan McGee. One more secret shouldn't really matter, should it? Sandy couldn't process while she was tumbling around in his green gaze. She averted her glance to the floor, mentally tracing the pattern of rectangles on the throw rug at her feet.

Ryan sat up, startling Sandy when he laid a hand on her shoulder. She turned around again but settled her gaze just to his right rather than chance what she might read in his eyes.

"There's a lot I want — need to talk about. Just..." He played with a strand of her hair, weaving it through his outstretched fingers. "I don't want to think about anything right now but you and me."

She laid her hand against the worst of the scar. The pale uneven flesh was warm under her fingertips. Tears threatened but she bit them back. Whatever had caused such damage had been major. She understood why he wouldn't want to talk about it. Hadn't she begged for a similar concession just days earlier? But she already knew she would tell him about Mick one day. Ryan might never talk about his past. She saw two clear choices before her: push him for the answers or back off and be patient. Scratch that, one option: back off. Patience might be considered a virtue, but it was also the safer decision.

"Does it still hurt?"

Ryan jerked when she traced a finger along his scar. "Not so much. Not for a long time."

* * *

An hour later, Ryan still slept. He'd been exhausted but restless, finally relaxing into sleep only when she'd let him hold onto her. To the sound of his snores — which she planned to give him crap about later — Sandy rose quietly and pulled on a pair of gray sweatpants she found folded over the back of a chair. With as much stealth as the sticky old wooden dresser permitted, she opened the top drawer a bit farther, looking for something to wear. She smiled at the neatly organized clothing, folded briefs on one side, T-shirts on the other, and smiled, thinking of her jumbled storage system. She chose a plain white T-shirt and slipped it over her head.

Her hand was on the drawer, about to push it shut, when she spotted the manila file folder with a single bold, black A in the tab. It had to be his file on the woman he'd been searching for. What had he said her name was? Amy? No, it was something else.

Sandy lingered with her hand over the folder as she fought a battle against curiosity. She shook her head. He'd taken the angel out of his car. He'd told her the other woman would never be an issue between them and she hadn't been sure she believed him. But if she opened the folder, she would be the one making the mystery woman an issue. With determination, she pushed the drawer closed, picked up her boots, and silently left Ryan sleeping.

Chapter Thirteen

The bitter smell of fire hung in the air as Sandy let herself out the door. Late afternoon sun bathed the yard in gold, hitting the scraggly shrubs planted along the front porch and forming squat shadows. Black scars of scorched grass zigzagged across the field beyond. She forced her gaze away as her mind delighted in painting greedy orange flames into the picture, raising the hairs on her arms and bringing on a shiver.

"Afternoon, Ms. Sandy." Comfortably slouched in a wooden rocking chair, Justin sipped lemonade from a tumbler then set his drink on the table beside him — next to a nearly full pitcher and two clean glasses. Either he was in the habit of being prepared for unexpected visitors... or he'd been waiting for her and Ryan to emerge from the bedroom. Instant heat flooded her cheeks.

But he seemed not to notice. "Will you sit with me?"

Why not? She hadn't really wanted to leave so soon, and it was Mel's night on schedule. She could always get Charlie to help with what few customers might drop by the bar on a weekday.

"Thank you." She settled into the rocking chair opposite his and gestured to the clear sky. "Looks like we have a nice evening ahead."

He poured a second glass of lemonade and added a sprig of mint, then offered it up. "Would you care for some?"

"Yes, thanks." Beads of sweat already forming made the glass slippery as she accepted it.

"My son getting some rest?"

Heat pushed up her neck into her face. *Well, you were the one who decided to brazen it out.* She took a drink before responding. "It took him a little time to unwind enough but he was asleep when I left him."

Justin chuckled. "Plenty of times his mother and I had to unwind the same way."

The heat infusing Sandy's face kicked up to searing. "Oh, crap. I mean, no. That is, I'm sorry, Mr. McGee. I didn't — we didn't—"

"Sorry?" The old man laughed outright. "For what? Loving my son?"

Well, that rocked her world. The word she'd been avoiding had rolled so easily off his tongue. Her body deflated into her chair. "Is it obvious?"

"Probably obvious to a blind man." The smile settled into his eyes first, the way Ryan's did sometimes. "And I'm not blind. You know, Ryan could do a lot worse on many counts, Sandy. But he'll never find anyone better than you."

"I thought — some people would say we don't know each other — that I'm easy or... after something." Sandy spread her hands helplessly, looking out at the blackened hay field because it was easier than letting Ryan's father look into her soul, to risk him seeing the things she wasn't sure of herself.

His voice was kind, his words gentle. "Are you? Easy or after something?"

"I've only just met him. But sometimes it feels like we've known each other for a lot longer, more like years." She lifted a shoulder. "I can't explain it."

"Some folks just fit together right off." Justin reached out and touched the back of her hand. "Some hearts are lucky enough to make an instant connection. I see something special between you two. My son's a lot like his mother. She always dove into life headfirst."

"You're saying he's not careful with his heart."

Justin toyed with the beads of sweat on his glass. "He never had to be. Always knew what he wanted and if it was right. But something happened to him while he was gone, something he hasn't talked about yet. It changed him. He still knows what he wants. But now he starts looking for the ways his heart can break instead of keeping his eye on the potential for happiness."

Sandy set her drink down. She didn't know if it helped or not, to know that he hadn't even talked with his father about the things that still hurt him. "I can't promise I'll never hurt Ryan, Mr. McGee. But I'll never do it on purpose."

"I know you won't." Justin's steady gaze paralyzed her. "I see in you the same I see in him. You know what you want. But sometimes you see only the obstacles and none of the joy."

The denial was formed on her lips but the words stuck in her throat when Justin raised an eyebrow. With a wry smile, she acknowledged the truth.

"He's got trouble here, girl, and his troubles are spilling onto you."

Sandy stiffened. "I don't see it like that."

"My son does," Justin said softly.

She drew a deep breath to steady herself. "I haven't told him yet, but I do love him. We're together. He's not alone with this trouble."

"He can't let you get hurt because of him, Sandy. It would kill him. He takes care of the people he loves." Justin directed a look at her as though to be sure she got the point.

She picked up her lemonade and sipped. "Maybe it's time he lets someone take care of him back."

Justin nodded his approval. "He did that today, you know. Letting you fix him up. Was a time he would've run off and licked his own damn wounds."

Sandy looked into her glass, swirling the liquid around. "Sometimes it feels like I'm his second choice." Heat slid into her face when she looked up to see Justin watching her. "I don't know why I told you that. He says I'm not, and I want to believe him."

"Something stopping you?"

"I know next to nothing about him. He doesn't share much." She laughed. "I got mad at him because he ran to my rescue this morning. But I know he did that because he — cares about me."

"That's the way he's built — he's got a chivalrous streak as wide as this state."

Sandy studied Ryan's father, noting the physical similarities to the man she loved. "I know exactly who he gets that from."

Justin's color heightened slightly. He pulled out one of his cigars. "Do you mind?"

"Of course not."

He took his time trimming the end, lighting the cigar, enjoying his first few puffs. Wisps of white smoke sweetened the leftover smell of grass fire.

In a gravelly, emotion-filled voice, he spoke, so quietly Sandy had to lean forward to hear. "Leaving here when he was a boy cost him more than he'll admit. He thinks no one knows how much he still hurts over that. When my son loves someone, it's a hundred percent. He'll give up anything for the folks he loves, even his life if it's needed."

Sandy drew in a tremulous breath as she absorbed the meaning of his words. Ryan held nothing back when he loved someone. She knew that already; it was one of the things she loved the most — and the one she found most frightening. "He could have died today. When he saved me."

"We lost his mother when he was twelve." The end of the cigar glowed orange and a translucent cloud surrounded Justin's face for a few seconds before billowing away. "The boy was always mature, always the big brother looking out for Sean. But losing his mother the way he did made those instincts stronger."

"What happened?"

"It was branding season." Deep sadness colored his voice. "The whole outfit was up in the open range. Back then, three ranches around here were all working together in a co-op. It was the only way the smaller ranches could compete with the big-time operations."

Justin sipped his lemonade. Absently he rubbed a hand across his chest, as though soothing an aching heart.

"My Bethany wasn't born to ranching but she took to it. She could ride, pull a calf when its ma couldn't get the job done, round up the bulls, even rope calves with the best cowpokes. She hated branding, called it cruel. But she understood the need. I met her when she was up visiting her half sister, Alice. We got married a month later."

Sandy blinked. "Alice MacKay?"

Justin nodded, took another puff. "The same. Back then, Brody MacKay and I were part of the co-op, along with Colton Ford, Senior. Beth and Ford went off after some cows in the woods. When Beth's horse showed up and she wasn't on him, I sent Ryan to look for them."

Justin stopped talking. He looked out at the ruined field but it didn't take much effort to realize he was seeing something entirely different. His deep sigh was one of the loneliest sounds she'd ever heard.

"Lot of spring rain and flash floods up there." His voice took on a distant quality, as if his memory of that time hadn't faded at all. "The creek was running real high. Beth must have fallen or gotten off her horse. She ended up holding onto a dead tree branch to keep from getting washed into the creek. Ford was working at getting her out. Ry came on them both in time to see Ford slip. They were both holding on but the branch was breaking." Justin shook his head. "He was only twelve. I should have gone, not him."

"He tried to save them..." she guessed.

Justin nodded. "According to Ry, Beth knew she wasn't going to get out of there. She told him she loved him. She told him to tell Sean she loved him and to be good, and she told him—" Justin's voice cracked and he drew a heavy breath. "She told him to tell me I was the only man she'd ever loved. She held on long as she could but the end of the branch snapped off and she just washed away."

"Oh, Ryan," whispered Sandy, thinking of the little boy. "What happened to Mr. Ford?"

"Ford knew Ryan couldn't save him so he chose to save my boy — told him to get back off the muddy riverbank and when Ryan did, Ford just let go. Took us four days to find their bodies. They washed up some miles downstream."

Sorrow branded itself on Sandy's heart in a flash of white-hot pain.

"Alice blamed us all for her sister's death. Brody seemed to feel the same. Truth is, I always felt a little like Brody wished he'd met Beth first so maybe he felt her loss a bit harder. And Bull, well, he never needed a reason to hate Ryan. He just did from the day Ryan was born. But MacKays have full-on hated McGees ever since that day we lost my Beth. All except the younger MacKay boy, Mac. He looked up to Ryan. My son was always kind to him, patient with his tendency to stutter. So Mac — he refused to hate anyone. Was always sneaking over here to see Ryan even though he was a couple years younger."

"What about the Fords?"

"Ford's wife, Kendra, just stepped up and took over running the ranch with her children, Colt Junior and his little sister, Livvy."

"So they didn't — blame Ryan for Mr. Ford's..."

"Nah. Nothing to blame him for and they knew it." Justin stared at his cigar for a beat then looked up with a sad smile. "There's more to the story about the sorrow between Ry and the MacKays, but that's for him to tell. The thing is, if you're with him, you're taking on a huge grudge. And it runs deep."

"I love him." And that was getting easier to say.

"I can see that runs deep, too," said Justin, widening his smile. "On both sides."

"Your boys are Alice's nephews," she whispered. "They're Bull's cousins."

Justin nodded. "Hard to figure, isn't it?"

It was time to get out of there. How had she not picked up on the relationship? Why had Mel kept it from her? She pushed to her feet. "Thank you for telling me. I wish I could stay but I have to get to work. Ryan's, um, well, he's likely to be mad because I left him sleeping."

Justin's eyes twinkled. "Without a doubt." He reached for a box sitting next to his chair. "This here's a two-way radio. We use them a lot now. All the ranches out here. This is set to Cross MC frequency." He changed the setting. "This here's the direct line to the sheriff's base."

Justin touched her on the arm. "My boy had some bad moments today. We all saw it. He's not right unless he knows you're safe. I'm thinking you can carry this when you're out riding, and even keep it in the truck. There's a dock for it above the windshield between the visors. Those cell phones don't get a lot of service out here."

Sandy accepted the radio with hands that weren't quite steady. "Thank you."

Justin tossed her the keys to his truck. "Tell my son to bring you to dinner this Sunday. We'll barbecue."

* * *

The sleek red pickup was a dream to drive. Sandy almost wished hers would be held up for a long while with the state police. As she pulled into the bar's parking lot, glare from the dying sun reflected off a cluster of five cars parked near the front entrance. So many cars on a Tuesday?

Mel popped her head out the back door of the bar just as Sandy hopped to the ground. "The whole town knows about the fire."

Well, that likely explained the extra customers. Too bad it wasn't the new and improved menu bringing them in. Probably wasn't a great business tactic to get involved in small-town uproars to capture a little attention. She offered a shrug.

"Don't even think about pulling a disappearing act until you tell me about it," warned Mel. Then her eyes widened. "Are you driving Justin McGee's truck? He must *really* like you!"

The sound of something striking the ground drew Sandy's attention and she stooped to retrieve a long-handled screwdriver. Standing up, she tucked it into the toolbelt slung on the hook just behind the seat, then closed the cab door with a thunk.

"He's letting me use it until mine comes back from impound. I'm just going to run upstairs and put on my own clothes. I promise I'll be right back."

Mel wagged a finger. "Okay, obviously you are ignorant of the rules. You can't use words like *impound* and *own clothes*, and think you're going to just walk away from the conversation."

Sandy sighed. "Melanie, the last thing I would dream of doing is walking away from filling you in on all the *gossip* of the past..." She checked her wristwatch. "...eight and a half hours. Just let me put on something I can work in. Something not screaming *look at me, I just had my clothes ripped off during wild animal sex and had to wear my boyfriend's clothes home*, okay?"

Mel's mouth formed an O. *Direct hit!* Grinning, Sandy galloped up the rest of the steps.

* * *

Sandy quickly changed into a loose-fitting filmy dress with a random pattern of black and tan swirls. She took extra care with her makeup and for the first time in her life double-checked it in the mirror. Then she tore down the outside steps and into the kitchen.

"Hi, Charlie," she called out, angling for the bar.

The cook lifted one hand without glancing up from brushing barbecue sauce on a rack of ribs.

One more pause at the swinging doors to catch her breath and shake her arms; she willed her muscles to loosen up. *Stand up straight.* Squaring her shoulders, she schooled her expression.

The stainless steel chilled her palm as she pushed through. Hopefully her nerves weren't showing. Tonight she could show no weakness. Tonight she had to wow the world. One person at a time.

With a stack of menus strewn before her, Mel looked up as Sandy stepped through the doors, an expression of abject boredom on her face. It didn't last. Her jaw slackened and her eyes popped as she performed a double take worthy of a Saturday morning cartoon.

First objective met.

A glance over the floor revealed a half-full house — though oddly no one lounged at the bar. How many people had arrived while she'd been upstairs primping?

And how many had recognized Justin McGee's bright red pickup parked outside her door?

Fighting nerves all the way, Sandy sauntered to her normal place behind the bar, conscious of sidelong glances and hushed whispers.

"I'm going to want overtime if I have to work through another of your shifts so you can have a hot date," Mel murmured, sliding the menus into their holder.

Sandy sighed and affected a pout. "No hot date tonight. He probably won't wake up for another few hours."

Mel raised an eyebrow and spread her hands in an expectant gesture. "Don't you have some details you'd like to share?"

"You sound like you already know." Sandy picked up the bar rag and began wiping the spotless bar down, just to keep her hands occupied.

"Only as told to me by Sarah Jessup, whose son Jess is with the VFD. But I also heard bits and pieces from Mamie Schmidt, who got the stories from Gloria Pratt and Walter Blackstone. I'm sure there are details you can fill in."

Sandy shook her head. *Gotta love small town grapevines.* "Okay, in a sec. Any of these tables need seeing to?"

"Not a one." A smile bloomed on Mel's face as she checked her watch. "At least not for another five or so minutes, when I'll make the rounds again and see to their refills. Now spill."

To her credit, Mel leaned against the bar, showing absolutely no reaction while Sandy recounted the events of her very busy day. Professional poker players could take lessons from the woman.

"So, since my truck is considered evidence, Mr. McGee is letting me borrow his for a while." Sandy gave a little shrug for effect.

"Wow," Mel whispered.

"I know." Sandy suppressed the urge to giggle as she wiped her hands on the rag before tossing it back under the bar. "It does seem like a lot happened in the past couple of days, doesn't it?"

Shaking her head, Mel heaved an exaggerated sigh and began a slow clap. "I was just thinking most teenagers would envy your storytelling skills. You got through the whole thing without one mention of the hot sex I know you've been having with Ry McGee."

"Oh, that."

"Oh, *that*?" mocked Mel. "What's the matter, does he come up a little... um, *short* in that department?"

Sandy cringed at the pun as the heat in her face kicked up a notch. "As far as I know, he's not short in any area, but, um..." This time the giggle wouldn't be contained. "Honestly, I don't have firsthand knowledge of that particular, um, trait."

Mel gave a snort. "Right." Then she peered more closely into Sandy's face. "You're *serious*? *No* knowledge?"

Sandy tossed the bar rag into the sink and shrugged. "None," she confirmed over her shoulder as she ambled toward the jukebox.

* * *

An insistent chime drilled its way deep into Ryan's brain via his audio nerve. He couldn't reach the cell phone to turn it off, but covering his head with the pillow only muffled it and had the added disadvantage of suffocating him. As he tossed the pillow aside in irritation, waves of searing agony danced along every nerve in his left arm up to his neck and down to his fingers.

He flopped back onto the bed, his plans of smashing the phone abandoned. By remaining perfectly still, he was able to get his ragged breathing under control. The pain lessened some; at least he wasn't still seeing red and purple flashes in his peripheral vision.

Definitely not the best way to awaken from a deep slumber after the most pleasurable massage Ryan had experienced in his life. Sandy's soft hands had been pure magic as she'd worked at the knots of tension in his shoulders and back. He would have gladly given the same treatment back, eased some of the stress he knew she felt. But when she'd finished, she'd simply lain at his back and held him to her, cocooning him with her warmth and humming softly. Falling asleep in her arms had seemed like a requirement, and he'd allowed himself to drift with thoughts of forever on his mind.

But the other half of the incredible experience seemed to have disappeared. At least she was no longer in his bed. A folded sheet of paper about the size of a small photo provided the answer.

Sleeping Beauty–
Much as I'd love to stay until you wake up, it's my night to close the bar. Stay home and rest. I'll see you tomorrow.
Sandy

So he should rest, huh? Not damn likely with Bull loose and on a vengeful rampage. What did she plan to do if the asshole came to her door again? Invite him in for coffee? She should never have left the safety of the ranch. She needed to stay where he could watch out for her.

Muttering a string of curses under his breath, Ryan grabbed the first pair of jeans he laid his hands on, hopping around his bedroom as he struggled to get into them one-handed. The fire in his arm had his stomach jumping. If he'd eaten dinner, he'd be puking already. He had to do something to control that pain. He managed to fasten the jeans as he stomped into the bathroom. He pulled open the door to the medicine cabinet and grabbed the bottle of painkillers. Swallowing the whole thing probably wouldn't help, but hopefully the two he took would take the edge off the molten agony currently reminding him of the danger they were all in. The danger Sandy was in.

Tossing the rest of the water into the sink, Ryan set the plastic cup to the side and returned the bottle to the cabinet. When he swung the door shut, hard green eyes stared at him from the mirror. If anything happened to Sandy, he'd kill Bull, slowly and painfully.

Donning a shirt sucked and was managed only with beads of sweat forming on his forehead and dripping into his eyes. Too bad he had no time to just hit the bed to recover. Setting his jaw, Ryan slid his watch onto his left wrist, grabbed his wallet and car keys off the dresser, and as an afterthought opened his cell phone to see whose call had awakened him. He frowned at the L.A. area code. Joe — again.

"Sorry, Joe." Why should he give a flying hoot about a woman who had disappeared and obviously had no desire to be found? The phone went into his pocket, the call unreturned.

The pungent scent of cigar smoke hit his nose about the same time he hit the door to the porch.

Shit. He was going to start parking out the back and using Sean's teenaged escape route down the tree outside his window.

"Evening," his father greeted easily.

"You let Sandy leave." Ryan tossed the words at his father without stopping.

"Was I supposed to stop her?" Justin calmly surveyed him.

Ryan paused his forward momentum and glared. "Yes. She's safe here."

A pained expression crossed Justin's face and he slapped at a mosquito on his neck. "She's got a business, boy. She has to tend to it or she won't have it long."

"She needs to be safe — I need her to stay safe." Ryan moved toward his car.

His father's quiet voice stopped him. "Ryan, I haven't been in a position to give you advice in a lot of years, so maybe you'll think it's late for me to be starting now."

With an inward groan, he met his dad's eyes. Now or later, one way or the other, he was going to have to suffer through some kind of lecture. Might as well get it over with. He jangled his keys against his thigh, impatient.

Justin pulled out a cigar, studied it, then sighed and slid it back into his pocket. "Maybe if I'd spoken up more when you were younger, things would be different. But I can't change the past. I can see you love this gal."

"Yes, I do." *And trust you to notice.*

"Son, you came home missing something. Or maybe missing some*one*. Did you go looking for what you're missing — maybe hoping to find it in Miss Sandy?"

The car keys fell to the porch with a clink. Frowning, Ryan bent and scooped them up. Only the fear that echoed his father's question kept his anger at the invasion of privacy in check. Still, he couldn't keep the chill out of his voice. "She say something to you?"

Justin chuckled. "Nothing I didn't already see." He shook his head. "She doesn't deserve to be your second choice, son. And as long as you keep yourself walled off, separating the pieces of your life you don't want to talk about, you aren't making her your first."

"What the hell does that—?" He huffed out a breath. Trust Justin McGee to pick up on *that,* too. "It's not like that. We haven't had time—"

Justin's pointed stare halted Ryan in mid-denial. There had been plenty of time, lots of opportunities. He'd just always found a way around the subject, reasons not to talk.

"You know..." Justin picked up a half-empty glass of lemonade and drew lines with one finger in the condensation.

Damn, if the man ever said anything straight out without pausing for effect, Old Faithful would probably stop spouting. *One, two, three, four, five—*

"Love comes with a lot of things." Almost in slow motion, Justin raised the glass and took a long drink. "Happiness, responsibility. Fear. Open up to her. If she loves you, she'll understand anything you have to tell her. But don't smother her with everything you're feeling right now, son. She isn't one who's going to take easy to that kind of love."

Forcing himself to take a deep, calming breath, Ryan waited a beat then asked, "Are you telling me not to see her tonight?"

Justin shook his head. "I'm strongly suggesting, son, that if you woke up from your nap, missed your girl, and wanted to see her, maybe hold an enlightening conversation, she'll take it a lot more kindly than the attitude you're wearing right now."

The emotions gripping Ryan suddenly drained out of him, and he nodded. Then he chuckled. "You're the second person today to give me that advice."

"Really..." Justin said in a droll tone. "Who would be the first?"

Ryan drew a deep breath, blew it out. Avoiding his father's sharp stare, he mumbled his answer. "Sandy."

Justin's hearty laughter followed Ryan to his car. "You know, a lady usually likes to get a call first before a gentleman drops in on her. Gives her time to spruce up a mite."

Smiling, Ryan reached for his cell and pulled up Sandy's number.

* * *

Dusk was settling into night when Ryan bulleted into a parking spot about as far away from the front door of Valentine's as it was possible to get. The place was hopping. He'd almost forgotten how current events could alter the lives of the locals, pulling them away from their satellite TV and backyard fire pits to gather where they could talk and analyze and keep score. If they were lucky, they would catch sight of some of the players in the drama.

Which probably explained the endless rows of cars and trucks parked in front of Sandy's place on a weeknight.

Small town gossip had never bothered him when he lived in Orson's Folly as a kid. He'd certainly been the subject of it on plenty of occasions. He had to admit it wouldn't bother him now. Except for his family. Except for Sandy. The shitstorm that always seemed to find him was swallowing the people he loved.

Ryan was halfway to the door when a figure emerged from the shadows, extra large and moving like a train in his direction.

"Aw, shit," muttered Ryan. Just one night, one damn night without a MacKay would have made his whole year.

"You stay away from my boy!" shouted Bull. The blue-white light in the parking lot turned his angry red face a deep purple.

"Bull, now settle yourself down." Reason probably wouldn't work but he had to try. "Ricky helped put out a fire at our place is all. I told him thanks and he left."

"He's got no business out near your place." Bull's gait was none too steady, but his eyes held enough hatred to overcome any drunk he had going on. "Unless you enticed him out that way."

"I never met him, didn't even know he existed until today." *Keep calm. He doesn't have to know when today.* "He showed up, helped out, introduced himself, and left. You don't want him out our way, you tell *him*, not me."

Bull faked right then left, swaying side to side in a blocking tactic, his hands balled into tight and very effective-looking fists. "The boy's got no call fighting a fire on McGee land."

Through narrowed eyes, Ryan assessed his situation. His old nemesis was bigger, meaner, and well past rational talk. He was also blocking any avenue of escape into the bar. The door remained closed. Didn't look like the cavalry was going to arrive any time soon, either.

With a mental shrug, Ryan decided to go fishing. If he was going to have to fight, at least he could get some information. "Why not? Boy was just being a good neighbor. You'd have done the same thing, wouldn't you, Bull? Unless you started the fire." He thought about Brody Senior's threats from the night before. "Or maybe your old man decided to pitch a match our way?"

Bull's bark of laughter rang across the parking lot, but his forward motion faltered. "You don't know what you're talking about."

"Don't I?" Ryan's gaze slid to the bar's entrance, willing someone to step outside, preferably his brother. "Old Brody was full of threats last night."

Bull frowned. He looked in the general direction of his truck. Had his adversary not been aware of the threats his father had made? The information seemed to throw him off balance.

"You know, you've got a good son there. Real considerate and helpful."

A startled expression flashed in Bull's eyes just before his belligerent mask fell back into place. And that flash made Ryan particularly curious, so he pushed a little harder.

"If he *is* your son."

Bull's response was the roar of an enraged animal.

Pay dirt!

The charge wasn't unexpected, and Bull telegraphed his intent to lead with his right. Gravel crunched under his feet as Ryan easily ducked aside. But he was still on the wrong side of the parking lot, with Bull between him and the door, and he couldn't duck those mean, meaty fists forever.

"Ricky's *my* boy!" Bull took a step forward. Damn, had he grown a foot in the last decade and a half? "My brother had nothing to do with him. And *you're* not touching him, McGee." He stumbled sideways.

The anger was wearing Bull out. The beer Ryan could smell from several feet away was probably beginning to work its magic as well.

Crouching into a fighting stance, Ryan circled back, holding on to his intent to keep his adversary off balance. "I heard you and Brenda don't have any more kids, Bull. What's the deal? Can't get it up or she won't have you?"

"Maybe I don't touch *her*. I don't want anyone's damn leavings."

So that was it? Had Bull just confirmed he wasn't Ricky's father? Triumph surged, lending Ryan a bit of energy. He'd decide what to do with the knowledge later.

Icy awareness entered Bull's gaze. "He's not Mac's boy. He's never been and never will be." So the asshole had added two and two and managed to get it right. Sure was pissing him off that Ryan had figured it out in a lot less than twenty questions.

Time to end the standoff. Ryan edged to the right, found himself blocked by Bull's quick sidestep. *Shit.* "How much does a hooker go for these days?" he goaded, hoping to throw his opponent off again.

"How much does that slut you're doing charge?" countered Bull.

Oops, wrong direction. Ryan slid a glance right and stepped left.

Bull blocked again, a leer contorting his already ugly face. "How about I do *her* and see whose name she calls out when she has a real man on her?"

Ryan clenched his teeth. "Not gonna happen." If the fight wasn't going to be avoided, he might as well be the one to draw first blood. Feinting with his left, he slammed Bull in the nose with his right. His knuckles stung. Direct hit. Blood spattered, then gushed. Ryan followed with a quick left to the jaw, then another right, connecting solidly in Bull's left eye.

Bull spat. Blood and what might have been a tooth sailed in a shallow arc and landed on the ground. Breathing heavy but with a full-on mad, Bull seemed to puff up, and then he rushed, catching Ryan in the middle of his chest.

Ryan registered his feet leaving the ground, then he was airborne, flipped over Bull's shoulder. He rolled into the landing, somehow protecting his head as he landed on his back, winded. Before he could roll over, Bull was on him, fists pounding, his drunken aim hitting far more than it missed. The bigger man was sloppy, though, and he tired quickly. The opening came and Ryan got an arm between them. Bull's weight pinned him down, but Ryan was lean and fit. And not drunk off his ass. With the next punch, Ryan moved his head aside so Bull connected with the gravel. That gave him the opening for a pop to the temple. Dazed, Bull toppled sideways.

Rolling in the opposite direction, Ryan pushed onto his hands and knees. He didn't quite make it to his feet before Bull plowed into him again. Ryan lost track of how many kicks he took to the ribs. The stomp to his chest made his vision dim briefly. When Bull pulled back for another kick, Ryan grabbed his leg and toppled the jackass like an old oak tree.

Once again Ryan rolled forward and thrust to his feet with a grunt, forcing back the tight sensation in his chest that stole his breath. When Bull rushed him again, Ryan ducked left and landed a hard gut-punch with his right. Bull doubled over and Ryan stepped back. With any luck he might just pull out of the fight relatively intact.

Light flashed off the door to the bar, catching his eye.

Something slammed into him from the side. Excruciating heat barreled along his arm, tearing a grunt from deep in Ryan's throat. He stumbled.

A knowing gleam entered Bull's eyes and he struck again in the same place, then again. White-hot torture rolled over Ryan in waves, unchecked by his rush of adrenaline. Bull took advantage of the weakness to grab Ryan at the site of his injury, twisting painfully, a malicious grin distorting his face.

Ryan slumped in Bull's big-handed grip. Whimpers were torn from his throat as he struggled to get away from the fire in his arm. Still holding the arm he'd destroyed, Bull hit Ryan in the face with a series of quick, hard jabs.

"I'll give your little slut the best ride of her life." Bull gripped Ryan's arm tighter, pushing his face so close his stale, beer-laden breath soured Ryan's stomach. "Then I'll beat the shit out of her like I just did to you. Teach her a good lesson. I'll make her forget you exist. And I'll do it whenever I want." He flung Ryan away from him. Gravel sliced into his cheek.

Sandy. Have to keep her safe. Can't leave her alone. Can't let him get to her.

The ugly thoughts spurred Ryan back to life. Core adrenaline kicked in, giving him the energy to drag himself to his feet. Rage born of fear pushed him past the threshold of agony. He rammed his fist into Bull's gut. When the big man doubled over, Ryan clasped his hands together and aimed the double fist to the bottom of Bull's jaw, knocking him backward. A feeling of pure disgust coursing through him, Ryan grabbed Bull by the collar, pulling him up and glaring into his eyes.

"Like. Hell. You. Will." He accentuated each word with alternating left-right blows to Bull's face. "You sorry—" With a grunt, Ryan rammed his knee home into Bull's unprotected groin. "—son of an ugly *bitch*." He rammed his knee home one more time for good measure, staggering backward with the force of his own blow, landing on his ass. Bull collapsed to his knees, puking.

Shouts came from behind him. Gasping for breath, Ryan's head went light. Purple fog begin to overtake his vision. He sagged to the side just as a pair of strong arms closed about him and lowered him gently to the ground. He looked up, relieved when he recognized his brother's eyes. "What... the hell... took you... so long?" he panted before the merciful blackness took him away.

Chapter Fourteen

Everything was going to be okay. Sandy tried hard not to dwell on Ryan's phone call and his cryptic request to find them a secluded table where they could have a conversation without too much distraction. Either he was ready to talk about his secrets, or he was coming to break things off. The way things kept swinging back and forth between them, she only wished she could be confident it was option number one.

In the meantime, she tried to concentrate on the story Justin had shared. How could she have lived in Orson's Folly for six years and known none of that history? She closed her eyes as the answer worked into her awareness. Because she'd had her head and her heart wrapped up in a man who had died the year before she'd found the small town.

During a lull in serving, Sandy cornered Mel. "Do you know anything about Bull having a brother?"

The younger woman edged sideways to peer around Sandy. Was she seeking an escape route or trying to make sure no one overheard them? The trapped look in Mel's eyes suggested she'd rather do anything than answer the question.

"Mel? What is it? Where is Bull's brother now?"

"Um, there's lots of rumors," Mel began slowly. "But, well, ahh... he's—"

Frantic shouts from the doorway interrupted the conversation. Mel's relief was palpable. As every bar patron rushed outside, one word repeated in the crowd's collective murmur: fight. No use hoping Ryan and Bull weren't the ones going at it.

"Damn it!" As she pushed through the mass of humanity clogging the entrance, she shouted for Mel to call the sheriff's office.

* * *

The fight was over before Sandy got outside, but the aftermath provided a clear picture of exactly how violent it had been.

She spared a glance but absolutely no sympathy for Bull, who was cursing in falsetto as he writhed on the ground in a pool of blood and vomit, both hands clutching at his crotch. Blood streamed from his nose and he spewed more from his mouth with every vile oath he squeaked.

The crowd parted. Ryan sprawled half on the ground and half in Sean's arms. Only the deep purple already blooming on his swollen face kept him from appearing pale as ash in the bluish light.

"Oh, no, no, no!" She sank to her knees next to the man she loved more than life. A metallic tang assaulted her nostrils, and she gagged back her dinner. "God, it looks like his face was shoved into a wood chipper." Blood gushed freely from his nose and bubbled from the corner of his mouth. More crimson liquid oozed from a flap laceration at the top of his cheekbone. It was probably a blessing for him he was unconscious.

But his breathing was too shallow and from the gurgling in his throat, he was choking.

"We have to protect his airway. But I don't know if his neck is injured. Help me. I have to get him off his back without turning his head." She met Sean's gaze and held it until she was certain he understood.

He gave a sharp nod but said nothing.

She showed him how to keep his brother's head in line with his body while she rolled Ryan toward her, onto his right side. Like the miracle he needed, she managed it in one smooth motion. Sean pushed his knee beneath Ryan's head like a pillow. A gasp tore through the air, and then he sucked in a burbling breath. The trickle of red at the corner of his mouth became a gush, but he stopped choking and his ragged breaths seemed to come a little easier.

"This is a lot of blood." Sean's voice shook.

"It's probably all from his mouth and nose." *I hope.* She laid her hand against his neck, releasing a sigh of relief at the pulse beneath her fingertips — staggering but fairly strong. A cramp speared her calf. As she shifted to a less awkward position, her hand brushed his arm and came away wet.

"Oh, dear God." The dark cotton fabric had hidden the bleeding, but his shirt sleeve was saturated. "He must have pulled the stitches out. I have to make sure he's not hemorrhaging."

"Cut it," said a deep voice over her shoulder as a hunting knife was pushed into her hand.

"Here, I had this in my car." Bertie Higgins dangled a dark damask throw pillow in front of Sean, who took it and slipped it a centimeter at a time beneath Ryan's head as he eased his knee away.

Confident Ryan was as secured in place as possible, Sandy sank her teeth into her lower lip and began to work on his arm. She cursed violently in her head as she lifted the shirtsleeve and punched a hole with the knife tip just below his shoulder then slid the blade around until the sleeve was mostly off. Then she sliced downward until the cloth laid open butterfly style. Dark blood flowed from the wound she'd repaired earlier, a steady burgundy stream, but it wasn't pulsing. She tore the rest of his shirtsleeve free, folded it, and pressed it to the heaviest bleeding.

"It's not arterial but he's losing a lot." She leaned over and murmured in his ear. "Don't you go anywhere on me, you hear? You stay with me, Ryan."

Someone laid a hand on her shoulder. Sandy looked up to see Deputy Penelope Sherwood standing behind her. "Life Flight's en route. ETA about ten minutes."

Ten minutes. Did he have ten minutes? She pressed harder on his bleeding arm. *Not again, not again, not again.*

Across the parking lot, Bull was on his feet but hunched over. Bruises decorated his face and his nose looked broken. His hands were cuffed behind him and a couple of men flanked him. He wasn't going anywhere.

In civilian clothing, she almost didn't recognize DC as he crossed the parking lot toward them. "Sandy," he growled. "What the hell happened here?"

"I don't know." She flicked a glance between Ryan and Bull. "I got here too late to see anything. But isn't it obvious Bull—?"

"*Bull* is over there saying Ry started this. He's claiming self-defense."

A terrible icy rage washed over her as she leveled her gaze on the sheriff. "He was mad enough to start something, but I don't think he did." She shrugged. "I know he's been gone awhile and you don't know him anymore, but if he was going to do something, he wouldn't have gone after Bull *here*. Not in *my* parking lot."

"No witnesses. And two men with bad blood between them kicking the shit out of each other."

"And a sheriff who's giving the wrong one of those men the benefit of the doubt. Go ahead, ask Bull about the mess he made of my truck. Or about the fire out at the ranch." She scanned the crowd, knowing pretty much the whole town was there. "Walt Blackstone!" she shouted, grabbing Sean's hand and pressing it to the makeshift bandage on Ryan's arm.

"Sandy," murmured Sean. But then he looked around and his lips thinned. Instead of the warning she'd expected, he only gave her a curt nod.

The mechanic cast a nervous glance at the gathering crowd as if in disbelief that she'd called his name.

"Yeah, Walt. Why don't you explain what happened to all your damn tires, how you were so willing to think Ryan was involved, how you accused him of starting the fire in the lumberyard even though I told you he was having lunch with me!" She swept her hand in a gesture indicating Ryan. "Well, look at him. Do you think he got what he deserved? A man comes home after a long time gone and instead of a welcome, he gets blamed for everything. Like all that shit wasn't going down before he even got here? Please, we all know it was. And we all know who's been doing it. Do you think he caused it from wherever he was before he came back?"

"Sandy," DC said, shaking his head. "You need to calm down."

"No, I don't." She cried, pushing her hair off her face. "You say you're his friend. But you make him prove himself every time. Every. Damn. Time."

DC stepped closer, his face a mask. Probably going to arrest her, but she didn't care. Maybe if she was in jail with Bull, she could kill the bastard.

"Ryan didn't do nothing wrong." A voice rose from the edge of the crowd.

The group of onlookers shifted in one fluid motion, like a giant single-celled organism. The lights overhead flashed on red hair as Ricky walked forward until he stood looking down at Ryan. He trembled, then faced his father.

"Bull was waiting for him." Ricky's voice was tinged with a mix of misery and defiance. "He was mad at me for helping with the fire today. Mad because the McGees let me help. He brought me here to show me what he did to people who cross him. When Ryan got out of his car, Bull jumped him. Ryan tried talking to him but Bull was yelling. He wouldn't listen."

From ten feet away, Bull lunged against the arms holding him back. "You shut your mouth, boy, you hear me? You shut your damned mouth or you know it'll get shut for you."

"You wanted a witness." Ricky squared his thin shoulders. "I'm your witness."

"Damn it, boy, shut the f—"

One of the men guarding Bull slugged him in the belly and he doubled over.

DC motioned to his deputy. "Get him out of here, Sherwood. Book him on assault. Call Doc Trent to have a look at him. I don't want him bleeding all over my jail."

"Easy, son." DC placed an easy hand on Ricky's shoulder. "I'll see you get home."

Ricky shook his head, regarding Bull with hatred blazing in his eyes. "No, I'll get myself home. Just keep Bull away from me. He's not my father." With the backs of his hands, he scrubbed tears from his eyes.

The sound of a helicopter landing in the church parking lot across the street interrupted the exchange.

More than seven years had passed since Sandy had given report on a patient. Somehow she managed to untangle her emotions enough to give an objective case presentation to the middle-aged flight nurse in a dark blue jumpsuit. His badge identified him as G. Wilcox, RN.

As she spoke, Nurse Wilcox worked to finish stabilizing Ryan. Sandy helped get him onto a backboard, closing her eyes when the endotracheal tube was placed.

"Are you a doctor or a nurse?" asked Wilcox.

"EMT, retired."

"Still certified?"

Sandy nodded.

"We're riding one short tonight," Wilcox shouted over the sound of the helicopter. "It's against protocol, but we sure could use a hand getting up to Jackson."

"I..." If Wilcox had been aware of her relationship with the patient, he'd never have asked her along. It would keep her in the loop she would surely be left out of as soon as the connection was discovered. Still, Sandy hesitated, torn between the life she'd tried to forget and the man she loved.

"Go, Sandy," urged Sean. "I'll let Dad know what happened and meet you up there."

Accepting the mantle of professional EMT, Sandy nodded and climbed into the helicopter. They were at the trauma center in Jackson in less than twenty minutes, and then she was relegated back to observer status as Ryan was whisked away for evaluation and treatment.

She sank into a blue chair in the waiting room, the generic kind made of plastic and metal and so common in emergency rooms. Hot tears streamed from her eyes, soaking her cheeks.

* * *

A gentle hand touched her on the shoulder. Sandy started. She must have fallen asleep. Quickly she looked at the console but the red light remained dark. A throat cleared behind her and she spun around. The man with one hand on her cubicle wall was tall, well over six feet, with hair that reminded her of a pepper shaker. His firehouse dress blues told her he was on official department business. Deep compassion shone in his warm brown eyes.

"No," whispered Sandy. "Not yet, please."

"Alexandra, I'm Chaplain Hindson with LAFD," he introduced himself formally, no smile, no offer of a handshake. "I understand you've been talking to one of our men."

"He's been calling in every so often, trying to conserve the battery on his handheld," Sandy said. "His name is Mickey."

Chaplain Hindson nodded. "How are you holding up? You've worked almost twenty-four hours."

"Only about twenty-one so far."

The red light on the console popped on.

"Hey, Angel, I'm checking in. Are you there?"

"As promised," she sang out, instilling brightness in her words. She spared a glance over her shoulder at the chaplain. "Mick, there's someone here who wants to talk to you. Chaplain Hindson."

The radio squawked, but Mick was silent. When he finally spoke, his voice was thick with emotion. "Okay, put him on."

She stood and exchanged places with Chaplain Hindson so he could operate the comm system, but she lingered nearby, shamelessly listening in.

"Son, is there anyone you want us to call?"

Mickey took an even longer time answering. "There's a letter in my locker for my family. Call them... afterwards, okay, Padre?"

"Son, we might be able to patch you through, let you talk to them."

"No! This is for them, Padre. They can't do anything to help, to change things, and they'll hate that. Best to leave it until it's over. Lieutenant Ryder has all my particulars in my employment files."

"Okay, son, it's your call. Is there anything else we can do?"

"No offense, Chaplain Hindson," Mickey said between gasps. "But I'd really like to go back to chatting with my girl. I'm not getting out of here, and I'd really like for her voice to be the last one I hear."

"Of course, son." The chaplain motioned for Sandy to take her seat again. "I don't think he has much longer. Thank you for doing this. I'll be here in the main office if you need me."

"Hey, Mick, I'm back." Her voice sounded too brassy but she couldn't seem to temper the forced sparkle. She was losing her tenuous hold on her emotions. Tears blurred her vision and she hastily wiped them away, suppressing a little sniff.

"Hey there, girl. Those better not be tears for me I'm hearing."

"Now, what makes you think I would cry for you? Maybe I jammed my toe on my desk."

He chuckled. "Are you a klutz, Angel?"

"You know it."

"I mean it about no crying." His voice grew serious. "I've lived a good life, gotten into my share of trouble. I have a family I love. And I'm even more'n halfway in love with you, Angel. I've had it good. I just wish I would have got to kiss you."

* * *

A gentle hand on Sandy's shoulder startled her. She looked up, surprised to see Ryan's green eyes regarding her solemnly. No, not Ryan, her tired brain finally registered. Sean.

"Any word?" he asked.

Sandy looked past Sean to see Justin settling into the seat next to her. The old cowboy looked out of place in the hospital. His face — an older version of Ryan's, she realized — was pale. He had deep shadows in his blue eyes.

"They took him for a CT scan a few minutes ago to check for damage to his internal organs and for bleeding in the brain. He hasn't woken up yet." Her voice cracked and next to her, Justin took her hand. "They're watching his heart because he took a bad blow to the chest and if he develops bruising or swelling in the pericardium, the rhythm can—" She pressed the heels of her hands into her eyes, then lowered her arms and met Sean's gaze. She finished in a whisper. "His heart can stop."

Justin's hand tightened spasmodically, and Sandy turned hers over to clasp their palms together. Sean slumped in his seat and let his head roll back against the wall.

* * *

Waiting was always the worst. Sandy took a small measure of comfort that this time the subject of her vigil was actually receiving medical care, rather than waiting for rescue that would never come.

She even found herself laughing when Sean shared stories about growing up as Ryan McGee's baby brother. She knew she wasn't fooling anyone with the lighthearted optimistic act, but he seemed to need to keep talking.

When Sean finally trailed off, Justin stood, stretched. "I never was a good one for waiting. I saw something looking like it might pass for a coffee machine on the way in." He clutched his hat by the brim as if it was the only thing holding him upright. "If—" He broke off awkwardly.

"We'll find you if we hear anything," Sandy promised.

When he was gone, Sean looked up into Sandy's eyes, seeking answers. Though he didn't voice the question, she understood he wasn't looking for her to give assurances if there were none.

"The testing can take a long time," she said. "Best case will be by the time the tests are done, he'll be awake and surly because he wants to go home, but his mental status will be clear. He's going to hurt for a while."

Sean said nothing. Without a doubt he'd recognized her omission of the worst case scenario.

"Why did they put a tube down his throat?" he finally asked.

"He was choking on his blood." She spoke quietly, maintaining outward calm she didn't feel. "It was just to help him breathe." *And in case his throat swells closed.*

"Is he going to die?" Sean blurted. His face displayed stark terror, mirroring what she felt.

Sandy could only offer a helpless shrug. "I don't know." A tear slid down her cheek, followed by another one. With a sniff, she cleared her throat and dashed the wetness from her face. "Sean, that was a horrific beating. A lot of hate went into it. Your dad told me how you lost your mother but this hatred of Bull's... it feels like more. It runs deeper. What happened between them?"

"You have to ask Ry."

With a determined shake of her head, Sandy glared at him. "No, you don't get to put me off. I'm asking *you*. Ryan said there were things I needed to know, things he wanted to tell me. He would have told me tonight. That's what he was coming to my place to do. But we never got the chance to talk. So I'm asking his brother to help him out here."

Sean stared indecisively for a minute. Then he gave in. "Bull and his parents are convinced Ry killed Bull's brother, Mac. And I think — at least a little bit — Ry accepts the responsibility."

"No," she whispered in dismay. "What happened? Was there an accident?"

"We all called him Mac but his name was John, Johnny when he was younger. Somewhere along the way, Ry called him Mac and it stuck. Mac decided Mac MacKay sounded cool."

Sandy blinked in surprise. *Mac MacKay?*

"Copy you, 9-Bravo. Who am I speaking with?"

"Mick-" More static, then, *"Mic-key."*

Frowning, Sandy stared across the waiting room. The stark white walls, lined with pictures of the mountains, spun out of focus, replaced by a messy dispatch station, a notebook with messy handwriting.

She jotted the name into her notes. "Mickey, you're breaking up badly. How many do you number? How long have you been trapped?"

He hadn't corrected her. It was just a weird fluke that the name was so similar. Mick Mickey was just so close to Mac MacKay that her memory was playing tricks. Right? *Could* he have actually said "Mac MacKay?" The radio connection hadn't been great. She shook her head. No, that would be too much of a coincidence, wouldn't it? To end up in Mick's hometown? She *had* gone looking for his description of a place with plains and forest nearby. And what were the odds she would stumble onto another person in Wyoming with such a similar name who was also dead?

"Sandy?"

She forced her attention back on Sean. "Sorry, my mind was wandering."

"So I noticed." He sat still, his head angled, just looking at her. She shifted under his scrutiny, wondering if he had any idea how like his father he was.

Finally he picked up the story again.

Sandy's heart broke for the battered sixteen-year-old. And for the not-quite-man who'd tried to rescue his abused cousin, in the process turning his back on his family rather than involving them in something that would only bring on more MacKay wrath.

"How did Mac die? Why does Ryan feel responsible?"

"After they did a tour in the army, Ryan and Mac became firefighters," Sean said.

Sandy nodded as things began to fall into place and she blew out a relieved breath. *Not the same man.* "Right.

Walt Blackstone said Ryan fought oil fires." Sandy busied her hands by flipping through a magazine without looking at it.

"He did for a while, before Mac came of age and they joined the army together," Sean explained. "But this was after they left the army. They mustered out at Fort Irwin. Ended up in L.A."

Sandy's hands stilled in mid-flip. A chill started in her chest, rippled out to her arms, down into her belly.

"Apparently someone from their army unit got them into the training program for L.A. City Fire Department."

She shivered.

"You're pale. Are you okay?"

Drawing a deep breath to shore up her nerves, Sandy nodded and whispered, "Go on."

Sean stood and began pacing in the tiny, deserted room. "Mac's whole life, what Ry did, Mac did, too. My brother was his hero."

Sandy's heart squeezed just a little for Sean. Clearly Mac wasn't the only one who'd always looked up to Ryan. "But just because Mac decided to be a firefighter, too... that doesn't make his death Ryan's fault."

"They were partnered up," Sean explained.

Little pinpricks began to crawl along her skin like thousands of unseen insects. Setting the magazine down, she rubbed her arms, trying to dispel the feeling.

"Are you cold?"

"No," she said quickly. "How — how did Mac... die?"

"Earthquake," Sean answered. "You remember the big one in L.A. about seven years ago?"

"Oh, man. No..." She couldn't keep the shaky warble from her voice as the room began to spin. "I remember."

"They were clearing a building after a gas explosion when it collapsed. Mac died when— Whoa!"

Bones and muscles melted into a puddle, and Sandy slid off the chair. White and beige floor tiles rose up toward her face.

* * *

"That was a strong one," Mick said.

"A strong what?"

"Aftershock. Feel it? It's still moving."

Sandy looked around the room. Coworkers were manning the other boards. All was silent. And still.

"Aw, damn," whispered Mick. "'The course of true love never did run smooth.'"

Sandy instantly recognized Lysander's line from A Midsummer Night's Dream. *"It can,"* she insisted. *"It will, Mick!"* Tears welled.

"Angel... I'm sorry. I think — we could have had something good—"

Crashing and crunching sounds came over the comm, followed by a burst of static and then nothing. Not even the hiss of open air. The connection had been abruptly severed.

"No!" she shouted in frustration. Around her, other dispatchers stared openly. Two of them averted their stares, murmuring and shaking their heads.

Frantic, Sandy worked the buttons on the outdated radio system, trying to reestablish a connection, but the link remained silent.

"It's okay. His battery died, that's all," she told herself.

One by one, the clock ticked off the minutes of radio silence.

Sandy stared at her console, willing it to light up again. But when it did, it was just an outside call, and one of her coworkers picked it up.

"They got through!" someone shouted.

"They made contact," said Ellen at the next workstation. She listened to the report, one hand on the link in her ear. But as the happy grin on her face began to fade, dread gripped Sandy's heart.

Then the chaplain was at her side.

"No!" she exclaimed. *"Don't you say it. I was just talking to him. He was fine!"*

"They got through a few minutes ago," Chaplain Hindson said gently. *"I'm sorry. They were both gone when search and rescue got to them."*

Sandy closed her eyes against the burn of tears. He hadn't wanted her to cry. She stopped breathing, drowning in a tsunami-sized wave of pain. She'd known this was a possibility; worse, it had been the likely outcome. But she'd never given up hope. And now... she had no more hope to hold onto. Mick had no more hope. He was gone before she'd ever had a chance to really get to know him. Drawing a deep breath, she forced her eyes open.

"Thank you for letting me know." She forced the words through stiff lips as she checked her watch. The digital readout swam into focus: 7:21. Tears she refused to succumb to burned her eyes as she made a final notation in her log: Duration of contact 23:57:00.

Numb to everything, ignoring the stares and the whispers around her, she pushed past friends and strangers and stepped into the parking lot. Alone, she set loose the hot tears.

* * *

Sean's face, even paler than it had been earlier, hovered above her, his green eyes clouded with worry.

"You think you can sit up, girl?" Justin's gravely voice brought her to the present.

She tried to piece her revelation together. "Not Mick. It *was* Mac. Mac MacKay." She pulled in deep breaths of air, not interested in meeting the floor so up close and personal again. "Mac..." She tested the name on her tongue, finding it foreign after years of him being *Mick*.

"I'll go get help," said Sean.

"No!" she said sharply. She sat up, took Justin's hand and let him pull her to her feet. "I'm, um, I'm good. I, ah, need to tell you something."

Justin cupped her elbow and helped her back to her seat. She smiled and assured him she was fine.

"I was an EMT dispatcher for Central L.A. during that quake. We all did rotations on both sides of the job." She drew a shaky deep breath, blew it out. "I was the dispatcher who sent them — Ryan and Mac — into that mess. I... met

Mac right before he died. We were going to go out. I had —
feelings for him. I knew he was from Wyoming, but I didn't
know exactly where. But he's the reason I came here."

Sean's brow drew together. "You knew Mac?"

Sandy nodded, brushing at the tears burning her eyes.
"I didn't know he lived *here*. I didn't know exactly *where* he
lived. He talked about Wyoming a lot but in general terms.
He loved it here, missed it so much. I came here to see the
Red Desert because he mentioned the sunsets were
amazing."

Sean exchanged a puzzled look with his father before
turning his attention back to Sandy. "If you didn't know
where Mac was from, how did you end up here?"

"I stopped at Valentine's for some dinner. I was so
tired of driving around, knowing no matter where I went, I
wasn't going to find Mac. Tom had a help wanted sign behind
the bar and suddenly I just wanted to put down roots.
Orson's Folly seemed as close to anything Mac had described
as anything else." Sandy spread her hands, helpless to
explain why Orson's Folly had felt like coming home. She
picked at the hem of her dress, frowning at the rusty smear
across her lap that didn't quite blend with the fabric's
pattern. Ryan's blood. She brushed at it but it had long since
dried.

Sean crouched in front of Sandy, stilling her hands.
He searched her face, speaking softly. "Ry doesn't know, does
he? He doesn't know you were seeing Mac."

Sandy shook her head slowly, still feeling dazed. "I
don't see how he could. I didn't realize it myself until you told
me the story." She stared at the bloodstain. It would never
come out. She'd never be able to wear the dress again. Not
that she really wanted to.

Sean squeezed her hands. Releasing one, he reached
up and placed his thumb beneath her chin in a gesture so
like Ryan's that fresh tears welled. Gently he raised her face
to meet his eyes. "Hey, you okay?"

"It's mind-blowing... weird ...all the coincidences, the
connections. Suddenly everything feels very complicated."

"We'll all get through this, Sandy. You and Ryan love each other."

But doubt had become a constant companion recently, and once again it crept over her, invading her mind, dispatching reason into exile. Would they really get through it? Or would they end up each other's painful reminder of the past?

"Family of Ryan McGee?" A green-clad doctor with thinning gray hair and horn-rimmed glasses stood in the doorway.

When the three of them looked up, he closed the distance between them.

"Mr. McGee is stable. His injuries are severe but not life-threatening. He's a lucky man. He only *looks* like he was run over by a truck. He's more exhausted than anything else. He woke up for a few minutes but he was agitated, so we had to sedate him. He'll probably be out the rest of the night. You can all see him for a couple of minutes. Then you can take turns sitting with him, one person at a time. Maybe when the sedation wears off, he won't be as agitated if he sees a familiar face."

The doctor began to lead the way but hesitated in the doorway. "He kept — asking for chicory. We thought maybe he was experiencing expressive aphasia but he insisted he was saying what he meant to say. He wants someone to make sure the chicory is safe."

Tears broke free and streamed down Sandy's face. "That's me. He's talking about me."

* * *

Justin insisted Sandy sit with Ryan. "He asked for you. It's you who'll be able to ease his mind the most."

She couldn't let go of Ryan's hand. With it cradled in hers, she noted the faint bruises on his knuckles and the raw abrasions, which were already scabbing over. The tube had been removed once the bleeding from his nose had stopped choking him. Now his breathing was deep and even. His face was hard to look at. Even cleaned up, he still looked like he'd run headfirst into a wall. The stitched-up C-shaped laceration just below his left eye was going to leave a scar. His eyes were closed in deep, drug-induced sleep, but Sandy didn't think they would open very far even if he was awake.

He's alive.

"I know it'll be awhile before you can ride but I want to race across the plains with you. I want to go out at sunrise and get home just as the sun's going down." She had no idea what, if anything, he heard, but she kept talking. "I want to go camping in the mountains with you and stay in the cabin up there. I want to make love with you at night with all the stars above us."

His hand moved in hers. "Stay," he whispered weakly. Then he drifted off again.

She kept talking. Every so often he would surface from the darkness that gripped him. It never lasted longer than a moment. His words were slurred and thick, difficult to understand, but it was always the same plea to stay with him.

"I'm not going anywhere."

When he grew agitated, she gently rubbed the sensitive spot on his temple with her thumb. "I'll wait right here. I promise. I'll wait until you come back to me."

* * *

Hanging at the edge of consciousness, Ryan didn't want to wake up. He could listen to her talk forever. Her words painted the color into his dreams.

"I want to kiss the most beautiful girl in the world," he mumbled. His mouth was stiff; his tongue felt swollen. The words came with difficulty. "My girl. Stay with me. Don't go away, please. Please don't go again."

Her promise to stay with him sounded like it was coming from the other side of a wall as he sank into the blessed blackness again.

* * *

Ryan fought to resurface at the sound of the familiar voice. She was here. Promising to stay. With a mighty effort, he clawed and pushed his way out of the void. Frantic, he searched the room with eyes that didn't want to focus.

A figure sat next to the bed. She held his hand, stroking the pain away from sore knuckles, making assurances that she would stay with him; she would be there. With agonizing slowness, his vision cleared, the room brightened. Little flares of light seared along his optic nerves, each flash a hot needle stabbing into his eyes. As his vision began to normalize, the pain behind his eyeballs diminished. The room gradually whirled into focus. His eyes settled on the woman next to his bed.

"Hey, you," he croaked.

His brain finally kicked into first gear and he registered Sandy's face, Sandy's clear, amazing eyes looking at him with... love, he realized. Sandy was making promises and talking about the things she wanted them to do together.

Ryan tried to smile but his aching lips turned the action to another exercise in torture. It had been Sandy sitting with him, talking to him. If his head was a little disappointed, his heart was doing handstands with pure pleasure. His girl with the amazing eyes was waiting for him to wake up. He flexed the hand she held and she stopped talking.

"*You*... waited for me," he whispered. He tried to clear the hoarseness from his throat. It felt like he'd walked for days across the desert with no water. "My... Chicory. You didn't... disappear."

"I'll never leave you, Ryan McGee."

Relief bathed him in warmth. She was safe. She was there, not going anywhere.

"I'm sorry, Chicory. Sorry about... the fight at your place."

Exasperation heightened the color on her face. "You're an idiot. But you're my idiot. I won't tell the boss about the fighting. This time." She leaned over and gently kissed his cheek.

Tears shimmered in her eyes. Tears he wanted to wipe away, only he couldn't move his arms.

"You rest now."

Her warmth spread through him, Ryan tried to smile again, but the effort of keeping his eyes open was becoming too much. He gave in and let sleep overtake him.

Chapter Fifteen

Ryan forced his eyes open with a groan. It didn't hurt as much as the last time. Softness caressed his fingers and he shifted his gaze to find his hand fisted in Sandy's cloud of dark hair as it spilled around her face. How long had she slept in the chair next to his bed? Makeup streaked her face, reminding him a little of the way she had looked smeared with soot. How long ago? He had no idea how long he'd been under, but from the sore and stiff muscles when he struggled to move, maybe a long time.

Memories of another hospital awakening, followed by long months in rehab, intruded on his current reality. No one had waited for him then. No one had slept next to his bed and stroked his hand.

Sandy stirred and drew a deep breath. Rubbing the sleep from her eyes, she sat up, pushed her hair from her face. She arched her back and stretched like one of the barn cats, thrusting her breasts against the loose, filmy fabric of her dress.

For a few sensual moments, Ryan enjoyed the view. A profound sense of relief followed as a critical part of his anatomy stirred in response to the gorgeous picture of Sandy waking up.

"Hello, beautiful," he whispered. When she graced him with a slow, sizzling smile, he sighed. "What's a guy gotta do around here to get a beer from the pretty bartender?"

Tears filled her eyes but she blinked them back.

"Hey, this is a no-cry zone." Struggling to sit, he was dismayed to find himself knotted up in tubes and wires. He tugged on one. "What the hell?"

"Take it easy, cowboy." With a gentle touch on his hand, she stopped his movement and used the controller in the railing to raise the head of the bed. "One step at a time. You've been in and out all night and half a day."

Damn. He flexed his hands. "Concussion?"

She shook her head. "Exhaustion and sedation."

"Good. Then I can leave. I hate hospitals." He squinted up at her. She sure was a mess. Beautiful, but a mess. And she was shaking her head. "And I meant it about the beer."

Her smile looked less than understanding as she held up a Styrofoam cup filled with ice water. "How's your imagination?"

Ryan eyed the cup with distaste. "Not *that* good." But he reached for it anyway.

A long drink eased the dry sensation in his throat. When the nurse came to check on him, he insisted the tubes and wires be disconnected. Refusing to utilize any sort of bedside facility, he made a very shaky trip to the bathroom, thankfully getting there before he embarrassed himself all over the floor. As he washed his hands, he glanced up, startled by the battered man peering back at him from the mirror. Shaking his head, he took stock. Two black eyes, a row of Steri-Strips closing a crescent-shaped cut on his cheekbone, and a road rash along the right side of his jaw. "Holy hell, I look like a frickin' raccoon that got run over by a lawn mower."

He staggered sideways, barely managing to catch himself on the doorjamb. Yeah, that would make a great impression on the love of his life. As if having the shit kicked out of him by the town bully wasn't enough, wouldn't it just make his day if she found him sprawled out on the bathroom floor? Spent, he stumbled into the hospital room and crawled back into the bed.

A nurse approached with an injection, murmuring soothing words about taking away the pain.

"No." He waved her off. "It doesn't hurt. I'm just weak. How do I get out of here?"

"I'll call your doctor." The nurse tucked the blanket around him, checked his vital signs, and then hurried out.

Sandy stood at the window with her back to him, apparently extremely interested in something on the other side of the glass.

"Hey," he called softly. "Come back over here. I miss you."

When she approached, he caught traces of shadows in her eyes before she distracted him with an exaggeratedly sexy walk in his direction. Then she was close enough to touch, so he took her hand, laced his fingers through hers. "What's on your mind?"

"Not a thing now that you're back," she said a little too casually as she perched on the edge of his bed.

She kept staring over his right shoulder. Frustrated that she wouldn't look at him, he held on tight when she tried to extract her hand, refusing to release her until she met his stare. Then he almost wished he hadn't pushed things. Worry haunted her eyes but the rest of her face was constructed into a careful mask. She was hiding something.

"Don't." The word came out in a croak. "This is me, Sandy. Tell me what's wrong. Is it Dad? Sean?"

"No," she said quickly, glancing over her shoulder toward the door. "They're right outside. Do you want me to get them?"

Slowly he shook his head. "I want you to talk to me."

* * *

She wanted to put it off, preferably forever, but at least until he was further on the way to recovery, maybe even at home.

"Sandy." His voice was hoarse, but his tone was no-nonsense and his green eyes, even behind twin bruises, were compelling.

So it was going to be now. She tried to swallow but her mouth was suddenly bone dry. Something brushed her lips and she realized her hand hovered there. Was she hoping to push the truth back inside?

"Okay." Sandy straightened. She wouldn't insult him by trying to play down the impact of what she had to say. It would be best to just rip off the band-aid in one quick motion.

"I told you I fell in love very quickly once," she began.

A muscle working in his jaw was his only reaction.

"Nothing ever really happened. There wasn't time. But it was going to. At least I thought it would, and I'm pretty sure he felt the same way. He said he did, anyway." She paused, considering her next words. "I lived in L.A. at the time and he was a firefighter. Ry, he was your cousin, Mac."

* * *

Ryan stared, unable to believe what he'd just heard. Sandy continued to talk, explaining, rationalizing. He knew she was talking because her lips were moving, but everything past the bomb she'd dropped on him was just more blah-blah-blah. So Ryan said nothing, partly because he didn't know what he *could* say, and partly because the emotional sucker punch had rendered him without air in his lungs. Somewhere, some cosmic being had to be having a good belly laugh at his expense.

He forced himself to pay attention.

"I didn't know until I asked Sean why Bull hates you so much, and he told me why you left home in the first place and where you ended up."

"You're saying Mac is your twenty-three-hour man." He spoke with caution, keeping his emotions hidden until he could process what she was telling him.

"I didn't know, Ryan. I wouldn't have kept that from you." Her eyes begged for his understanding. "We danced around the subject some, you and I, but we never got around to really talking about where we were before we met."

He stared. He blinked. He searched for something to say. He had nothing. She was looking at him for reassurance when every good thing in his life had just been uprooted, like a delicate plant plucked from the ground that sustained it.

Every self-inflicted wound surrounding his decision to run off with Mac had been systematically reopened. But her revelation took it to an all new level. Chicory, part of the new beginning he thought he'd found, stolen from him by a past he couldn't seem to leave behind.

Fiery pain exploded in his heart.

He'd suspected Mac was seeing someone but he'd never met the girl. Sandy didn't seem at all like the type Mac usually went for. The thoughts continued to race through his mind, speeding up to the point where they no longer made sense. He wanted to ask what Sandy felt about her revelation, but he was afraid of what he was already reading on her face.

And damn it! Why did it have to feel like he'd been poaching on Mac's memory?

"Sandy..." He shook his head. What could he say? "I, uh, I don't think you were trying to keep anything from me." He rubbed at his tired eyes, wincing as sudden sharp pain reminded him of his raccoon eyes, bringing him to full awareness of where he was and why. Damn Bull and his big ugly fists. "I'm sorry... my mind's still fuzzy. Give me some time to absorb this, okay?"

She looked away but not before Ryan caught the spasm of pain. Then she took a deep breath. Her head lifted and she met his gaze again. "Okay." She stood, straightened, and walked to the door, where she cast a glance over her shoulder. "I understand. Take all the time you need, Ry." Then she was just gone.

Unbe-freaking-lievable. In the space of less than a week he'd finally walked away from his past only to have it chase him down and ruin his future. He flopped back against his pillow and shut his eyes, waiting for memories of Mac to surface. But it wasn't his cousin's voice he heard.

"Ryan, you can't control what happens to you, but you can always control your reactions."

"Mom!" He bolted upright, shooting glances around the room. Of course she wasn't there. She couldn't be. But those had been her words to him on more than one occasion. They must have stuck in his head, waiting for just the right time to surface.

Impeccable timing.

Could he have handled things any damn worse? What in God's good name was wrong with him? He didn't know exactly what he should feel about everything, but he didn't want her to leave.

"Sandy!" Ryan swung his shaky legs out of bed, cringing when his bare feet hit the frigid tile.

When the door swung inward, he sagged with relief. But it was his father's tall, lanky frame filling the doorway.

"Sean's takin' your lady home."

The room began a slow spin.

"Geez!" Justin rushed forward and caught Ryan around the shoulders before he went down. "Let's get you back into bed."

"No. Get me out of here!"

"Settle down!" His normally easy-going father pushed him back toward the bed. "If you keep this up, they're going to come in and sedate you again. Now, listen to me."

Ryan sat on the edge of the bed and held his hands up in surrender, taking a deep breath and forcing calm. "I screwed up. I promised I'd never want to leave her and then I just sat here like a jackass when she needed me to tell her everything's okay. There are things she needs to know — things I need her to understand, but I couldn't talk to her." Shit, he was twelve years old again, needing his father to help him make sense of life. Ryan met Justin's eyes. "I can't lose her, Dad. Please help me."

"No one's losing anyone, son." Justin laid a weathered hand on Ryan's shoulder and squeezed lightly. "Sandy flew in with you on the helicopter and never left your side. She told us you asked for some time and she's giving it to you. That's all. Sean's taking her home to get cleaned up is all. She'll be here when you get yourself together."

"I am together, Dad. Maybe more than I've been for years. I was surprised by what she told me. But I—" He drew a deep breath and finished in a whisper. "Sandy's it for me."

Justin smiled. He squeezed again and warmth radiated from his touch directly to Ryan's heart. His dad got it. Sixteen years of lost time formed a knot of emotion in Ryan's throat. "I love you, Dad."

When Justin's arms closed tightly around him, another lock snicked open in Ryan's heart. The last time he'd felt his father's hug, he'd been almost seventeen and nursing a broken heart over Jenny Valentine's engagement to a boy she'd met at college. Sean had been right. Justin hadn't been the one to set up the emotional barriers. With jerky movements, Ryan returned the hug.

"Son, she's not going anywhere, I promise."

The words slammed into Ryan like a truck. From out of nowhere, tremors rocked him. His breathing simply stopped. Ryan was on the edge of mental instability and he knew it, but he had no idea how to keep himself from plunging into the dark abyss. Once before, someone had helped him cling to life when hope had seemed lost.

As if sensing Ryan's deep need, Justin held on tighter. "What is it, boy?"

He felt like he was being strangled. "I've heard it before. Heard the promises. She didn't mean it and it hurt like fire, Dad."

Justin stepped back with a frown, confusion clouding his eyes. "Who didn't mean it? Sandy?"

Ryan shook his head. "It was in L.A., when Mac died."

His father sat on the bed next to him, and Ryan began to talk about his search for an angel.

* * *

In mid-afternoon light, Valentine's looked like it always had — friendly, welcoming, and solid. It had been her anchor since she'd first started tending bar for Tom

Valentine. Sandy had cemented her place in the community when Tom had retired and sold the place to her. And if Ryan didn't call? Couldn't get past his feelings about Mac? She'd have to leave, Sandy realized as another wave of dread chilled her. If he couldn't accept her past, and she stayed, Ryan might leave his home and family again because of her. She wouldn't let that happen.

"Hey. It'll be okay," said Sean as he stopped the truck. "I told you, Ryan's adaptable."

"I keep seeing the look on his face." Sandy's tears threatened again. "He felt betrayed."

"You got it backwards, Sandy. He's been gone a long time but he hasn't changed much." Sean switched off the ignition and twisted to face her. "I'm guessing he feels like he betrayed Mac by falling for his girl."

She rubbed her aching head. "But he has no reason to feel like that."

"He'll figure things out." Sean's lips curled into a one-sided smile. "And if he doesn't, I'm pretty sure Dad'll help him reach the right conclusions."

"I love your father." Sandy stopped fighting the tears.

"He loves you, too. We both do." He touched the top of her hand. "Should I walk you up?"

She shook her head. "No, DC said Bull's bail was denied. There's no more threat. But Mel's here in the bar if you want to stop in and see her."

A slow smile tugged at his mouth and he shrugged a little sheepishly. "Naw, not just yet. I'll stop back later."

It was so cute, the way his accent thickened with his emotions. The same way his brother's did.

As she slid from the truck, her cell phone fell from her lap and hit the pavement. "Damn it. I've broken more phones by dropping them." She picked it up and activated the screen to make sure it still worked. The little green happy face icon indicated she had voicemail. "Someone must have called while we were in the mountains." She punched in the number to retrieve the message and listened.

"Hey, Chicory, I'm getting out of here tomorrow. So get lots of rest tonight and wear something sexy when you come get me, because I plan to get very physical with you as soon as I see you." He waited a beat before he added softly, in his exaggerated Wyoming drawl, "And sweetheart, don't do too much thinking — unless it's about all the ways I'm going to be lovin' you."

Delight rolled over her like a tidal wave. "He wants me to wear something sexy when I pick him up tomorrow."

"Told ya." With a wink, Sean started the truck and then drove off in a cloud of dust.

She watched after him for a moment then started toward the bar. Ryan's blue Corvette sat where he must have parked it the night before, looking a little forlorn. Someone had shown the decency of having the gravel parking lot sprayed down, leaving no visible traces of blood. A stray piece of crime tape clung to one of the bushes lining the walk to the door. Fluttering on the gentle summer breeze, it reminded her of how easily Ryan could have died. Anger, fright, and sorrow blended into one intense amalgamation of emotion, and Sandy snatched at the bit of yellow, crumpling it into a ball.

Her thoughts drifted to the night before, her imagination filling in the gaps. Ryan, a little irritated because she'd ditched him earlier, plotting how he'd make her pay, walking toward the door with his cocky half-grin, tossing his keys in the air and catching them over-handed the way he did when he was feeling frisky. Bull approaching unseen, belligerent, making nasty comments, throwing punches. Ryan fighting back, probably making some comments of his own. Getting overpowered. Ryan down. Bull not stopping. Ryan helpless.

Her breath caught in a sob as memory kicked in. Ryan cradled in Sean's arms, unconscious, blood gurgling. So much blood, his face so pale in the bar's exterior lighting.

She felt a touch on the arm and screamed.

"Sorry!" The woman jumped back a split second before Sandy recognized her.

"Brenda." Sandy slowly let out her breath. Blood rushed in her ears but after a couple of deep breaths, her heart slowed to nearly normal. "I didn't see you."

"You looked like you were thinking kind of deep," said Bull's wife, the kindness in her tone overshadowed by the trouble in her eyes.

Sandy appraised her, the woman who had married Bull just after her sixteenth birthday and borne him a son well before her seventeenth. The ensuing years hadn't been remotely kind to Brenda. According to Sandy's math, she and Brenda were roughly the same age, but the other woman looked at least a decade older.

She had probably been pretty once, with her ash brown hair, pale blue eyes, and heart-shaped face. Now she only looked defeated and tired. Used up. Mousy hair was pulled back tightly from her plump face. She wore absolutely no makeup on her pale skin, emphasizing the dark circles beneath her red-rimmed eyes.

Her formless floral print dress, with the prim collar, looked like it had come from a 1930s version of *Prairie Wife* magazine. The dress hung loosely, even with Brenda's plump frame, and hit her legs mid-calf. It had to be eighty degrees out but she was wearing a faded denim jacket. On her feet she wore what Sandy's grandmother had always called "sturdy shoes," black Oxfords with rubber soles.

The woman could use a little fashion advice from her always smartly-dressed mother-in-law.

"Sorry, yeah." Sandy answered slowly, aware she had been silently staring. "A lot's happened in the last few days."

Brenda looked at the ground. "I came to ask you to talk to Ryan McGee, to see if he'll consider dropping the charges. I heard how he's gonna be okay and all."

Sandy simply stared at the other woman, unable to believe what she was asking or that she had the guts to ask it. Any sympathy she'd mustered for Brenda began to fade. "Your husband beat Ryan so badly he had to be taken to the hospital in a helicopter. He's only just regained consciousness and part of the time we weren't sure he'd make it."

"I'm aware of that," said Brenda. She drew circles in the gravel with her toe. "If it's about the cost and all, I know Bull's folks'll pay the bills."

"Pay the bills." Sandy tried to stem her outrage. Adding a cat fight to what had already gone down in her parking lot wouldn't help the situation any. "Y'all think they can just pay the bills and everything Bull did just goes away?"

Brenda flinched at the bite in Sandy's words. But she didn't back down. She chewed her lip as, for the first time, she met Sandy's gaze. "Thing is, I need Bull to come home. My boy needs him home."

"Ricky told DC he saw the whole assault, saw his father provoke the fight." Sandy shook her head. "Why aren't you afraid for how Bull's going to react? For what he might do to your son?"

Tears filled Brenda's eyes. "I thought you'd feel that way. But it's not like you think. It's not like anybody thinks." Shoulders slumped and head down, she shuffled toward her car.

No one should look that pathetic and downtrodden. *I'm going to regret this.* But human decency gave her a nudge. "Wait!" Sandy caught up in three strides and reached out to stop Brenda.

The sleeve of the denim jacket pulled up and exposed angry reddened skin over a good portion of Brenda's forearm, but she yanked the sleeve back into place before Sandy got a good look.

A chill rippled through her gut. "Oh, you're hurt. What happened?"

Brenda tugged on the sleeve. "It — it's nothing. I spilled some hot water yesterday."

Sandy hesitated. It was a reasonable explanation. But why was Brenda so nervous about it, so determined to hide her arm? "If it's not like anybody thinks, Brenda, then how is it? Does Bull *hurt* you?"

"Bull keeps us safe," whispered Brenda. "I have to go."

With a sigh, Sandy relented. "Okay, I'll give Ryan your message, but I'm not promising anything."

She watched as the dejected woman walked heavily back to Bull's tan pickup, and found her outrage had been replaced by sympathy. It was no secret Bull largely ignored his wife. Could he be abusing her? Why on earth would she want to stay with him?

* * *

Showered, dressed in her more typical attire of jeans and tank top, Sandy stood at her usual place behind the bar. It felt almost as though the past couple of days hadn't happened.

Except they had. And now she was left with an inexplicable feeling that Fickle Fate had never stopped toying with her.

"Do you think that spot might be clean enough? You've been wiping it for ten minutes." Mel set a plate of chicken fingers and sweet potato fries in front of Sandy. "Eat something."

Sandy glanced at the rag in her hand and tossed it aside. Frowning, she picked up a fry and twirled it between her fingers until Mel pushed her hand toward her mouth.

"Sean told me more about the bad blood between the MacKays and the McGees. Sounds like one of those clichéd family feuds."

Mel rolled her eyes. "Not so clichéd, really." She began stacking cocktail napkins. "Not many people know the details. Mostly they keep it close between them."

"Because it was a long time ago?" Sandy shot Mel a pointed look. "Or because Ricky is Mac's son?"

Melanie's hands stopped moving. "Did someone tell you that?"

Sandy popped a chicken finger into her mouth and chewed thoughtfully. "After the fight, Ricky told DC that Bull wasn't his father. At first I thought he was just mad and disowning Bull. But other things I've heard are beginning to add up." She pulled a bottle of water from the refrigerator under the counter and cracked the top. "And Ricky doesn't really look like either one of his parents."

"No one's ever said for sure," Mel admitted. "But everyone kind of accepts that's how it is. He looks just like Mac."

That explained Ryan's reaction when he'd first seen the boy at the baseball field. But what had Brenda meant about things not being the way most people thought?

"Has Sean ever told you what brought Ryan home?"

Mel pushed a hand through her hair. "Sean said he wrote a letter asking him to come back for a couple of weeks. He didn't say why, but I think it might have something to do with the thing at the high pasture."

Sandy picked up another fry. "They aren't using the high pasture."

"Well, no, not now they aren't." Mel began sorting through the stack of menus at the end of the bar, clipping in an insert outlining the Wednesday specials. "About a hundred head of cattle were picked off with a hunting rifle this past spring." She frowned. "Sean doesn't want it to be common knowledge. He's been trying to play it down because he's afraid he'll lose his boarders."

Sandy caught her breath. "The calf we found. Ryan said the mother was injured but he never did say how, just that he had to finish her off. Afterwards, he was... well, different."

The trouble had started before Ryan came home. A chill ran the length of Sandy's spine. Had he been lured home with trouble at the ranch? Had Bull planned to hurt Ryan all along?

The door opened and Ricky MacKay hesitated on the threshold, scanning the room. When he made eye contact with Sandy, he sucked in a deep breath and walked toward her with an air of determination in his steps.

"Miz Sandy." His soft voice was guarded and polite. "Do you have any work for me?"

Oh, crap, this could get thorny.

"It just keeps hitting the fan, doesn't it?" Mel murmured for Sandy's ears only.

"Ricky, I'm not really sure your parents—"

"Please, Miz Sandy. I need work real bad. I'll do anything."

He was just a boy, a teenager. She doubted he had anything to do with slaughtering cattle. He'd helped extinguish the fire. He had told the truth about the fight. It had also taken a lot of courage to ask her for work. But thoughts of her encounter with his mother made her wary.

"Why are you asking me?"

He looked down, shuffled his feet. "I like you. You're always nice to me."

"So this doesn't have anything to do with your father?"

Ricky stiffened. His head snapped up. "I don't have a father." He swallowed convulsively then whispered, "I'm a—I'm a bastard."

Sandy recoiled, feeling like she'd just been sucker-punched. Bastard. The word echoed through her head. Did anyone even use the term any more? *He's probably Mac's son.* She hadn't been able to help Mac. Maybe she could do some small thing for his son.

"I can't formally hire you on." His face fell, and she held up a hand. "But I do need the floors mopped. Can you get it done before five o'clock?"

Ricky nodded eagerly.

"Come on, I'll show you where we keep the mops and buckets. You can hang your jacket in the back."

What was it with the MacKay family and jackets in eighty-degree weather?

Sandy met Ricky on his way into the main area with the buckets and mops. He quickly stepped off to the side, angling himself awkwardly away from her, cursing under his breath.

But he hadn't moved fast enough to hide the fresh blisters on his arm.

"Ricky, what happened?"

Sandy took the buckets from his hands and set them down. She held out her hand. Hesitantly he extended his arm. She ran her fingers around the painful-looking sores, and her rage stirred again.

The teenager said nothing, just stood still, looking at the wall.

"Did you get burned fighting the fire at the ranch?" she asked with gentleness she wasn't feeling.

It was impossible to miss the look of intense relief on Ricky's heavily freckled face. "Yeah, some sparks got me is all."

"We have some burn salve in the first aid kit. You go on in the kitchen and ask Mrs. Charlie to help you with this before you start on the floors."

As he shambled through the swinging doors, Sandy took the buckets out to the main floor. Everything she'd learned in the past week about the MacKay family boiled through her brain, none of it lining up with the image they presented about town. Maybe it was time to go to the source. At least one of them. She pulled out her cell phone and punched in Sean's number.

"I know you just left, but I really need your help. I just hired Ricky for a casual job and I need to run an errand. I'm not comfortable leaving Mel and Charlie here on their own."

"I'll leave right now."

* * *

The keys in Penny Sherwood's hand jangled as she ushered Sandy into the holding area. "The trooper can let you out when you're finished."

"Thanks," murmured Sandy, looking around. *What the hell?*

Surely she had stumbled into another Orson's Folly time warp or maybe the set of the same Old West movie that had generated the cabin in the mountains. Apparently the quaint western Wyoming town hadn't quite made it all the way into the twenty-first century. A state trooper sat in a gray metal folding chair at a gray metal desk in a corner of the dimly lit room. Dull gray walls seemed to push inward. Either someone had an affinity for the color gray or they'd scored a good deal at the paint store.

Come on, even prisoners ought to have a little color in their lives.

The trooper looked up from the local newspaper he was reading when the door behind Sandy whooshed shut. With a smile, he set the paper aside and stood, politely offering the chair. She declined with a wave and he resettled himself behind the sports page.

Bull sat on the edge of a narrow cot behind the heavy gray bars in the only cell. His orange jumpsuit — ah, a bit of color — left him resembling a crumpled Halloween decoration.

"Come to see me off before they transfer me up to Jackson?" At one time, the hard stare he directed at her would have struck a chord of fear, but not so much at the moment. "I got nothing to say to you, Sandy. On the advice of my lawyer." But he stood and limped toward the bars.

She studied him in silence, the man who would have killed Ryan. Dirty dark brown hair looked like he'd been running his fingers through it. A row of surgical strips closed a cut on his chin. Two black eyes flanked an obviously broken nose that was swollen and red with more strips across the bridge. At least Ryan had gotten in a few good hits.

"I'm not here about Ryan," she said, stepping forward. "You know, you and I always had an understanding. When you aren't drunk, you're actually not unlikable."

Bull snorted and rolled his eyes. The stiffness in his shoulders eased until he was slouching. For a split second, Sandy thought she caught a tinge of regret in the big man's eyes before his expression became wary.

"I know I've done some things that weren't right. I shouldn't have come by your place Sunday when I was drunk."

"No, you shouldn't have come by at all. You have a wife... and a son you love at home."

Bull's head snapped up. A distinct flicker of pain entered his eyes, but he said nothing.

"Bull, I've heard the rumors. I know what people think about Ricky and you. But I know you love him. He may or may not really be your nephew, but he's your son in every way it counts."

He moved stiffly back to his cot, lowering himself onto it with a grunt. He sat staring at his hands, clasped between his knees. They were swollen and abraded. Did the sight bring back memories of pounding them into Ryan? Sandy didn't even bother to stem her satisfaction at his injuries or the obvious physical and emotional pain. He deserved it and more.

But she hadn't come to gloat.

"Brenda came to see me at Valentine's this afternoon."

Bull tensed then drew several deliberate breaths. His lips drew into a thin line, as if holding in words he'd rather not say.

"She told me she and Ricky need you at home."

Bull lifted a shoulder and let it fall. "And *you're* gonna tell me I should have thought of that before I beat the shit out of your man."

"Nope. I don't have to. You just told yourself." Sandy shook her head. "Bull, she said things aren't like most people think, and she said you protect her and Ricky somehow."

He shrugged again and sniffed. "She don't know what she's talking about. She ain't always right in the head. Fact is, living with me's been bad for her. She and the boy should go home to her folks."

His reaction didn't come close to what she'd been expecting. Maybe a different tack was in order, given his obvious apathy regarding Brenda.

"Not long after Brenda's visit, Ricky showed up looking for work. I hired him for the day to clean my floors." Sandy raised an eyebrow. "Do you have any problem with that?"

Staring at the floor, Bull drew a deep breath, blew it out. "No," he said in a low voice. "No, that's not a problem for me. You always did fair by him."

So, he does care about the boy.

"He has burns on his left arm. Fresh ones. He wants me to think he got them fighting the fire at the McGee ranch."

Tension showed once more in his shoulders and neck, but he said nothing, didn't even look up.

Ugh! She hated the feeling of pulling teeth. But she pressed on. "Thing is, when I saw Brenda today, she had burns on her arms, too, only not as fresh. And she wasn't fighting the fire at Ryan's place. Bull, Ricky's also got *old* burn scars. The kind a person might get from the end of a cigarette."

A muscle worked in his jaw and he clamped his mouth shut. For a moment Sandy was certain he was just going to close down and shut her out. He pushed to his feet, rose to his full height without slumping, and stood with his damaged fists clenched.

"How fresh?" he demanded, his words strangled. For the first time since she had entered the jail, he met her gaze directly.

She wasn't prepared to feel sympathy for the deep suffering reflected in his eyes. But there it was. Where in heaven's name had *that* come from?

Sandy held his attention as she spoke, making sure to keep her voice level. "Hours old. I didn't see much of Brenda's arm because she's hiding it. She said she spilled some hot water. But Ricky's looked really fresh, at least six of them."

"Do you know where my mother was when Brenda was talking to you?"

"Alice?" Frowning, Sandy shook her head. "Brenda didn't say. Why?"

Bull's fingers worked agitatedly, flexing and releasing. "I need to talk to DC."

"Bull, what is it? Does Brenda hurt Ricky?" Sandy paused, watching him closely for his reaction. "Or does your father hurt them both?"

Bull jerked upright. "I need to talk to DC." Shaking his head, he clamped his mouth shut. He was done talking.

"Okay. I'll ask Gloria to call him for you." Sandy walked away from the bars and waited for the state trooper to let her out of the confinement area.

"Sandy," Bull called out as the trooper inserted his key in the lock. His next words seemed to be ripped from his mouth. "Brenda's right. It's not like everyone thinks. And Ricky... he's *not* my nephew." He watched her face closely. "He's not my son, either. But I do love him like he was my own. And if Mac would 'ave known about him, he wouldn't have stayed with McGee."

He turned away just as the trooper opened the door. She hesitated but then sighed and stepped through the opening. She wouldn't get any more from Bull, and what she'd gotten had only managed to raise more questions.

Chapter Sixteen

Some detective she was! She pulled Justin's truck into her parking spot behind Valentine's and shut it down, convinced she'd just wasted an hour of her life. Not only had she not discovered anything new, she'd added to her list of questions. And she couldn't shake the feeling that she'd just stirred a pot of some kind. Hopefully nothing too stinky.

She slid from the cab, thinking about Bull's last statement. If Mac had known about Ricky, he wouldn't have stayed with Ryan? Was he implying Ryan was somehow responsible for Ricky? That made no sense. Ryan wouldn't have done anything with Mac's girl. It just wasn't in him.

But what could Bull have meant, then? She slipped through the kitchen with a wave for Charlie, and found Mel on the floor, delivering a meal to an older couple sitting near the door.

With a light laugh, Mel left her customers to their food and carried the tray back to the bar. "Ricky's a hard worker," she said with a nod toward the jukebox where he lingered, trying — and failing — to look as though he wasn't watching them. Mel slid the empty serving tray onto the stack behind the bar. "He finished the floors and cleaned the men's bathroom, too. Seems like a good kid."

Sandy motioned for the teenager to join them. "Would you be interested in working dinners doing light food prep? Mrs. Charlie could use help in the kitchen three days a week, Thursdays, Fridays, and Saturdays, maybe three hours a day. We're closed on Sundays. But you can pick up extra shifts cleaning on Wednesdays if you want."

Mel's eyebrows shot up.

Ricky's eyes widened in surprise. A hopeful grin splashed across his face. "Are you giving me a job?"

Sandy nodded, smiling. "Looks like. How old are you?"

"Going on sixteen."

So still only fifteen. "Okay, we can work with that. You aren't allowed behind the bar or in the liquor storeroom for any reason. You can't even move a hand truck with anything alcoholic on it or stack cases of anything alcoholic. I don't even want you to look sideways at anything with alcohol in it, and you can't bus tables if there's been drinking. I'll lose my liquor license if you don't follow those rules."

Ricky's blue eyes widened, taking over his pale freckled face. His voice shook with what might be hope. "You trust me?"

Something twisted in Sandy's heart, and she knew she was doing the right thing. "I do, Ricky. I know you won't let me down. I'm only paying minimum wage to start but if you prove yourself, I'll bump you up by a dollar in six weeks. When you go back to school, we can adjust your hours any way you need to."

Ricky looked at the floor. "I was... I wasn't going to go back to school."

Sandy shook her head briskly. "No, that's a deal breaker. If you don't stay in school, you can't work past the end of summer."

Ricky's head popped up. His hands balled into fists but he slowly relaxed them. Emotions worked on his face, astonishment battling with fear.

"I'm not going to give you the school-is-important lecture." She smiled, aware she had his attention even though he wouldn't look directly at her. "But it is. If there's a reason you can't go back, I want you to come talk to me about it by next week. Otherwise, when school starts, if you stay in school, you can keep your job and I'll give you an extra fifty cents an hour."

Mel choked on something but Sandy ignored her, keeping her eyes on Ricky while he fought his inner battle.

He swallowed hard. Finally he looked at her and nodded. "Okay."

"Good." She held out her hand.

With a slight hesitation, Ricky took it and the deal was sealed.

"We need to get one of your parents to sign a work permit, since we serve alcohol here," said Sandy. "I can talk to your mom if you want."

The cautious optimism drained from his face. "She won't do it."

The front door opened and DC was momentarily silhouetted against the late afternoon light filtering from outside. Sandy watched him search the room and wondered if he was about to let her have it for her visit to Bull.

"I'll talk to your mom, Ricky. I'll convince her." Sandy laid a hand on his good arm. His flinch when she touched him cut her emotions to ribbons. "Excuse me, I need to talk to DC."

"Hello, Sandy," said DC. "How's Ryan?"

"He's a little sore but better. I'm picking him up early tomorrow morning."

"I hear you dropped by the jail for a visit today."

"I'm sorry you weren't there, DC. I didn't go to harass Bull. I just needed to ask him something."

DC negated her need to apologize with an easy wave of his hand. "It's okay. The man's allowed visitors and he agreed to see you. But he had some things to say to me after you left, and now I need to speak to the boy."

"Brenda was here this morning." Quickly she related the incident, describing her brief glimpse of the burn on the woman's arm. "DC... the other day I bumped into Alice MacKay at the drug store. She dropped some of her purchases and I helped her pick them up. She had a carton of Reds and a six-pack of Black Mountain."

He snorted. "You think old Alice MacKay is out starting fires in hay fields? Or whizzing on your truck and slashing tires?" DC shook his head. "Lots of folks smoke those cigarettes and drink that beer, Sandy. And in case you don't remember, whizzing wasn't the only thing done on your truck."

Sandy leveled an unblinking stare at the sheriff. His eyes sparked with recognition. The brand names meant something to him. "Just telling you what I saw," she said coolly. "Alice said the Reds were for Brenda."

DC nodded and sighed heavily. "I'm sorry, Sandy. Things are edgy here. Thanks for letting me know. I'll add it into my notes. Right now, Bull asked me to look in on his wife and boy, and that's what I'm doing."

* * *

For the first time in her life, when Sandy's morning alarm went off, she was already out of bed and in the shower. She agonized in front of her closet. Wear something sexy, he'd said. But sexy what? Practical and sexy or feminine and sexy?

"Oh, screw practical." She pulled out one of her sexiest dresses. Sliding it over her head, she shimmied to adjust the fit, then regarded herself critically in the full-length mirror. The dress was outrageously short. Sheer black material splashed with tiny red and tan flowers lay over a black satin slip. A peasant style neckline connected to ballooning sleeves that started off the shoulder and fell to her wrists. The fabric was loose but clingy in all the right places and Sandy did a happy dance, watching in the mirror as the fabric swished and swirled around her bare thighs. She was already picturing the gleam Ryan would have in his eyes when he saw her.

After fastening an elaborate braid of shiny red beads around her neck, she slid on a matching bracelet. Her hair she pulled into a messy, loose ponytail and secured with a filmy red scarf, the style Ryan seemed to have so much fun undoing. Next she added subtle makeup. Finally she slipped into her favorite red Western boots.

She twirled in front of her full-length mirror, happy with the result.

"Girlfriend, you are quite the trollop," she said to her reflection. Her appearance sent a definite message of her sensual intent, and Sandy hoped Ryan was up to the things he'd promised in his phone message. If he wasn't, she certainly could improvise. She smiled and her heart tripped in happy anticipation. He'd obviously made peace with her revelation about Mac.

The soft knock on her door bumped Sandy's pulse up a notch, and she took a moment to settle her nerves. Bull was in jail. She was safe. Still, she peeked through the window. When she saw Mel's cap of pale hair, her muscles sagged in relief.

"Hey, I left my storeroom keys at home — whoa!" Mel stared. "That's hot! Are you sure you want to risk giving your man a heart attack? He is just getting out of the hospital."

"And I intend to bring him all the way to a full recovery." Sandy grabbed a set of keys from a hook near the door and tossed them to Mel. "Thanks for waiting on the deliveries."

With a laugh, Mel dragged Sandy toward the door. "Go get him. And by all means, do everything I wouldn't do." She grinned. "Just be ready to tell me all about it."

Excitement sent out tiny ripples as she climbed into the truck. The sun had already begun to heat the air, but the days of oppressive heat were still a month off. Sandy opened the windows in the cab, thrilled by the wind whipping through her hair. It was almost as good as riding across the plain on Domingo's back.

She cranked the radio up and sang along with the variety of popular country artists as the red pickup began to eat up the miles to Jackson. Too bad she hadn't driven Ryan's hot little sports car. That machine probably took these mountain curves without slowing down.

She saw the white truck as she rounded another curve, parked not quite far enough off the road to be safe. Pulling in front of the disabled truck, Sandy stopped and jumped to the ground.

The door to the other truck pushed open and Alice MacKay hopped out, a look of profound relief on her face.

Sandy groaned inwardly, almost wishing she hadn't stopped. Alice had always been a bit distant and lately was even more so. Still, it wouldn't be right to just leave the older woman on the side of the road.

She pushed what she hoped was a friendly smile onto her face. "Alice, what are you doing all the way up here?"

"Oh, thank God!" Alice wrung her hands and started babbling out her explanation. "I've been stuck up here for over an hour and you're the first person I've seen. Brenda had one of her spells last night, and we used near all her medicine keeping her calm. I left Brody watching her so I could go to the nervous hospital and get her prescription. But then I got this far and the truck just died. I can't think what might be wrong with it."

"Did you try looking under the hood?"

"Oh, I know absolutely nothing about engines. I wouldn't even know what I'm looking at."

Sandy made a face. "I probably wouldn't, either. Have you tried starting it again?"

"Not for the last fifteen minutes or so." Alice smiled. "The engine just turns and turns and turns. Brody's going to kill me."

Sandy felt a twinge of apprehension at Alice's words. She didn't doubt Brody would be capable of killing. She thought of him at home with Brenda, and the twinge of apprehension turned into a winter-cold blast of fear. She shook it off. DC knew something was going on. Surely Brody wouldn't hurt Brenda. Still, it would probably be best to help Alice get back home, just in case.

"Oh, I'm sure it'll be okay. It's not like you broke down on purpose. Here, let me give it a try. Maybe I'll have better luck."

But the engine only spun without catching, just as Alice had described. Sandy went back to Justin's truck and retrieved her cell phone from her purse.

"Hmm, no service." She changed position, held the phone up over her head squinting at it.

"I've walked all around this place, even walked back down a ways," said Alice. "I don't have service, either."

Sandy checked her watch and sighed. She was going to be late, but what could she do? "I'll take you back to Walt's. He can send out a tow truck."

"Oh, no." Alice shook her head in protest, but she looked apprehensively around the deserted stretch of road. "I can see you're on your way someplace. Just leave me here and as soon as you have service, you can call my husband for me."

"Alice, don't be silly. I can't just leave you here. It's almost an hour to Jackson."

Alice sighed heavily, her face troubled. Then she brightened. "Brody has a cousin who lives just a ways further up. Could you take me to his place? It's about a mile off the main road."

Sandy smiled. Driving one mile out of the way beat the heck out of twenty. "Do you think he'll be home?"

"It won't matter. I have a key so I'll be able to use his landline to call for help."

"Okay." Sandy motioned to Justin's truck.

Alice reached into the white truck and came out with an oversized purse. Offering a weak smile, she joined Sandy.

"It's kind of hard to spot," said Alice about a mile and a half later as she peered intently at the side of the road. "There it is!" She pointed to a narrow track.

Sandy turned left onto the tiny trail, wincing as branches scraped along the side of the truck. *I wonder what a new paint job costs.* "Are you sure this is it? It doesn't look like anyone's been along here for a long time."

"Braden likes his privacy. He's a little standoffish."

That would explain why she'd never heard of Brody Senior's cousin. Maybe. Why would anyone want to be so disconnected from humanity?

The trail narrowed. If that kept up, she'd never get the truck turned around to get out. According to the odometer, they were a little over a mile in. As it was, she'd probably have to back up half of that before she could turn. She slowed the truck to a crawl.

"I don't know, Alice. It's getting tight through here."

"Just a little farther now."

The track had become next to nonexistent. Light spilled through a break in the trees up ahead, so Sandy aimed for that. Loose sand sucked at the tires, sending them into a sideways slide. She struggled with the wheel and played with the accelerator. If they stopped, the sand would swallow the wheels. Maybe even the truck.

They burst out of the woods amid more scratching branches. About twenty feet ahead, blue sky loomed — and nothing else. Sandy jammed her foot on the brake, stalling the truck's engine but coming to a stop in a spray of shale only a few feet away from the edge of a cliff.

She took a deep breath and blew it out. Leaning forward over the dashboard, she chuckled nervously. "Okay, that was definitely a wrong turn, Alice."

"No, it was the correct turn."

Sandy angled a glance toward her passenger, smiling. "Are you sure? It must have been—"

The long barrel of a very large revolver was leveled directly at her chest.

Her smile deserted her as chills settled low in her belly.

Alice MacKay's mildly anxious countenance had been replaced with grim determination. Emerald eyes, cold and calculating, watched her. They were the eyes of someone who had nothing left to lose.

"I'm sorry, Sandy, I really am." Alice apologized as though expressing regret over missing a social engagement. "But you're about to have a terrible accident, and I'm afraid you won't survive."

"Alice... what are you doing?"

"You've just become too big a liability. I overlooked it when you helped the McGees with starting their horse boarding business. That wasn't going to save their ranch. But you shouldn't have started going about with Ryan McGee. That just got you more attention than was good for you." Her gun hand jerked with her agitated speech. "Oh, I know you talked to DC about your concerns for Ricky and my daughter-in-law. But I've been putting people off that trail for years." Drawing a deep breath, Alice seemed to calm herself. She shrugged and added in a considering tone, "Now I'm thinking that losing you will devastate Ryan. He'll probably drive that fancy car of his over this same cliff in his grief. That's even better than shooting him."

Sandy struggled to breathe against the dread filling her. She frowned, unable to follow all of Alice's disjointed rambling. "Alice, are you and Brody responsible for the incidents at the Cross MC?"

"You like those? Some of them were pretty creative." A serene smile curved Alice's mouth. "Brody... he didn't think any of it would work."

"But why? Were you trying to get Ryan to come home?"

Alice's face clouded and the barrel of the gun dipped slightly. "It was Sean I wanted to kill. I almost had him when he was up there moving the herd off the range. He had to come up with fancy plans to expand their ranch. I figured with Sean dead and Ryan still gone, old Justin would never follow through. If the McGee ranch goes under or near enough, they'll sell that range land along the Green River. Got a buyer all lined up for MacKay land up there, but they aren't interested unless they can get all of it or at least the mineral rights. Sean McGee flat out refused to sell to them so they stopped the deal."

"You want to kill Sean over a land deal?" That *was* straight out of a Western movie. Sandy forced herself to breathe slow and easy. "What's up there that makes it so appealing? It's almost impossible to get to."

"Coal," snapped Alice. "Green River's got a rich vein but not many folks around here want a mine in their back yard."

"The McGees will never sell." Sandy remembered the sheer love for the land she'd seen on Ryan's face.

"Justin will, once he's got no more sons to leave the great McGee legacy to," said Alice coldly. She shook her head. "Those McGees. Always in our way. Always acting like they're better than everyone else in the county. I'm glad it's them I had to deal with. Means I can finish what I started years ago. I was going to kill one son. Now I can get them both. I really didn't think Ryan would ever come back here. But then he did and right away he took up with you." She brightened. "Now that he's here, I won't have to worry about him showing up later. I wanted to get you together but my son had to go off on him." Her teeth flashed in a cunning smile. "He did good that night, though, even if it was too soon. If people would have just minded their own damn business and stayed inside, he might have finished it."

No denying it anymore. Alice was completely insane. The way her emotions ran her up and down like a roller coaster, it was a wonder no one had ever noticed her instability before. And she was clearly losing what shaky hold she had on reality.

"What did Ryan do?" Sandy tried to swallow but her throat seemed paralyzed. "Do you hate him for taking Mac away?"

"Goodness, no." Alice's smile and pleasant tone made their conversation an obscene parody of afternoon tea between friends. "I hated Johnny. Never wanted him. But Ryan taking him off like that drove the final wedge between our families. I made sure of that." The chill in her eyes intensified as she spoke in a falsely sorrowful tone. "Oh, I just don't know why he'd take off with my boy like that. My poor, poor baby. What could Ryan McGee want with him?"

Sandy stared. How could that wonderful man she'd fallen in love with have possibly come from this madwoman? "But Mac was your child."

"So?" Alice tilted her head and regarded Sandy thoughtfully.

"Then is this about Bethany's death? Ryan was only twelve. He tried to save her. She was his mother."

Alice's laugh reverberated in the pickup's cab. A startled hawk took off from its perch in the top of the pine tree just outside Sandy's window. "I was glad he couldn't save her." She leaned toward Sandy, her tone becoming conspiratorial. "How do you think my sister came to slip into the creek in the first place?"

Sandy's jaw slackened. "You killed your sister."

"Now see that? You're a lot smarter than these local folks, aren't you?"

"Why?"

Alice shrugged. "She caught my husband's eye."

"They were having an affair?" *Keep her talking, stall for time, look for a way to escape.*

A snort from Alice echoed the contempt reflected in her eyes. "I doubt she would have seen it that way, but sooner or later, he'd have had her. He wouldn't have been able to stop himself."

"I don't understand."

"Of course you do. My Brody takes what he wants. *Who* he wants. He wanted my sister, and I couldn't have that."

Surprise propelled Sandy forward a couple of inches. "So you *killed* her?"

The gun jerked.

"Sorry." Sandy held up her hands. "You surprised me."

"You're in no position to judge me, the way you parade around half-dressed. You're a tramp, just like all the others. It was only a matter of time before Brody turned his eye on you, the way you carry on at that bar. But you whoring yourself with a McGee brought it on that much sooner."

Despite her attempt to remain calm, the bitter taste of bile gurgled into Sandy's throat. "Alice, there's nothing between your husband and me."

A bark of harsh laughter shook Alice, and she rolled her eyes. "You think this is about a relationship? It's all about what he hungers after. And you being with the McGee boy, that's made him hungrier than he's ever been." Her smile faded; bitterness settled over her face. "He'd come at me brutal 'most every night, but it was your name he was moaning as he finished with me. Same as when he wanted my sister. Why do you think he was in your parking lot the other night? He'd have come for you then, but you were with Ryan."

"Did Brody tell you about that?" Panic swelled, choking off her oxygen. She struggled to steady her breathing. Fear wasn't going to get her out of anything.

"No. He keeps that part quiet unless things get out of hand and I have to clean up. My daughter-in-law's mother works in the sheriff's office. She's such a shameless gossip. It helps to know what investigations are active and the direction they're taking. Helps me keep tabs on who's going to be where." Alice's smile was cunning and self-satisfied, and Sandy wanted to wipe it off her face. "She couldn't wait to tell me you were going to pick Ryan up early this morning. She thought I'd be relieved he was going to be okay."

So that was how Alice had known where to catch her. Sandy's hands turned to ice. Each revelation tightened her anxiety. Things couldn't end well. *Keep her talking.* "Your husband has liked other women, hasn't he?"

Alice shook with silent laughter, her eyes glazing. "He's taken a few companions up to the McGees' cabin for a nice little getaway."

"He hurts them, doesn't he?"

This time Alice MacKay's laugh was loud, bordering on maniacal. "Nothing but trash. He takes what he wants when I let him. By the time Brody's finished with them..." She shrugged. "Believe me, I'm doing you a favor ending it this way."

"No, you're not." Sandy kept her voice even. She had to find a weapon of some sort, or she had to figure out how to open the door and get out of the truck before Alice decided to shoot her. "You don't care about me any more than you cared about your sister. You can't let him hurt me because if he starts hunting women in Orson's Folly, that investigation's going to end up on your front porch."

"See? I told you, you're smart."

"Where does Brenda fit into this? Why did you let her stay?"

A flare of nostrils and a very slight narrowing of the eyes were Alice's only reactions.

Sandy leveled her gaze on the crazed woman. The more she talked, the less attention she seemed to be paying to her surroundings. Was it possible to reach the tool belt behind the seat without drawing attention?

"Mac isn't Ricky's father, is he?" Sandy asked quietly, holding Alice's eyes with her stare. "You didn't have a choice. You had to let her stay. Did Bull force your hand?"

Alice sighed heavily. "Bull always did exactly what I told him. Until Brenda had that child." Her eyes were looking in Sandy's direction but focused on something she saw in her head. "I wanted Brenda to die in childbirth." Again her voice took on false sorrow. "So sad, my boy's gone, and now so is my daughter-in-law and her baby... my grandchild..." She snorted. "When she went into labor and started having trouble, I thought she would. But Bull defied me that day. He took her to the hospital himself."

Slowly, without taking her eyes off Alice, Sandy slid her hand toward the rear of her seat. If she could just keep Alice occupied and off balance long enough to get her hands on that tool belt. A screwdriver wasn't much of a weapon compared to a gun, but it was all she had. She stretched a little more, almost there.

"I wouldn't do that if I were you."

Sunlight flashed on the gun's barrel just as the butt smashed into Sandy's forehead, leaving her stunned. Vaguely she heard Alice rummaging around in the truck's cab. Then she was alone. Seconds later, the driver's side door was wrenched open.

Sandy tried to sit up, but her brain couldn't seem to animate her body. Rough hands shoved her forward into the steering wheel. She connected with a painful jolt. Her teeth sank into her bottom lip and the metallic taste of blood flooded her mouth. Alice was coming at her like a wild woman, carrying something big. *Move!*

Moaning, Sandy rolled her head, managing to dodge the worst of the blow as Alice slammed a rock into the back of her head. Pain exploded like a bomb. Little star bursts of fiery agony blurred her vision. Dimly she saw Alice raise the rock again.

* * *

Dressed in the stiff new jeans and dark pullover shirt his father had insisted on purchasing for him the night before, Ryan waited. He paced from the bed back to the window, looked out at the parking lot, seeking any sign of his dad's bright red truck. The wall clock registered noon. He'd been waiting four hours.

Something's wrong. She'd left a message at the nurse's station that she would be there at eight. It took just over an hour to get from Orson's Folly to Jackson. Even if she hadn't left her place until eight and had run into traffic, she wouldn't be four hours late.

He dialed her cell number again, and again it went straight to voicemail. Did that mean her phone was off? Or was she in the mountains with no service?

Ryan erupted into a string of violent cursing that he punctuated by an open-palmed slap on the marble window ledge. He had to get out of there. Still cursing, he punched the speed dial for Sean.

"Melanie's waiting at the bar for a delivery," said his brother. "Let me call over there, find out when Sandy left. Maybe she was delayed."

When the nurse came to check his vital signs, Ryan waved her off then called her back.

"Is there someplace close I can rent a car?"

"About a block away," the young nurse replied. "But your discharge instructions recommend against driving."

"I'll take that under advisement."

By the time his phone rang again, Ryan was just signing the papers on his rental.

Sean got right to the point. "She left just before seven."

That was no surprise. If Sandy promised to be somewhere at eight, she would be there at seven-fifty. But it was more than that. Something was wrong. He felt it with everything in him.

"Do you want me to come up and get you?" Sean asked.

"I want you to drive up this way and watch for the silver Grand Prix I just rented," Ryan said, slipping behind the wheel. "We'll probably meet halfway, but if she's stranded on the road, you might reach her before I can."

Tossing his phone onto the passenger seat, Ryan stomped the gas pedal and squealed out of the rental company parking lot, heading toward home and, he hoped, the woman he loved.

"Damn it," he muttered as he hit the main highway. The brush along there was so thick in places, it could easily swallow a vehicle whole and pop back into place. If she'd gone off the road, finding her would take keen eyes and patience to look thoroughly. He definitely had none of the latter.

As Ryan had predicted, he met up with Sean at the halfway point between Orson's Folly and Jackson. He pulled his rental into a scenic overlook and waited for Sean to turn around and join him.

"I didn't see anything on the way up," Sean said in response to the unvoiced question. "I saw Alice MacKay coming back from Jackson, flagged her down, but she said she hadn't seen anything. She must have been about thirty minutes ahead of you."

Ryan paced to the road, looked in both directions, willing his father's red pickup to appear from around either of the bends in the road.

"Bull still in jail?" he asked without turning around.

"Transferred to Jackson late yesterday evening," said Sean with a hint of satisfaction. "I got the impression that's where Alice had been."

"Damn it!" Ryan punched the hood of his rental, not caring about the fist-sized dent he left. "Where is she?"

Sean touched his good arm. He held the radio from the cab of his truck. "Ry, it's time to call DC," he said gently.

* * *

The sheriff was already in his office when the brothers pulled in, one behind the other.

"I've reported her missing under suspicious circumstances," DC told them before the door finished closing. "They're going to take a long, hard look at Brody MacKay Senior because of Sandy's visit to Bull yesterday and the report I filed about concerns for the welfare of Brenda and Ricky."

"Wait, wait!" Ryan held up a hand. "What the hell are you talking about?"

DC brought them up to speed about the events of the previous afternoon. Ryan's gut began to eat at itself.

"The boy had fresh burns on his arm," DC reported grimly. He looked at Ryan as he spoke. "Six round burns in a line on the underside of his arm between his elbow and his wrist. He said he got them from fighting the fire at your place."

Ryan shook his head. "No way. I asked if he was okay, looked him over before he left. I would have noticed burns like that." His mind was racing. Burns on the kid, probably Mac's kid. "Old man Brody has a history of using cigarettes for discipline," he murmured, more to himself.

But DC heard him. "I know," he said, meeting Ryan's eyes with a haunted gaze.

"Did you tell the MacKays it was Sandy showing concern for Brenda and Ricky?" asked Sean.

DC shook his head. "No. The request to check welfare came from Bull."

Ryan started as though he'd been slapped. "Bull?"

"He seemed pretty worked up after Sandy left," admitted the sheriff.

In a lightning move, Ryan swept the pile of papers from the edge of DC's desk. Sheets of white glided to the floor like dozens of unfolded paper airplanes. "What did they do to her?"

The sheriff pushed the papers into a pile with the toe of one boot.

Ryan's cell phone rang. *Sandy!* He fumbled to answer it, saw Joe's number, and hit reject, his spirits deflated. "I should be out looking for her. But I don't know where to start." He pressed the heels of his hands into his temples. His head was killing him. Not knowing what had happened to Sandy was killing him quicker.

The door to the office opened and a pair of state troopers entered. The one in the lead shook his head in response to DC's question of whether they'd made any progress. The building closed in on him. With profound claustrophobia assaulting him, Ryan stepped outside while DC spoke with the troopers.

He used his cell to check in with his father while he paced around the parking lot.

"Have you tried calling her?" Justin asked.

"Several times. It just goes straight to voicemail."

"On the radio, son. The other day, I sent her off with one of our handhelds."

At last, something else he could try. Ryan sprinted to Sean's truck, reached in and grabbed his radio.

He checked the frequency on his way back inside.

Chapter Seventeen

A deep, throbbing ache swelled in the base of Sandy's neck, flowing like molten lava up over the top of her head and down into her shoulders. She desperately wanted to go back to sleep. Instead she began taking inventory.

She was slumped forward, her chest pressing into something hard. Her lungs burned. Her brain was starving for oxygen. She needed to breathe. Raising herself against gravity as much as she could, she sucked in huge gulps of air.

Her arm felt too heavy when she lifted it and clumsily sought the cause of her agony. When she finally found the source, she wished she hadn't. Touching the back of her head started a series of bright explosions behind her eyeballs. She allowed her hand to drop, knowing the stickiness on her fingers was blood.

"Damn it." The words sounded like a whisper breaking through the ringing in her ears and it took Sandy a moment to realize she'd been the one to speak.

Convincing her eyes to open took effort. Slowly images swirled into focus. Gearshift. Steering wheel. Airbag? She was in a vehicle. A truck.

Yes, Justin McGee's truck.

She tried to sit up straight but the cab leaned forward at a very unnatural angle. She lifted her head and saw the dark green of pine boughs splayed against the windshield. Had she driven into a tree? Where had she been going?

Ryan! She was supposed to pick him up. Had she gotten him? Was he hurt? The muscles in her neck protested when she twisted her head to the right. The passenger seat was empty. No, that's right. She hadn't picked him up yet.

Her right arm tingled. Circulation was cut off. Willing the muscles to work, she moved spasmodically, reaching for her side. She had to get the seatbelt off before the freaking thing strangled her.

"Cross MC Unit 1, this is Sheriff Cooley. Sandy, do you copy?"

Where was that voice coming from?

"Sandy Wheaton, this is Sheriff Cooley, performing a status check. Please respond."

The voice was tinny and small. "That's a radio. Keep talking, DC."

Silence.

A moan escaped Sandy's throat, becoming a wail of despair. Pushing through the anguish, she continued to reach for the seatbelt buckle.

Finally her fingers connected, fumbled. After a little effort and a lot of cursing, she depressed the button. The loud click reverberated through her brain. Released from the confines of the shoulder harness, Sandy flopped forward and landed with a gasp against the steering column again. The horn blared. Bracing herself against the wheel, she pushed but her hand slipped on the powder from the deployed airbag, impelling her forward to land with a breath-stealing crunch.

She would just rest a moment. Rest until she could catch her breath again. Her eyes were so... heavy.

* * *

Ryan stood behind Deputy Sherwood while she worked the citizen's band radio, contacting ranches and homesteads along the route to Jackson, advising them of a missing person. His chest squeezed with each call she made until he had to vacate the office again.

Outside, he leaned against his rental car and spent a long time staring up the road to Jackson. In the distance loomed the mountains he'd always loved, now shadowy and menacing. The sun was beginning to kiss the tops of the tallest trees. They were on the morning side of those mountains. Once the sun edged behind the trees, night would be on them. For the first time since coming home, he missed the always-lighted city.

Footsteps crunched the gravel behind him. Ryan knew without looking that his brother approached.

"They've contacted the Forest Service. Search and rescue is being called out."

Two pickups pulled into the parking lot. Ryan recognized Gus Hanson's blue rust bucket, saw the old ranch foreman getting out, then his father rounded the rear of the truck and headed straight for them.

The warmth of his father's touch on his shoulder provided a margin of comfort. When Ryan raised his eyes, his father was regarding him with a steady, reassuring gaze. "We *will* find her, son. And she'll be okay. Nothing else is acceptable."

"How does a bright red pickup just vanish?" Ryan asked.

"It wouldn't, son. Not without help." Justin rubbed his jaw as he studied the parking lot that was quickly filling with volunteers.

Ryan squeezed his eyes shut, then opened them.

Pickups and SUVs pulled in, one after another. More vehicles lined the street. People called out to each other as they moved toward the building. Some had been at Valentine's and found it closed and the owner missing. Others had heard through the grapevine. Perfect strangers were reporting to the sheriff's office to aid in the search.

The sun lost its battle, and the veil of darkness slipped over Orson's Folly. With it, a sense of menace slipped over Ryan.

The county road crew arrived with high-powered nighttime work lights. Flashlights were handed out. Brother Bobby drove the church van, hauling volunteers up to the mountain road where human chains were formed to search for Sandy.

They'd wasted so much time. The longer she was missing, the less chance they had of finding her alive. Ryan hovered in the parking lot, unable to tolerate being inside.

DC sent off another group of volunteers. His steps were labored as he approached. "I'm sorry, Ry. I should have paid more attention to your concerns."

"DC." Ryan fought to get the words out. "The pictures in your office. The ones of the missing women..."

The dismayed expression on DC's face told Ryan his old friend had already considered that scenario.

"Don't go there, Ry," said DC quietly. "We're not ignoring that possibility, and I've notified the FBI, but don't go there in your head yet."

Headlights swung into the parking lot and a white pickup pulled next to the sheriff's cruiser. Brody and Alice MacKay climbed out.

"DC, we just heard about Sandy." Alice was a lot more vocal than the last time Ryan had seen her. His radar went up.

"We're here to help with the search," Brody said gruffly. "I've got the light bar up on my rig. We can start looking along the lumber roads up on Diamond Peak."

"Get away from here, you miserable sack of shit." Ryan's muscles bunched as he prepared to strike, but he found himself up against the considerable bulk of his baby brother, planted firmly in his way.

"Don't." Sean walked him backward a few steps. "You won't be any good to her if DC has to lock you up."

Ryan abruptly released his fists and lifted his arms in a gesture of surrender, and Sean stepped back. Ryan aimed a malicious glare at Brody.

Alice gave back a sweet smile.

"Just give me one reason," whispered Ryan. "One reason to take you out."

DC looked at the MacKays through a narrowed gaze, apparently appraising this new source of assistance. Finally he nodded. "Thanks. We can use the help. I'll assign some extra eyes to go with."

MacKay's malevolent eyes glittered his triumph at Ryan as DC stepped back to the office.

Flanked by his father and brother, Ryan followed DC.

"Penny!" DC scanned the room until he spotted the deputy. "Take Wendell and ride along with Brody up by the old logging camp."

"Wendell's out with the VFD," said Penny. "I'll go solo."

As his deputy passed by, DC touched her on the arm and murmured in her ear. She nodded and kept going. DC made subtle hand motions to a lean man with black hair and black eyes standing near the door. The man nodded and slipped outside. Colton Ford Junior, a good choice for backup.

Ryan pushed through the handful of people lingering in the office and intercepted DC. "Why are you letting them help?" he demanded. "What if—?" He choked on his next words.

DC considered Ryan for a long moment before answering. "Because if he's helping, I know where he is and what he's doing."

A white foam cup of something hot was pressed into his hand, followed quickly by a sandwich to his other hand. The rich tangy scent of coffee tickled his nostrils and turned his stomach.

"Mel and Charlie brought food." Sean closed a hand over Ryan's shoulder and gave a little shake. "You have to eat, Ry, just a couple of bites. You're a liability if you're running on empty."

Ryan bit into the sandwich. He might as well have been chewing the coffee cup. Taking a long drink of the dark liquid, Ryan found his eyes bugged out. The stuff was extra strong and insanely sweet. He smiled. It would probably give him an extra couple of hours.

* * *

She stepped outside, blinking, holding a hand above her eyes against the harsh glare of midmorning sun. Hot waves shimmered off the blacktop parking lot. But even L.A. heat wasn't enough to push back the cold that had rooted in her core.

The acrid tang of smoke from recently extinguished fires lingered. After a beat, the scents of settling dust and the rotten-egg stench of thick L.A. smog joined the mix. Heavy construction equipment droned in the distance. Cleanup had begun.

How long would it be until the earthquake's scars were erased from the city? And would the scars of the past twenty-four hours ever be excised from her aching heart?

A flash of navy blue caught her attention just as someone touched her on the arm. Sandy forced a smile on her face for her boss. Ebony skin glistened with fine perspiration, but Renee's hair remained slicked and neatly twisted into a perfect picture of professionalism.

"Hey." Sandy scrubbed the remaining tears from her face with the backs of her hands. "Turns out I'm not cut out for this work after all."

Renee regarded her with obvious compassion. "Don't make the decision just yet. Take some time."

Sandy shook her head. "I have four weeks of vacation. I'm going to use that in lieu of notice. I'm sorry."

With a sigh, Renee nodded. "I understand. I just talked to Marcus. Our condo was flattened. He's done out here, too. Looks like we're going back to Baltimore."

Sandy smiled. "It really was good working for you."

Renee squeezed her hand. "If you ever get to Maryland, Alexandra, you look me up."

Promises were superficial, but Sandy made them anyway, knowing in her heart she was going to Wyoming.

"Would you like me to call you when the funeral arrangements are made?" asked Renee.

Sandy hesitated. Mick had touched her more deeply than anyone she'd ever known. He'd been right. They would have had something good.

But she had never seen him in life. To see him in death would be a hollow substitute. The parts of him that he had shared with her, his last thoughts and feelings, hopes... dreams... were all gone. There was simply no meaning to be found in visiting the shell that had once held all he'd been.

She shook her head. "Thanks, but no. I have someplace to go."

* * *

With a sharply indrawn breath, Sandy came awake. The damp mountain air surrounded her. She shivered. So cold. The truck's window was open. Why couldn't she see anything? She forced herself to slow her breathing. Gradually the absolute panic edged back. She began to make out nearby shapes. Black on dark. Nighttime.

She had to move. Her position was cutting off circulation to her legs. Mustering a sense of determination, she pushed against the steering wheel, mindful of the powder-coated airbag this time. As she moved back, an ominous rumbling began and the truck shook violently.

Quake! Her heart stalled. But as her movements stilled, so did the shaking. "Okay... Oh, man!" She tried to slow her rapid breathing, but her heart pounded so hard she thought her chest would burst.

More shaking, then the already cracked windshield creaked, popped, and a pine bough burst through in a shower of tempered glass. Instinctively she covered her face as chunks rained over her. With a series of jerks, the truck shifted, and Sandy cried out, flailing her arms as she tumbled sideways.

The groan of distressed steel ricocheted through the cab, and the truck remained still and silence fell again. Sandy's arm was twisted beneath her. She rolled until it came free with a pop and a painful toothache feel in her shoulder. She flopped back and the truck jiggled, then jolted in a sudden downward movement. Sandy froze.

Wherever she'd landed, the truck wasn't on solid ground. What had happened to her? Fearful the truck would drop, maybe with deadly consequences, she forced herself to remain still while she tried to piece together what had happened.

Someone had been with her. Who? Thinking brought on a throbbing ache in her temples. "Oh, God, please..." She needed an aspirin. Maybe a whole bottle of aspirin.

"Sandy Wheaton, Cross MC Unit 1, this is the sheriff's office, do you copy?"

She scowled. The radio again. It sounded like it was coming from somewhere above her.

"Sandy, this is Gloria with the Orson's Folly Sheriff's Department."

Justin's radio! She'd plugged the handheld unit into a charger dock in the truck's overhead console. She reached upward, but in the darkness there was no way to tell if she was within reach or far off the mark.

"Sandy, if you can hear but cannot respond, be advised that search and rescue is in place. We're looking for you, hon, so you just hang on wherever you are."

They're looking for me! Hope surged.

Which means they don't know where I am. And was just as quickly smashed.

How could they find her if she didn't know herself where she was?

She reached up again but grabbed only air. Exhausted from her efforts, she let her eyes close. *Just for a minute...*

* * *

"You just got out of the hospital," Justin reminded Ryan, pointing at a green vinyl chair next to DC's desk. "Park your butt for at least an hour. I know you're not going to sleep, but you're not doing yourself or her any good pacing like a caged animal."

How many times had his dad tried to get him to rest? At least a dozen. And his old man was probably right. Ever since that first shock of coffee had worn off, his muscles had screamed with exhaustion. With a sigh, Ryan sat.

Many of the searchers had come in to take a break during the darkest part of the night. A few were conversing over sandwiches and coffee. A handful of volunteers who lived close to town had gone home, but with promises that they'd all come back out before first light. Trying to continue the search now was not only dangerous for the searchers, but too much evidence could be missed, or worse, destroyed by people walking over it in the dark. Ryan had participated in enough searches to understand that concept.

But those operations had all been part of his job. They hadn't been his whole heart. He watched the people left in the office. As soon as his old man turned his back to talk to a neighbor, Ryan got up and slipped out into the darkness.

He stood against the back of his brother's truck, staring in the direction of the mountains where he knew without a doubt Sandy waited, unable to communicate, perhaps trapped, likely injured. But it wasn't the intimidating behemoths of rock he struggled in the dark to see.

It was her face he conjured.

Sandy's face, with the chicory eyes flashing fire at him on a mountain road. Sandy, flirting with him at her bar, performing a sexy song and dance. Sandy looking over her shoulder with that half-smile, enticing him to follow her. With eyes darkened by passion when they kissed. Her face showing her vulnerability while she slept. Eyes that held compassion for a defenseless baby animal. Her face, streaked with soot and set with defiance... lit by concern as she sat a vigil by his bed in the hospital. Then as he'd last seen her, eyes filled with hurt because she'd misunderstood his astonishment when she'd told him about Mac.

"I know you're out there," he whispered into the night. "You're out there somewhere and I know you're still alive. Sweetheart, I *will* find you."

Not for years had he felt the sort of connection with another person that he had with Sandy. Without her in his life, he might as well be dead, because he sure as hell wouldn't be truly alive.

Headlights sliced across the blackness of the parking lot and Ryan stood, prepared to meet the newcomers. But a sudden sense of misgiving kept him pinned to the safety of the shadows.

When he recognized the MacKays, his stomach heaved and he was glad he'd stayed put. He watched old Brody park directly in front of the door, as if he were somehow entitled to the best parking. Then MacKay and his wife entered the sheriff's office, Deputy Sherwood on their heels.

A figure slipped through the darkness and joined him.

Ryan was taller than average, but Colt Ford had a good three inches on him. Broad-shouldered, with muscular arms built by years of hands-on ranch work, he nonetheless carried himself with cat-like agility. Because Colt was four years Ryan's senior, the two had never really traveled the same circles, but they'd always been friendly on the few occasions their paths crossed.

Ryan nodded. "Ford."

With typical reserve, Colt nodded in return. "If DC's not looking hard at those two, he should be. Something about them…" He shook his head. "She's batshit crazy and he's too quiet."

Interest piqued, Ryan focused on Ford. "What happened?"

"We were up by the old logging roads." Colt adjusted his Stetson. "That's an area that bears another look in the light. The old lady was pretty anxious that we officially mark the area as already searched."

Ryan's head popped up. "Go on."

Colt shrugged and shook his head again. "It's just a feeling. But if I'm right, McGee, we don't have much time to find your lady."

His message delivered, the taciturn man strolled toward the building, leaving Ryan alone in the dark, with a renewed sense of urgency squeezing his lungs.

The earliest fingers of dawn were just beginning to creep into the eastern horizon when the first of the returning volunteers arrived.

Ryan pulled a weary hand down his face, wishing he could wipe away the exhaustion that was as much mental as physical.

* * *

Daylight filtered into the cab when Sandy opened her eyes again. The sharp scent of pine sap had become a dismal companion throughout the dark night, and with the coming of dawn it was easy to see why. At least a third of the cab was occupied by the branch that had crashed through the windshield. One leg was cramping. She had to move it. Praying the motion wouldn't set the truck into more shifting, she managed to straighten the leg so it wasn't underneath her. Blood rushing into the foot burned as though she'd walked over hot coals. She closed her eyes and took deep breaths until the searing eased.

How long had it been? Why hadn't someone found her yet?

And Ryan! Did he think she'd abandoned him?

Yellow-orange rays of sunlight touched the edge of the driver's door window.

She could make out the radio overhead but it was beyond her reach. Every time she tried to stretch, the truck teetered and the tree outside the window groaned. In frustration, she slapped her hand on the seat, then froze as she felt the truck rock. How high up was she? It could be anywhere from several inches to a couple hundred feet. She wasn't keen on the idea of answering that question with a long fall to the bottom of some canyon.

Slowly, moving mere centimeters at a time, she managed to settle herself, lying crossways on the seat. It was marginally more comfortable than being bunched behind the steering wheel. Her foot brushed something at the end of the seat. Justin's tool belt.

Stopping every time the tree groaned or the truck shifted, it seemed to take forever, but at last she managed to hook the tool belt with the pointed toe of her boot.

"Oh, thank you, God."

It took even longer to work the tool belt up her leg until she could reach it with her fingers. When it was finally in her hands, she explored the contents. Wire cutters, pliers, a couple of screwdrivers, a utility knife, and a pair of gloves.

One of the screwdrivers was just long enough to touch the tip to the radio. She should be able to slide the radio out of its dock.

Sandy drew in a couple of deep breaths to steady herself. She had one chance at it. If she popped the radio out of the dock and it landed out of reach, she might never be able to retrieve it.

"One, two, three!" She stretched up with the screwdriver in hand and caught the handheld radio on the side by the strap. It was so anticlimactic when the little radio was finally nestled in the palm of her hand that she cried with relief.

* * *

Ryan's cell phone rang, ripping through the tense silence that had fallen in the sheriff's office during the briefing by search and rescue. Joe again. This time, Ryan answered.

"You're hard to get hold of," said Joe.

"Hey, man, this isn't a good time."

"McGee, wait! I found your Allie. We had her name wrong."

"It doesn't matter any more. I'll give you a call next week and explain."

"Ryan! She moved to your hometown. Her name's—"

From across the room, the citizen band radio squawked. "Orson's Folly Sheriff Department, this is Alexandra Wheaton, operating Cross MC Unit One on your frequency. Please show me Code 60, unknown location. Over."

The voice he'd been seeking for seven years was coming from the sheriff's base unit. "Angel?" Ryan's cell phone slipped from boneless fingers.

Chapter Eighteen

A cheer went up at the sound of Sandy's voice, but Ryan was processing her message. She'd reverted to L.A. dispatch lingo. Code 60 meant she was in imminent danger and needed urgent assistance.

"We read you, Ms. Wheaton," responded the ranger manning the radio. "This is Will Fremont of search and rescue. Can you give us your general vicinity?"

In a daze, Ryan approached the radio station. He needed to hear her voice again.

Was it her? Could Sandy really be the woman he'd been looking for since he'd been plucked from the ruins of the L.A. Convention Center? Had she been here in his hometown all along? His heart wouldn't stop bounding up into his throat.

"My location is unknown," said Sandy.

Ryan sucked in a huge breath. His gut wrenched. It *was* her.

Sean appeared at his side. "What is it?"

Ryan shook his head, in shock, unable to put it into words.

"I'm trapped in my truck. I think I'm over a cliff but not at the bottom. The truck slides every time I move. I can't see any landmarks. I'm stuck in some pine trees. Be advised that I have a head lac and I have had positive loss of consciousness, unknown number of episodes or duration."

"Copy that, Ms. Wheaton. Stay calm."

"Angel," whispered Ryan.

"Holy shit!" Sean gripped Ryan's forearm. "It's her, isn't it? *Sandy's* the girl you were looking for in L.A."

Ryan nodded wordlessly as violent shakes consumed him.

"We're going to get to her, Ry," said Sean.

Fremont spread a topographic map of the area over DC's desk. Search and rescue leaders gathered around. DC used a yellow highlighter to outline the road to Jackson. As he gestured at an area on the county map, Fremont tapped another area then drew a large circle in red marker.

Ryan approached the radio. Before his quaking legs could give out, he fell into the chair vacated by Fremont.

His trembling hand mirrored his shaken soul as he pushed the pressel on the transceiver. "Angel? Is that you?"

Silence.

Ryan huffed out a breath and tried again, louder. "Angel, you there?"

Finally Sandy spoke, her words a mere whisper, difficult to hear but clear. "Oh, my God. It was *you*. It wasn't Mac, it was *you*." She was obviously as shaken as he. "But it can't be. You died."

"It's me, Angel. I promise. 'O, it came o'er my ear like the sweet sound, that breathes upon a bank of violets.'"

"You're not dead!" She was half crying, half laughing. "You're not dead and you're quoting Shakespeare."

Ryan could hear the tears in her words. He had to get her to hang on, to help them find her. He knew time would work against them with the truck balanced over a cliff. If she moved the wrong way or too much... He closed his eyes against the images in his head and brought his focus back to the radio.

"Not dead, Angel. Not even close. I've been looking for you for seven years." And now that he'd found her, losing her wasn't in the plan. "Those better not be tears I hear, sweetheart," he mocked in a stern tone.

"Not crying anymore," she said, her voice stronger. "I'm just trying to get my mind around the fact that the only two men I've ever loved are the same person."

The oxygen left Ryan's lungs with a whoosh at her words. "Angel, you hold onto that thought. When we get you out of there, I'm going to kiss you all over."

She was quiet for a moment, then he heard her soft, sexy laugh. "You have to do better than that, cowboy. I seem to recall a trip to a chapel in Vegas being mentioned seven years ago."

"Is that a proposal?" His heart skipped a beat. "What kind of crappy proposal is that?"

"Sorry — can't get down on one knee at the moment since I don't want to end up with a damn truck up my ass."

Ryan's smile widened, recognizing her spoof of his own words to her seven years before. Panic eased its grip. Her morale was high — half the battle. But now he had to pick her brain to find her. "What happened, Angel? How did you end up over a cliff?"

"I... don't know. I was coming to get you. That's all I remember."

So she was probably off US-189.

Commotion and loud voices near the door drew Ryan's attention. "Hold on a second. There's something happening here."

Walt Blackstone held the door open and Ricky MacKay tumbled through, landing in a heap at Justin's feet.

The boy's face was bruised and swollen. His hands were covered in dirt and dried blood. His bare feet had left bloody footprints on the tile. Ryan's heart lurched into his stomach then violently up into his throat. If a man could do that to his own kin...

Justin crouched and settled a steadying hand on the boy's shoulder. "Someone get him some water. Did you walk all the way from your place, son?"

"Yes, sir." Ricky gulped in air. "She said she'd kill my mom if I didn't help them. But I can't do it anymore. She burned my shoes so I couldn't go anywhere but I had to get help. My mom's real bad off. Grandma, please help us," he cried out just as Gloria reached his side. Then he began babbling but the only words Ryan heard made his gut writhe with terror. "She wanted me to help her kill Miz Sandy."

"Someone find MacKay." DC's hand rested on his weapon, as if itching for an excuse to use it.

"His truck's not out there," Blackstone said from the doorway. "Ford's truck's gone, too."

"Penny and Colt went outside right after Brody and Alice left, about five or ten minutes ago," Gloria told the sheriff.

As Ryan watched, his father laid both hands on Ricky's thin shoulders and searched his face. "Where is she, son? Do you know where Ms. Sandy is?"

The boy shook his head then swayed against Justin.

"I think he's telling the truth," murmured Sean in Ryan's ear. "I'll be right back."

Justin cradled Ricky against him. "This boy needs a doctor."

Ryan rubbed his jaw. Colt's words from the night before were suddenly making sense. If the MacKays wanted the logging trails marked as searched, they had a reason. Ryan's gut heaved again.

Obviously Brody and Alice were on their way to finish Sandy off, with the advantage of already knowing where she was.

"DC!" He waited for the sheriff to look in his direction. "Last night Ford said they were checking the logging roads and Alice seemed anxious for that area to be marked as clear."

A flurry of talking erupted. DC's mouth set into a bleak line.

Torn between the twin needs of racing out to rescue Sandy and staying to talk to his Angel, Ryan shifted from foot to foot, throwing glances at the door. Then Sean was next to him with his handheld.

Relief at such a simple solution kicked his heart rate up a notch. "Angel," Ryan said, "can you tune your handset to the ranch frequency?"

"Yes."

"Do it. You'll get Sean. Okay?" He flicked a glance at his brother to confirm the plan. "If you don't connect to Sean right away, flip right back to this frequency. Got that?"

In ten seconds, Sean had her on the ranch frequency. He handed the radio to Ryan. "We got us a posse. Let's roll!"

Ryan climbed into the cab of Sean's truck right behind his father. Several grim-faced volunteers jumped into nearby pickups, and Sean took off, tires shooting gravel, with a line of trucks following behind.

"Sandy, we have a general vicinity for your location," said Ryan into the radio.

Silence.

"Angel?" Panic began to swell into his throat. Ryan swallowed, pushed it back. "Angel, you there?"

"I'm here, cowboy." She chuckled softly. "Just appreciating the irony. Guess I need you and your white horse after all."

Ryan smiled, but the gravity of the situation quickly returned. "Sandy, do you remember maybe running into Brody MacKay yesterday?"

"Brody... no," she said slowly. "But..."

Ryan took a deep breath and stemmed his impatience. Angel was clearly struggling with a spotty memory.

"Wait!" Sandy's excited voice came over the radio again. "Alice! Her truck had broken down. I picked her up and I was taking her... somewhere."

"Alice? *Mrs.* MacKay?" Ryan's apprehension renewed itself, but he couldn't let Sandy pick up on it. He white-knuckled the handheld as he strove for a calm tone. "Angel, I know it's hard, but it's important that you remember where you were taking her."

Justin sat forward and swiveled in his seat. "What is it, son?"

"A big piece of what we've been missing," Ryan said through clenched teeth. "Ricky said 'she.' When he told us someone threatened his mother, he said 'she,' not 'he.' *Alice,* not Brody."

Sandy's voice came back, frantic. "Ry! I was taking her to see Brody's cousin. She said he would get the truck running or take her back home. She had me turn off the road. You can barely see the track."

"Good girl. Did she give you a name?"

"Umm... I can't..."

"Come on, sweetheart, you've got this." *Where did she take you? What cousin?*

"Maybe... Brandon? Brendon?"

"Braden." Justin gave a grim nod. "I know where we're going. It'll be a left turn just beyond Diamond Peak. Braden is — *was* MacKay's cousin. He died in a riding accident on the trail heading up to the high pasture from Devil's Wash. Happened before either of you were born."

"We know where you are, Angel," said Ryan into the radio. "Hang in there."

"That's apparently what I'm doing," she responded with a nervous chuckle. Then, "I love you... Mick."

"Back atcha." Ryan blinked away the burn behind his eyelids. He would not lose it and bawl like a baby.

Sean hit the accelerator hard, squealing around the switchback curves as they tore up the mountain toward the Diamond Peak overlook. With every switch, the truck swung close to cliff edges protected only by narrow steel guard rails set so low, the high-profile pickup would probably flip over them.

As they skidded toward a patch of gravel beyond which showed pine tops and cloudless blue sky, Ryan tensed, preparing for the truck to become airborne.

"Crickets on a cracker, boy, don't drive *us* off the damn mountain," growled Justin, bracing himself against the dashboard.

Sean's only answer was to increase their speed upon pulling out of the turn, but he hung closer to the mountain for the next two switches. Suddenly he let up on the gas and nodded at a two-track off to the left. "Diamond Peak."

Justin leaned forward and squinted through the windshield. "Braden's trail used to be about a hundred yards past— There!" He pointed.

A sapling had been cut and arranged into an arrow, just off the road. Barely slowing down, they hit the path with a bone-shattering jolt, and the truck bounced violently to the right then the left.

"Damn it," ground out Sean, wrestling with the wheel.

"Angel... Sandy." Ryan forced himself to keep his voice calm, though his heart was still lodged in his throat. "We're almost to you. But honey, Alice and Brody are up here ahead of us."

Sandy's voice came over the radio again, sounding very calm. "Ryan, Alice wants me dead. She hit me. She must have pushed the truck over the cliff." Her tone sharpened. "Ryan! She said she would kill you, too. She'd make it look like you were so overcome with grief that—"

"She won't hurt me, Angel. You hold on. It's not only me on my white horse coming for you. It's the whole damn town."

"I'm scared." Her voice shook and so did his heart.

"You hold onto me, Angel. Hold onto my voice the way I held onto yours."

The truck dipped into a rut, sprang back out. Ryan slammed into his father, grunting when lightning erupted from his newly re-stitched wound and spread down his left arm. Lurching to the right, they barreled into a clearing that ended in a sharp drop-off.

"Shit!" Sean stomped the brake pedal, spinning them to a stop in a spray of loose rock.

MacKay's truck was there, and so was the burgundy pickup that Ryan recognized as Colt's. The occupants were nowhere in sight.

Along the cliff's edge, an obvious gap scarred the line of pine tree tops reaching up from below. Tire tracks in the layer of dust and shale ended at the cliff's edge.

More trucks pulled into the clearing, the men in back jumping to the ground before they came to a complete stop. The sheriff's cruiser roared into the clearing and halted behind MacKay's monster pickup. Asshat wouldn't be going anywhere in that for a while.

With confidence he didn't feel, Ryan spoke into the radio. "We're here, Angel. Just a few more minutes. Are you holding on?"

"I'm here. Where else would I be?" she finished under her breath.

Despite his fear, Ryan found his lips twitching into a smile. *That's my Angel.*

Clutching the handset like the lifeline it was, he inched his way to the cliff edge. It was just a shelf of crumbling shale, and he had no way of knowing how unstable it might be. He held up a hand to warn the other volunteers back. Then he dropped to the ground and crept forward on his belly. Screw the safety gear; he had to get to Sandy.

Justin's pickup was a bloody red wound amid the dark pine boughs. Shit. Not good. Drawing a fortifying breath, he forced his swelling emotions into a cocoon of objectivity, then blew out slowly.

"She's maybe fifty feet down," he called over his shoulder. "With about another seventy-five feet to the bottom. Truck's lodged between the top half of a blackjack pine and this cliff. It's listing sideways and it's not even close to stable." He eased back until he could be certain the ground beneath him was firm then spoke into the radio. "Angel, we're gonna get you. Just don't move. Can you give me your status? You said you had a head injury. Any other injuries? Broken bones?"

Her response was lost amid the sharp crack of breaking wood. Ryan froze. The sickening sound of rocks falling followed. His objectivity faltered. With a final groan of bending metal, the sounds and movement abruptly ceased. Ryan cautiously let out the breath he'd been holding.

"Sean, what kind of gear you got in your truck?" Ryan called out.

His brother shook his head. "No climbing gear, man. Better wait for search and rescue."

"No time!" Ryan strode toward the back of Sean's truck. "You got any rope?"

The bushes on the other side of the clearing rustled.

A grim-faced Justin leveled his rifle at the sound, raising it quickly when Colton Ford stepped into the clearing.

"I've got climbing gear," Colt called out, crossing to his pickup. He popped open the back window on the cap and pulled out orange nylon climbing rope and two harnesses. "Who has climbing experience?"

"I do," Ryan said quickly. "Mostly off buildings but some rock face."

Colt eyed Ryan critically. "You're pretty banged up. You good for this?"

He had to be. There was no one else, and they were out of time. He nodded once. "I'm good."

Colt began clipping connectors and testing them, fitting one harness onto Ryan and adjusting it. He spoke quickly as his hands performed their efficient work. "It's not an ideal cliff with all that loose rock. We'll do a dual top climb using a belay system. Let me set the anchor, then we'll go from the side. You'll go down first and get her out and I'll guide and run safety. Yours is a tandem harness." He tapped a connective clip on the blue harness. "When you get her out, use this to secure her in place with you. It's going to be awkward."

Ryan nodded. "Got it."

Ford lifted the radio from Ryan's hand and passed it to Sean. "She has to be ready to go. We need to know what side she's on and if the window is down or up."

"Ask her about injuries. I didn't catch her answer when I asked." Ryan double-checked his harness. "Back and neck, arms or legs. She's an EMT. She'll have self-assessed. We need to know how much help she's going to be getting her out."

Sean spoke into the radio, listened to Sandy's answer, spoke again.

"She's stiff because she hasn't been moving," he relayed, frowning in concentration as he listened for more. "She's changed position from where she first found herself and doesn't think she has any spinal injuries. She's lying across the seat with her head on the passenger side. The window's up but she can reach the handle. She's moving very carefully to roll it down now."

Colt nodded. "Good. Let's go."

"Ry!" called Sean. "There's a tree branch through the windshield."

"Okay."

The minute Ryan's feet swung free of the cliff, his training kicked in, and he surveyed the truck with an objective eye from his fresh perspective.

"The damn thing's barely hanging on," he called up to Ford. "We're only going to get one shot at this."

What had started as a mild stinging in his arm took on the tone of a colony of fire ants. Very angry ones. He gritted his teeth and pushed at the searing agony but with little success. A gallon of morphine might cut the torment. His descent halted.

"What's the hold up?" he called out.

"Just making an adjustment," answered Colt.

Taking advantage of the delay, Ryan drew in a deep breath and blew it out, clamping down on the burning. After a few breaths, he started moving down again, but the wait had been enough for him to build a mental block against the pain.

As Ryan drew even with the passenger window, it became obvious the truck was listing so badly it would be more of a topside extraction than parallel. At least she'd gotten the window down.

"Sandy, I'm out here." He spoke just loud enough to be heard, keeping his voice even. The angle of approach made seeing inside impossible but according to Sean, he should be near her head. A strong breeze tickled the pine trees and the truck wobbled.

"Angel?" He kept his tone even as he announced his presence.

"Still here," she sang out, her voice a little pitchy.

Ryan leaned back and caught Colt's attention. "If I touch the truck at all, it's gone."

"Okay, change of plan."

Colt lowered another nylon rope, with a clamp and pulley attached above the loop tied on the end. "Drop this through the window and have her loop it under both arms," he called. "She should be able to do that without moving too much. Once it's secure, we'll drag her up and out."

It took two tries for Ryan to hit the open window with the rope. Nothing like dangling in the air and wishing his lassoing skills weren't so rusty. He spoke calmly as he worked to get the rope to her, relaying Ford's instructions, reassuring her.

The moan of stressed metal grew louder and more insistent, as if he needed reminding of the truck's precarious position. Loose gravel fell from above.

"Crap!" Ryan shied away from the gravel's bite on his neck and arms.

"What's the matter?" Sandy called out from inside the truck. Fear resonated in her voice.

Before he could respond, a deafening crack sounded and the tree branch gave way. The truck fell another three feet, crashing into the next branch down with the deafening crunch of breaking wood.

Sandy shrieked.

Ryan eased back into breathing when he saw the branch was holding. "Still there, Angel?"

She took a moment to answer. "Have I told you I'm terrified of heights?"

He held onto his objective professionalism until he saw her. Already half out the window, she hadn't had time to get both arms through the loop. The only thing keeping her from going with the truck was a loop of rope under one arm and her white-knuckled grip on that rope with both hands.

"Keep holding that rope." When she nodded, Ryan heaved. Fire shot through his injured arm. He clenched his jaw and breathed through the worst of the pain. Above him, Colt cursed and adjusted the pulley system. Steadily, Ryan hauled Sandy up. Finally her feet were clear of the truck. Colt guided her closer to Ryan.

"Don't let go, sweetheart."

She held his stare, her eyes huge blue sapphires set in ivory colored skin. Then she was at his level and Ryan used the rope to draw her in. She hummed softly but didn't speak.

"Crap. Damn it." His fingers fumbled as he fought to secure her into the dual harness. Finally he slid the clip into place and twisted it closed. "All set!" he called out.

Colt began the process of raising them to the top of the cliff. Sandy hummed a little louder and it took him a second to figure out why it sounded familiar.

"Rock-a-Bye Baby?"

"Singing keeps me calm. But that's the only song I could think of." Her lips curved upward as she put the words to the tune. "When the bough breaks..."

The branch beneath them cracked and the truck slipped again. Sandy angled her head to look downward and shivered, her musical interlude apparently forgotten. "Oh, crap."

"Sandy! Look up here. Look at me. Don't look down, don't think about anything but moving up this cliff with me."

She nodded and locked onto Ryan's gaze again as she followed each instruction. He kept talking, soothing, encouraging, not knowing exactly what he was saying but using his voice to keep her attention on him.

Then Colt disappeared over the top. Sandy's hands tightened on Ryan's waist, her nails digging into the skin beneath his shirt as she clung to him like a kitten. Sean reached out to help her over the edge of the cliff.

"You're okay, Sandy. You won't fall."

Very slowly, one hand at a time, she released her hold on Ryan and took Sean's hands.

Flat on his belly, Colt reached over to assist Ryan, and then he was on the shale. Moving as quickly as his half-dead arm would allow, he scrambled away from the fragile edge.

Breathing hard, more in relief than with the exertion, Ryan pushed to his feet. At the sound of movement, he spun around. There she was, standing in front of him, tears freely rolling over her cheeks. He brushed a strand of hair behind one ear. "Sandy," he whispered. "Angel." As he leaned his forehead against hers, the last of his adrenaline drained in a rush, leaving his legs weak. The tears he'd staved off earlier threatened again.

He pulled her closer into his embrace, sliding his hands along her back and pulling her tightly against him. "Are you okay? Are you hurt?" He couldn't tell if the sobs that shook them were coming from her or from him. He'd waited so long to hold this woman, his Angel. He might have lost her without ever knowing he'd found her. What had once been an endless spiral of searching had become a closed circle.

"I'm okay." She drew back and their gazes collided. She made no move to stem her tears. "I'm fine. Now."

"All those years of looking and you were right here. Thank God I found you again." Ryan took her lips. He'd meant the kiss to be gentle. But she kissed him back fiercely, her hands fisted in his shirt. With a groan he matched her ferocity, one hand planted in the small of her back, the other sliding through her hair to cup her face.

He leaned back and noted with satisfaction the glow of a woman who had been well and truly kissed. Anything else would have to wait.

Sandy's laugh was weak. "*That* was a kiss worth waiting seven years for."

"Guess I'm starting to do it right." Ryan smoothed her hair, cupped the back of her neck, pulling back swiftly at her sudden sharp intake of breath. Angling her for a better look, Ryan took in the large purple swelling at the base of her skull, the long jagged cut in the center, the ooze of fresh blood.

A strong desire to murder Alice MacKay settled over him, darkening his soul.

Lifting her easily, Ryan strode toward Sean's truck.

"No hospital," she murmured. "Please."

"We're just going to take you up to Jackson and get you checked out."

She remained firm. "I want to go to the ranch. I want to go home."

Ryan's arms tightened around her. "Okay, Angel, I'll take you home." And if they happened to take a detour up to the hospital in Jackson...

"Ryan, put me down and listen to me. It's important." Sandy spoke with a sense of urgency as she struggled. "It's Alice. It's been Alice and Brody causing all the problems at the ranch."

"I know, honey." He settled her on her feet but kept a hand in the small of her back. "She and Brody came up here to finish you off."

"You should have stayed away," sneered Brody from behind him. "I warned you people would get hurt if you didn't leave."

Ryan spun around, shielding Sandy with his body.

But Penelope Sherwood already had Brody MacKay cuffed and on the march toward DC's patrol car.

"Exercise your right to remain silent, MacKay," said the deputy. "Or you're gonna have an accident that involves needing your jaw wired shut."

"Where's the old lady?" Ryan asked, his fists clenched. "Where's Alice?"

"She slipped off into the woods," Penny said. "Colt was tracking her, but I sent him back to help you."

"She's right here." The grim voice belonged to Dale Pratt, Brenda's father. As he spoke, he propelled a subdued Alice MacKay forward by her arm, twisted tightly behind her back.

"Sandy, I'm so glad you're okay." Alice's voice was too pleasant and it didn't match the crazed look in her eyes. She'd lost and she didn't seem to know it.

The woman deserved to be chucked off the cliff. Fists clenched, Ryan took a step in her direction.

Sandy laid a hand on his arm and squeezed, whispering, "Stay with me."

Dale shoved Alice's arm higher into her back and her next words were nothing but a strangled garble. A state trooper stepped forward, secured Alice with handcuffs, and took custody. A second trooper assisted Brody into the back of his cruiser.

DC split a glance between Ryan and Sandy. "You up to coming in and making a statement?"

"She needs a doctor," said Ryan.

But Sandy was already nodding her head. "Yeah. She told me things you need to know." She captured Ryan's gaze. "All of you."

Chapter Nineteen

A TV news truck out of Jackson awaited them at the sheriff's office.

"So not ready for any of this," muttered Sandy.

Cameras flashed and questions were shouted. She hid her face against Ryan's chest, grateful for the protective arm he threw around her shoulders. Together they pushed through the crowd of reporters and search volunteers, into the sheriff's office.

As Ryan helped her to a metal folding chair, Sandy caught the aroma of coffee. Toes curling in delight, she pointed at the pot. "I need some of that. Black and extra sweet."

Mel pushed a cup into her hand and Sandy gratefully chugged it down. Its heat coursed through her along with a good caffeine kick.

On the far side of the room stood Brenda, an apparition in a light pink dress that hung loosely, nearly to her ankles. Her ashy hair looked like wild animals had been nesting in it. Her face was bruised and coated in a layer of dirt, streaked with tears. She was huddled with her son, who also looked like he'd just been in a battle with a grizzly.

Doc Trent ambled in Sandy's direction. He was the cliché of the town doc, had probably delivered many of the residents, and still carried a leather bag filled with medical mystery cures everywhere he went. His steel-gray paintbrush mustache and wide wrinkled face never failed to make her think of a walrus. But his gruff mannerisms hid a heart as big as a continent.

"Let's see what you've got here." Gently, he pulled Sandy's hair away from the back of her neck. He grunted, poked at it.

"Ow!" Sandy ducked away from the probing fingers.

Doc grunted again then went digging in his bag.

"Wait, what are you doing?" Sandy eyed the old man suspiciously as he rummaged. "I'm fine. I can clean it up when I get home."

A movement caught her eye. Ryan, finally looking less shocky and more like himself, was trying hard not to laugh. She glared at him through narrowed eyes.

He ignored her silent warning. "EMT Wheaton's not such a good patient. I doubt DC has any Jack Daniels tucked away here. Got a lollipop in that bag, Doc?"

Smiling, the doctor pulled out an assortment of suckers and handed her an orange one. Sandy looked from the sucker to Ryan, then back to the sucker. Sugar won. She unwrapped the candy and popped it into her mouth, moaning as the sweetness washed over her tongue.

"I'm just going to clean this up a bit. It's been bleeding, but head wounds tend to do that."

"Doc," she said quietly, focusing on the battered pair across the room, "Brenda and Ricky need you a lot more."

"They'll be going to the hospital as soon as DC's finished talking to them." He pulled her hair aside. "Someone told me *you're* refusing to go anywhere but home. Now lean forward just a bit."

Sandy caught the glint of his scissors and winced, but did as he asked.

In the tiny room, it was impossible not to hear what Brenda was saying. Sandy let Doc Trent cut a bit of hair away and clean her wound, distracting herself with unashamed eavesdropping on Brenda's story.

"He raped me. Brody." Brenda's eyes were dry, but it was obvious she'd been crying. "The night Mac ran off. I was fifteen. I'd never been with anyone before. He told me if I said anything, he would find Mac and kill him. I believed him, so I pretended like nothing happened. And then I found out I was pregnant. By... *that.* Everyone thought it was Mac's baby. I wanted an abortion. I didn't want the baby. Didn't want any reminder of—" Her chest heaved as she visibly struggled. With a shudder, she continued. "Alice went to my mom, begged her to make me have the baby. She said it was a piece of her *son.* My mother believed it was Mac's baby. And I couldn't tell anyone the truth because I was afraid for Mac. I didn't know where he was, but Alice said *they* did."

Gloria made a tiny sound of distress, but her husband squeezed her shoulder and she clamped her mouth into a thin line.

"All finished." He directed a pointed look at Ryan that had Sandy rolling her eyes. "Swing by my office on the way out and have Amanda do a skull series. We'll go from there." Then Doc patted Sandy on the hand. "Do you want something for the pain?"

"No, thanks." What she wanted was to hear Brenda. She shook her head then wished she hadn't. But she stood, reaching for Ryan's hand. Together they walked across the room and joined the little group around DC's desk.

"I didn't know what to do," said Brenda, picking at the fabric of her dress. "They all forced me to marry Bull, to pretend it was Bull's baby. Even when the town talked, everyone always thought Bull was just doing right by me for his brother. That Mac had abandoned me and his baby."

Ryan jerked upright.

"None of this was your fault," murmured Sandy, threading her arm through the crook of his elbow and drawing him close.

He nodded, but said nothing. He probably couldn't, considering the way his jaw was locked as he breathed rapidly thorough his teeth.

"But Bull — he ..." Brenda's voice softened. "Bull was nice. When he could be, anyway. When he wasn't drunk, when his mother wasn't making him—" She took a deep breath. "And then I had Ricky and it didn't matter where he came from. I loved him."

Gloria was crying openly. Dale looked like he would commit murder if the MacKays were in the room.

"Alice made me do things by threatening to hurt Ricky," said Brenda. "She said she would hurt him and then prove it was me, that I was on drugs. People would think I was an unfit m-mother. She said they'd put me away and she would have my Ricky. She told people I was crazy. And everyone believed her. *Everyone.*" She cast an intense stare at her mother. "I was alone. I was afraid if I left she would find me and take Ricky away and hurt him. And when he got older, she made him do whatever she wanted by hurting me. He'd do anything to get her to stop."

"Oh, my God," whispered Sandy, sickened.

Brenda turned toward Sean. "She made my boy do things, bad things, at your ranch. He started the fire because she forced him. I'm so sorry. Please, Sean, please look out for my son. He's a good boy, and he really likes you."

From the door, Penny caught DC's attention. "The ambulance is here."

As Ricky was loaded — amid many protests — onto a gurney, Alice MacKay's ramblings began to filter back into Sandy's memory. Many of them started to make sense after she'd heard Brenda's story. Closing her eyes, she struggled to recall exactly what Alice had said.

A touch on her arm startled her and she blinked to find DC in front of her.

"Do you think you can give a statement?"

Brenda and Ricky were gone, and so were Brenda's parents. Good. Neither needed to hear what she had to say.

Her voice warbled as she talked. She told of meeting Alice on the road, of being assaulted. "She planned to kill me."

Standing behind her, Ryan tightened his arms around her waist, and she covered his hands with hers.

"She started bragging about all the problems she and Brody had caused the McGees. Alice told me they wanted to make a deal with a coal mining company to sell their open rangeland up in the mountains."

As her memory cleared, Sandy added details. DC wrote on his clipboard, his face becoming grimmer with each new revelation. Sandy stopped talking, not sure how to finish. She knew she was about to open wounds that were decades old.

"What is it, Angel?" asked Ryan.

Sandy twisted to look up at him, clasping his hands in hers and squeezing. She spoke haltingly, with tears streaming, but kept her gaze locked onto his. "It's about your mom."

As she told that part of the story, his face went pale, emphasizing his multicolored bruises. Sandy held onto him, letting him absorb what she'd said. Tremors rolled through him, and he kept shaking his head as though in denial.

"I'm so sorry, Ryan," she whispered.

The muscles of his jaw twitched as he pulled her tightly against him and buried his face in her hair. He was shaking like he'd never be able to stop.

"Alice?" Sean appeared too stunned to be angry. He looked like he was leaning on his father for support, but Sandy's sharp eyes could see it was mutual.

Justin's face was unreadable, but through the sadness in his eyes, she saw strength. He was going to be there for his sons the way he always had been.

"What's going to happen to Brenda?" Sandy asked. "And to Ricky?"

"God only knows," Sean answered, sadness tingeing his words.

"Mac will take care of them." Ryan finally broke his silence. "If he'd known this was happening, he'd have come back for her. For them. He sent letters to her parents' address, and they were returned. When he found out she married Bull, he thought—" He shook his head. "Mac will take care of them now. I'll set up a trust fund for the boy. Make sure they have a good lawyer, and they'll both get the help they need to get through."

"Mac's insurance payout." Sean nodded in approval. "Good call, Ry."

The world began to spin, blur together in a whirl of color. Sandy leaned into Ryan's arms. "I think I need to lie down. Please take me home."

* * *

Dark wood wainscoting and walls the color of a clear Wyoming sky faded into focus. Late afternoon sunlight filtered through cream-colored curtains, illuminating the room in a golden glow. Ryan's bedroom.

Sandy stretched, inhaling deeply. The soft sheet gliding over her bare arms and legs was like a lover's kiss. The scent of him lingered enticingly in her nostrils. Ryan's bed.

Warmth flowed over her with the memories of his loving touches the night before, when he'd patiently taken care of her, wiping her tears and drawing her bath, and then giving her privacy. He'd left a pair of sweatpants and a soft white undershirt in the bathroom, and when she rejoined him in his bedroom, he'd brushed out her hair. She'd never felt so pampered in her life.

All night long, he'd held her lightly against his chest. He had shushed her with soft whispers, and every time she'd startled herself into wakefulness, he'd soothed her back to sleep with long delicate strokes along her arms. They hadn't had sex, but he'd made love to her just the same, through his gentle caring.

But now she was awake and he was nowhere to be seen. Where was he? Her Ryan, who was also her Mick? How had she not recognized his voice? How had she not known him? She sighed, thinking about her body's instant reaction to his. Perhaps some part of her had always known.

She ached for him, desperately needed to see him, touch him. To make sure she hadn't been the victim of a cruel dream.

Putting a hand to the base of her skull, she felt the lump and winced. Okay, that part at least hadn't been a dream. Gingerly she shook her head, pleased when the movement brought on no pain. She closed her eyes and lay back against the pillow, wishing she had her makeup and some fresh clothing.

"You've been one hard lady to find, Angel."

Sandy's heart pounded madly. Her body began a slow all-over tingle. She kept her eyes closed, delighting in the sound of his voice.

A slow smile pulled at her lips. "Do I hear a sexy cowboy lurking nearby?"

Sweeping her eyes open, she rolled over to find Ryan McGee lounging casually against the doorframe. He was all masculine cowboy in his faded blue jeans and pale blue denim shirt with the sleeves rolled over muscular biceps. Not even the white bandage on his left arm or the bruises on his face could ruin the effect. Her eyes drifted downward, sliding over his waist to his lean hips. She licked her lips and wiggled her eyebrows, eliciting a husky chuckle from him. Warmth burst through her in little explosions.

"Angel..." The voice of one man collided with the face of another, merging into one reality.

It hadn't been a dream.

"You're beautiful," she whispered.

That earned her another chuckle. "I'm the one who's supposed to be saying things like that to you."

A giggle slipped out. "Then you'd better get to it, don't you think?"

"You're beautiful." He stepped across the threshold and set an overnight bag on the floor. "Mel sent over a few things from your place. She said I'm to reassure you she put your best makeup in here."

Sandy didn't take her eyes off him. "Go, Mel."

He hovered just at the door, emotions playing across his face. Incredulity. Uncertainty. And love. So much love, she almost forgot to breathe.

"I can't believe I didn't recognize you," he whispered.

"I didn't recognize you, either." Sandy frowned as another question nudged. "But you said your name was Mickey. I was calling you Mick. Is that— Were you using an alias because of... Mac?"

Ryan's wince became a sheepish smile that tugged at her heart. "Naw... nothing like that. I said I was McGee. I don't think I ever gave you my first name." Staring at the hardwood floor, he scuffed the toe of his boot along an old crack. Then he looked up and met her gaze. "And I... kind of liked when you started calling me Mick — felt like your own personal name for me."

Tears welled. Seven years of pain washed over her cheeks. "Ry, back in L.A., I would have been there. I would have come to you and stayed until you told me to leave... They told me no one made it out. They said they got through and found everyone dead."

* * *

Ryan crossed the room and sat on the edge of the bed, his heart crowding his chest at the sadness in Sandy's voice. He surveyed the bruise on her temple. She'd almost been killed because of him, not once but twice. And still she was with him because she wanted to be.

He traced a finger along her forearm. "That last shock, when the building fell, I slipped a little farther down — a lot farther down, actually, into the next lower level. But falling probably saved my life. When I woke up, I could breathe easier and I wasn't pinned. I'd lost the radio so I couldn't call for help. But I survived, Angel. Because of you." His throat tightened, choking on every emotion he'd held inside for the past seven years. "They found me almost a day later. I held on for you."

"But I wasn't there," she whispered, her eyes mirroring distress.

He brushed his fingertips against her lips. "You're here now. *We're* here now. We've come in a circle, back to each other. We're where we're supposed to be."

With a shudder, Sandy pulled one of his fingers into her mouth and sucked, teasing with her tongue. It was such a sensual move, his body went into instant horndog mode.

He needed to touch her. Cupping her shoulder with one hand, Ryan rubbed his thumb in a gentle back and forth rhythm. He couldn't resist her. Leaning close, he replaced his fingers with his lips, pushing her backward and following her down until he rested on his elbows, cradling her beneath him. He sought her lips and prolonged the kiss, freeing all the love and longing he'd held onto for seven years, blending it with the fire that had been lit since his first sight of her on the mountain road.

When Sandy would have deepened their connection, Ryan pulled back, smiling at the confusion in her eyes. He sat up, pulling her with him. "Much as I'd like to continue this, we have someplace we need to be and you're gonna want to get dressed for the occasion."

"What occasion?"

"Our dinner reservation. You wanted Italian."

He pushed her toward the bathroom, trying not to enjoy too much the thought of having her off balance. Though if he had his way, he'd keep her just a bit off balance for the rest of their lives.

* * *

Sandy stared at the blue dress Mel had packed for her. Simply cut, with a rounded neckline and long flaring sleeves, it lovingly embraced her upper chest, lifting her breasts and thrusting them front and center, and then flowed in a swirl of diaphanous fabric to mid-thigh. How had her best friend known? How had she chosen to send the perfect dress?

As Sandy shook the dress out, a slip of paper fell to the floor.

This was in the back of your closet. The only time I ever saw you wear it was also the only time I ever saw you drunk and crying, just about six years ago. Now I know your story, I understand. I hope this dress works for your first date with your fireman.

Love, M.

"Oh, Mel, you did good," whispered Sandy.

She held the dress in front of her and looked in the mirror. She'd seen it in a store in Jackson, its intense blue reminding her of Mick's love for the mountain sky. She'd bought it — knowing he could never see her in it — for the same reason she'd come to Wyoming, to feel close to him.

She was halfway down the stairs when he entered the foyer from his father's study. Her mouth went dry then watered at the sight of him. Dressed in a dark Western-cut suit, with white shirt and string tie, he wasn't an L.A. firefighter. But he wasn't her cowboy straight off the range, either.

He devastated her. His gaze was like a physical sensation, a whispery soft caress on her skin. And even better, his long indrawn breath and the gleam in his eyes told her he liked what he saw.

He held out a hand. Feeling like royalty, she finished descending the elegant old staircase and slipped her hand into his. Pulling her close, he bent and took her lips in a gentle toe-curling kiss, lingering just long enough for her to want more.

* * *

He loved the soft look of her, the gentle curve of her lips when she smiled for him alone. The blue of her dress intensified the blue of the incredible eyes fixed on him as she walked into his arms. And he loved the way the filmy material of her dress swished around her legs, stroking her hips with each step.

Ryan swallowed hard. He'd thought about doing this for seven years. Her voice, her spirit, had kept him hanging on, clinging to life when hope of life was gone. It was some kind of fairy tale ending to a seven-year search for the voice of an angel. At least he hoped his plans for the night would give him that fairy tale ending.

"Time to go," he murmured, almost, but not quite, wishing they could stay in after all. "We're running late."

"I'm sorry. I tried to hurry."

His eyes twinkled. "Angel, we're about seven years late for our first date. Catch up, will ya?"

Her jaw went slack for a moment.

He tilted his head to look in her eyes. Good, still just a little off balance. Then that slow predatory smile crept over her features. Apparently he'd awakened the sleeping cat.

She rubbed against him and lifted her face, finding his lips and tracing them with her tongue before pressing a heated kiss there.

They almost *didn't* leave the house.

* * *

"Where are we going?" Sandy looked out at the miles the little sports car was eating up.

"You said you wanted Italian on our first date. Again, catch up."

"But we're going away from Jackson."

In the dim lights from the dash, she caught the curve of his lips in a secret smile. "We're not going to Jackson. Just taking a short ride into Orson's Folly."

"But there aren't any Italian restaurants in—"

"Chicory, if you don't stop fretting, I'm going to have to stop the car and kiss you quiet." He glanced at her before returning his attention to the road. "And you already know what DC thinks about making out in public. Besides, we're here."

Sandy looked out at the over-crowded parking lot of her own bar. "Oh, you're really funny, ace. Reservations? Italian? Valentine's has neither."

"Oh, didn't you hear? I know the boss. All I had to do was drop her name and the staff was quite accommodating."

Ryan winked as he held the car door open for her. "Even if she does have a reputation as a ball-buster."

She swung her legs out but just sat there, staring at him in disbelief.

He quirked an eyebrow, mischief glinting in his eyes. "Still catching up?" But he smiled when she accepted his hand. Tucking it into the crook of his elbow, he gave it a pat, and with their steps in perfect sync, they walked to the door.

Sandy didn't know what she'd expected. But it wasn't for her normal weekend crowd to fall into a hushed silence at her entrance on Ryan's arm. The band on stage abruptly stopped playing.

From somewhere in the center of the crowd, one person began clapping. Slowly, others joined in. Then people stood, and the applause rose to deafening levels as Sandy found herself in the center of a standing ovation.

Out of nowhere, Mel was at her side, a wide smile lighting her face. "Welcome to Valentino's. I have your usual table ready."

Sandy raised an eyebrow. "Valentino's?"

Mel giggled. "Just for tonight." She led Sandy and Ryan to the secluded table in the corner, where they had shared dinner not so long ago.

Around them, the band went back to playing, the crowd went back to drinking and conversing. But Sandy was acutely aware she and Ryan were the center attraction.

Mel had outdone herself with the table. A white linen tablecloth lay beneath white tapered candles set in crystal holders. Sandy raised her eyebrows at the cloth napkins and fine silverware, set for two. A bottle of blush white zinfandel waited on the table next to a gold florist's box tied with a dark blue ribbon.

"Your meal will be here shortly," Mel said as Ryan held Sandy's chair. Then she was off.

"I'm almost afraid to ask if we're about to add Italian cuisine to our menu." Sandy looked up at Ryan, knowing he'd orchestrated the evening and all the extras for her. Not for any reason other than seven years ago, she'd told him she wanted Italian on their first date. "Thank you."

Ryan slid the slim gold box toward her. "I recall a promise of daisies."

With hands that weren't at all steady, Sandy lifted the lid, her breath catching when she saw the bouquet of white daisies and blue chicory. Raising them to her nose, her eyes widened. In the center of the wildflowers, tied with a pale blue cord to a single dark red rose, was the crystal angel. Her eyes flashed to his. "Oh, Ryan..."

He touched the tips of her fingers and gently shook his head, his eyes never leaving hers. "She's you. She's always been you."

* * *

Dinner was spaghetti and meatballs, excellently prepared by Charlie, who obviously deserved a raise.

As Sandy sipped her wine, she watched Ryan over the rim of the glass, enjoying the easy way he moved and smiled. They talked of little things. How she'd grown up in the Blue Ridge Mountains and lost her parents in a car accident. How she'd moved out west with friends and worked as a dispatcher for the L.A. Fire Department. They spoke of Ryan finding himself in a world he hadn't wanted but had made the best of. He told her about his dream of returning home to the family ranch, and how beautiful Wyoming was in all seasons.

Before she knew it, the meal was finished and Mel was clearing away their dinner dishes. Next, a waiter in dark pants and white shirt with a dark tie hesitantly delivered their dessert.

"Ricky." Sandy smiled, happy to see him, relieved his injuries had apparently not been serious. "I hope this means you still want to work for me."

Ricky nodded eagerly. "Yes, ma'am." The teen's awkward hesitancy faded. "I brought your dessert." He set a plate in the center of their table then disappeared.

"Canolli!" Sandy laughed. "I can't believe how much you remembered."

"I remember it all," Ryan said. "I've remembered it over and over for seven years. You're everything to me, Sandy. Just everything. Not only from back then but — from now, too."

Sandy smiled. Feeling suddenly shy, she concentrated on the cannoli.

"'Such is my love, to thee I so belong...'"

"You do know that when you quote Shakespeare, I'll do anything for you. Even share my cannoli." She swept her gaze up to look at him.

In his hand, extended toward her, was an antique engagement ring, the rose-colored gold gleaming beneath the sharp sparkle of the modest diamond.

The room fell into absolute silence.

"Oh, my." Sandy's hand hovered about her lips. She met his gaze and her heart fluttered as he bared his soul to her.

"This belonged to my mother. And before her, it was my great-grandmother's." Ryan picked up her left hand and held it gently. "I sure would like it if you would wear this and be my wife... my Angel... my Chicory."

"Ryan," she whispered.

An unsteady grin flashed. "Still catching up, sweetheart?"

She shook her head. "No."

Surprise etched his features. His face registered disappointment. "No?"

"Yes."

Surprised morphed into confusion. "Yes, you're saying no?"

Sandy shook her head, realizing she wasn't making any sense. "No, I'm not still catching up. And yes, I want very much to marry you."

The huge grin sliding across his face made her think of kids in candy stores. Ryan slipped the ring onto her finger. It fit perfectly.

A cheer rose from the crowd. Sandy looked around, seeing all the regulars and a few who rarely showed up. Seated at his normal spot at the bar where Mel worked was

Sean, and next to him Justin, who smiled and winked when he caught Sandy's eye.

She didn't think she could be any happier.

Ryan stood, tugging Sandy to her feet. On stage, Ray Dan led Cowboy Blue into a slow number about finding perfect love. After a very sweet kiss, Ryan led Sandy to the dance floor. No one joined them.

Emotions wound through Sandy, her love for Mick fusing with the passion she felt for Ryan. Tilting her head up, she smiled into his eyes. "You're my everything, too, Ryan Mick. I love you."

At the end of their dance, Ray Dan began talking to the crowd. "What do you say, folks? Don't you think she owes us a song?"

Sandy groaned and hid her face as shyness washed over her. She smiled and shook her head. But the crowd was roaring their agreement and a chant began. "Sandy! Sandy! Sandy!"

Helplessly, she looked up at Ryan and found him smiling broadly. He wasn't going to be any help. He released her and gave her a little push toward the stage. And suddenly she knew exactly what she would sing and to whom she would sing it.

* * *

Ryan watched his new fiancée speak to the bandleader, who nodded. Then she stepped up to the microphone. She smiled, her gaze settling on Ryan, and he was the only person in the crowded room. A single note began to play on the piano.

As her chicory eyes eased themselves into his soul, Sandy sang the song she'd begun seven years earlier, "The Rose."

About the Author

Kay Springsteen grew up in Michigan but transplanted to the south at the turn of the century and now resides in the shadow of the Blue Ridge Mountains, where she enjoys photography, gardening, hiking and camping, and of course spending time with her terrific family. She is a firm believer in happily-ever-after endings and believes there is one out there for everyone; it just may not be exactly what you expect or think you want.

Don't miss the wonderful sequels!

Elusive Echoes

Abiding Echoes

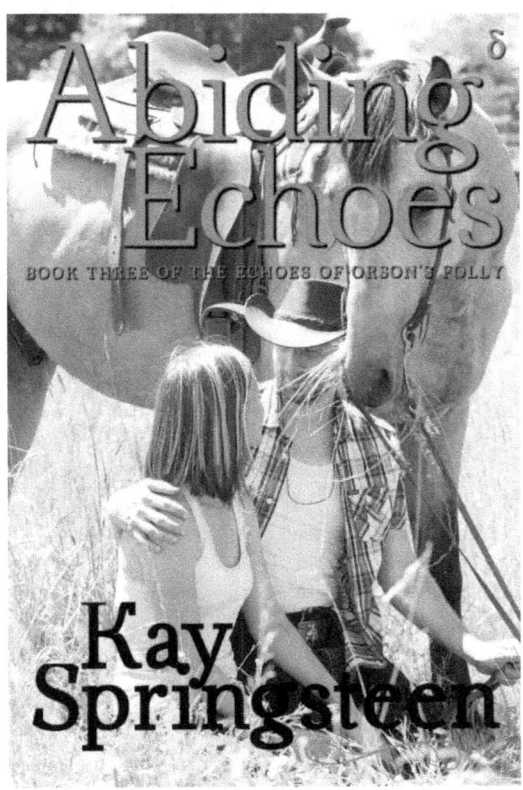

Also from Dingbat Publishing

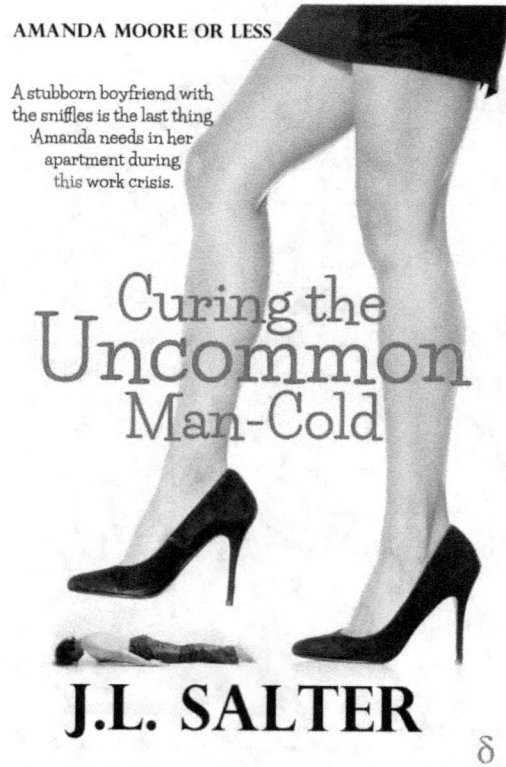

AMANDA MOORE OR LESS

A stubborn boyfriend with
the sniffles is the last thing
Amanda needs in her
apartment during
this work crisis.

Curing the
Uncommon
Man-Cold

J.L. SALTER

δ

Chapter 1

August 10 (Monday)

"I don't think I can hold up..." Amanda's eyes were full. "Jason just left the doctor." Her apartment suddenly felt smaller.

"What on earth is wrong?" Her friend Christine had just arrived and already plopped down on the small sofa. "Cancer? Paralysis?" She probably pictured even worse diagnoses because Christine zealously read supermarket tabloids.

Amanda groaned softly.

Christine grabbed her younger friend's shoulders. "You'll feel better if you talk about it." She moistened her lips slightly. Medical news was known to be among her favorites, along with stories about nasty divorces.

Amanda looked for her nearest tissue box. "It's... a... man-cold."

Christine sighed heavily. "Don't wind me up like that. I thought this was a real *situation*."

"It is!" Amanda had been home from work about twenty minutes and still had her heels on. "I don't know what I'm going to do."

"Just ship that basket case back to his momma." Christine snapped her fingers. "Let Margaret wait on him hand and foot for the next week."

"More likely two weeks. Remember when he was sick in January?"

"I thought he had triple-Nashville-man-ditis or something."

Amanda nodded. "Totally helpless. He could barely use the bathroom by himself."

"Look, Jason was overindulged from the get-go. I bet Margaret nursed him too long. Ship him back."

"I can't." Amanda closed her eyes. "She absolutely won't take him."

"His own momma?"

"The last time a sick Jason stayed at her place, it nearly put Margaret in the hospital." Amanda lowered her voice. "She said Jason moaned every waking hour. Hardly ever moved from her couch for over a week... and he *limped*, for cryin' out loud!" Amanda shook her head. "I can't live with that."

"You can't let him stay here! You won't survive two days with Jason's sick-over." Christine sputtered. "There's got to be somewhere else... somebody else. Maybe he can bunk with a buddy."

"A buddy? Just picture irresponsible Kevin trying to assist helpless Jason who's down with a deadly illness. Kevin would hightail it out of his own apartment so quick you'd think he just spotted a fumigation fog sliding under his door."

"Slow down and rethink this." Christine touched her friend's forearm. "Do you really know this person well enough to nurse him back from near-terminal man-sniffles?"

"Know him? We've been sleeping together since the Halloween party last year. My place *and* his!"

Christine leaned in closer, even though she should have remembered this development. "At his place too?"

"Three times." Amanda was prepared to list the dates.

"Hmm. That is serious, I guess." Christine waved her hand briefly. "Okay. So you do have an investment, so to speak. The issue is how to tend Jason enough that it even registers with him, yet not so much that the effort kills you."

"Now you understand why I'm freaking." Amanda moaned again. "Not to mention these are my Hell Weeks at work."

Verdeville was about twenty miles east of Nashville's Interstate loop. Amanda Moore's current crunch was reviewing applications from every Greene County agency seeking federal grants. Some thought she was too inexperienced, at age twenty-eight, for such a significant role and she was not taken very seriously in county government offices because of her shapely legs and hips.

"Okay, back up. Let's say you were in-the-bed ill, with doctor-ordered bed rest." Christine's hand went horizontal. "Would Jason take care of you at *his* apartment?"

"Are you kidding? He'd tell me he'd been evicted and show me a cell phone picture of a notice on his door."

"Okay, you're catching on. So, tit for tat." Christine Powers crossed tanned arms beneath her augmented bosom. Divorced for about four years, she was financially secure because of her lucrative alimony settlement. Frankly, she had too much free time on her hands: brunette Christine had lots of urges and often followed up on them — she behaved more like a redhead. "In fact, if you were the one sick, I'll bet Jason wouldn't even help you here at *your* place."

Amanda merely shrugged.

"Of course not." Christine showed a satisfied smile. "I'm glad I was able to talk sense into you."

"You realize I've got to help Jason."

"Why? He's obviously not worth it."

"I do actually love him, you know." Amanda sighed.

"Give me one reason." Christine rolled her eyes. "And don't go way back to him rescuing you at that New Year's Eve party. Jason did real good in a scary situation, but you can't let him coast forever on a single night of good ole boy gallantry."

Actually, Jason had been Amanda's very chivalrous knight that memorable evening nineteen months ago, and his rescue was both literal and figurative. However, Amanda loved Jason more for the connection they'd made since then. "Well, right now I can only think of his eyes — they're deep and soulful... and loyal."

"A spaniel has interesting eyes and loyalty. Get a dog." Christine was uncommonly pragmatic at times. "And that's his most endearing quality?"

It was sometimes difficult to ignore Christine's negative attitude toward the man in Amanda's life. *Why does she have it in for Jason?*

Christine frowned. "So you actually intend to cancel your own home life for the next two weeks and baby Jason?"

"Don't really have a choice. I can't totally refuse to help my boyfriend. But I don't think I'll survive his sickness."

"Okay, the only workable option is he stays in his own apartment and you bring deli soup each evening."

"You must be joking." Amanda bent forward until her face nearly met her knees. "He'll be on Facebook and e-mail telling everyone he's been abandoned to die. Somebody would probably start up a blog to raise donations for his cure."

"Yeah. He does tend toward the dramatic. Probably got that from his momma, too. When boy babies nurse that long, they suck in a lot of drama." Christine didn't explain her certainty that Jason had spent more than the typical phase at Margaret's breast. "Plus, I thought guys who played all those team sports didn't get sick. This is weird."

"You know, it is pretty suspicious that he fell ill during the one sliver of August when none of his leagues have any games scheduled."

Christine's mind obviously churned. "I still say there's got to be another solution."

"I've been pulling my hair out, looking for it." Amanda tugged on the longer front tresses of her inverted bob cut — honey brown coloring this year. "I hate guys getting man-sick. If you and I had a cold like that, we'd just keep on going." She moaned again. "I'm in for total misery with no escape. He'll sit around in his jammies all day, contemplating what's inside his jammies. Guess what he's thinking about while I'm at work all day."

"Sex... with you."

Amanda nodded and closed her expressive blue eyes. "One time in that January siege, I was up all night bringing water or pills... or just listening to him whimper. I dragged myself to work, put up with nine hours of B.S. from my boss, and then crawled home. There was Jason — a stupid smile on his face, sprawled on the couch in those ratty jammies."

"Just hand him the December *Cosmo* and tell him you've got a headache." Christine looked into her friend's tear-stained face. "You didn't fall for that old routine."

"I did, back then, but I've wised up. So it's mainly a matter of extra guilt." Amanda recalled the previous occasion. "Don't even get me started about the mucous and coughing... plus he hadn't showered in two days. Yuck."

Christine's expression clearly indicated she shared that characterization.

Amanda slowly toppled over onto the vacant cushion. "I feel sick myself. Maybe I'll go home to *my* mom."

"Arizona? In August?" Christine poked her friend's shoulder. "Just pull up your big-girl panties and tell him no. Jason cannot stay here with you, period. Just break the news quick and steel yourself against his whining."

"I can't. I've been trying to tell you: he's already on his way over. Right now."

Christine quickly began gathering her belongings. "You've got two choices..."

"Suicide is one. What's the other?"

"Seriously. This is the time to decide if Jason's going to remain part of your life. Because if he does, this ultra-high maintenance side of him is going to kill you."

"What's the second choice?" Amanda tried to look hopeful.

Christine shrugged. "Become his nurse, errand girl, and sex slave for the next two weeks."

Amanda's tears gathered again. "Well, there's one thing I won't do. Absolutely will not do."

Christine nodded solemnly. "I wouldn't do that, either, 'specially if he hadn't showered."

"No. I mean I'm not going to call in sick for him." Amanda clamped her jaw shut. "Jason can make his own calls every morning."

"Oh, I thought you meant the other thing." Christine held up her hand, signaling a new subject. "Well, if Jason does stay here, he sleeps on the couch."

"No, too much in my way out here. Back in my guestroom."

"You couldn't fit a sick hamster in there."

"I cleaned it up, a little." Amanda had not intended it to sound so defensive.

"Show me."

Amanda escorted her friend down the short hall to the guestroom. Boxes were stacked along one wall and a single bed occupied a corner. Extending from another wall was a treadmill with a long row of clothes hanging on each handrail.

"I didn't know you also had exercise equipment in here."

"Mom insisted on leaving it here when she and Dad moved to Tempe." Amanda shrugged. "I only use it for closet overflow."

"I did that with Daniel's treadmill for a few years. Works better if you stack bricks under each back corner." Christine pointed. "That helps level out the handrails so the clothes hangers won't slide down to this end."

Amanda fleetingly wondered where she could find some free bricks. "Well, anyway, a human can certainly fit in here."

"Okay, I guess so, since you've got that path through all those boxes. Might need a map, though." Christine obviously didn't approve. "Although now that I think about it, you don't really want him too comfortable. So maybe this hamster nest is a good idea after all."

"It doesn't matter where he stays, really. In this tiny apartment, he'll never be more than about twenty feet away. Coughing, whimpering, calling for whatever kind of attention."

They left the cluttered guestroom and returned to the living space. Amanda crumpled to the couch and curled into a crescent. She knew the dreaded uncommon man-cold was incurable — so nobody even tried. They just gritted their teeth and stuck it out... or they packed up and left. Not many options. "You've got to help me."

"Sorry, there's no cure." Christine started to leave, but stopped suddenly. Her eyes brightened and her fingers twitched slightly. "Unless..." She sat again. "Well, it's a long shot, but theoretically possible."

Amanda straightened slowly and pulled hair from her damp eyes. A few strands stuck in the corner of her mouth where drool had started to collect. "Do you have a plan?"

"Scare him."

"You mean, like... boo?"

"More subtle." Christine lowered her voice. "Remember that movie with Kathy Bates and James Caan in a remote cabin? He's a writer."

"*Misery*? You call that subtle? You want me to scare Jason with a sledgehammer and a stub of lumber?"

"No, I'm still on *subtle*. But you might need the hammer later." Christine nodded. "If this works, you'll get Jason out of your apartment and might even cure him of man-colds forever."

"Okay, I'm on board." No hesitation. "Tell me your plan."

"Fear is a powerful force if properly applied."

Amanda heard a noise outside. "He's here! What's your plan?"

"We're going to give Jason the Scare-Cure."

"The what?" Amanda looked out the window. "Hurry! He's nearly at the door."

"The Scare-Cure." Christine seemed to like its sound even though she obviously had no strategy yet developed to implement that devious term. "I've got some research to do."

"You're leaving me alone with Mister Sick?"

"I'll call you tomorrow at work." As the doorknob twisted, Christine whispered, "Don't feed him anything besides really thin soup and those nasty crackers your mom left last year. You have any other yucky food?"

"There's a soy hotdog leftover from July 4th."

"Perfect. That's Jason's lunch tomorrow. No bun. Hide everything else." Christine opened the door.

Jason Stewart was slumped over like he'd been at hard labor on a chain gang for weeks without food or water. He looked up pitifully, saw who it was, and waved lazily. "Hi, Christine. Where's Amanda?"

She turned her head to indicate the interior of Amanda's apartment. Christine moved down the walk — partly backwards and partly sideways. She noticed how much more debilitated Jason looked when Amanda came to the door.

Scare-Cure. This could be interesting.

Amanda took in the pitiful sight. Jason seemed like an abandoned kindergartener clutching his teddy bear as he looked for Mommy at the house next door. It might have been endearing, except her boyfriend was no longer in preschool. At 32, Jason seemed in no hurry for their serious relationship to grow deeper. He obviously adored Amanda and loved being with her, but his notion of commitment had some leftover adolescent one-sidedness. Could he become a responsible mate? Nobody knew, including Jason... apparently.

Good-looking and leaning toward handsome, Jason had a boyish face and thick, dark hair that would look better combed the other direction. His blue eyes, occasionally dark and soulful, were bright with zeal when he participated avidly in basketball, softball, soccer, and flag football. About average weight for his frame and medium height, Jason's strength and athleticism were belied by a slight paunch, due to his predilection for junk food, beer, and frequent snacks.

She remained in her doorway, blocking his entrance. "I'm sorry you're under the weather. But like I said on the phone, these are my most horrid work weeks all year. Already stretched to the limit. I simply can't deal with anyone staying here."

Jason looked puzzled at why he was still on her threshold. "I won't be in the way. You won't even know I'm here."

"Trust me, I'll know." She frowned. "Even without the bell you auditioned in January."

"The concept was good; maybe the tone was off."

"If you'd rung that bell once more, I would've stuffed it up a... really... dark... place."

Jason's muscular shoulders slumped. "But I don't think I'm well enough to drive."

"You got here all right and your place was closer to the doctor's office."

"But I shouldn't be alone when I'm sick."

Whiny is quite unbecoming in a lover. "It's a cold, Jason. How bad could it be?"

"Doctors miss a lot. I have complications." He coughed to illustrate. "And fever."

"Well, I'm sure this is the worst cold in all of middle Tennessee." She sighed heavily and felt his forehead. No discernable warmth. "Okay. Wait right here and I'll get a thingy to check your temp."

When she returned from her bedroom, Jason was sprawled out on her couch and already had the TV on. She paused to consider *where* to insert the thermometer.

After an hour of channel surfing, Jason entered the hall bathroom. Moments later, he emerged wearing floppy socks, a very old tee-shirt with several holes, and pajama bottoms with a sprung-out waistband. He headed toward Amanda's bedroom.

"Hold on, Mister Germs! Not in *my* bed!"

"Huh?"

"These are my Hell Weeks. I can't get sick with all those grant apps stacked on my desk. The boss would bring files to my hospital room." Amanda ground her teeth slightly. *Why can't you wait 'til after Labor Day to get sick?*

"So where do I sleep?"

"Your own apartment."

No reply from Jason.

Amanda shrugged and pointed to the guestroom.

"All the way over there?"

"It's forty-two inches across this hallway."

Jason peered in. "That's not enough room for a five-year-old."

"Well, stop acting like a five-year-old." Amanda sighed. "You'll be safe enough if you stay on that path."

Supper was a few hours later. As per Christine's instructions, Jason's complete meal was a small mug of chicken-flavored consommé with one stale, generic rye crisp cracker.

It was a long night for Jason. Highlights included: loud groaning, coughing fits, sneezes like backfires from a rusted exhaust manifold, and snoring which rattled the inside wind chimes. On numerous trips to the bathroom he even managed to click the light switch with amplified noise. Beginning around 2:00 a.m., he spent another hour flipping through TV channels.

Amanda netted about three hours of sleep.

* * *

Thanks for reading! Dingbat Publishing strives to bring you quality entertainment that doesn't take itself too seriously. I mean honestly, with a name like that, our books have to be good or we're going to be laughed at. Or maybe both.

If you enjoyed this book, the best thing you can do is buy a million more copies and give them to all your friends... erm, leave a review on the readers' website of your preference. All authors love feedback and we take reviews from readers like you seriously.

Oh, and c'mon over to our website:
www.DingbatPublishing.Weebly.com

Who knows what other books you'll find there?

Cheers,

Gunnar Grey,
publisher, author, and Chief Dingbat

δ

Dingbat Publishing